# Shadow Tears

A.J. TUPPS

Halo Publishing International

ISBN 13: 978-1-61244-310-2
Library of Congress Control Number: 2014917660

Printed in the United States of America

Published by Halo Publishing International
1100 NW Loop 410
Suite 700 - 176
San Antonio, Texas 78213
Toll Free 1-877-705-9647
www.halopublishing.com
www.holapublishing.com
e-mail: contact@halopublishing.com

This book is dedicated to my loving husband and children. Their support and love have been my inspiration. They have given me the strength to step outside of my comfort zone and follow my dream of writing. This story laid dormant until an illness entered our lives. My children needed to be entertained in the hotel across from the hospital that my hubby was in. After my husband survived the colon cancer my children wanted to read the book that I had told stories from. It was a surreal moment. They were right. This series needed to be shared. I love books and so do many others. Thanks to Tyler, Meggan and my darling hubby, Chris, this book is finally a reality. I love you with all my heart unconditionally. Thanks for allowing me to give life to my dreams.

# CONTENTS

# PROLOGUE

**The flickering** of the sun through the branches became clear as Shep stood outside of the gates of the cemetery. With a quick survey of his surroundings, he found the caretaker at the very site he planned to visit. The caretaker removed the dead flowers from the ground and left. Once the man turned behind the mausoleum, Shep took a step closer. He quickly looked at his large wristwatch and could see time was moving too fast again. Suddenly the wind blew hard, blinding him. Shep stepped back and surveyed his surroundings once again. Cautiously he made his way towards the two graves. The bright, white stones stood boldly among all the darker ones.

The whistle of the wind was filled with a single wind chime sounding from near the grave. Shep knelt in front of the first stone with the name ANALEASE. Shep laid the fresh neon bouquet of flowers in front of it. With a deep breath Shep began to speak. "It's been a long time, Analease. Sorry, I had to visit. I've been careful..." Shep bowed his head as the memory forced its way into his mind. A memory from ten years ago appeared...too painful to stop.

***

He and Sarah had arrived at the wrecked car to see the horror set before them. The beat-up car was hanging off the cliff by its back wheels, teetering. The only thing that had brought Shep back to reality was Selena's wailing. He and Sarah had rushed to rescue her, but could do nothing for Analease and Jared. It had been a decision Shep would regret for the rest of his life. Jared had ordered them to take Selena to a safe place, and they had obeyed. There had been no choice. Shep remembered the feel of the car under his hand just before it plunged into the edge of the fishing lake below. In a matter of seconds, Shep and Sarah found themselves to be parents. Unfortunately, the result would not be a happy ending. Shep had seen that their family was in danger and had to be protected. Jared and Analease had a plan already in place for such a terrible circumstance, and this was Shep and Sarah's reality. Shep had assured Analease this would never happen. They would never be found. He had been wrong. He had been overconfident in his role.

Shep remembered looking at the sweet little girl nestled tightly in the men's jackets that Sarah, his wife, held. He watched. It had been a grueling three years. It seemed like the world was out to claim everything they had to offer. Things had already gone horribly wrong. Jared and Analease were gone. The events had been unbelievable. What was to come next would have to be faced, no matter what the result. Nervously Sarah glanced around through the autumn leaves with hopes that no more could possibly happen. If it did, he wasn't sure what she would do.

She would have to manage. Delbert had taught her that with his love. Sarah had a unique perspective when it came to loved ones.

It felt like their world was crashing in around them. What was worse was that the day wasn't over. There still remained a major undertaking in order to secure their new daughter. In a few minutes Sarah would be forced to give up the small child nestled so snuggly in her arms. With a nervous glance to Selena, he could see bruising still forming on her naturally pale skin around the cut on the child's cheek. Sarah didn't look too well herself. Her clothes were torn, and the bruising on her beautiful tan skin was clear to see. Sarah jerked with dismay as two men appeared from the shadows, looking somber.

At that moment, Shep felt his guts wrench. For the first time in his life he felt defeated. Hastily he shook this feeling from his mind. He had to show confidence so Sarah and Clark could do their parts in this ploy. If they didn't deal with this correctly, all could be lost. He steeled up his muscles and forced what he hoped was a determined expression to his face. Sarah always stated she looked to his eyes to know the truth. He needed her to see fire there.

"Give her to me. It's time." Selena's grandfather rushed forward with a look of defeat as he kissed the child's cheek anxiously. "Be strong my precious treasure… be safe." The child seemed to stir as the man's mustache tickled her skin.

"He…" Shep knew what Clark was about say, but he understood what his son, Jared had ordered. Shep was shocked at his own voice. "We can't take a chance. I must leave now. I can take care of the injury, don't worry. I have enough money to start out with, and I can get a job somewhere. You can't tarry. It wouldn't look right." Clark patted the child's hand as Sarah bent to place one last kiss. She fingered her daughter's cheek. "I checked for infection and found nothing. Everything is mending, but if you give me a bit…"

"There is no more time, Sarah. Things are bad enough. Please, don't make this worse. Our papers are finalized and we stick to the plan. I will contact you in…" An abrupt noise outside drew everyone's attention to the dirty window panes where a tree was shaking.

Clark moved to Sarah's side and tugged her back as he spoke. "He's right. Five years and we will be waiting." Shep stepped away from the grieving duo as the finer looking business man assisted with the duffel and suitcase. Carefully Shep shuffled his precious daughter over his shoulder as he adjusted the strap and lifted up a small suitcase.

"Thanks, I've got it."

The finely dressed man nodded. "Yes, you do Master Goodwin, but you need to know I placed the legal documents you will need to start your life within a box and it is in that duffel. The last documents will be placed where you and I agreed on earlier. Once I see that those are gone, I will return to our home and see to the rest of our legal needs. I won't leave there until you tell me differently." The man tugged on his fine cuff to reveal a chain tattoo. "As you see, the special seal is in place and I cannot reveal what has happened here. Be at ease. Master Martin and I will see to your wife."

Shep nodded with appreciation. The man was insightful and must have known he needed some reassurances. "Don't try to follow me or find me. I am cutting myself off from you all as soon as I leave. I love you, Sarah…I mean *we* love you. Clark, I'm counting on you. Take care of Sarah for us."

Shep shuffled the child up over his shoulder. Thankfully she remained asleep with her rag nestled safely against her cheek. Watching the room fade from sight, Shep wondered where he should begin. He couldn't take any chances. He had scouted around the previous night for a place to possibly call home. After a good search he had found three possibilities. With one last thought he closed himself off from all that was important to him except from his daughter who lay so still in his arms. He could feel the beat of her heart thumping soundly against his own. With a reassuring pat to the child's back, he took a deep breath. Could he really do this alone?

Stopping at a set of railroad tracks, he stepped out from the trees to look back down the road. He had to make sure he wasn't followed. With a deep breath in, his little bundle squirmed as he waited for any sign of trouble. "Can't leave yet." He couldn't believe he had said that aloud with no one to hear him but little Selena. Again he patted his precious bundle as he rocked. Hesitantly walking away from the railroad tracks, he could hear the sounds of people nearby. Their comments sent a chill over his skin.

"I can't believe this is happening!" Police officers were pressing people back from the site, trying to assure all that there was nothing to see. The loud creaking of metal upon metal was followed by a shout that the car had been found. Dead man's curve had claimed more lives than any place should have been allowed. "Any bodies?"

"No, but the car seat is still inside, and no baby!" The crowd went ballistic and the men were flinging the car doors open in search of the child. "She's not in here, sir. Nothing…the bodies must have been pulled out of the wreckage. We will have to dredge the water." Reassuringly Shep patted his daughter as he continued to look around at the crowd while pulling his hood further down. Many looked grieved beyond belief. The mixed sentences began to garble as he turned his back on the scene to walk away into the woods. Familiar voices whispered with panic. "What are we to do?" "How will we survive?" "What…"

Shep remembered leaving with tears streaming down his dark skin. This was a test of strength for him. Then he remembered deciding on his least favorite location to rear his daughter. It had been the right choice, he now knew. Jared would have agreed with him. The community had healed not only Selena, but his heart as well.

In the late evening they had arrived alone for the first time in ages. He stood with his daughter to face the great lake where a storm performed proudly with its beauty. He took a deep breath and trudged up to a house that was newly built, with a "for sale" sign still in the yard.

His first steps into their new home had been hard. Shep's father's voice had rung loudly as he and Selena had settled down into the empty shell of a house. His father was a large, well-muscled African American man. "Son, you only have time for your first only once, and you have to make the most of it." Shep missed his father and his sweet mother. Still, he had done exactly what he intended to do. He made a home and his daughter was happy.

The first year had been full of nightmares that brought them both to their knees. Selena had to attend a daycare after he started his job. The Muirs and Parker had become close friends within the new neighborhood. He and Parker had to rear their daughters together since neither of them had a female to support their precious girls. Thankfully, Chelsea Muir along with Shep's secretary, Cassidy had given the girls the attention they felt they needed. The girls never seemed to be lacking, especially with the Muir boys acting as big brothers. He remembered how the time had flown since that incident, but most of all, he was able to keep her safe for ten years.

Shep shook himself free from the bitter memories. "Analease, Selena is growing up. She is absolutely beautiful." Suddenly his throat constricted. The thought of his daughter made him smile. "I had to ask for help, Analease. She's maturing. I needed Sarah and Clark's assistance again. The sanctuary is interfering, and you know I can't do anything about that. Selena has to be *protected*." Shep's fist clenched as he bit his hand to keep quiet. He didn't want to be noticed yet.

"I'm sorry, Analease. I have no choice. Please keep an eye on us." Shep could sense the caretaker returning. He had to leave.

Before he could do so, he stopped in front of the second stone, which read JARED. This time Shep spoke loudly. "I won't fail this time, Jared. I made you both a promise, and I will die before something like this ever happens again. You gave me your most precious daughter, and she is the most wonderful gift I have ever been given." With that, Shep jerked to a flicker of darkness in the trees. Hopefully he hadn't been spotted.

Once within the safety of the forest, Shep turned to see the caretaker return. The man stopped upon seeing the fresh bouquet, with its ribbons flapping in the air. Anxiously he surveyed the area but found no one. Shep smirked as he left.

An hour later Shep stepped out of the forest behind his home to see his daughter in the yard with her two best friends. Hopefully they hadn't been up to no good. Selena shouted her greeting to him as she ran towards him happily. Her hugs were warm. Quickly he kissed the top of her head.

"Where have you been?" Shep chuckled at his daughter's demand.

"I took a walk. I needed to think."

Selena shoved back as she began to tug his hand. "John and Parker have a bonfire going for a cookout at the beach. We have to go." Shep laughed as her two partners in crime encouraged him to follow swiftly.

# CHAPTER 1.
# SELENA

**It was** another unbearable hot summer's day. No rain clouds were in sight and the grass was only bound to get browner. It had been one of the hottest summers in half a decade. We lived in a small town close to the U.P.—that's in Michigan. U.P. means Upper Peninsula, not "up". We are one state that is surrounded by water on three sides. I live with my dad, Shep. He adopted me when my parents were killed in a car accident back when I was five. He had known my parents for a long time and had been appointed as my godfather. That was a good thing since they died in such a tragic way.

Shep is a nice guy. I have to admit, Shep isn't the ordinary parent. In fact, he is pretty cool for a good-looking, middle-aged African-American man who is naïve to most around him. It always irritates me how he doesn't seem to notice these divorcee women throwing themselves at him. You can tell they think he is from the olden times because he has manners. A "gentleman" is what they used to call it. I guess it is rare. I sort of worry that he didn't date because of me.

I have always looked at Shep as my dad. I really never had a chance to know my genetic father. From what I understand, they served in the Peace Corps together or something like that. Evidently, Shep knew my mom first, and from the few stories he had shared, was quite leery of my father. He says my dad could win over a monster if need be. I always enjoyed his stories of my parents, but never brought the subject up much because I could see how painful the memories were for Shep. For some reason I can tell he feels responsible, but I'm not sure why.

I only have one picture of my family, and it is very special to me. I'm not sure why there is only the one, but still I have it. This picture looks so familiar to me that at times it almost looks like the area we live in now. In the background there is a large hill, and the grass is just as brown in it as it is here in Empire. If I didn't know better, I would say that our little cul-de-sac is the same place as in the picture, just not as developed. Shep says that is impossible. They never lived here. Although, the pine forest looks the same; just not as mature as it is now. At times I look at this photograph and wonder what they were doing there. I imagine that working in disaster areas for most of their time contributed to the lack of photo opportunities. Maybe the reason this picture looks so familiar to me is because I look at it so often. All of these thoughts are just making me sentimental. I wonder what is wrong with me today. Lately I've felt strange and moody. Maybe I should just focus on chores? I wonder what Heather is going to do today. As I wandered into the kitchen, I found our calendar hanging on the fridge. Unfortunately, it proved to only remind me that school was barely a month and a half away. Why does time seem to fly when we were off from school and not when we were in school? In many ways I dreaded the return, even if I did enjoy it. Shep says, *They teach you a lot, but there is even more to learn in life than just book learning. Life isn't easy but full of many different experiences. Sometimes it is wonderful, and other times you just have to endure.* When I think about Shep, he is almost like Yoda from *Star Wars*. There always seems to be more to what he is saying, but he never comes right out and tells you. It would make my life easier if he did. I wonder why.

Slowly I began neatening things up as I checked our home. With it just being the two of us, it didn't take much to manage. Shep and I were both kind of neat freaks in some ways. Sitting down at my piano bench, I couldn't resist but to play the melody from my favorite piece, *Canon in G*. Shep loves music and so do I. He had me taking piano lessons when I was five. We both love to compose our own music, and I recognized this as one of his sweet ballads. When chords are rolled it is the richest sound a person can hear. I would need to get a practice in today, but the sun was shining so bright that I wanted to go swimming instead. It would have to wait.

With a quick glance towards the window I knew it wouldn't be long before Heather or Mike called me. I was sure they were itching to be outside too. They both were my best friends, and in many ways, more like my brother and sister. We rarely spent any time apart, not that I would want to. The abrupt ring of the phone drew a small scream from me. With the house being so quiet I wasn't expecting the noise. "Hi Heather, what's up?"

"We were just wondering if you wanted to meet us at the end of the cul-de-sac. I know Shep left for work already, so come join us, sleepyhead! Mike is jumping his bike ramp for now, so don't make me wait long." As usual, Heather sounded bored. She didn't like watching Mike practice anything, especially if she didn't feel involved in the activity.

"Maybe we could go for a bike ride?"

"Sure. Why not?" she said. "I'll see you in a few."

As I made my way into the garage, I was pleased to see my old Star- Spangled Banner bike that Shep had won a long time ago from our old grocery store, Cox's. The ladies in there were always talking to him, and I sometimes wondered if they didn't fix the drawing that year. I was always in there looking at the little extra home decor and outdoor stuff. It was nothing like what we have today with Super Wal-Mart and Meijer. It was just an old-time grocery. They even had bag boys take your groceries out to the car. These days I was lucky if I could drag Shep along to get the groceries. Hasn't anyone heard of chivalry?

With one glance at my bike, I knew it was time to buy another, even if I did find it sentimental. I had definitely outgrown this one. With this old bike my legs would hit the handlebars if I wasn't careful, but I still liked how it felt when I did bike tricks. A quick glance to the clock proved it was close to noon. This day seemed to be slipping by too fast. I had to be back by five o'clock for dinner duty or Shep would be questioning me on why I hadn't informed him he was to be cooking. To me it would just be easier not to have to eat. It would be nice if you didn't have to waste so much time cooking and eating and cleaning up. Maybe someday we could take a pill or something in its place.

Heather said to meet them at the end of the cul-de-sac. I hoped they had a bit more planned than just jumping Mike's bike ramp. With Heather around, I was sure it would be more. I truly did want this summer to be special. Before long we would graduate and head off to college. Who knew if we would attend some place together or each take our own road, only to see each other from time to time when visiting our parents. To me that sounded truly depressing. That was why I didn't want to miss a minute with them. We had been friends since I could remember, not to mention how we felt about each other. We acted more like siblings than Mike did with his own brothers.

At least the Muirs treated us like family. I was sure it was because Heather and I didn't have moms. Chelsea, Mike's mom, treated us like we were her daughters while John, Mike's dad, protected us like we were fragile dolls. I do believe he did look at females as very delicate and breakable. To be honest, I sort of enjoyed his bellows at the boys when we were around. He always referred to us as ladies.

Slowly the garage door opened. It felt nice to feel a strong breeze blowing in. I didn't exactly live in the country, but I certainly didn't live in the city either. We lived in this small subdivision that had the best of both worlds. I truly love the feeling of wind in my unruly honey-blonde hair. My hair was another thing to think about before biking off. I don't think it will ever thicken or grow long like my best friend's. Heather has long, brown hair with lots of wave. I just pull mine back and pray that it will stay in place if I clip it. Shep says my hair is so soft it reminds him what angels' hair must be. What a laugh. He knows I am no angel, but one can always wish! Allowing my bike to glide down the drive, I felt like I could fly. Wouldn't that be cool? Maybe today we will go to the bluffs and see if we are brave enough to jump them.

A quick look towards the end of the cul-de-sac and I could see Heather and Mike were already jumping with the help of one of those store-bought plastic ramps. John, always saw to it that his boys had any sort of sports equipment they wanted. He was one of those men who didn't want his sons to ever seem girlish. He would even compete against them and push them to their limit. It was funny when we first started hanging out with Mike that John actually tried to convince him that he needed guys as friends, not girls. Within the first couple months, John had softened and pretty well treated us as if we were his own daughters. Not to mention that Mike's brothers, Andy and Josh, defended us as such. Josh was on the rough side—captain of the football team, but still he had a heart of gold underneath. Andy, on the other hand, was sweeter but was the intellect of the three. Unfortunately for him, he had come down with pneumonia the previous year and had missed so much school he had to repeat a year.

Mike definitely has a look of a basketball player. His blondish-brown hair is pretty short today. He always cuts it short, then lets it get real long. His mom is pretty cool when it comes to things like that. When Mike stood to watch Heather attempt a jump I realized he was growing taller this summer by leaps and bounds. Before long he was going to be as tall as his dad. Even if his body was maturing, it hadn't helped his mischievousness any. I could tell by the way he was teasing Heather about being so lame.

Upon hearing Heather scream, I watched as she about fell over when the ramp moved across the pavement. Heather tried to do jumps, but the only reason she did was because she didn't want to be teased. She won't ever go too high. She is afraid of falling. It made me wonder how safe those ramps really were, but it didn't matter to the Muirs. Bumps and bruises to them were just par for the course, Mr. Muir would say. Mike hit the ramp hard, causing the plastic thing to jump forward again. I wondered if that was what their big plan was for our afternoon. I sure hoped not.

I hollered out my hello as I sped towards the ramp, drawing their attention to me. As I landed, Mike let out a whoop of praise at my brazenness. I had to admit, I did like the feel that entered into my stomach when doing something I considered dangerous. Mike began explaining to me that Heather had an idea, and it was a lot better than jumping his old ramp. His grin was almost contagious. "She thought we would go out to Crystal Lake. It is only a thirty-five minute hike out and thirty-five minutes back. If we watch the time we should be back without any problem. What do you think? It has been a hot summer and the water should be nice." They both already knew my answer. I loved swimming.

Shep said my mom never learned how to swim and hated the water. My dad, however, was thrown into the dirty Ohio River and you either swam or slept with the fish. For several reasons I had the strong feeling that Shep and my father's family had enjoyed the outdoors. I would only hear now and then about something they had done together. Overall, Shep didn't like to talk about anything. The only thing he did talk about was how things had been with us after my adoption. Some people get all bent out of shape or think how sad it must be to have never known my genetic parents, but I didn't feel that way. In fact, I felt just the opposite. I was fortunate even if I only had a dad, for he was a good man and a good father. He took care of me and I was sure my parents would be very happy with our relationship.

After a quick glance to my blue jean shorts and shirt, I decided they would have to do. Today there would be some white caps since the wind was up, and usually the lakes were choppy anyhow. The white caps would be good for riding in our little blow up rafts. Towards the end of the hike, I always enjoyed looking down the side of the cliff to see the clear water. This was going to be a wonderful day. The sun was shining and I was with my best friends. What more could I want?

Mike didn't waste any time heading into the water. Heather, of course was heading to the sand to get a suntan. I declare, that girl is going to get skin cancer as much as she lies in the sun and puts actual cooking oil on her skin. Not to mention that she uses a blanket that looks like Reynolds Wrap. At least she doesn't look like a dried prune yet. Searching for my favorite raft, I was glad to see it was still filled with air. I had to admit, I felt rather lazy today. It wasn't a surfboard, but you could sit or lay down as you ride the waves into shore. It was odd how the caps were pretty foamy today when there was no sign of rain. It must be raining out on Lake Superior somewhere. Lake Superior has a finger into this little lake and is known for most of the freaky shipwrecks. The storms come up suddenly and disappear just as fast.

Mike was already bobbing to shore, and it looked like our friends Maymie Jean and Karen were joining us too. I wondered if Cory might be around. In ways he was the neighborhood pest *and* pet. Which one, I wasn't sure, for in many ways he was a likeable guy when he wasn't looking at you like a predator.

I tried to paddle out a little further than most since I wanted a long ride in. Gradually I continued to push out towards the horizon. It always amazed me how one could possibly think that it was the border of our world. In today's society we had disproved so many myths like the earth being flat. A pretty good wave was coming, making it so I could just lie down and let it wash me into shore, but only if I could jump it. Hopefully my skills were good enough. As I drifted, slowly my mind wandered back to the incident at school when my athletic skills *weren't* good enough. My shiner from the softball hitting me was finally gone. Shep was none too happy with the news. He had lost his temper. Somehow he arrived at the school before I even made it to the office.

The seagulls were gliding in, and by their sounds you would think they were screaming for us to feed them. They were a little scary. Tourists love to feed them, and once in a while something bad happens to them. I sometimes help Heather's dad, Parker, out on his tour boat that shows off our beautiful bluffs. He only runs his tour boat twice a month during the tourist season. Suddenly, interrupting my thoughts, the bottom of my raft began dragging across the sand bottom. Snap, I had already made it into shore.

"Hey Heather, come on into the water. It's warm and the waves are coming in fast now. Stop lying on the beach. You're going to get skin cancer for crying out loud!" She pointed to the yellow flag, which was a warning to swimmers that the water was not calm. Thankfully, after a bit more pleading, she finally gave in and joined me. Still, she was enjoying it. Heather had never been a strong swimmer, even if we had spent most of our childhood here on this lake.

We rode the waves longer than we should have; the sky started to prove that rain was on its way in. Hastily we put on our clothes. If there was anything I knew about Michigan, it was that weather changes suddenly, and it is usually not mild when water is involved. By the looks of the sky, this was going to be a bad one.

For some reason, this looked like something I had witnessed before. The clouds were rolling as they normally do, and yet the storm didn't appear on the horizon like the weather usually does around here. *Okay, I just need to stop thinking and start running*, I mumbled to myself.

"Come on Heather! You're a fast runner. Get a move on! Mike, Maymie Jean, Karen, and Cory are already out of sight." Heather may have been my best friend, but she didn't like being told what to do, even if it was for her own good. Heather never did well in the woods, and she hated insects and other junk like that. This is why she dances around so much. As we left the beach, I tried to reassure her. "If you're afraid of the webs getting on you, just put your hands up in front of your face and run. When we get back, I will check you for ticks and spiders...anything. Just move it. I don't want to be caught out in the woods during this storm. I don't know, something isn't right with it and Shep is going to be upset." Heather began complaining that she was one of the clumsiest people in the world and she didn't want to reel her ankle again. She *was* clumsy. "Alright," I agreed, "but can you stop stopping every time you run into a web?"

Thunder belted out over the water and the clouds looked like they were rolling in fast. Now all I needed was to see a ghost or a ghost ship. I love folklore and yet, I really don't want a death omen today. Leave it to me to see intrigue in something like this. Another strike of thunder brought reality back to me swiftly. This time I could see the lightning inside the clouds and it was now reaching to the horizon. Boy, this is going to be a downpour. Maybe we should stop and find a safe place to stay out of the storm. It was getting dark too fast.

"Heather, we are never going to get back to the cul-de-sac before it hits!" The wind picked up, whipping my wet hair into my face. Suddenly out of the corner of my eye, I thought I saw a person, but it was just a shadow. Sometimes the light and shadow seemed to play tricks on my eyes. I had a terrible habit as a child of talking to the shadows around me like they were real people or something. Shep had never liked the idea of my believing in the boogey man. He was adamant that shadows were never anything to fear.

And then it happened: Heather fell and reeled that ankle again. Great, just what I needed, and to top it off, we were next to a grouping of white ash trees. This type of tree makes a great lightning rod. Now my best friend is unable to walk, and my imagination is getting carried away with me. By the looks of the ankle, it was already swelling. That was just great. We were going to have to wait this out, but where? My mind began ticking over all the possible places we might find safety. The first thing of importance was to get away from these white ashes. Then we could hold up against the back of one of the steeper hills or rocks or something. Helping Heather up, I asked if she could put any weight on it. Again, I saw a big black shadow out of the corner of my eye and jerked to look. Maybe we were not alone and there was a stranger following us. This was exactly what I needed, to get spooked. Instantly I decided to keep this to myself. The shadow had to be me seeing the trees move or something better, like my imagination.

The sun was almost completely darkened out by the impending storm. A glance to the sky proved that this storm was rolling in faster than I thought possible. I had never seen the sky darken so quickly. The rain clouds were moving in faster than normal, which was a really bad sign. With any luck it wouldn't turn into something like a tornado. To my relief, I suddenly thought of a little den in the side of one of the hills where we could maybe seek shelter from the rain. It was not a cave, but our two little bodies should be able to stay dry in it. Hopefully this storm would roll over as quickly as it came in. That way maybe we could get home before dusk.

One thing I didn't relish the thought of was spending the night out there. I am so not a tent type of camper. Pop-up campers, RV's, and hotels are all I will do. Well, that isn't totally true. Shep made me learn how to tent camp when we went into the backwoods once a year. He was always concerned that I be able to handle any situation I might be presented with. I had the strong feeling that he had spent a lot of time tenting with my parents when they worked in the Peace Corps Group, or whatever it was. I had seen a picture once of Shep and my parents working in the backwoods. They had posed to show how tired they were. It looked like they were having fun in spite of the surrounding conditions. There had been another lady in the picture, but when I asked Shep about her he just frowned, saying she was a good friend. He hadn't let me look at it long, and when I went back into his room the next day, the picture was gone. I never saw it again.

"Well, here we go," I said, telling Heather to lean on me as we began walking slowly down the dirt path.

"Where are we going, Selena?" We began stumbling up the wet dirt path. Heather tumbled again, almost taking me with her this time. I had to figure out where to take her, and that den was looking like the better of my choices.

"We are too far from the cul-de-sac. I think there is a little hole in the side of one of these hills."

"How do you know?" Heather pleaded as she pressed her hand firmly against her leg. I knew she was trying to ease the pain, but right now we had to make it to that shelter.

"I don't. I seem to remember seeing something like that once. It was a little further up the hill and then down its side." This time Heather looked worried.

"Are you sure? It looks so dark ahead." With Heather complaining all the way, we finally made it up the next two hills to the one I remembered having the hole in its side. While looking over the edge, I had to agree it really did look dark and forbidding. The ferns were blowing quite hard, and I could hear the rustle of the trees as the storm was moving into shore. She was right: it was scary. But I couldn't let her think that.

"Hey, you have to trust me." I think I was trying to convince myself as much as Heather. "I am sure it is over this side. Slide down on your butt with your foot up." I jumped over the edge and fell into a slight jog until I hit the bottom with a final slip. I could see the shadows moving and still wondered if there was someone following us.. This place really looked familiar, but I didn't think I had ever been here before. I ventured forth, reached my hand out against the taller vegetation, and found a cool breeze. Heather screamed, causing me to jerk around and see her sliding down the incline, flailing the whole way. Goodness, she truly could be a clown without even trying.

"Good grief, give me a heart attack why don't you? Come on, Heather, it's here. I found it." Suddenly the thunder cracked again, and the lightning seemed to be hitting shore now. I draped her arm over my shoulder with my hand around her waist to make sure we would have no more accidents. After finding our balance, she looked over at the hillside, questioning where this safety supposedly was. As I pointed in front of us, she started shaking her head that she didn't see anything but a lot of tall weeds. We limped toward the dark vegetation, which seemed to move the closer we came. Immediately she dragged me to a stop.

"I'm not sure I want to go in there, Selena. What if there is an animal or a lot of bugs?" Heather's squeamishness was showing quite clearly. Hastily I encouraged her to move. She was actually stronger than I expected. "Selena, are you sure we couldn't just go back up to the path and take our chance in the rain?"

"Heather Dawn, are you listening to that storm? It is full of lightning and the wind sounds strong. We need to seek shelter and wait it out. We won't make it back up the hill with your ankle." Lightning struck real close as the wind rushed around us. Heather grimaced as the ferns blew enough for her to see the dirt interior.

When we were through the vegetation, there was a hole just like I remembered—not very large, but still big enough for us. At any rate we would have a ledge over our heads and it seemed to be a comfortable temperature. "It doesn't look like a cave, and if it's mud we might get messed up with the ground giving away above us." Heather had a valid point. After asking her to steady herself, I carefully went into the hole. Luckily it appeared to have some rock in it, which meant it was solid. I returned to grab her around the waist as the ferns and trees started rustling with what one might call a land wave. We watched as the vegetation all leaned in a rippled as the air crossed our shivering forms. We made it inside barely in time before the rain came down in a sheet. Heather and I both looked around the forest floor. We were praying we weren't witnessing the beginning of a tornado. According to my memory though, it was always quiet with a tornado, and this was definitely a noisy thunderstorm with a lot of electricity, which meant we were in danger.

The angels must have been having fun, getting strikes in heaven because the lightning was cracking loud. Safe finally or were we? I had forgotten for the briefest moment about the shadow.

***

We could hear and feel the thundering of the storm, and we both wished we were home. It was a complete torrential downpour with no end in sight. Heather was rubbing her ankle, wishing for some ice and Tylenol, while I kept staring out through the tall ferns, wondering if I was going to see some stranger looking for us. At least in this place I could see out, and more than likely they would not be able to see in. The smell of must was coming in strong now, and I could see steam forming from the rain when it hit the ground. What was that? I saw a shape in the mist, definitely not a person. That was it—I could keep Heather's mind off her ankle by playing a game. "Heather, let's see if we can make different shapes out of the mist like we did with clouds when we were little. It will help us pass the time."

As I looked into the mist I could see many different things like animals, eyes, and shapes like people. All right, I could see absolutely nothing but mist. I kept telling myself that for a while. Heather interrupted my mental breakdown, wanting to know what I was looking for. Carefully I scooted back against the bank and realized I didn't have enough room to stretch out. "I was just trying to see how dark the sky is." Heather scoffed. I knew that was obvious by how the dark was enveloping us. Besides, the evening never came this early in the summer. When we had left the shore it was before five. I wondered if Mike had made it home safely.

Scooting back to the vegetation, I carefully peered out and this time saw nothing but a sheet of rain. Heather seemed to have found a comfortable spot to lean back into and had fallen asleep. How unusual that was. Heather hates sitting on the damp ground, let alone dealing with bugs. She really must be scared to try and escape by sleeping. The rain was making a nice rhythmic sound, which was soothing. Still, there was no way I would be able to go to sleep right now. Heather's ankle still looked really bad, and I could see that shadow in my head. I was listening intently to all the noises around us. If I heard the crunch of leaves or undergrowth, I could peek out and see what it was. My senses were on overload. Trying to distract myself, I decided I should take off my shoes and socks so I could use my socks as a cold compress. I would get them wet in the rain and place them on Heather's ankle to try to help with the swelling. Picking up my socks I had to giggle at what I was thinking about doing. Shep would say if it works then do whatever it takes in an emergency. This will really gross her out when she wakes up.

She really did have the worst luck with her ankles. Parker was always complaining that she should keep a brace on her left ankle so he wouldn't spend so much time running to the doctor's office to find out if she had broken it yet. Heather would sometimes make up the excuse that she must have her mother's ankles because the doctor told Parker it was an inherited problem with the joints.

Parker hardly ever talked about her mom. We didn't know much about her, just like I didn't know much about my birth parents..

Slowly I peeked out of the fern and crawled out into the storm and saw no one. Thank heavens. For a moment I relaxed until thunder hit above me. In a rush I scrambled over to a puddle and dropped my socks into it, hoping the coolness of the rain would reduce the swelling. As I was looking through the trees in the mist, I thought I could see the outline of a body. The harder I stared, the more I realized the body was transparent, almost like a ghost. He had very strong features, and his eyes had color. They were…blue eyes. His hair was short and his face was clean cut. He looked at me like he knew me. A tremor coursed through my body. When I looked back at where he had stood, he was gone. Immediately I began to shake my head in hopes of clearing my mind of the ghostly image. What was it I had told myself as I was leaving? That it would be nice to see a ghost? Well, I was wrong. That was the one thing I didn't want. I couldn't afford to let my imagination get carried away with me. Once again I looked, but found nothing. The only thing to be seen was the swirl of the mist. Unfortunately, I was totally soaked and my socks were thoroughly wet. Tilting my head back I let the rain hit my face, for it felt warm to my chilling skin.

I sat there for I don't know how long. Finally I decided I was only going to make myself sick or set myself up if someone was stalking us. A worse thought came to mind: how long we were going to be here? The rain was not letting up and there was no sign of the sun, for it was completely blocked out by the storm. None of this was good. The sun didn't go down until nine most of the summer. Once again, I lowered to my knees and crawled back into our shelter. Our area needed this rain anyhow. Several farms had to start irrigating their fields artificially. Farmers were just starting to get concerned that we were in for a dry summer. I guess this proved us all wrong. This area usually stayed pretty green and did have thunderstorms.

I wondered what Shep and Parker were thinking. It has to be close to five o'clock. Shep would get home and see I was not there and call Heather's house. I do spend a lot of time over there. Then both men will become upset and probably call Mike. Great, this is going to upset the whole neighborhood. I can see it now: "Two Girls Go Missing." Oh please Shep, remember not to let Parker blow this out of proportion. You know I like the woods and have gone camping a lot. I know to seek shelter and not to move until the storm has passed. As soon as the storm is over we can get home. Suddenly a thought went across my mind, almost like I could hear Shep say, *I know you're safe*. This day certainly has been really…unique.

Carefully, I leaned back against the rough wall thinking about the man's gentle face that I saw earlier. It made me wonder why I thought he had blue eyes. His face looked so familiar. I am sure I have seen it somewhere before. He looked sort of happy, but something else too. Again my eyes were drawn to the mist.

I could still make out shapes in the swirl. It had to be my vivid imagination. There were animals of all kinds, bodies dancing, and eyes, but not everything looked friendly. Hastily I closed my eyes as the thunder shouted at me, almost as if demanding for me to look. That was something I didn't want to do. How was Heather sleeping through this? I knew she was a sound sleeper, but this was ridiculous.

Again the air ricocheted with the sounds of lightning and thunder, forcing me to jerk my eyes open. My body was screaming how tired I was. I wanted to block all of this from my mind but couldn't. I wondered what all this forest has seen? Slowly my eyes fought to shut as I allowed my mind to wander. I could imagine voyageurs, soldiers, and Indians passing through here. This area was loaded with history. There had to be plenty of stories this forest could tell. In fact there was a piece of folklore about our little area that I always wondered about because of my interest in the supernatural. This piece of lore dealt with shadow people and super humans who lived together for a time in peace. But a war broke out and they were pitted against each other supposedly trying to save their world. What was it from? Shep always told me this story and I had heard it so many times, why would I forget it now?

The thunder and lightning seemed to get louder as if it was concentrated right over us, and Heather still did not wake up. As my mind relaxed I became aware of angry voices, but I couldn't tell what they were saying.

My eyes flew open and adjusted quickly. A fog was rolling towards our shelter, and in the fog, an arch seemed to be growing, intertwined with branches and vines. It had a triangle top, not a round arch found in traditional architecture. To my surprise I could see three men standing at it and a bright light bursting through. The fog was rolling towards them, and in the fog I saw many dark shapes. They were coming closer and closer to the men. I spotted another human within the darkness. His eyes looked strange, almost like they were swirling. He was arguing with the three men. By the way they were dressed I could assume they were voyageurs. Two of the voyageurs seemed to be moving their hands, which made the fog swirl around feverishly. Suddenly one of the men began shouting at the abnormal one. It was obvious he wasn't going to allow the man to exit the arch. The shadow's eyes changed from a swirl to a vibrant green as he smirked. Evidently he felt confident in pushing the issue as he was joined by other silhouetted forms. Abruptly he turned into a dark form, with flashes of light jumping on the man in front of him. I heard the man's neck snap with sounds of electricity echoing in the surrounding area. Shouts from other voyageurs drew my attention as they rushed in, waving their hands frantically at the opposing crowd. The fog and shadows seemed to be moving back through the tree, slowly fading from sight in the blur of the rain. The storm around them was getting worse. I hadn't noticed it before, but there were women there too.

What was happening? I needed to get out of here! The thunder clapped really loud as lightning struck a tree not too far away from us. I watched as it zigzagged across the purple sky. When I looked back to the fight, I found nothing but swirls of mist. Luckily I had been dreaming. In a rush I reached over towards Heather to reassure myself that all was fine. We were still in our little shelter and we were safe. I then felt an icy coldness that startled me when I found myself looking beside Heather at a woman wiping Heather's head, smiling. At that moment I realized it was a mist, and it evaporated. This dream seemed so real. Come on, Selena. Get a grip. No more dreaming.

After I checked Heather again, I settled back into my spot, not feeling as comfortable as I did before. I couldn't afford to lose it. Heather depended on me to be the levelheaded one. I had been thinking about fur traders and Indians right before I fell asleep, so that had to be the reason I had made such a dream. Leaning against the entrance, I looked out into the rain. It was letting up at least. Now I could distinguish the trees that were set off to the side of this small shelter. They were formed into a circle around a mound. We had seen that many times when Shep and I went camping.

I remember one year Heather and her dad joined us in Indiana. We stayed at Mounds State Park. They had wonderful hiking trails, and there were historical markers all over the place. She insisted on wearing some boots that she thought would be good for hiking, and the heel broke going up the devil's spine trail. Who in their right mind would go hiking in heels? When we finally made it up the hill, we came to many different mounds. Some were grave markers, and others had been fire pits. There was a large coliseum mound where the tribes had met. They even had a long entrance into the center of the bigger mound that functioned as a stage. Some would say the entrance reminded them of a spoon. They had performed meetings and rituals there. I imagine they had brought their horses down in a long processional. The entrance into the large mound was huge. I wonder if this mound might be a burial site. Shep will have to see it. I wondered what he would think.

Hearing the rain hit the leaves on the vegetation was peaceful, but sleep still was not going to happen. I wished I had a flashlight. The breeze was picking up as the trees were creaking while they swayed back and forth. I began concentrating again on listening to everything around us. It was almost like the pines were whispering, "Watch." Michiganders say pines whisper and they are loud. The noises of the trees were getting worse causing me to have to strain as I stared into the darkness. I could see the trees and they seemed to be growing into the arch again. This time, however, it was different. The arch held a closed door. It wasn't a wood door, just solid darkness. Hmm… Fog rolled in and I saw people laying things in the ground and crying. Cautiously I crawled forward so I could see what was happening. Oh my goodness, it was the voyageur I had seen killed. This must be his funeral. I watched the group's activities not hearing much but felt I was intruding on something personal. The sky was clear with stars and I could see the Leo constellation. It seemed there were small fires throughout the woods with small groupings of people around them. To my surprise I could smell the fires too. Suddenly the smell changed and I recognized the smell of fall. This time I turned back to the dead voyageur only to see one mound covered with fall leaves and seven saplings arranged in a circle around it. This was not right. I could not be seeing these things. Wake up. Come on wake up…..

Once more I found myself sitting out in the beating rain on my knees. The rain was subsiding as the sun started to rise. The rain felt like ice even if it was lighter. How did I get out here? Could I have been sleepwalking? Rapidly I crawled back into the shelter this time shaking from the cold. My knees and legs were caked in mud. I tried wiping them off the best I could but it was of little use. I felt cold as I wrapped my hands around my knees in hopes of warming my body. Slowly my mind began to process the dreams. The last set was as unsettling as the first.

This had been the worst night in my life.

As I moved back into the corner I curled up with my back facing the entrance. I was trying to force my core heat to warm my extremities. This time I became too comfortable only to jerk myself awake. To my surprise the rain was done and the forest was bright with the sun. I had fallen asleep after trying not to after that last dream. Slowly I crept out and stood up to examine how terrible I must look. I was filthy and cold. Then again I remembered my dream as I looked around for the mounds and those trees. When I finally found them, there was a mist draping over them and a man standing with what appeared to be tears in his beautiful blue eyes. He lifted his hand up and made the sign that said, "I LOVE YOU." Then his form evaporated. Now I knew I had really seen that.

Immediately I began shouting to Heather as I slid back in to drag her out. I felt close to hysterics. "Have you gone crazy?" she shouted as I continued to pull her into the mud. "No, Selena. You were dreaming. I don't see anything but a mist." Maybe she was right. The sun was shining quite bright now, and it was filtering through the trees with a light mist rising. When I looked up at the top of the hill, I saw Shep standing there with a big grin on his face as he stared down at me. He looked satisfied.

# CHAPTER 2.
# SHADOW OF YESTERDAY

**"Shep,** how did you find us?" I felt total relief at seeing his smiling face. The sun outlined his slender, well-built form as he stood at the top of the hill.

"Selena, I'm coming down." He was down the hill in a flash and moved with such grace you would think it took no effort to get to us. "Do I even want to know what happened to your shoes and socks, Selena? I always knew it was hard to keep your shoes on you, but this is not the place to go barefoot," he stated while laughing. As Heather looked at me indignantly, she told Shep how she woke up with my cold socks draped across her ankle. Shep really started laughing then. "Heather, I think she forfeited her socks trying to make a cold compress to keep the swelling down on your ankle. But as far as why she looks like she went swimming in the mud, I have no idea." I was beginning to feel totally unappreciated when I realized how bad I really did look. Quickly gazing down, I could see my hands were dirty, my shirt was stained, my knees and legs were caked with mud, and who knows what my face looked like. Suddenly I felt extremely tired and stumbled back. Shep jumped to steady me as he began to look at me with concern. "Are you all right, Selena? You look like you haven't slept, and you're as pale as a ghost."

"I think I am overtired. It was a long night. I think with you here I was able to relax and it just hit me." We heard people shouting our names as Shep hollered to guide them towards us. The sudden weakness in my knees forced me to sit down and try to regroup my energy. I must have been more scared than I thought. People from the neighborhood came running from all directions and were ecstatic we were safe. It was like a block party was forming. I smiled weakly up at Mike as he came charging down the hill, demanding to know what had happened to us. Parker, however, was not in the mood to accommodate anyone's curiosity. Instead, he looked sicker than I had ever seen him; he looked like he was about to break. He kept kissing Heather's hair, and I was sure I heard him muttering a prayer of thanks.

When I looked around, I wasn't at all surprised to see John and Chelsea Muir coming up from the opposite direction of the others. It was evident they had gone towards the shoreline in search of us. John began hollering to the others that we were found and for all to return to the cul-de-sac. He pointed to Mike and ordered him to find his brother and tell anyone else he ran across. Mike took off up the hill like it was nothing as John kissed Chelsea on the cheek. "I'll go towards the boardwalk so we cover a large area. Chelsea, you will need to announce it on all emergency frequencies." Chelsea nodded as she smiled at me, and began announcing over the talkie we had been found. Today she looked even younger than normal. She almost looked too young to be in her thirties. Her hair was short, and the natural highlights almost made her look like she was in her twenties. Her tan sports jacket blew in the wind to show she still had the shape of a young girl, instead of a woman who had given birth to three boys. One thing about Chelsea: she wasn't easily pushed around by anyone but her husband. She was a strong woman.

Quickly my attention was drawn back to Parker as he began to growl for people to either help him or get out of his way. Shep was by my side and grinned down at me. "Would you like to be carried, too?"

"Of course… NOT" I huffed at him as I stood up. Gently he placed his arm around my shoulders and gave me a big hug as he whispered how happy he was to find us safe. Then he offered that he had no doubt he had taught me correctly about forest safety. What a smarty. Even though he was smiling, I could read the concern on his face. He started telling me all that had happened the night before. He had found Parker sitting on our porch when he arrived home.

"Mike was really upset. He didn't realize you were not behind him until he was at the cul-de-sac. He waited a few minutes, but the storm was raging, so he decided to run home and tell his mom. Chelsea got ahold of John. Of course John came home immediately and went out looking for you with one of the men from his agency, but visual perception was at zero and more than likely a search would only end in injury." Part of Parker's work was to help coordinate search teams that would later help in rebuilding communities hit by disasters. I was feeling slightly winded, so Shep insisted on us sitting down for a moment as he continued. He kept brushing my bangs back and swiftly wrapped his rain jacket around my shoulders. "Anyway, as soon as Parker pulled into the driveway, Mike informed him you must have lost your way in the storm and were in the woods somewhere. John was there with him when Parker went ballistic, wondering why you hadn't seen the storm coming and headed back sooner." Poor Mike. I knew he already felt bad, and I bet this had made it worse. "From what John tells me, it was near impossible to calm Parker down. He kept muttering he couldn't handle another time like when Athena ran off. John sent Mike home so he and his partner could talk to Parker. They were already working on a search team from their own place of business and had even called Chelsea's dad, Travis. Did you know that is how John met Chelsea? Her dad is a policeman or an agent, and John was a field agent and had been assigned to Travis, who is somewhere around here."

Shep seemed to act puzzled by this as he looked around. "He barely said 'hi' to me. All he muttered was that he would have you found within an hour. He wouldn't let anybody go with him." For a brief moment Shep seemed distant, and then suddenly he tapped my leg, wanting to know if I was ready to walk some more. Softly agreeing I could, we stood, only for me to feel how weak I truly did feel. As I encouraged Shep to continue, he wiped his hand over his bald head like he always did when concentrating on a problem. We slowly began to walk, but I felt his firm grip around my waist holding me tight.

"Well, John and his man went home to coordinate the search party that was here today. They were mixing professionals with neighborhood people. They didn't want anybody going it alone. After they left, Parker made a million calls. He never did say to who, though. To me he acted very funny about that whole privacy thing. Parker was hoping I had trained you well enough to be able to handle this type of circumstance."

Again we stopped as Shep rubbed his bald head and looked to me with concern. "Parker wanted to demand for the sheriff to come out during the storm. I convinced him to wait until the storm broke. I was sure they would be here at first break. The only problem we had was how far off the main path did you have to go to find shelter. You weren't going to be able to get away from the trees. Of that I was certain. You wouldn't head towards the water, either." This time, as we resumed walking, I could tell Shep was becoming more and more worried with the weakness I was showing. I hadn't realized how badly I felt until he arrived. I didn't want him to worry about me, so maybe if I kept pushing we would make it home soon.

"Parker figured Heather would be hysterical, but you would manage to keep her calm. We both made jokes on how you would probably turn it into a big adventure. I tried to get Parker to go to sleep, but he wouldn't. Even so, I made up a bed on the couch. He only stared out the window and kept trying to call a friend named Dracus or something." Shep continued to mumble for a moment, as if mulling over a problem with the name. "I believe Parker finally fell asleep around one-thirty."

Because Shep had been telling me this story the whole time we were walking, I hadn't realized we were back to the cul-de-sac. Several people rushed forward to wish us well while talking excitedly about our little adventure. I was shocked to see a shelter had been pitched and how people were crowded around it. I recognized several of my teachers, along with people from all over the community. To everyone's dismay, Shep and Parker insisted on getting us home and not prolonging our misery as John and his people began making a clear path for us to walk home.

John kept hollering that there was nothing to see and to shove off. He would be giving full details within the hour. John then turned and winked at me. "You can call me Shep when you do get the full story. I am sure it is a doozy. Good to see ya, girl. Next time, keep my son with ya though. I wouldn't have had to worry so much if he had been." John was a sweet man, but a chauvinist too. Abruptly I heard the honk of a car and registered that Parker was trying to pull out into the massive crowd. John whistled, and I saw Travis and Andy—along with several other people—start yelling for people to move so Parker could go to the hospital.

When I arrived at our home, I couldn't wait to just lie down. Luckily the couch still had the blankets on it to welcome me home. Quickly I laid down before my legs dropped me to the floor. Shep cuddled me in like he did when I was little and turned the fireplace on. The sound was very soothing as I watched it flicker for a while. Then I noticed Shep sitting in his chair, looking anxiously at me. I tried to assure him I was fine, but he refused to listen. Instead he insisted on me trying to sleep, which I did with great pleasure.

I don't know how long I had been asleep, but the sun was shining directly through our window. The blankets felt so warm and cozy that I didn't want to move. Shep was playing our piano quietly. "Are you all right, Selena?"

"Yes, I feel so comfortable and warm I just don't want to wake up yet."

"Then don't." He continued to rub my face until I fell asleep again. Shep always said that when I was a baby, the only way to get me to sleep was to rub my face. I guess that still holds true.

When I woke the next time, it was dark outside, and Shep was sitting on the hearth, seeming to talk to someone. "Hey, who are you talking to, yourself?" I asked sarcastically. "I knew you were getting old, but not that old yet."

Shep smirked. "So, you are finally awake little one. Would you like something to eat this time?" At the mention of food my stomach started growling. We both laughed as I jerked myself up from the couch, only to feel dizzy. Thankfully Shep caught me as I fell forward. "You sure you didn't have any liquor out there with you the other night?"

"The other night," I squealed. "How long have I been asleep?" This time I heard his muffled chuckle. "About two days. You needed the rest. Whatever happened during your overnight in the woods was difficult for you. Before you ask, Heather is doing fine. Unfortunately, she will be wearing her brace for the next couple of weeks. She has been calling to check on you. You will have to call her tomorrow."

I thought about how Parker had looked so unhappy when he pulled out of the drive. Heather didn't like upsetting Parker—ever. She always felt angry at her mom for leaving them without even leaving a note of excuse. Heather didn't ever want Parker to look at her in the same way he looked at her mom when she left; this episode came mightily close to that.

The smell of eggs and toast caught my attention. I usually don't like eggs, but I like Shep's. His were made with butter and tasted great. My only regret for this meal would be the cleanup. Shep loves to cook, but not to clean up, because that was my job. I am the one who has the pleasure of eating. So naturally I have the pleasure of cleaning the kitchen too. Shep sat down and enjoyed the feast with me.

For once he seemed to want to ask something, but he didn't. I hate it when he does that. I am not a mind reader. Although I could guess that this time he wanted to know what happened the other night in the woods. I know Heather couldn't tell them much since she slept the whole night. "You did a real good job with Heather's ankle the doctor said. He loved your idea of cold socks for a compress. Her foot wasn't too swollen when they got to the doctor and seems she was able to sleep through the pain. The doctor was amazed." Shep seemed to be studying me like he hadn't ever set eyes on me before.

"That is why I was muddy. I kept going out into the rain and getting my socks drenched and crawling back in. I tried to sleep, but I kept having very vivid dreams...some were even nightmares." I then shivered as I remembered the shadows, the fight of the voyageur, the funeral, and worrying about that stranger or animal in the woods.

Shep reached across the table and patted my hand. "Are you sure you're all right? Do you want to talk about this tomorrow?" I shook my head as he poured me more milk. His eyes were full of worry now, and I knew I couldn't torture him anymore. Taking a deep breath, I steadied myself and began the story. "We had been at the beach that day, and the storm came suddenly. There was no real warning. As we were running through the woods, Heather kept stopping because of cobwebs. I was pushing her to keep going, but the storm was too fast. I know this sounds funny...I thought I saw a person in the woods off to the side and it scared me. When I turned around, Heather had fallen, making it imperative to find shelter. We were in the middle of white ash trees, and I couldn't think of anywhere to go. So then out of nowhere, I remembered that little shelter we were in. I took Heather to where I thought it was and found it. She had a hard time getting to it, though. When we were inside, we propped her foot up and argued a little. The rain was pouring, and I went out to get my socks wet to keep the swelling down on her ankle. When I came back in, she was sleeping. The fog out there kept playing tricks on my eyes. At one point I was thinking about history, of course, and fell asleep. I had a dream about voyageurs and some kind of strange man. They were fighting over something, and this creature or man turned into a dark shape and killed a voyageur. I woke up and saw the socks needed to be soaked again, so I crawled out. Heather was still sleeping through that loud storm. While I was out in the storm I happened to notice a mound. It has a circle of seven trees around it. I think you and I should go look at it some time.

"Anyway, I told you my imagination was running away with me and I could see forms in the mist, a man...Anyway, I must have fallen asleep again because I dreamed about those old funerals they used to have in those days. It seemed so real. At one point when I was in the shelter, I thought I saw a beautiful lady taking care of Heather. Crazy, I know, but I wished my mom had been there to help me." Seeing that hurt expression on his face, I quickly apologized. "Sorry. The trees were even whispering like our trees do in the backyard at night. Everything just seemed so loud and real that I couldn't sleep anymore. So I waited for the sun to come out so I could help Heather home. It was a really rough night. In many ways I was scared." I wasn't about to tell him about the man on the mound using sign language to tell me he loved me. Shep would pack me up and take me to the hospital for sure. He would think I had hit my head or something. Besides, this thought seemed very personal to me.

We began clearing the dishes when Shep sent me to my room to get some sleep. It was clear he was worried, and if I didn't know better, a bit scared too. There was no way I was going to argue about not doing the dishes. Plus, I still felt drained. Once in my nice warm flannel sheets and fresh pj's, I laid there thinking about the man when Shep came in and sat down on the edge of my bed.

"Selena, your parents would be very proud of you, and so am I. I know you miss them, and everything you told me does not sound crazy. You know you can talk to me about anything and I will listen, and most of the time not interrupt. After all I am your favorite Protector. I expect you to follow the rules. Still, I want you to feel free to talk to me about anything. You might be surprised by my response. Sometimes things are not what they seem to be. Think about it, okay?"

Rolling my eyes I reminded him that he was my dad. He laughed as he covered his beautiful smile. "My parents made arrangements for my adoption, and I don't think they would mind if you call yourself my dad. Sometimes I don't think you want me to be your daughter." Hastily Shep jerked to kiss my head.

"No, there you are wrong. You're mine, and will always be completely mine no matter what. A father couldn't be prouder of his daughter." Gently he brushed my bangs back from my eyes as he ordered me to get some sleep, and tomorrow to take a shower because I stunk. It didn't take a command for me to acquiesce. Without much effort, I turned over and went straight to sleep.

The next morning I took a long, hot shower. There was no noise in the house so Shep must still be sleeping. The past several days must have been hard for him. Maybe I could make him breakfast for once. I pulled out some frozen waffles and dropped them into the toaster. That was the extent of my cooking skills. Suddenly I heard the sound of Shep stirring in his bathroom. He wasn't giving me enough time to do *anything* for him. In a rush I grabbed the syrup from the pantry along with plates and silverware on the way back to the table. Not a second later Shep came walking in and laughed since he knows I am no cook unless it comes from a box, bag, or can. At least I was trying to do something nice for him. Our conversation over the breakfast table was quite interesting since it involved a discussion of the history of the area, including Indians, voyageurs and the first settlers. We figured it was possible that what I saw was a real mound. Shep agreed we would go look at it on Saturday.

When the phone rang I rushed to answer it. I was sure it would be Heather, and I was right. Her voice sounded concerned as she continued to evaluate my health. She was wondering if I was part bear since I had been sleeping for forever. We laughed about the whole thing and decided to meet later. Shep, however, hollered in that he would prefer for us to stay around the house today. Hastily I informed Heather that I would see her tomorrow instead. Going back into the study, I watched him type frantically on the keyboard.

Quietly I sat down on the couch and turned on the little TV. A second later, Shep turned around to see what I was doing. His smirk was a sign that he was about to make some kind of wise crack. "Haven't you vegetated enough the past couple days?" Instantly I gave him a dirty look as I continued to watch TV. He seemed to get all his paperwork done in record time. Evidently, the day I had gone missing he had been on a call at a farm where he delivered a foal and a litter of puppies. Today he needed to go and check on the foal and wanted to know if I wanted to join him. Of course I wanted to go! I might see those beautiful pups and convince Shep to let us buy one.

As I was coming through the kitchen, I spied his vet bag sitting on the table and grabbed it. If he didn't have me he would lose his head. He was laughing when he saw what I had in hand and was grateful he hadn't left it. We drove for about thirty minutes before we pulled into a long drive that led to a farm. Ben was waiting there with a big smile, waving us in.

"Glad you got here, Doc. Susie and the foal are doing great. That little thing has been walking around and even jumping a little. Come on to the barn and see." As we followed him into the barn, my nose was assaulted by all the farm smells imaginable. I like animals, but I really can't stand the smell of pigs. Wrinkling up my nose, I started to back out, but Ben pushed me forward to look at the new foal. It was a beautiful brown horse. Shep went in and started giving them the once over when Ben motioned for me to come to the farmhouse.

He had a house full of boys. Jeremy was my age and came over grinning, wanting to know if I wanted to see his mom's Yorkies. We went into the kitchen to find several black pups. They were adorable. All Yorkies are black when they are born. Jeremy informed me they were going to sell them in about a month or two. I would love to have one. Hopefully I could convince Shep into letting me. Jeremy leaned back against the counter as I played with the pups. "I hear you and Heather got lost the other night." I gave a quick nod and continued to play with the pups. The way Jeremy stood there made me uncomfortable. It was like he was studying me or something. "Is it true that Heather slept through that whole storm?"

"Yep."

Jeremy winced as he knelt awkwardly beside me, only to brush his hand down my back. "It was a freaky storm, especially with the way it came in so fast. Most of the farmers are concerned this year. The weather isn't acting by what is the norm lately. It was almost like a tornado. There wasn't enough warning to secure anything." I was glad someone else had noticed how fast it came in. "It's the talk around town. Many feel it is like the storms that the Coast Guard are always worried about. Heather was just lucky to have you with her. I know you can handle most anything. Can't tolerate girly girls." Jeremy moved closer to me, causing me to scoot further off to the side. I had the feeling lately that he wanted to be more than friends. We had grown up together, and I just couldn't see myself dating him.

Luckily, Shep came in with Ben to take a look at the pups. "They're doing just fine, Ben." Within the next moment, Shep pushed Jeremy over as he offered his hand to assist me up. "Time to go little one. I've got business to attend to elsewhere. Ben, we have to be going. Susie and the foal are doing fine. I don't think they will need..."

Ben threw off his hat. "No, I want that foal checked on again. Just set me an appointment in that dang book for the same time next week. That little stallion is going to help with the bills when I can sell his services. With his lineage I already have offers."

As we left, we waved bye to the Bakers as Shep grumbled under his breath that Jeremy was going to be a problem. I was shocked at his statement, for Shep rarely grumbled about anyone. I wondered if he had sensed the same thing I had.

The drive into town was wonderful. Instead of using the AC we opened the windows and turned our music up loud. It may not have been hip hop, but it still was loud. Who says new age and classical didn't have a beat? If they only realized rock came from classical music, they would croak.

Arriving at the house, we sat at our picnic table in the back and ate our pizza and breadsticks. The breeze seemed to be just right, even with the sun going down. We always have a breeze around here. We get the lake effect. I think that is what they call it. I believe that is why we have so much wind. They say in Michigan you only have to drive ten minutes from anywhere and you will see water.

Shep commented it looked like I had recovered from my adventure and that he would be going back to work tomorrow. Which meant that Heather and I could do something. Since it was getting late, I decided to go do some laundry, read a book, and go to bed on time for once. Shep agreed that sounded like a good plan.

While sorting the clothes, I started listening to some more music. Music always makes chores go faster. The laundry was sorted, and I could finally start it. It was a good thing Shep wasn't doing the laundry since there were some red items today. I remember one time he did the laundry and there was a red towel in the load. Needless to say, he was wearing pink for the next couple months. All the staff teased him forever and suggested he find a wife. Poor guy, he was never going to live that one down.

The laundry was running, and this would give me a chance to read one of my favorite books: *Treasure Island.* Sitting down on my bed, I began to read while hearing Shep walk into his room, being quite loud. Wonder what he's doing? Slowly my posture slipped down further into my comfy pillows as the sun seemed to be setting by the look of the shadows coming through the window. My eyes felt tired and heavy. Unfortunately, my thoughts wandered back to the man in the woods.

The man was a true puzzle, for he hadn't looked like the others. In many ways he looked real. His eyes were very endearing to me. Shadows seemed to play on the walls, and they looked like they were dancing. A thought came to me of a city after nightfall, and there seemed to be movement in a little area to the left of me. After hearing their voices I went closer. They seemed to be talking about the death of a physician who had been murdered by G…I couldn't understand what they were saying. Evidently the physician had trusted these people and they murdered her. How sad; not only was she murdered, but another friend was killed at the same time with no apparent cause. This place was dark and gave me the creeps. At times it seemed to vibrate somehow. The sound of their discouragement was heartbreaking. They didn't seem to believe this Lovie could have been hurt in this way.

So Lovie was the physician's name. That name was really old-fashioned. The blare of the washer going off woke me from my dream. Hopefully this wasn't going to become a common occurrence every time I slept. Why had it been so sad? And the town was much older than most modern places.

Quickly I rushed to the laundry room and opened the lid of the washer and started grabbing the clothes out to throw them into the dryer. Since I had fallen asleep, I decided not to do any more tonight. I didn't like to have to wash things twice. It was a waste of water and money. After starting the dryer, I went back to my room and prepared for bed just in case I fell asleep again. So what if I had to iron something tomorrow? That would be fine. In the bathroom I looked in the mirror while brushing my teeth and thought about the dream I just had. Why were my dreams so strange now? Maybe my book had influenced my dreams. Come to think of it, the city did look a bit like something described in *Treasure Island.* Slipping back into my bed I found a comfortable spot and felt like I was floating on a cloud. Maybe this time I would not have any dreams.

It was really dark when I woke up. I knew I should go check the laundry, but I couldn't move. The thought that I might save myself from having to iron was strong, but I was too comfortable. Slowly I turned towards the clock to read it was two a.m. This meant I had plenty of time to sleep. I turned the radio on to the classic radio station and fell asleep again.

Once again I entered a dark passage, and I could tell there was a large group there. They seemed to be trying to go somewhere but couldn't. It was very crowded. People were shoving, and it felt real. They were grumbling that they had to make it through or there was going to be big trouble. I heard fighting and someone bumped me and made me hit a wall with my shoulder. I tried moving back where there seemed to be less pressure on my body. Still hearing the angry voices, I became scared and screamed when I realized I was falling. Next thing I knew, Shep was holding my shoulders and shaking me awake.

"Wake up, Selena. You're safe!" For a moment I thought I heard him growl something about sanctuary and abilities coming forth. My eyes flew open. I grabbed him so I would not fall any further, only to see that I was still in my bed. He looked at me, demanding to know what I had seen.

That was an odd question; why hadn't he asked me what I had dreamed? "I was dreaming I was falling. You know the dream where you are falling and there is no way to stop?" He nodded and laid me back against the pillow while he went into the kitchen. I heard the pan clank against the stove and knew he was making me warm milk. That is what Shep always thought took away bad dreams and tummy aches. I sighed with a smile as he came in with my cup of warm milk, demanding to know if I would be able to go back to sleep. "Of course I can. I have my milk and you. I'm fine. Sorry for scaring you. Now go back to bed. You have work tomorrow and don't worry, I'm fine." Shep reached down and rubbed my cheek, saying he could stay until I had a good dream. I knew he needed his rest.

Later, Shep went back to bed and I was left dumbfounded about why I was having these dreams. At least tomorrow I would get back into my normal summer routine, and maybe my mind would stop interfering with my dreams.

# CHAPTER 3.
# REVEALING

**The** next morning the sun was shining bright like an angel had been sitting on my windowsill. There had been no more dreams, and for once I felt rested. Turning over towards the clock, I realized my shoulder was sore. I must have slept on it wrong. It was a surprise to discover it was already nine-thirty a.m. I was supposed to be meeting Heather at eleven o'clock. Hastily I ran to the bathroom. As I reached for the shower knob I felt a twinge of pain again. Now I took time to rub my shoulder. Maybe the heated water could work the kink out. The water felt so good I thought I could stand there forever. I rinsed out my hair as memories of my dreams began to infiltrate my mind. The dreams had felt real in many ways. This thought totally unnerved me, especially when I remembered hitting my shoulder in the last dream.

Quickly I jumped out of the shower to take a look at the sore spot. When I wiped down the mirror I began to examine my arm carefully. To my astonishment I discovered a huge purple bruise appearing right where I had hit it. How could this happen? I mean, I get bruised easily all the time and I rarely know what I did to get them. Yet, this dream kept hammering at my mind. I had been shoved into a wall or something. I didn't understand why my dreams were so vivid or why they seemed to dwell on violent events. If Shep caught sight of my new bruise he would have a cow.

What to have for breakfast had to be my focus, for time was getting away from me. At that very moment the phone rang, and I knew it must be Heather. Instead of answering, I grabbed my towel and started getting dressed. My jogging pants and a soft shirt were all I was in the mood for. For a second I stopped in midstride as I rethought my attire for the day. If we went on a ride to the lighthouse or out to the new construction site, then I would need something heavier that might protect my legs. I really didn't need any more bruises.

After running to the kitchen I began making toast and poured a glass of milk. Once I was back in the family room I turned on the TV to nothing in particular. It was so I could have a little background noise to eat by. Most of the time I enjoyed the silence, but today it was unnerving me. Maybe my night in the forest had been a little more stressful than I thought. Hopefully a good bike ride would help me relax and wear out my body enough so I could sleep tonight, preferably without any nightmares. That would put me in a good mood.

Going into the garage, I grabbed a beef stick to carry in my pocket and a bottle of Mountain Dew. Most days Mountain Dew was my main refreshment. I grabbed my bike and made sure the brakes worked well. No accidents today. Shep would never let me out of his sight again if something happened. Slowly the garage door opened to reveal Heather already riding her bike towards my house. She didn't look like she was in the best of moods either. "Hey Selena, you scared me to death with all the sleeping you've done after our little adventure. What's up?"

"I'm fine. I couldn't sleep with taking care of your ankle, and the storm was so loud, I don't even know how you slept through it." I felt totally unnerved. Usually I was the calming influence. Heather watched me with concern creeping deeper into her eyes.

"The doctor said the sprain wasn't bad and you really did take care of it well. Maybe when you graduate you should be a nurse. I still get grossed out over what you did with your socks though. Did you get to see those puppies yesterday? Karen is talking about them. It sounds like her mom is going to buy one."

"Yes, they were beautiful! I am thinking about asking Shep if we could buy one too."

Heather seemed to bounce with excitement as she offered to help convince him. "We'll talk to him later. Mike is waiting on us. He said to meet him at the path into the woods right before you get to the city planks. We thought we would go to the sand dunes. He wants to see if he can jump his new mountain bike out there. I think I will just watch today. Riding my bike is about all I can manage with this brace on. I probably shouldn't even be doing *that*."

My mind ran over several possibilities of what Mike might be considering doing today. I could see him doing something stupid like trying to jump those sand dunes. Mike is a daredevil. Hopefully he was only considering jumping our little hill and not one of those bluffs. You can barely walk on the dunes, let alone ride on them. I just had this nagging feeling that something bad was going to happen.

Mike was already waiting for us at the beginning of the path. "Hey sleepyhead, how are you doing?" His cocky grin made me feel happier.

"Fine." Mike's grin twitched into a look of guilt. "Sorry I left you the other night I..."

"Stop, Mike, I don't want to hear it. I would prefer to go have a good day riding our bikes. I really didn't care about you leaving. Really, I just wanted to make sure Heather was all right. We both survived and no blood was spilled." We lifted our bikes up over the curb without another word and started down the path that led into the woods. When we were about five minutes from the entrance, we turned onto the planked boardwalk put in by the city for tourist and community walkers to use. Today we were going to use it to get to the beginning of the dunes where the sand, grass, and dirt all came together. As we were riding along, I was hoping we might continue out to the Point. It would be a long ride, but well worth it. Sometimes you can see ships on the horizon, and they look like they are barely moving. That would be awesome today.

It looked like Mike was determined to put his new bike to the test. Heather, however, stopped on the planks while Mike forged ahead. It was clear he wanted to go further in except that would be too dangerous, especially with Heather's injury. Mike waited on her patiently. His pride had sustained some damage the other night due to his lack of chivalry, and I was sure today he needed to make up for it in his own way. We began riding again, once Heather had made it clear that she wasn't going to be able to do much since her ankle was already throbbing. Mike didn't scowl or anything. He just shrugged his shoulders in defeat as he muttered that it didn't matter.

We had been riding for about fifteen minutes when we finally arrived at what many consider to be the easiest bike hill for beginners. This place had lots of pine trees to the side and sand grass surrounded us. You could see the dune we liked to ride over occasionally before going further to the more dangerous ones. This one had a well-trodden path. Even little kids from the neighborhood liked to ride over this one. Going off the path, Mike and I ran over our favorite hill, enjoying the plunge down the other side, while Heather left her bike at the planks and hobbled towards us. At the bottom, Heather and I started to turn around when Mike hollered for us to come on. I jumped off my bike and started shouting at him to stop. He hadn't even checked the next hill. Everybody who lives here understands that sometimes because of the sand drifts, you might be coming off a cliff instead of a hill. Mike was crazy. He started pumping his bike harder. Luckily he didn't have enough speed and slid back down. This time he went back to the first hill and told us to go watch from the bottom of the second while he tried it again. He muttered that Andy had ridden out here last night and told him he had to jump the second hill to reach the other side. One thing about the Muir boys was that they couldn't allow the other to do something that they hadn't done. This was why he had demanded to come out here. He had to be on a level playing field; that's what Mike always said when he felt he was competing against his brothers.

When I looked at the second hill, I realized that he had no clue how big of a jump it truly was. I didn't see how Andy had made it. It was so wide I wasn't sure that Andy hadn't lied. There was no way Mike would be able to pull this off safely. Heather and I began warning him as he slid back down, looking irritated with us. With that look of determination in his eyes, it was clear there wasn't much we could do. We both pleaded with him to think, but instead he laughed, telling us we worried too much. He muttered he just had to keep up the momentum he had from the first hill to manage the jump, even if it was wide. He ordered us to watch or we would miss it.

Mike took off, and we both followed him as he made it up the first hill and continued to peddle down the other side. When he reached the slight grade of the second hill, it did look like it was going better. That Muir stubbornness to take risk was peeking through today, especially with a challenge from his brother. It was a wonder these boys had survived their childhood without maiming themselves.

When I went to the other side, I had forgotten that Mike would have to jerk his bike instead of using a ramp to make the jump. All of this was getting worse by the minute. He was strong, but was he strong enough to manage this? The only positive thing was that there was more sand than dirt, and maybe that would soften his fall. We heard his bike whizzing up the hill. I saw him coming over the top, but the bike didn't fly out. It plummeted almost straight down. He was going to go face first into the ground. He hadn't understood he was going to have to propel the bike into the jump. He was expecting a lip to help shoot him up.

Instinctively I closed my eyes, whispering to myself. Without thought, I threw up my hands in offering to stop what was happening. I couldn't help but watch in horror as the bike began to fall precariously. To my great surprise, I noticed that Heather seemed to slowly gasp as things around me slowed down. I tried to convince myself this was not happening. Heather was starting to scream in terror at what we were seeing when the wind picked up and Mike began to move in slow motion. He was able to straighten the front of the bike up and slowly throw his body to the side in order not to have the bike seat break under his butt from the impact. My breathing began to speed up, and I found myself screaming as well. This was totally terrifying. Then everything seemed to go back to normal speed. Mike and his bike were on the ground. He rolled over, wincing in the pain from the hard landing .

As Heather went running over to him, I thought I saw someone watching the whole horrible incident from the shade of the trees. When I ran to Mike, he was sitting up, grabbing his knees, saying he was all right. Swiftly I looked around for the individual, only to realize I had been mistaken. No one was there.

"Mike, you are so lucky," Heather kept repeating as he shook his head up and down in agreement. We both agreed that everything seemed to happen in slow motion like in the movies. Solemnly, Mike admitted he had never felt anything like that before. Mike and Heather both seemed to shiver from our ordeal. Sometimes people say that when something bad happens, it seems to last forever. I hated to admit they were right.

Shaking his head with disgust, Mike promised not to try that again. Softly he admitted that he had landed far too hard on his butt. He was going to be really bruised. Heather and I had a fit of giggles to the point we thought our sides were going to bust when Mike winced as he tried to push himself up. He huffed as we each made some kind of sarcastic remark at his predicament. "At least you all are benefitting from my misery," he said. It didn't take long for us to see the error of our overwhelming laughter as we wondered if he could walk. He grinned before commenting that walking was all he was going to be doing for the next several days.

Gently we pulled him up and dragged his bike back to the planks as Mike decided to go home. Heather grabbed her bike and started teasing him that he would never sit again. I couldn't resist joining in on the ribbing too. "Yeah, you are going to be the butt of all of Heather's jokes for the next year, Mike!" Again I grinned, but I realized in my terror and relief that I had left my bike at the bottom of the first hill. With disgust I encouraged them to go on home and I would catch up with them later.

My two childhood friends were limping home instead of riding. This was a sight I had to laugh at. This made me wonder what was going to happen in their future. Sometimes I wondered if they didn't have a crush on each other, but they both always gagged when I hinted. I continued back to the hill and could see my bike on the other side. Slowly I walked back to it, still pondering how the wind had picked up at just the right instant, and how everything seemed so slow there for a while when he was in the air. Was I missing something? The past week had been very strange and I was beginning to wonder: what if things were not as they seemed? Hadn't Shep mentioned something like that once? Suddenly the wind picked up again and the pines started their whispering, and I felt like I was being watched. As a shiver went through my whole body I fought the feeling of panic that was building inside me. I tried to muster enough courage to turn around, but it was not coming easy to me. I closed my eyes, wishing time would stop so if there was something behind me, I could run.

Again the sounds around me slowed down and when I opened my eyes, it looked like the seagulls were flying in slow motion. And yet I seemed to be turning around faster than everything else around me. Why was this happening? It was not possible. This was something from the *Twilight Zone*. Beginning to breathe normally, I heard a low laugh from beside one of the pine trees to my left. To my surprise it was Shep. But there was movement behind him, like someone else had been there with him. He started clapping with a big grin on his face as he moved forward. "Maybe it *is* possible for something like slow motion to happen. Maybe you should stop wishing for time and breathe a little, because no one is going to hurt you while I'm around."

How could he have known what I was thinking? I had stopped breathing. My heart had skipped a beat I was sure. I felt my heart jump as it went back into its normal rhythm, as did everything around me. Shep came over to me and looked deep into my troubled eyes. "It is time we had a talk about what is real and what can be." Hastily I looked around as I tried to make sure I hadn't hurt myself and was making all this up. What if I was lying unconscious and this was...Shep shook me a little, and then I noticed that even the seagulls were back to normal. When I looked at him he seemed ecstatic, like he was going to burst. Why was he so happy about this? This was not a good thing.

"What is going on? Did you see what I did?" I felt like I was going to hyperventilate.

He touched my face and rubbed my cheek. "I have been waiting a long time for you to do something that wasn't normal."

"You are supposed to be at work. Why are you here?" Again Shep laughed. "Technically I am at work." With a great sigh he stared at me. Shep seemed happy, and yet he was leery too. He took me by the shoulders and said he didn't have time to explain things yet, but he promised he would very soon. "I will have to straighten things out at the office first." He encouraged me to go straight home and wait for him there. For the first time he looked around anxiously. "I don't want you going anywhere else. Do not talk to anybody that you don't know. If you see any of your friends, tell them you received a call from me and you have no choice. You have to go home immediately. Selena, you have to trust me and follow my instructions to a tee. There are things you do not understand. As you have seen, you are able to do things normal people cannot do. You have nothing to fear. You are being carefully watched over right now. Do you understand?" I shook my head up and down as my mind screamed for me to ask him a million questions. Nevertheless I knew better. I totally trusted him, and I would do exactly what he said.

Quickly I bent over to pick up my bike and realized Shep was no longer there. What happened to him? Suddenly I felt like I was going to cry as I pulled my bike to the planks and jumped on the seat. I took one last look around as I wondered if my life was ever going to be the same. For some reason I felt like I had lost something of great importance to me just then. Wanting to get home quickly I hit my pedals hard. I had never peddled so hard in my life. My mind was racing over how things happened today and how Shep had suddenly appeared. All of this was becoming overwhelming. What did he mean I wasn't normal? I already felt like I was nobody. I didn't need to feel like I was a freak too. Had I really slowed down Mike's bike? How was Shep there *and* at his office? Okay, I am just crazy. I need to calm down.

When I returned to the cul-de-sac I noticed Heather's bike parked in front of Mike's house and wondered how they were. Did they know there was something wrong with me? I didn't want to have to see anyone right now. And I knew if I started talking I would cry. With this thought, I peddled even harder to my house. As I flew up the drive, I ran to our key pad and punched in our security code for the garage door to open. It seemed to take its own sweet time. I waited impatiently as I held my bike tight and threw it in as soon as possible. Then I ran to the garage door opener and pushed it down and held it so it would close the world out.

I opened the door and went inside to sit at the table. Now it would be a waiting game. I looked down at the table and realized my knuckles were white from holding it so tightly. I needed to relax. If I let go, though, I wouldn't be able to stay still. I was beginning to panic when my cell rang. Thankfully it was Shep. "I'm headed home, Selena. Calm down. It is not that bad. In fact, it is totally expected and wonderful what is happening. I will be there soon. Relax, please. Love ya."

The phone went quiet and I realized he had hung up. Slowly I turned my cell off. Calm down? How? Wonderful—I was a freak. What else was not normal about me?

I don't know how much time had passed, but I was still sitting at the table when I heard the garage door open and Shep's car pulling in. He was taking too much time; my patience was fried. When he finally walked in, he sat down at the table, probably assessing that I looked like I was going to pass out. Maybe I couldn't handle what he was about to tell me. Maybe I really didn't want to know. He took my hand and rubbed it gently as he smiled calmly at me. I knew he was trying to help me calm down.

"Selena, you really need to stop panicking. It is perfectly normal for our kind." I shook my head no but nothing seemed to come out of my mouth. He smiled his sweet smile and leaned back in his chair and started to grin. *"I think this is going to take more time to explain than I originally thought."* Shep had said that, but I hadn't seen his lips move. He slid his chair back and went to the refrigerator. Not the warm milk again! That was not going to work this time. I was a freak and warm milk won't change that. A second later he slumped into the fridge, laughing harder than ever. That was *it*! I burst out, telling him this was not funny, until I heard his voice inside my head again. This time he insisted it *was* funny. He had waited a long time for me to hear his thoughts; it would make things easier for the both of us. My mouth dropped open in astonishment as he peeked around the fridge door with a dorky smile on his face. He was speaking inside my head and he was reading my thoughts. Really? Reading my thoughts? How dare he! I couldn't believe it. Could I do that too? He shook his head up and down, laughing even louder. *"Now you understand. I can hear your thoughts. We will get something to drink and go into the study to talk. There is a lot of information I need to convey to you, and it is not going to be easy to hear or explain for that matter."*

Looking at his face, I was still fascinated that his lips were not moving with the words. He gave me a cold pop and started walking towards the study. I followed. Once inside, I sat down on the couch as Shep took the swivel chair. His thoughts started pouring into my head like a running faucet. He turned back to the desk and pulled out a key. The key was small and very jagged. Cautiously he reached down and opened the one desk drawer I had never seen opened. I had always wondered what was in there but never pushed the issue. He turned around with a round box and a lot of little books that looked like diaries. The first thought I heard was that these books were my father's journals, and there was a lot of information in them that I was going to need. The box he held was a bit more complicated since it held my mother's locket. Did I hear that right? *Yes,* was his reply. I looked at him, and his mouth was still not moving. *"Selena, I have been hearing your thoughts since you were able to organize them. That is how I knew where you were when you were in the woods. As you now know, you and I are not exactly what we appear to be. In other words, we are not totally mmm...human. I mean we are, but we have special abilities that most humans do not. We are a little more advanced."* Shep threw back his chair as if trying to maintain his cool disposition. *"I knew it was a matter of time before your abilities would start manifesting themselves, and I was not sure how they would work since you are your father's daughter. You were born in the Mortal World for lack of better terminology, but you are not Mortal by any means. Your mother is from a different world. I don't mean "world," because she is from here, but not this exact plain or time. I knew this was going to be difficult for me to explain, and now I think I should have practiced this.*" He took a drink and settled back into his chair with disgust. I felt confused—and yet excited—as I stared at him. He began rubbing his head like he had a headache, and one thing I knew was when Shep rubbed his head he was upset.

Concentrating, I thought I would try to talk to him with my own thoughts. *"So what you're saying is my father was Mortal and my mom was not.*"

He smiled at my effort but shook his head. *"As you practice it will become easier for you to hear my thoughts and send your own. You will also have to learn how to guard them. But your father was not Mortal either. He also had special abilities. See, there are more than two types of beings in this world. Do you remember the night you were lost and the dreams you had for the next couple nights? Well, I was showing you two different beings beside Mortals. Some of them were memories shared with me by your family. Although, some of the dreams were not my doing and surprised me as well."*

"You were showing me those dreams!" I shouted. "Those were nightmares, and I thought I was losing my mind!"

*"Use your mind, not your voice. You need the practice. When you were little you were a natural with your telepathy, but I had to help you avoid its use. Slowly over time you didn't pay attention to it. It was easier for us to live among this realm if we didn't use what is natural to us. Now listen. Your father is easier to explain than your mother. Your father was also born in the Mortal World, but he has many abilities. His family is large and they are known as "Guardians." But you are very special. The earth seems to know when one of importance is about to be born and announces it with something spectacular in many ways. Not all Guardians—just special ones like you. Your grandfather's birth was during the sighting of Haley's comet. Your birth was announced with an eruption of Mt. St. Helens. To us, these natural events means a special person is being born. The more spectacular the event, the more powerful they usually are.*

*"No, don't interrupt. Listen. You know how sometimes you see shadows or come up with thoughts that seem to answer a much-needed question? That is another form of being, which is what your mother is. She was Shadow. Both Shadow and Guardian are immortal in many ways. That does not mean they cannot die, though. It takes either time or a great act to kill them. Mortals do have the means to kill us, too. It would, however, have to be done with help. Guardians have lived from the beginning, as have we. They stay in their own plain mainly. They look at themselves as protectors of Mortals, this world. They know history of the Mortal World better than the Mortals do. Each Guardian has special fight-*

*ing skills and telepathic abilities. Their telepathic abilities vary from person to person. The Guardians use the knowledge of chemicals, nature, and technology in the guarding of this world. While Shadows help a culture to advance with knowledge, the Guardians help by giving guidance.*

*"Shadows have different forms. You remember your Greek mythology where there were nine daughters born to Zeus and Mnemosyne? These daughters' names were: Calliope, Clio, Erato, Euterpe, Melpomene, Plyhymnia, Terpsichore, Thalia, and Urania. Zeus had other children, and there is much you have to learn between myth and truth. They are responsible for influencing poetry, history, love, religion, dance, comedy, astronomy and technology. Well, they are from the Shadow Realm. They were our beginning. We are like muses. We call ourselves Shadows. Yes, Selena, I am a Shadow, but there is no reason to fear me. I am and will always be your appointed Protector and father. I chose to be your guardian. Your parents are from two different plains and you are a miracle of two worlds. Something that is rare since you show signs of both types of abilities. The dreams you had in the forest were dreams about what happened many years ago, and the voyageur was actually from a Guardian group, not a human one. The man you saw killed was named Jonathan. What you saw were actual memories handed down from your father's family. Every Guardian can pass on his or her knowledge to the next generation. Since your father is not here, he entrusted me with these memories. The darker dreams were from the Shadow Realm. They were about the same event that involved the voyageur, except for one of your dreams, and..."* He looked squarely at me almost as if he was assessing me. *"All these memories are interconnected in some way. This did cause division and distrust between the Guardians and Shadows.*

*"You see, the Shadow who killed the voyageur was trying to break the rules. The name of the Shadow was Alexander. I never did trust him, and I am sure he was following someone else's directives. I suspect the killings that took place in the Shadow Realm were actually done by Alexander or someone from his group. Right now we do not have what we need to bring him to justice, or to even prove what happened that night. Because of the voyageur's death, his people placed extra safeties on the portals into the human realm. Guardians can pass through the portal under their own power. Shadows on the other hand must have permission to open and close any portal created by a Guardian. There are, however, some portals that were created by our originator, and those we can open and close without permission. Still, Guardians are able to seal the portals as long as there is danger, just not ones Shadows can access. Our originator did not create many portals from our realm though. Guardian portals are many compared to ours.*

*"Shadows have a physical form—a mist form—and a Shadow form. When we are in a Shadow form or mist, we are vulnerable to the one ability that all Guardians have: to prevent us from taking a solid form. As you remember from your dream, there were many voyageurs waving their hands around. They were pre-*

*venting the invading Shadows from taking human form and not allowing them to exit the portal. The story Alexander told once he was back in the Shadow Realm didn't match up to anything. That night, a sweet lady was murdered by the name of Lovie. At the time she was in charge of research that was to help a young aspiring doctor here in the Mortal Realm. Lovie had always bragged about her friendship with the Guardians and how we all needed to work more closely together. She felt this would bring progress at a faster rate. Many in the Shadow Realm believed the Guardians did kill her at first, but I know that was not true. The memory you saw proved that. This is a lot to take in all at once...would you like to take a break?"*

I know I must have been looking like I was dumbfounded and needed one. Nevertheless, I really wanted to hear more. The startling revelation that came to me through these dreams must have been related to my parents' death. Shep did not look into my eyes at my revelation, so I knew it was a part of it. Hearing him sigh, he then replied, *"This particular event did not cause your parents' death. They were here when they died. Now why don't we fix something to eat? You are going to need a full stomach in order to continue. Using a new ability will require a lot of energy. That is why you felt so drained earlier."*

We went into the kitchen, and Shep started rummaging around throwing this and that together. It smelled great. I hadn't realized how hungry I was until then. I set the table while Shep prepared a small meal in a matter of minutes. We sat down to eat as I started thinking again about the dreams. I wondered if my father was among the memories. Shep's mind answered my question. *"Your father did not arrive there until the Guardians had called for help. Your grandfather, however, was one of the three men who witnessed the incident. I know you must have a lot of questions, but enjoy your food first. We have time to talk afterwards."*

I was ravenous. I hoped I won't gain a ton of weight doing this. A chuckle from Shep led me to believe I wouldn't. He looked down at the dishes that had been totally decimated and wanted to know if I was ready to listen some more. I hadn't realized it, but I was using telepathy instead of my mouth. Shep looked at me and asked if I had any questions about what I had heard earlier. The most prominent question was why this Alexander had been so ruthless. Shep's reply surprised me. "*We will discuss that later, but I want you to think back to Alexander's eyes. They have a slanted starburst in the iris, and if you see anybody like that, I want you to stay away from them and summon me. Your parents had reason not to trust him, and I feel the same way. The death of Jared and Analease is still considered an accident by most of the public. We can't discuss this until the time is right.*"

As I looked at Shep, I knew I would get no more answers than I already had on that subject. It wasn't fair we couldn't discuss it anymore. Had my parents been murdered? For a brief moment I saw something flicker in his eyes that worried me. So I decided to ask him what the other things were that I would be able to do. I was sure that was a fair question. He smiled hearing my thoughts. "*You should be able to do a variety of things but exactly what each thing is, I don't know yet. You are of unique parentage. Your parents were Guardian and Shadow. The marriage of our two species does not occur often. Children like you either have Guardian ability or Shadow ability, but for some reason some have a mix and that is rare. We felt you had a mix before you were born. It became apparent, you might say. Your parents had not counted on that."* He chuckled as he continued to clear the table. For once he seemed to be enjoying his past memories. *"This will be a learning experience for both of us."*

My mind became flooded with so many thoughts at that point that I didn't know what to ask first. I was a mix of both worlds and no one knows what to expect from me. Great, no pressure. *"That means you don't know if anything else will happen?"* It suddenly scared me to understand that even Shep was a bit concerned with my mixed parentage. My abilities evidently were going to be a mix and would have to be refined before I could show the two abilities could live as one.

*"In the past month, Selena, your mind seemed to be able to block me from hearing you. I found this to be very disturbing since I had always been able to. I didn't mind being away from you when I was at work since I always could hear what you were thinking. By the way, I don't listen to you all the time now that you are older. I just listen to check on you now and then. It is important for me to do this in case you should accidentally have used an ability you had no control of. I knew you were about to do something unusual when you started blocking my mind from hearing yours. Because of that I started checking in on you physically. This required assistance from others of our kind. I am able to sense your essence because of your parents and because you are my daughter. Parents can always track their little ones if the need presents itself. There is one ability, however, that can interfere with that, but enough on that for now. We have more important things to discuss.*

*"See, when I became your Protector it gave me the knowledge and abilities of your parents that help guide their offspring into maturity. Your parents trusted me, and I hope I can do them justice. When you were caught in the storm last week, I had hoped to relay the dreams in a different way than what happened. When Heather was hurt in the rush I knew my plans had to change. The shelter you found was a piece of information your father would have known. Like I said, Guardians pass their knowledge down, and technically some of his knowledge you already possess. You just have to access it. Your father began sharing his memories and heritage before you ever exited the womb. He felt it was important for you to receive them quickly in case something ever happened. It was interesting to see that you took in the memories without any guidance. Jared would be proud; you would always have a part of him tucked inside. It was important to him to share everything he could think of with you. I sometimes felt...like he knew something was going to happen. I kept assuring him he would be around a long*

*time, but he never seemed to believe that, not with you."* Shep stopped talking, and I could see he was concentrating. Then my heart sunk as I saw that look of pain cross his face.

Shep shook his head and patted my leg. *"Most Guardians have to be physically taught many of their abilities, but I can see with you some things are going to come naturally. You were wondering what I can do. I can create storms and enter your thoughts or dreams to help solve problems, and I am a Protector. I was your mother's bodyguard, and that is how I became yours. I know it sounds strange, but I have been watching over your mother's family for a long time. It was only natural that when they could no longer take care of you I would step in. This morning I knew something was up when your thoughts became so jumbled. You were stressed, and knowing the way you react to things I knew anything could happen. When I heard your terror at Mike's situation, it took me a couple minutes to be there in the pines to watch. I saw most everything thanks to help from a friend. You stopped breathing. I would have stepped in if I felt you would need guidance, but I am not immune to your ability and it kept me at bay for a few seconds. I can guide you, but not with that ability. I had to have help. You gave Mike more than enough time to correct his error, plus the little wind you stirred up was a bonus. I don't know why you thought wind would help. Maybe you thought it might decelerate his rate of fall is all I can figure.*

*"I felt your fear. When you slowed things down and stirred the weather a bit, you sent out a beacon announcing the beginning of a new power taking form. We didn't know what abilities you would have, for we never had an interpreter inform us properly. Now let's see...I think maybe we should see if you can use your abilities at will."* Shep stood up and started towards the garage door, leaving me feeling slightly overwhelmed. I wanted to know if I was in trouble of some kind by acting as a beacon. Shep didn't volunteer an answer. Instead, he stood with his back to me as he waited for me to join him. I could tell he wasn't going to say another word. "Tomorrow I will tell you more. For now, I need you do what I ask when I ask, without question. Selena, I would be lying to say there are no dangers." Sadness seemed to plague his voice at this point, and that horrible look crossed his face and stayed longer than I had ever seen him allow.

"Alright," I said, trying to sound confident. "Where are we going to practice?" He chuckled as he motioned for me to follow. Once outside of the garage door, we saw Heather and Mike goofing off at the end of the street. Shep smiled just like everything was normal, but I wasn't good at being an actor. We were walking towards the path which led into the woods, and that meant I would have to talk to them.

"Hey, what happened to you?" Heather hollered.

Shep stopped to glance at her. "I called Selena to tell her I was coming home early. So we could do something together. Mike how's your uh...injury?" Shep chuckled so loudly that Mike flushed as he stared at me. "Selena told me you weren't using your brains today. It is a good thing you had something soft to land on, though." We all laughed as poor Mike grimaced at Shep's pun.

We continued to walk past them. It was strange that they were not tagging along like they usually would have. I wondered why not. I couldn't help but stare back at my two best friends in the world. Shep seemed to understand and placed his hand on my shoulder in a comforting gesture. *"I encouraged them to remain behind today so you and I can practice. I need to know what you are dealing with at this moment. The next couple of weeks we will have to be careful when we practice anything that might help show us what your abilities are. You could accidentally cause a storm or who knows what. I will go to work tomorrow and tell them I will be taking that long vacation they all have been encouraging me to do for so long. Then you and I will go someplace where we do not have to worry about interference."*

As we walked further into the woods, Shep walked off the path and I followed. "You mean I could hurt somebody by accident?" Nodding his head up and down, his reply wasn't comforting. "Yes, but I won't let that happen. See, you will have to learn to control abilities by will, not by circumstance. You have never been one to show your emotions because I know you think that shows weakness. So everything you have held back all these years is like a bomb waiting to go off. That is why we need you to work on sharing with me and controlling the ability physically. Do you understand? Holding everything inside is not always healthy, especially for you."

"Yes, I wouldn't want to hurt anybody. Do you think I have more abilities than what I have already used?"

"Of course. Both of your parents were gifted and I would expect you will have some of each. What I wonder about is how the abilities will work." I hadn't realized it, but we had arrived at a clearing in the woods that I was not familiar with. Shep rubbed his foot on a stone that had been covered with dirt and grass. I realized the stone had a design on it. That was curious. I noticed he seemed to be walking a square and rubbing the ground at each corner to uncover another stone. When he had completed the square he walked towards me. "Now I want you to try and build a breeze in this little area around us. Move the trees that are at the north end of the square."

# CHAPTER 4.
# PRACTICE MAKES PERFECT

**I tried** to clear my mind, but nothing worked. How would I make those trees move? How do breezes actually begin? At first I thought of the time I had tried to learn how to whistle. Parker had been trying to teach me by telling me to put my tongue close to the roof of my mouth while forming an "O" with my lips to blow. I began blowing over my lips, trying to feel what the air felt like going across them. Maybe if I could remember the sensation, that would help me create a breeze across my skin. I felt self-conscious and started getting upset. A shiver went up my body as I felt a strong cold breeze blow across me. Suddenly I felt the pressure of both of Shep's hands holding my shoulders as he began whispering to me not to be ruled by my emotions. "You need to remember the feeling," he kept repeating. "Control comes with time, but for now close your eyes and feel the air around your body. What does it feel like? Feel the movement of the air even when there is no breeze."

I thought of how cold I was, and all I wanted was to feel the sun. Soon enough there was no wind blowing across me and the clouds that had been covering the sun today parted and shined down on me. I was feeling the warmth when Shep made a satisfied sound. "You are doing well. Now try again."

Once again thinking about the air's touch across my skin, I could feel the breeze blow gently, but this time the sun was still on me. I didn't feel so cold. The breeze continued for a few minutes and I finally became bored with it. Could I make it pick up? As I continued to concentrate, I could feel the increase in the air around me. Softly Shep began speaking to me. His voice, however, held a clear urgency.

"We don't want to cause an unnatural weather change, Selena. Slow it back down." His voice was commanding but gentle. Concentrating, the breeze slowed down. Then I heard him request for me to stop the breeze altogether. This took more concentration than I felt it should, but as I thought about the feeling of no air, the breeze stopped. With a quick glance back at Shep, the trees seemed to be filled with noise, even as the sun flickered across his body. "That was a good beginning. Now you have to remember how you created the wind so the next time will be easier. You truly are the child of Analease." The thought that this would have made her happy made me smile more.

"Was my mom able to do this?" My question was hesitant. *"She was not very good with breezes, but she did have a mild winter ability. She could create fogs. Come to think of it, she could create mild misty rain too. Meteorologists call it slush. Shadows are able to manipulate the elements as well as influence other pursuits like math, science, art, or comedy.* You...*you seem to have the ability to influence the weather though. You didn't like the coolness earlier, which influenced the sun to warm you. Because of that, your wind pushed the trees out of the way enough for the sun to do as you pleased. You understand now what could happen if you wished for something that wasn't natural, especially for this time of year don't you? A definite pureblood."* I wasn't sure exactly what his last mumbled statement meant, but right now I didn't care.

"So, now what do you want me to do? Should I try to slow things down again? This ability could come in real handy, especially during Mr. Gequot's test," I jested. Shep threw me a sharp glance that meant I was not to do anything of the sort.

Abruptly, the small sounds of a chipmunk drew my attention. It was close. When I finally spotted the little guy, he was starting to run up a log that led out of the clearing that we were in. Maybe it wouldn't hurt to try with this little creature. It hadn't hurt anything this morning. Slowly I began to focus on him. To my dismay, he disappeared before anything happened.

How did one access each ability? If I was to be successful at this, I had to understand this basic skill. My mind began to study the effects I had created this morning and all that had been involved. At one point Shep said I needed to breathe. Could this ability be controlled with breath? My heart began pumping wildly at the thought. As I began to hold my breath, I found my little friend had reappeared next to the log that lay near me. As the little chipmunk began to move back into the forest, I watched as everything slowed down. The little creature poked his head into a hole like he was in slow motion. Sharply I heard Shep's frantic yelling in my mind to breathe. Instantly I took in a deep breath and found myself on the ground.

"I think we have done enough today, Selena. No more. I don't like how you make things slow down. You have to breathe to do it. You were holding your breath so long, you fainted." His statement shocked me. It didn't seem that long, and no one would hold their breath to the point of fainting. It had only been a few seconds.

As I struggled to move, I realized how weak I felt. Still I needed to know if I had succeeded. *"Did I do it though?"* I asked feebly.

"Yes, how do you feel?" Shep's voice was weak, and for once it sounded like he was scared.

*"I feel dizzy."*

He surprised me by growling with his frustration. Immediately he turned me around on the loose forest floor and tilted my head back to stare at my face. What was he doing? "Selena, do not block your thoughts from me." I could tell he was quite serious. Shep never spoke that way to me unless he was upset. When he started checking my pulse I knew he was scared.

"Please let me try again. This time I will do better. I will remember to steady my breathing to slow my heartbeat and not stop." It was evident to me that my pleading was doing nothing. He was not going to let me try. I watched as Shep went back to the last stone he had uncovered and tapped it until he had tapped every stone in the square.

*What is that all about*, I wondered.

*"I'll explain later."* Shep's sharp reply in my mind caught me off guard. It was a surprise to hear his telepathy sounding agitated. It was as clear as any voice. "Let's get you home." I didn't want to go home. I wanted to work on this.

The trees were swaying in a light breeze that was blowing our way as I studied them. Cautiously, I slowed my heart, but this time I was careful not to hold my breath. The effect was clear. Every tree in the vicinity moved as if a person was turning a page in one of those flip books very slowly. Then my attention fell to Shep. He seemed to be moving in slow motion too. The only difference was the complete look of horror on his face. Everything went black in that split second of time.

When I woke up, my skin was clammy and Shep was rubbing my cheek. We were at home in my room. He looked down at me. I couldn't decide if he was mad or just plain upset. "My dear…little one, I *told* you to follow my instructions to the letter. You tried to slow down your heart again and lost consciousness." Shep's voice was practically a growl with every word. "I was unable to get to you in time because of the change in speed. I told you this ability affects me. We're just lucky that when you passed out everything went back to normal. I had activated the quad of stones to limit your effects. You must never do that again. I am here to keep you safe."

His frustration was clear as he continued to pace at the side of my bed with his hand rubbing his bald head. The sun was shining brightly, outlining his biceps as they strained from the stress. "I won't do it again. Sorry I scared you. I…just want to learn everything I can."

He interjected his thoughts into my own. *"Safety is always first and every ability will have to be dealt with…with patience."* When I sat up I felt like a sledgehammer had been used on my head. Even hearing Shep's mild laughter hurt. *"Take this Tylenol PM and clear your mind so we can try again later. You must remember that each ability will have a physical effect on your body until you become accustomed to the changes."* As I started to roll over, my head swam terribly out of control. So I stayed on my back while listening to Shep walk down the hall to the piano. He was playing his ballad again, which was another sign he was trying to de-stress. Gradually I began to drift off to sleep, wondering how we had returned home without anyone noticing. Everybody would have noticed him carrying me. I would have to remember to ask him tomorrow.

Later in the evening I woke up to voices in the family room. I could tell one was Shep's, but who the others belonged to, I didn't know. One sounded a bit feminine. When I rolled over to look at the clock I read two a.m. Shep never had company at this hour unless it was Parker or one of the Muirs. Not to mention females. As quietly as possible I pulled myself up and sat still for a while to make sure my head would not spin out of control. I also could hear an older man's voice. It sounded familiar and yet not. Warily I crept down the hall towards the family room. It was obvious the fireplace was on, for I could see the flicker on the wall. When I peeked around the corner, I found Shep was sitting on the hearth carrying on a conversation, but I didn't see anybody else in the room. The shadows were jumping off the walls like they normally did. Tonight, however, I thought I could see more shape to them than should be.

When I looked to the corner where Shep seemed to be gazing, I thought I saw something. Frightened, I leaned back against the wall as my head spun out of control from the abrupt movement. To my own surprise I let a slight moan escape my lips. I sure hoped Shep couldn't hear my thoughts. It wouldn't be good for him to find me eavesdropping. I leaned back to listen for any signs of movement. It seemed he was still carrying on the conversation. He was saying my first special abilities were quite impressive but would need some polishing. He would be taking me to Billy and we could work on the ones that had already made an appearance. He was a little concerned that I had the ability to slow things down, especially since it could affect his ability to protect me. He was sure Billy would be able to manage me. He was so excited after my little performance with that kid, Mike. Billy's sons would be helping, too. Then a male voice said, "The child is at the floodgate of who knows what, Shep. You need to be prepared for anything. Shep…it is honestly time to give up this pretense of living here." The voice sounded familiar, and yet I couldn't place it, which bothered me. The man also sounded sincere in everything he was saying.

Shep and the stranger both agreed this could only mean that my next abilities would probably be even stronger, and maybe another should be sent to help. My ears started ringing as I began to feel nauseous. Shep came running around the corner and carefully leaned down to pick me up. "What are you doing there? I should have realized I could not hear you again. You are going to be a handful now, but not any more than your mother was."

I felt confused. "Shep, who were you talking to? I didn't see anybody. I know there is a man on the far side of the room. Can't I meet them? And who is that female? You never let any female around unless it is Chelsea or Cassidy." Trying to peek over his shoulder as he carried me, I could find no one in the room. He let out a low sigh as he began to transfer his thoughts to me.

*"Do you remember I told you we are keeping a close eye on you? Well, I am your main Protector, but there are others who are helping. We are a mixed group of Shadow and Guardian. I was relaying the events of the day to them since I am in need of assistance. Most Shadow abilities I can handle, but Guardian abilities*

*are not in my repertoire. They are very excited and yet...we need to make sure you do not draw too much attention to yourself. We want to present you when you are in control of your abilities to make sure things are safe. When I realized I could no longer hear you, I sensed you were not in bed. Now here you are, using yet another ability to listen in on a private conversation and have drained yourself once again. Really Selena, you need to rest. Help me out and sleep. If you are strong enough tomorrow we will work on wind, telepathy, and see if there are other abilities you have been using without realizing it. Plus, we will have to let everybody think we are going on a vacation. School will be a complication. Nevertheless, I am sure we will have things under control by then. We have a lot to plan and there is still so much to discuss."*

He carried me to my bed, making me feel childish. Yet he was right—I had no energy to fight him. When he laid me down he wished me sweet dreams as usual. At that moment I couldn't resist saying I had enough dreaming for one week. He agreed. I felt slightly troubled as I watched him leave. He kept referring to himself as my Protector, but he was just my dad.

I was about to drop off to sleep when Shep came back in with one of those cave rock lamps. He didn't plug it in or anything; he touched it and a light came on. He looked very pleased with himself as he whispered that would do the job. What job? I wanted to ask but was too tired to do so. It had a beautiful orange glow to it, and I felt the heaviness in my eyes. Shep shook his head and sat down on the bed. "I am your father. I will always love you, but I am also your Protector. None of what has happened today changes that we are family. You will always be my little one. Now sleep." He leaned over and kissed my forehead, knowing he had answered my worried concern.

"That's good because I love you too, old man." Sleep had finally overtaken me.

***

My body felt so warm and comfortable in my flannel sheets, I didn't want to open my eyes. I could hear Shep doing something loud out in the garage. Then it donned on me what Shep had said the previous day. One day I would be able to hear his thoughts as easily as he could hear mine. Maybe I could hear his thoughts if I concentrated. I tried to listen for Shep as I cleared my mind. Lying there, the only noise I seemed to hear was the banging around he was doing in the garage, along with a small alarm of some kind. I continued to listen to my heartbeat as I worked on clearing my mind. That was a good idea. Everything with my abilities yesterday was triggered by physical or emotional feelings. What would help here? My heart started pounding a little faster as I tried to think of an emotion I connected with Shep. He had always been a dad to me. He chose to adopt me as his own. This made me feel special. Shep had to fulfill the roles of both mother and father. He loved to take me to the park when I was little so I could swing. I could feel him behind me pushing me and laughing. I can remember when my feelings were hurt and he would listen. I know he didn't really feel like it was important, but he still listened to me and tried to make me feel like my feelings were important.

*"Selena is a very bright girl. She has the ability to adjust to using her abilities quicker than anyone I have ever seen. I am not sure of what she is capable of, but one thing I know is that she is driven to do everything she possibly can. We will have to be very careful. Do you sense th…?"*

Shep came bursting into my room, and I realized I had been hearing his thoughts. I was in trouble. Quickly I pulled my sheets over my head as I heard my bedroom door hit the wall. "You were listening, little one." He accused. "I was afraid you would learn that ability quicker than the others." He sighed. Sheepishly I pulled the covers down and tried to look innocent, but that didn't work. He was half smiling and half irritated.

"You were talking to somebody. So who was it? There is no need for secrets anymore, Shep. Besides, I didn't mean to eavesdrop. I just wanted to see if I could sense you like you sense me. It's only fair." Shep smiled and walked over to my window while placing his hand on his hip. I then heard his thoughts very clearly.

*"We respect each other's privacy and you can practice, but please let me know when you do. Besides, you should only use it if you need to find me. How did you manage to do it?*" Very softly I began to explain. He looked at me with so much curiosity that I lowered my eyes as I told him the memories I had been thinking about. As I looked out the window, I was surprised to find a gloomy day taking shape as I proceeded to tell him he had always been there for me and he was the best parent anyone could have. In a rush he flew to my bedside and sat down, taking my hands into his.

Suddenly a thunderstorm burst outside, causing the rain to pour while shadows were being cast upon my wall. Shep looked out the window and stood up to study the weather. The raindrops looked huge on my window, and I could tell Shep felt perplexed. He looked over at me with confusion in his expression. "We've got a lot to do today. I'll see you in a bit. Be ready when I get home." Without another word he walked out of the room.

Still lying in bed, I rolled over to look out my window. *What if I did a little practicing?* I wondered.

Then I heard Shep as if he was in the room hollering, *"No practicing without me*!" Immediately I punched the pillow before trying to go back to sleep.

The next time I opened my eyes, I realized I must have been successful in going back to sleep because I could hear no noises in the house. Shep must be at work now. With a quick glance towards the window, I noticed the raindrops still hitting, but there was a small fog and a man there with blue eyes staring back at me. Instead of screaming, I jumped out of my bed and ran to the window. Abruptly Shep's voice echoed in my head, demanding to know what was wrong. As I searched the pane of glass, I found no man's face staring back at me. Was it my imagination? At first I was tempted to see Shep get home quickly. Instead I took a steadying breath and replied it was nothing. I wondered if he believed me. I looked around the room, half expecting to see Shep, but it didn't happen.

Slowly I walked towards the kitchen to check the locks before grabbing some breakfast. I didn't even feel like putting together a bowl of cereal. Oatmeal and milk would do nicely. As I passed the front door I checked to see if it was locked again before heading back to the family room. Maybe I could figure out who Shep had been talking to. In fact, he had been talking to two people, not just the man. With a look at the hearth I became amused as I looked for someone—Shadow, or maybe a pair of eyes—but saw nothing. Lazily I went to the hearth, finishing off the last bite of breakfast, and sat where I had seen Shep sitting the night before. I had the feeling I should be able to see somebody or something there. I traced my finger across the bricks and wondered if the fireplace would need to be on in order to speak to whomever had been there the night before. With some trepidation I opened the chain curtains and reached over to the switch that turned on the fireplace.

Gradually I scooted down to the floor and slid back to stare at the fire. How did this work? Or did you have to know the person with whom you wanted to communicate? Shadows started flickering around the room like they always do when the fireplace is on. Carefully I pulled my knees up into my arms while studying my surroundings. Nothing unusual seemed to be happening. I reached for my warm teddy bear blanket on the sofa so I could stay warm and watch the shadows bounce around the walls. This was going to be one of those lazy, rainy days, but my body was surging with the excitement of learning something new.

With a nervous glance to the corner at the far end of the room, I saw a shadow that did not seem to be dancing like the others. Slowly standing up I dropped the blanket to floor. My heart felt like it was skipping a beat as I started to walk towards the shadow. My body was trembling. My assessment was that the shadow did not seem to move. It was then that I realized my body was blocking the light from the fireplace. "You seem familiar. Do I know you?" There was no response. Shep's voice echoed in my mind as I recalled what he said I should do. Call for him. My mind immediately started calling to Shep and to my surprise, a shadow on the opposite wall started to take shape. Shep stumbled out of the darkness into the room, looking frantically around to see what I was concerned about. "So who was she?" I asked.

Shep looked at me with amazement. "How did you know she was a female?"

"I don't know. She looked familiar to me. I wasn't sure, but it just seemed like that. Is she always here?"

Shep sat down on the hearth as his thoughts began flowing quickly into my mind. *"There is always someone keeping an eye on you. We are not trying to invade your privacy, but your abilities are running faster than what is normal. What were you doing*?" With an embarrassed look to the fireplace, my cheeks heated as I retook my seat. Shep grunted with frustration. "I better get back to the office before anyone misses me." He walked to a part of the wall that was filled with darkness and faded into it.

Again I looked at the fire, only to wonder where the person was that was supposed to be watching me. This made me uncomfortable enough that I had to make it clear how I felt. "I'm going to get cleaned up and dressed. I don't expect to see any peeping toms around. If I do, I promise you will regret it because I will physically harm anyone who peeks." To my horror, I heard a slight laugh. Unfortunately the fire crackled, causing me to practically jump out of my skin at the sound. Steadying myself, I walked into my room to collect my things and headed to the bathroom for security. I spent the next hour soaking in the shower while letting it pound on the bruise, which was still very prominent on my shoulder. I wondered what I would need for our trip. My hand was rubbing the sore spot when I realized that the shower was creating a mist in the room. Didn't Shep say Shadow people use the mist? Instantly I felt uncomfortable. I climbed out and grabbed my towel, looking around for anything that shouldn't be there. After wiping down the mirror, I started brushing my hair until I heard the phone ring in the other room. After pulling my clothes on over my wet skin I made a mad dash towards the phone. The caller ID said it had been Heather.

She would have to be told of our surprise vacation. I bit my lip with reluctance as I tried to gather my thoughts on what to say. This wasn't going to be easy. Usually we told Heather and Parker in advance about a vacation and would see if they wanted to join us. When Heather answered the phone, my throat dried as I stuttered through my lie. I mean, it wasn't all a lie. Still, Heather and I never kept anything from each other—nothing. "Hey…Heather, Shep has decided on taking a vacation. They finally convinced him. He won't tell me exactly where we are going."

"Yeah. I imagine Dr. Owen and Cassidy forced it. They feel he has been too stressed out lately."

"Uh…yeah. We need you to keep watch over the house and flowerbeds. Sure… I'm sure Shep will want to pay you and that should help you have more money for your school clothes. Sure, no problem…I plan to go shopping with you like usual. I'll bring you something back to add a little bling to accessorize with. No, I don't have time to come over today. He wants me to start packing and do the laundry… sorry." Sometimes I love to talk on the phone, but Heather was like a sister to me and I didn't want to lie to her about anything. How was I going to keep this a secret from her? She knows me too well. "Hey Heather, the dryer is going off. I'll give you a call later. Love ya." Good, I didn't have to lie to her completely. Now what was I going to do the next time?

A glance to the front door window proved it was still raining, and knowing Heather, she wouldn't attempt to come over. She hated the rain for the most part.

This was another gloomy day. Going back to my room I started collecting some music I love to listen to and other items that I thought I would use while I was gone. I felt quite excited that I would be learning how to use these new abilities. I went into the study to get a book to take, when I looked on the desk and saw my dad's journals with his name boldly embossed with gold. Hesitantly I found I was drawn back to those tattered looking books. Slowly I went over to look at them. I couldn't tell which one I should read first, so I picked up the first one I laid my hands on. This one had a lot of drawings of different plants and the medicinal uses, while other pages had personal entries. This one looked interesting:

*July 3*

*Today Analease woke up sick again. I wonder if she needs to return to her Shadow form. She hasn't been home in a long time. She has been acting funny. I think I will suggest we should go to the Shadow Realm for a visit. We will travel through the Soo Locks and on up into the U.P. today.*

*July 4*

*We didn't make it to the U.P. yesterday. Analease has been keeping something from me. She is beginning to concern me. She definitely does not want to go home. I know that people think we are a strange match but it works for us. Occasionally we do run across some that do not like us as a couple, but Shep even likes me now.*

*July 5*

*I am so excited and frightened. Analease is pregnant. This type of pregnancy doesn't happen very often and we do not know what to expect. One thing she is certain of, she cannot strain her abilities right now. She is so beautiful that she does seem to glow. The Shadow Realm and Guardians still do not completely get along and this might have to be kept to ourselves for now. I have to keep Analease and the baby safe. I don't think anyone would intentionally hurt them. Yet with Alexander still being a Guardian hater, I can't take any chances. My father still believes he killed one of his own men and Lovie that fateful night a century ago.*

I flipped ahead in the book.

*July 28*

*Analease has set up our home in the backwoods of Michigan. She is bound and determined we stay in one place for a while. My family agrees with her. They are just as excited as we are. This child will be a blessing of great magnitude. My father, however, feels safety is also an issue with Alexander. Many feel this child will bring both realms together. Dad even speculates the child might not have any abilities or will have unfathomable abilities that complement both species. Analease and I really don't care as long as the baby is born healthy.*

*September 6*

*Shep and his wife arrived today. They were thrilled, but I could see Shep had the same concern as my father and I. Shep's wife is great in the medical arena and I am sure she will help Analease bring our little one into the world. Even Barry is going to assist. We both had a talk with Analease about her keeping our child a secret for too long. It was dangerous.*

*October 2*

*The elders have given me a leave of absence to protect our most precious treasure, my little one. They seemed as excited about our pregnancy as I am. They feel this could bring everything into fruition that many from both sides have strived for. A mixed child hasn't been born in a long time from any rank such as ours. Kenny and Wayne will be taking on my duties for the next two decades. Analease will be pleased—as if she could be any happier right now. I am so thrilled that she does not hesitate about anything.*

*October 31*

*Today was almost too real for me. Analease lost control of her abilities but thankfully Shep was able to help her gain control. It looks like our little treasure is going to be a handful. It is evident the child will be Seheirenel—another secret Analease shouldn't have kept. Shep and Dad are both thrilled, but this just adds to my bucket of concerns for my baby.*

*November 2*

*Alexander's men appeared in Texas a few days ago. They were looking for Analease. He said he had a message from her father. We know Analease's father would not send him. He knows we do not trust this group no matter whose house they are of. We figured he had heard Analease was pregnant and that they would confirm to others we were all compatible. My brother Billy went to see him and offered to deliver the message for him. Unfortunately, he became angry at this. Billy said he threatened Analease and our little one if she was going to have a Guardian child. All our fears have been confirmed by his flight into fury. Luckily no one was hurt, but we are definitely going to have to take precautions. Shep, Anthony, Drew, and Billy are going to help me do so.*

*December 26*

*We have had no problems and Analease is happy as all get out. She is constantly singing and dancing about even though she is definitely showing. Her smile seems to affect the sun.* Michigan usually has very cold winters, but this one has had the warmest temperatures in six years. She knows something is up but says she only wants to think happy thoughts so our little one will always be happy. I love her and the little one. We have been toying with names from Selena, Miranda, Lucas, or Jensen.

*January 6*

*Today was a big day. We could hear her mind developing. The little one is very happy. Analease* was right. Our little one will have very strong abilities.

Flipping through the book, I could see it did not have my birth month in it. I searched the other books and finally found the correct journal.

*March 18*

*Our little Selena was born today. I knew it would be soon because for the first time in centuries Mt. St. Helens volcano in Washington became active. This was to be the herald of her birth. I could not be any prouder than I am now. She is absolutely perfect and Analease is doing fine. She cannot stop smiling. Selena weighed seven pounds even. She was twenty-one inches long. She arrived at eleven a.m.*

*May 31*

*A select number of elders have arrived to give their blessings to our little one. Normally there would be a great celebration, but to keep my family safe I asked only four be sent. They complied. They feel our little one will have to be safe-guarded until she is well-trained in our abilities. Shep reminded them Selena is also half Shadow and had a Protector from the Shadow Realm who is very powerful. I had to grin at that. He wanted to assign his protégé but we saw things differently. Drew can assist. Drew is similar to Shep with being highly gifted. Like Shep, we both are concerned with what the future holds for Selena. Analease has become a little sad. She has made it very clear that Selena has to return to her home and take her place there. It doesn't hurt that he was Analease's Protector. Shep's family has been with Analease's mother's family for eons. I greatly appreciate his help. The elders agreed Shep and his wife should help in Selena's protection and training. Maybe later they will bring their protégé onto the project.*

I couldn't read the handwriting for the date, but then I found this little notation in the margin.

*Shep was sealed to her permanently as her Protector. Terah pointed out the fact that Shep had never been sealed to a charge. I am grateful for that. Our little one will have the four of us to take care of her. I am sure she is going to be a handful anyhow. She is the most wonderful gift I could ever have been given.*

There was another section that had been added much later. The ink was even a different color.

*July 5*

*Shep has returned from the Shadow Realm and is very concerned about how things are being stirred up. He feels we will need to change our location soon. Analease's' mother wants to see the baby, but sent a message to Shep not to tell anyone where Analease and Selena are. She also told Shep not to trust anyone and she would fill him in when she sees him.*

*July 21*

*Selena's mother, Terah, has arrived and Alec is not with her. She naturally thinks Selena is the most beautiful grandbaby she has ever seen. I would like to have known what she saw when that cold breeze surrounded her and Selena, but she says the future does not always need to be told so that it may change if need be. She is a strange woman but I love her anyway. She does seem to be worried about us though.*

*August 4*

*We received news that Analease's mother is dead.*

I jumped when I heard the garage door open. I could hear Shep rushing towards the study. "Selena, I see that you have been reading your father's journal. I wanted to be with you when you read that particular one." He looked down at his shoes and shuffled nervously. I had never seen him look so uncomfortable. I don't know what he wanted me to say, but I didn't feel like saying anything at all. I felt a large lump in my throat and didn't know how to get rid of it. He sat down beside me and said there was a lot to understand, and that I was the greatest gift my parents could have ever hoped for. He could read my thoughts and I really didn't want him to. Shaking his head he asked, "Do you want me to tell you what happened?"

# CHAPTER 5.
# SACRIFICE

**"Your grandmother** was murdered by an ability that only a Shadow could have had. This piece of evidence was disturbing even more than you realize. Your grandmother was very strong. She would have had to trust the person in order for them to have murdered her in her own home. Your father and I went to the Shadow Realm and tried to investigate the murder. Unfortunately, all we were able to prove is that it was done sloppily. Many things pointed to a person we didn't want to believe would do this horrible act of violence. Who that is, we will not discuss right now. We had convinced the ruling authority to start investigating Alexander and his head of house; that was all we managed. A few hours later we confronted Alexander. He admitted to us he had killed Lovie, but no one would be able to prove it. He laughed maniacally about your grandmother and said he had not killed her, but the same person who had ordered Lovie's death was responsible.

"When the authorities arrived, he escaped. We knew it would only be a matter of time before he would come after Analease and you. He was a great danger. That was when we rushed back to you and started taking precautions. We changed states, and things seemed fine for a while. Then one day, a battle erupted around us and we found ourselves outnumbered. We were barely able to escape with you. At that point in time, we knew we would have to separate up to draw Alexander off your path. You were about two years old then. We felt a mix of abilities had been what was saving us every time we were trapped. My wife and your father tried to draw their attention while you, your mother, and I worked to find a place you could grow up safely. You were not showing any active ability, and that was a great help in hiding you. Sarah and Jared drew them out to California. They were successful in luring Alexander's group into a battle with other Shadows and Guardians we trusted. California hadn't seen a fire resembling the Great Fire of 1848 in a long time. The battle had been very destructive. Luckily, we were okay and even able to take prisoners. Yet, when they arrived in the Shadow Realm, they died mysteriously or disappeared. No one knows how.

"Your mother and I had safely hidden you away in a farm town in Indiana. When Sarah and Jared joined us it was decided we would take on normal human jobs and live as two separate families in this community. Back in the Shadow Realm, Guardians and Shadows were working together to find out who was causing all this chaos and why. To my dismay, things were moving too slow, proving the danger was well-guarded. The Guardian Council of Elders was involved in arranging protection for our family. They have been a great help, even to this day. Jared's family has always been one of the prominent families, and at times they have been on the council. When your father approached them with the knowledge we had about your abilities, they became very nervous. You would be the first active mix abilities in a half century. This meant your safety would take priority over anything. Your father proceeded to see to legal matters involving us, including your adoption. Jared was a good man with much foresight. Sometimes it concerns me how he and Analease dealt with the family affairs, almost as if they knew they would die. Analease had one experience with the breeze the morning you were born. It has always bothered me the way she looked at Jared's mother in that moment, a look of complete despair. I had no idea. Jared and Analease became very secretive and we all knew it involved you. Terah had seen to my permanent assignment to you before she died.

"One night we all went to the county fair and had a wonderful time. Your parents decided to head home before Sarah and me. Since nothing seemed out of the ordinary. I didn't expect anything to happen. Jared was driving and your mother felt the presence of someone near. They didn't want to risk exposing themselves by using telepathy, and I was no longer attached to her mind. I imagine that was the mistake. Remember, both Shadow and Guardians are telepathic. We immediately started out by using the shadows to travel by. I could feel your mother's fear, and the storm was similar to a small tornado. By the time we reached your car it was perched over a hill with only the back wheels holding you back from the plunge into the water below. The car was pretty beat up. You were crying and had a terrible gash across your cheek, but you were alive. We knew this patch of road had many accidents on it all the time. The people there called it dead man's curve. We knew this looked like it was just another accident that happened during a storm, but I knew better. The signs were too obvious—our people would know. We had to get you to safety; there was no choice. Your parents wanted you safe. We had a responsibility to perform. You were now our daughter, not my charge. All the legal documentation would happen immediately upon your parents' death.

"Sarah went to the Shadow Realm to keep up the pretense that I had been killed in the accident along with your family. While there, she would take care of watching for the leader of Alexander's group. I would continue to raise you in this realm in safety. When the time came, I would see to your training along with a select, chosen group. We were not going to allow anyone to kill another member of our family. You were a little less than five at the time. Now you're fifteen, and we have been successful in keeping you safe thus far.

"Very few knew you had survived the attempt on your life, and the ones who did have been loyal for many years protecting you and helping me raise you. Now your abilities are presenting themselves. These could betray our secret before we want anyone else to know. That is why you must not use them unless a need arises or we are practicing. Our home is surrounded by safety precautions, so we can use our abilities safely here, but outside is another thing. See, your abilities are so strong they stand out like a beacon from a lighthouse. Now a place has been chosen to teach both of our ways without letting anyone know. Well..."

I could feel tears dripping down my cheeks and the lump in my throat was worse than ever. Shep looked so helpless that he reached over in an attempt to dry my eyes. His hug was tight, and I could feel this was hurting him as much as it was me. Quickly standing up, I left the room for my bedroom without a word. I hoped he understood I just needed some time to accept my parents were murdered. Upon entering my room, I didn't know what to do, so I turned the radio on and turned it up loud. The rain outside seemed to be getting worse, but I didn't care. Its pounding was more soothing than anything else. I pondered over everything I had just learned. They had loved me. They had been excited about having me. I never knew how hard I had made their lives and Shep's. I wondered if Sarah was still alive. The two of them had sacrificed so much to protect me. Was I really worth it? I sat back on my bed and watched the rain cascade down the panes. I could barely distinguish anything outside.

I don't know how much time had passed, but there had been no noises for a while. It had stayed dark outside and the storm had not lightened. I wanted to sit here forever and not do anything. Suddenly a light knock on my door startled me from my morbid thoughts. Shep came in looking as badly as I felt. I wished I could take all this pain away from him. I had been the cause of so much.

"You have been worth everything, Selena. We wouldn't have it any other way. Sarah is alive and well and we communicate...a lot. In fact, you saw her the night you were in the woods with Heather. She was the lady wiping Heather's forehead. She was helping you take care of her. We couldn't let you know who she was. I know you recognized her. We could feel your recognition. To be honest, it thrilled Sarah. By the way little one, don't *ever* think you're not worth the sacrifice. Every family would do no less to protect their own. We are family, and one day Alexander will be brought to justice for all he has done. Besides, when your abilities are completely developed and you are well-trained, we will be able to resume our normal lives. "

When we heard a knock on the back door, I couldn't help but jump from the surprise. Shep smiled softly as he muttered it would be the extra help he had called for. "We all have waited a long time for this day. It'll just be a moment." I heard the knock again and wondered why they weren't using the front door. My mind began to wonder what tomorrow would bring if we were expecting a guest tonight. Shep hadn't said a word about it.

The door opened and I heard excited voices and loud slaps on the back. Shep's mind encouraged me to come in. I knew that wasn't going to happen. *"Just leave me alone...please."* Someone was coming down the hallway and somehow I knew it wasn't Shep. Without so much as a knock, my door flew open to reveal a tall boy who looked about my age, grinning from ear to ear. He started snickering, and I recognized that snicker. "You!" I hollered as I jumped into a seated position on my bed. "That was you earlier today, wasn't it?"

"Yes, it was me. I was sitting next to the door that leads to your basement. Shep helped me in. I was to keep an eye on you today while Dad ran an errand. By the way, I would never peek, plus I don't have Shadow abilities. I am a Guardian. Well, I am being trained to be, like you will be too. Besides, you and I are cousins. My name is Tyler." At that moment I was totally angry, especially with him still laughing at my astonishment of his audacity. Oh, I wanted to slap him!

"Now that your blood is boiling with life again, why don't you come out and meet my dad? Everybody calls him Billy." Shock ran through me at the mention of his name. I was sure the emotion was plastered across my face. I had read his father's name in my father's journal several times. He was my dad's older brother and one of his dearest friends. It was almost frightening to meet the brother my dad had loved so much. Tyler came over and took my hand as he dragged me off the bed. I was grateful for his help. It gave me the boost I needed to not feel sorry for myself, or even better, not to feel scared. Hesitantly walking down the hallway hand in hand, I could hear the two men's excited voices in the family room. It sounded like Billy was thrilled with my ability to slow things down.

The sound of his voice was almost familiar, along with the jovial twang that ran smoothly with it. He still seemed to be the very happy man my father had envied. Upon turning the corner, I saw a middle-aged gentleman look up with a twinkle in his blue eyes. He looked so familiar. I knew those eyes; they looked just like my dad's. The one picture I had of my dad shows the same twinkling blue eyes. Tyler's eyes they were the same color. The older man came over and gave me a big hug. He said this had been a long time in coming. He carefully tugged me over to the couch to sit with him as their minds began telling me how they had kept watch over me for the past year. They had never been allowed to introduce themselves. The faces of many were floating into my mind.

"I'm afraid you all have me at a disadvantage. You know me, but I don't know you. It feels sort of creepy thinking so many have watched me carry on my humdrum life and I didn't even realize I was being followed. How boring that had to be for you."

Tyler grunted that it had been fun in many ways. "Shep has been the main one, and every once in a while one of us would help. We mainly made sure no one with ill intent would find you. Anyway, you and your friends can be quite entertaining. It wasn't like we were physically walking behind you; you would have noticed us. All of this has actually helped me work on some of my own skills. Besides, you sing wonderfully in the shower!" Lucky for him, watching his cousin wasn't a chore. He actually seemed to be genuine in his reply. Shep stood up, announcing for us to come into the kitchen while he fixed us all dinner. Slowly I followed behind. They seemed to be completely at ease about everything that had been going on around me. Billy sat down and his laughter filled the room. As I looked around, I found that everything had slowed down except for me.

Billy winked at me as I stared around the room with disbelief. He was still moving normally while Tyler and Shep weren't. "I see Shep is right. You can slow things down, like me. Funny, huh?" Everything went back to normal and Tyler shivered.

"You can slow things down, too?" I knew the sound of astonishment sounded childish, but I couldn't help but grow excited.

He nodded as my mind filled with questions. Billy held up his hands, indicating that we would have to take one thing at a time for now, and he would be training me with this particular ability. "Yep, if you have the ability to slow things down, you are not able to be affected by it. When the object of slowdown is a living creature, you are in effect slowing down their body. Humans do not realize it much, but if you are a Guardian or Shadow you are aware something has occurred. This ability can take years to manage. From what Shep tells me, you are already able to create the effect but still need to learn control so you do not hurt yourself. How do you think you created the slowdown?"

I took a moment to collect my thought before answering. "If I wanted things to slow down, then I would have to control my own body, breathing in particular. Am I right so far? When your breathing slows down you get cold." Billy didn't seem to react to my hypothesis so far. Instead, he looked aimlessly around the room.

"You realize how atoms are affected when they become cold. They slow down. Correct? When we learn about our abilities, it is important to know the scientific implications they will have on the physical. We don't just guess at this stuff. Tomorrow we will travel to a location that should be safe for us to practice this ability specifically. I know you are excited about all of this, but you must be patient."

Shep clanked his pots and dishes around. I could tell by the dishes that he was making our famous pie pizza. I pulled out the plates we would need from the cupboard. I realized there was another question I wanted to ask Billy, but I didn't know how to ask. Suddenly Billy's voice rang in my head that communicating can be between two people, not everyone in the room. He understood I didn't know how to accomplish this yet, so he offered to ensure our privacy. Shep called Tyler over and involved him in some conversation about video games.

*"Were my parents murdered? Shep didn't exactly say that. And did my dad have the ability to slow things down?"*

Billy looked at me with a glint of sadness in his eyes. *"There had been attempts on our family, and it did lead to you being raised by Shep. As to the second question, your father did not have this ability. I used it on him a lot in our teen years. In fact, I had made him a little scared. He would have freaked out with having to deal with this ability with you. I am sure he would have called me to help, too."*

At least he had given me a partial answer. Tyler seemed to be totally enthralled with the conversation Shep had started on the new video game system. Billy looked at me and asked if I wouldn't like to go play that Xbox thing, or whatever the system was. I grinned as I told him I knew how to take a hint when I wasn't wanted. He smiled and said maybe I could teach that to Tyler.

Tyler and I went into the video room and picked out a game. He couldn't believe I wanted to play Dr. Mario instead of Dead Rising or Halo or something better. I couldn't resist but to tease him. "You just don't want to verse me because I might beat you."

Instantly he scowled with contempt as he grabbed the controller. "Get ready to eat dirt."

I wondered why it was so important for Shep and Billy to talk without us. Why did it seem that everybody was still keeping secrets?

Tyler's response took me by surprise. "Because they are keeping secrets"

"You don't know either?"

He shook his head as he continued to play the game as if his life depended on it. Typical for guys to only be able to focus on one thing at a time. Tyler looked at me with a grin for a brief moment before returning his attention to the game. "*I've learned that if they want us to know they'll tell us, but not until we need to know. It's like beating your head against a rock without using any explosives.*"

"Wait a minute. You were listening in on my thoughts? Stop that!"

*"Sorry, but you think awfully loud. It's almost like you're shouting at me. I have been helping Dad keep an eye on you lately, and I have grown accustomed to your thoughts. I wouldn't listen if you could just lower your volume. Except that parents are always able to pry if they see the need, but most of the time they respect our privacy."* Immediately I paused the game and looked at him. He became irritated with the sudden action. "Why did you pause, the game?"

"You mean, if I don't want you to hear my thoughts I just have to not want you to hear them?"

"Sort of. The stronger your emotions, the louder your thoughts are. The more you control your emotions, the quieter your mind is. You have to relax in order to keep them low. You have to want to hear the person's thoughts in order to hear somebody else, and the more familiar they become, the easier it is to hear them. There are no mile limits to this telepathic ability, except between portals. Most of us start using this ability when we are real young. It's hard to believe you haven't discovered it until recently."

Shep's call from the kitchen was loud, and Tyler flew in like there was no tomorrow. To be honest, I was right behind him. I was starved. Billy hollered as we took our places. "Take cover, teenagers on the move!"

"Ha-ha, funny," Tyler and I both said at the same time. It only took about fifteen minutes for us to devour the meal. I felt stuffed. Excusing myself, I went to the guest room and made sure everything was in order for our guests. I pulled some sheets out for Tyler to sleep on the couch while Billy could have the guest bed. When Shep came back, he voiced how pleased he was with me taking the initiative to see to our guests' needs. Shep took Tyler's sheets from me, stating he would take care of this if I wanted to head to bed. It didn't take much convincing, for I truly was feeling a bit exhausted. Today had been an emotional day in too many ways. My head was even hurting.

Once I brushed my teeth I headed to my bed and climbed in. Grabbing my pillows, I piled them around me and found a good spot to fall asleep in. When I finally began to relax, I could only stare at the ceiling. Evidently I wasn't as tired as I felt. Maybe I needed to take a Tylenol PM to help. Suddenly I had the uncomfortable feeling of being watched. It took me a moment to convince myself to look around my room and prove myself wrong. I could see nothing unusual until I looked out my window. I let out a squeal of shock. Someone was watching me, and this time I was certain I wasn't dreaming it. His figure wasn't clear, but with a flash of lightning I knew he was there. I collided with Shep after jumping from my bed. The others came running into my room in order to find out what was wrong. Shep changed into Shadow form and left the house while Billy grabbed my shoulders and led me into the family room. He looked at Tyler with concern as I heard him warn that if anything should happen to take me to the prepared safety zone, especially if we didn't hear from him within an hour. Billy began muttering, "Selena, child, you are acting like a beacon. We were expecting that possibility. Still, we hoped you wouldn't be this strong this fast. It has to be your heritage. Some of our kind could possibly have been traveling through and caught your essence. But normally they would have introduced themselves politely." He turned and ran out the back door like hell's fire was licking at his feet.

I stood there in surprise for a few minutes. I don't know how long I was standing there. When I finally started to leave the family room Tyler caught my arm. "Please don't leave, Selena. We need you to stay in here until we hear something." It was then that I remembered seeing the man earlier in the day. I thought it had been my imagination. I had seen those same eyes in the storm. My whole body stiffened as I shivered. "Selena, you saw the same person earlier today, didn't you?"

Hesitantly I walked towards the hallway until Tyler blocked my path. "Stop listening to my thoughts, Tyler. It is not polite."

"I know, but like I told you, I can't help it, especially when you are upset." Pushing my way past him I headed for my room. It took me a moment to even be able to step into the doorframe. A shudder ran through my body as I looked out my window, fully expecting to see the drenched man again. "I thought his face… was my imagination." Tyler carefully placed his hands on my shoulders as if trying to comfort me. He pleaded for me to go back to the family room. I could feel his desperation. Hastily I grabbed my housecoat and socks before returning. He kept looking over his shoulder and never did say another word.

Once back in the family room, I asked Tyler why anyone would be looking through my window if they were a Shadow. They could just as easily be in my room. He looked at me and stated that he felt they might want Shep and his father to know so they could trap them. "That is why my dad said to take you to the safety if we don't hear from him within an hour." Tyler looked sick as I glanced at the clock. It had already been forty-two minutes. Tyler patted his pockets as he tried to settle his nervous hands. "Where's your phone?" A nod of my head pointed him towards the kitchen. With a soft voice he requested I come with him. At this I grumbled. Tyler acted very serious as he glanced between the rooms. "You stay right here. Don't move."

I listened as he dialed the phone. Quietly I slipped into the hallway and grabbed my shoes and a jacket. If Shep had fallen into a trap, maybe I could help. I would at least distract the man; after all, he wanted me. "Grandpa...We've had a disturbance here, and Dad has been gone almost an hour. I am going to head to the other portal with Selena in ten minutes." Knowing he could hear my thoughts if I was too excited, I started thinking about the cold rain, hoping he wouldn't realize what I was about to do. Since the front door was the closest, I pushed it in so it would not make a noise as I opened it. As I slipped out onto the porch, I felt the wind gust hit me like a ton of bricks. I barely had time to jump off the porch when I landed in a puddle as Tyler's panicked voice shouted that I was leaving. I heard the phone hit the wall and knew I didn't have much time to hide. Luckily I knew this area better than he did. Crawling under the steps, I slid under the porch and watched as he came running down the wooden steps. I could hear him calling my name softly. He was trying to convince me that I didn't know what I was doing and he only wanted to keep me safe. When he rounded the corner of the house, I slipped out, heading for Heather's backyard. For a moment I stopped to listen to the sounds around me. All I could hear was the whispering pines.

Once at the back fence, I climbed it quietly. Carefully checking to see if Tyler was anywhere near, I could hear him still calling my name softly. This time he was desperate. *"Selena, I don't like this any more than you do. But we have to do what we are told. Alexander is dangerous and you don't understand. He will kill both of us."* I hadn't thought I was endangering him. Suddenly I felt someone grab my mouth and pull me back. *"I knew you wouldn't want me to get hurt. Don't scream, you will give us away. Now, you are coming with me so the others can help Shep and Dad."*

Tyler was pulling me along the tree line behind my neighbor's home. We almost made it to the end of the cul-de-sac when I felt the same uneasy feeling I had earlier. When we looked to our right we saw a mist with the form of a man. "Run!" screamed Tyler. We started running while slipping and sliding through the mud puddles. Suddenly I was pulled into darkness and couldn't help but whimper.

*"Selena, Tyler it's me. I want you not to move from here. Billy and I almost have them trapped."* Tyler was now lying on the ground next to me, but he

reached over with a firm grasp to hold my hand. With a quick glance up I watched Shep's Shadow form gracefully moving through the darkness. A second later Tyler forced my head down, warning me not to watch. *"Don't think about him. You are giving his position away."* It was then that I realized what I had done. I continued to keep my head pressed against my arm. Again I felt the presence of the stranger, but now he was behind me.

We both jumped with the clap of thunder and lightning. My head began to pound with a headache and what I saw terrified me. *"Shep, Dad, he is here with us!"* A mist was rolling towards us and I felt ice cold.

"Stop!" I tried to pull away from Tyler in hopes of distracting the man from harming him. I began to run towards the mist. For some reason I was no longer afraid. I could save everyone. Tyler's strong hands halted my movement and began to pull me in the opposite direction. I hadn't realized how strong he was until I found myself being dragged back against my will.

The rain started pouring in a sheet, and lightning hit the tree in front of me. Feeling dazed, I realized that Tyler was pulling me deeper into the woods, muttering he needed to focus in order to find the portal. I was barely able to keep up. Finally tripping, Tyler pulled me into a sitting position behind a fallen tree.

"Selena, I have to concentrate. I need to sense for a portal. I know there is one in these woods, but I have to relax to find it. I need you to not move, and I mean it." He took some deep breaths and closed his eyes. The storm was clapping overhead and it reminded me of the last time I was in these woods. Suddenly I heard a horrible hissing noise and Tyler hollered as he grabbed me. He wanted to make sure I was still beside him. For once *his* mind was screaming.

A minute later Shep appeared in front of us, and Tyler started saying he had heard a portal open and close. Shep left again, taking Shadow form. "When he does that it is called shadowing, Selena. It is a way for Shadow forms to travel." I appreciated the lesson. He was very sweet. A moment later we heard running feet. I was surprised to see Uncle Billy headed straight for us. Shep had now returned, and both men were looking at each other with disgust. "They're carrying on a private conversation telepathically. I imagine they are going over what happened. Evidently Shep released some of the traps he had placed. He wanted to make sure others who are protecting you had a safe route in," Tyler informed me. With a simple nod of my head, my wet hair began to cling to my face as the wind howled through the trees. Shep sat down beside me, pushing the water from his bald head as I sensed his frustration. Without thought, I reached for Shep and scooted closer to him.

"Selena, I need you to stop blocking your thoughts from me. As your Protector and father. I can always force you to allow me to hear you, but I would prefer not to. You can block from others, but never me, okay?"

"I don't mean to do that...I'm sorry."

"Selena, in some families there are members you will have special relationships with. These people will be able to hear you most of the time like a parent would. For some reason, it looks like Tyler and you will have this type of relationship and I'm glad. What Tyler doesn't realize is that you are hearing him as well, but his thoughts are quieter because he is not a novice." When I relaxed, I realized Shep was right. I could hear Tyler too. Tyler straightened up as I heard Billy chortle with laughter. Quickly I opened my eyes to see Tyler staring at me like I was strange.

"I guess this is a two way street. We will have to work on the privacy thing, Selena," Tyler stated with obvious irritation. When I told him I would think about it, our fathers began to laugh hysterically.

"What happened to the Shadows?" Tyler demanded.

"They left," I said without thinking. "I can't feel him anymore. I guess he was not a part of my imagination after all." Shep grabbed my hands and pulled me back to face him. "You saw him earlier?"

"Remember earlier in the day you felt I was scared and asked what was wrong? I saw his eyes in the storm out my window, but I thought it was my imagination." Shep draped his arm around me as we began to walk back to the house.

"Selena, until you understand our two worlds better, maybe you should tell me every time something strange happens and let me decide if it is your imagination."

Once back at the house, Shep asked why we left the front door open. I felt Shep take in a deep breath. "Selena Marie, don't ever think I would want you to distract them to help me."

Hastily I walked into the house as Tyler zipped by me. "Now you are in trouble." Seconds later we all were greeted by an urgent knock on the back door. Since when had our back door become our front? Shep ordered me to stay where I was.

I heard the back door open, only to hear another man's anxious voice. Once again the slapping of hands on backs proved Shep was fond of this person too. "We were fine but had a close call." Shep walked in with another man around Shep's age. He was smiling from ear to ear. What shocked me were his eyes.

"Hi, I'm Wayne Martin," he said, offering his hand. As I reached out to shake it, I realized I was soaked in mud.

"Sorry, I wouldn't want to get you dirty. I'm Selena." Before I knew it, I found myself in another bear hug whether I was wet or not.

"Selena this is another of your dad's brothers." I was going to have to become used to everyone doing this. *"Yes, you will. Our family is a tad bit overfriendly,"* Tyler informed me with a self-satisfied smirk on his face.

"I don't mean to be rude, but I need to change," I said as I excused myself to go to the bathroom where I continued to listen to the men talk. Billy was explaining what had occurred and how the small route into the neighborhood would have to be tightened. When I walked into my room, I went directly over to my window and shut the blinds. Quickly I found some fresh pj's and closed my door in order to dry off. After I dressed I still felt uncomfortable. Carefully I looked around my room because something wasn't right. Within the next second my door flew open as Shep barged in.

"Selena, what's wrong? You blocked your mind from me again right before you noticed something." Billy and Wayne both were scouring my room suspiciously.

"I don't know. My room feels funny. I imagine I am just a little creeped out from what happened tonight." I grabbed the picture of my parents before sitting down on my bed. With shaking hands I gently placed it back on the nightstand while fingering its frame. Shep sat down next to me and asked if I had been looking at my parents' picture before the incident happened.

"No, I must have knocked it when I jumped." Shep draped his arm around me, and I knew there was something seriously wrong. Gradually he reached across me and picked up my picture. Billy came around and looked down, stating he remembered when it had been taken. A surge of excitement ran through me as I begged him to tell me.

"We were near here in Michigan. Your mother loved this area. I think this picture was taken about five years before you were born. Anyway, we all were on vacation. Shep and Sarah were with us too." Shep nodded his head at the memory. "In fact, many of Analease's family were with us. I remember Drew and Jared could not stop picking on each other. They both were acting like boys, short-sheeting the beds and jumping each other. Your mom wound up teaching them both a lesson, though. She set a trap and they both wound up spending the night out in the fog. Your mother had mild winter abilities, so they were a bit cold too. We heard them hollering all night to release them, but she wouldn't give in. In fact, if memory serves me correctly, Shep threw in a decent thunderstorm to drown out their voices."

We all were laughing by the time Billy was done telling the story. Shep was still holding the picture in his hands, rubbing it nervously. "Selena, I had never thought about this until now, but I need you to let me take this picture. We wouldn't want anyone from another realm to find this. It would be the evidence they want to prove who you are. I will keep it safe, and when this is all over, I will give it back."

My world was caving in on me as I felt tears sting my eyes. Wayne knelt down at my knees and gripped my nervous hands. "Selena, it won't be forever. We need to keep you safe. Shep's right—this would be a dead giveaway." Shep was rubbing my cheek. He looked as upset as I was with this turn of events.

"Please..." I knew Shep wouldn't have the heart to take it if I pleaded with him.

"Shep, this is the only thing I have of them."

He nodded with understanding. "But we have to keep you safe." Gently I took the picture from him to take one last look and held it to my chest as my tears burned my eyes. I didn't want to give it up. If I did I might forget them. Wayne very gently pulled the picture to him and handed it to Billy.

"It's alright love. I won't let anything happen to it. I promise one day I will give it back," Wayne stated emphatically. I could see it was hurting him as much as it was, me. Shep pulled me to him as I wept.

Around midnight I finally made it to bed. Listening to the chatter of the men in the kitchen I figured I would never be able to sleep, even if I wanted to. With a feeling of despair I looked back at my nightstand to find a vacant spot where my parents' picture used to be. It was like a hole had been made in my heart. It was all I had of them—the only picture I had ever seen—and it wasn't that good even.

Shep reentered my room looking miserable. *"We will give it back as soon as we can little one. Now I want you to go to sleep because we have a big day tomorrow."* Leaning over, Shep pecked my forehead, walked over to my window, and peered out the blinds suspiciously. *"You're safe, and we will use our telepathy so you and Tyler can sleep."*

The next morning when I woke, I could hear the guys goofing off in the garage. I imagine they were getting ready for our trip to who knows where. I dressed quickly and ran into the hall, only to bump into Tyler who was grabbing my belongings that I had put out the night before. "This everything?" he asked sarcastically. I threw him my bathroom supplies. "What, a duffel of beauty products? Dad thought *I* packed a lot." Sneering at him, I went to the garage to see if there was anything I could do. Then, of all things, the doorbell rang. I knew who that would be. Billy and Tyler scurried into the garage.

As I walked to the door I heard Shep's voice sounding in my mind. *"We don't want her to see Billy or Tyler."* Cautiously I scanned the entryway as I waited to make sure that Billy and Tyler were out of sight and quiet.

"I thought maybe you weren't going on your trip," said Heather somewhat hopefully as I opened the door.

"Well, it was raining and we didn't want to leave in that type of weather, but we're almost ready to go now. I really have to help Shep get the car packed. I'll call you in a day or two." Heather looked like she was going to plead with me to stay, not realizing I didn't have a choice this time. "You're abandoning me to have to do whatever Mike wants for the rest of the summer, so you'd better come back with a nice souvenir for me," she jested. Waving goodbye to my best friend felt a little sad. Would I ever be able to be the same with her again?

Back in the garage the boys had finished loading the car. Billy and Tyler looked at Shep, stating they would see us when we arrived, which made me wonder why they weren't coming with us. They all grinned at me as Shep climbed into the driver's seat.

"Get in Selena. It is time to start an adventure of a lifetime." His bold statement made me feel a bit apprehensive, even though I knew I had nothing to fear with Shep.

"What about Billy and Tyler?" I asked as I watched them enter the kitchen.

"We will see them later, don't worry." They had left the garage before we pulled out, leaving me dumbfounded.

"Are you ever going to explain?" Shep just grinned at me as he hit the door genie. It wasn't much of a surprise to see Heather waiting to wave goodbye to us. As we passed Heather I realized I never did get my answer. Once we left our subdivision I leaned back into the seat, trying to find a comfortable spot. The sky was still cloudy and threatening to rain, making me think I needed another pillow to lean against.

The rain started coming down as the fog seemed to be rolling lightly in around us. I asked Shep if it was going to be a long trip. He said, "Just the usual," which meant it would take all day.

"Will we be there tonight?" He mumbled again, and I decided I better let him drive. This time I grabbed my player and turned it on as I placed my earphones in my ears.

We had been driving for hours, and I hadn't been paying attention to where. I really should have been watching, but the only thing I needed was to stop soon. I heard a low, muffled laugh before he told me to get my shoes on and we would stop at a rest area soon and eat. "What, we are going to eat in the car? You never do that."

He pulled into a rest area a couple minutes later. I tried to see what number it was, but at that moment the rain came down in a sheet. When he finally parked I didn't care how hard it was raining; I needed to get to the bathroom soon or we were going to have water inside the car. Rushing out, the rain lightened to a gentle spray. Well, at least I wouldn't be soaked. Thankfully the restroom was clean and modern. I hate the old toilet houses because they stink. When I returned to the hallway, I noticed the building was being remodeled and I couldn't even look at a map to see where we were.

I had the specific feeling I was not supposed to know where we were headed, and it would be useless to ask. Moments later a car entered the area as we drove away, and I noticed the rain started getting heavier. I had a sneaking suspicion that Shep was in control of this storm. He evidently didn't want anybody to notice us. He was deliberately not telling me everything. I crawled into the back and placed my headphones on again. Somehow I had fallen asleep. When I woke, it was definitely dark, and we were still driving.

"Shep aren't we going to stop soon?" It was almost like he knew this would be what I was wondering, and he said he was going to go a little bit further before we stopped. Again I laid back into the pillow and fell asleep.

The next time I woke up I found myself in an RV—one of the real nice ones you see with stars. I stumbled out of the bed and walked down the hall to find Billy sitting at the little table cleaning his gun. I was relieved to see the bathroom was actually pretty nice. That meant no long hikes to a shower room in the middle of the night. When I exited the bathroom, I was presented with food and told to hurry up if I wanted to do some practicing. Warily looking at Billy, I wondered if his gun would be involved. "Of course not," he informed me. Then he turned around with a huge smirk as he walked out the door. "But if you want we could."

"No thanks," I muttered. It looked like I had the RV to myself now, so I swiftly darted back to the room I had come from to find my belongings. Quickly pulling on some clothing, I ran out the door and was met by a lush, mountainous terrain. It was absolutely beautiful and desolate. We were in no campground. To my astonishment there were two other RV's besides ours, and outside of that, nothing—not even a road.

Shep walked over grinning as he reminded me we had to train in secrecy. "We couldn't do it near people. What did you expect? Let's walk to where Billy has set up a quad for us to practice."

Time seemed confused to me. I bet Shep was pleased with that. Inside the box, Tyler was sparring with another boy his age. They were practicing some kind of karate. Was that what I was going to learn today? Shep looked at me and shook his head no. A sigh of relief escaped my lips. Billy walked over to me and hollered for the two boys to stop sparring. They responded immediately, like someone had actually jerked them apart. Slowly the boys walked over to me, looking quite cocky as they seemed to share a private conversation. I was sure it had something to do with me. Then I noticed a lady also heading towards me.

Billy introduced her as his wife, Betty, and his other son, Kirt. Shyly I greeted them as I silently wished I didn't feel like everybody already knew everything about me. Betty spoke into my mind, assuring me they hadn't pried into my secrets. *"We respect your privacy. As you become better at telepathy you will understand what we mean."* She did help to make me feel a little better.

*"I'm working on it."*

She smiled a smile that gave me the feeling of great love. I bet she was the perfect mother. They all seemed to be very genuine. I think most of our modern culture lacks that real understanding of love and family. They really wanted me to know that I was family.

Gently guiding me, Shep led me into the square. As we did, I noticed Betty,

Kirt, and Tyler leaving the area. That was truly a relief. Shep sat down on the ground, and I did the same as Billy entered the square. "So what are we going to do now?" Suddenly he threw a ball at my face. By instinct I reacted by holding my breath while covering my face to duck. When I looked up the ball was traveling very slowly towards the outside of the square.

This time the slowdown was different; I didn't feel dizzy. Billy laughed, while praising me aloud for my quick reflexes. He looked to Shep with a wink, muttering that I was a natural with slowing. "This must have been one of her first true abilities from Jared." He acted thrilled with that. "She has a part of him. It makes me very happy to know that." For a moment he looked sad, but he quickly drowned it into happier feelings.

The next thing I knew, Billy picked up a handful of leaves and was throwing them around. To my amazement they looked like they were forming a very slow tornado. "I'm doing that, Selena. You have to relax. You do not have to stop breathing—just control it. We can do with less oxygen than anybody else outside of those with water abilities. Once you have learned control, your respiration will be slower than the normal person."

Picking up some leaves and debris, I tried to slow them down the way he was. I always stopped breathing. Billy would let out a yip to remind me to breathe, and within about four hours I seemed to slow things down without holding my breath. Still, the leaves didn't have the graceful appearance that Billy was able to demonstrate.

I sat down next to Shep, discouraged. "I will never get this."

Shep sat up and wrapped his arm securely around me as he squeezed me tight. "You are not passing out anymore, and that is a sign of improvement. This all will take time. None of this will be easy; it requires persistence. You are doing things a couple of days ago you would have never expected to be able to do. Your basic instincts are good. They seem to kick in when you are stressed, but we want them to work on command." Shep and Billy decided to go back to the campsite and help with lunch while I remained behind to rest. After they were out of sight, I started practicing again until I felt someone slap my arm.

When I spun around, I found Tyler grinning. "See, training is fun, but you have a lot to catch up on. I can help you if you want." I looked at him questioningly, then asked him what his ability was. To my surprise he pointed towards the forest, and out poked a large cat. Instantly I became frightened and jumped back behind him out of fear. He proceeded to walk towards the mountain lion like there was no danger. He encouraged me to come with him, but I flatly refused. After a minute, a deer came out very close to the cat. Tyler was able to pet both animals without their natural instincts taking over. Then I remembered what he had told me the night before: to listen. When I did, I discovered he was communicating with the two animals. They were not sticking to their own instincts to flee or kill the other.

Cautiously I went over and felt their fur and was amazed by the textures. The deer left, and quite a bit later Tyler allowed the cat to leave. It was then that I realized he did not want the deer to be hunted.

"That was really cool. How long did you take to learn?" Tyler's smile was weak. "Not long—it took about a year for me to keep control, but now it is no problem. My telepathy is stronger than most." I shivered at the thought of those poor animals killing each other. I could tell he wanted to know how things went for me. I picked up some leaves and threw them out in front of me. I tried to slow them down into a graceful swirl when I happened to notice Tyler's face twisting into a grimace. That was when it hit me: he would be affected by what I was doing.

At that thought, everything went back to normal. I could see he was a little mad at what happened. "Sorry, I forgot you would be affected, Tyler. It wasn't intentional." I started laughing as he went straight inside the square.

"That's alright" he muttered. "I'll remember the next time I run into the mountain lion."

Again I picked up some leaves and threw them up much higher than before. Before long I started feeling the breeze pick up and things began moving in a swirl with a beauty I had never seen before. I heard Tyler gasp as he started clapping his hands. When everything had landed back on the ground, even the breeze had stopped. Tyler came over and praised me loudly.

Abruptly we heard the sound of ringing. "It's time for lunch." Hastily we made our way back through the trees. I felt extremely hot, and for some reason I knew I wanted a light breeze. When we reached the table at the campsite, Betty stated she would like to keep the food warm. Without realizing it, I had created a strong breeze to stay cool by. I stopped immediately as everybody started laughing, including me.

# CHAPTER 6.
# SHADOWS

**After lunch** I wanted to practice; instead we were told to relax. They made it perfectly clear that a group from the Shadow Realm would be arriving, and Shep needed to check the boundaries once more.

Tyler and his siblings went back to sparring out in front of the RV's. Their offer to let me join made me squirm. "Absolutely not," I moaned. I watched my little cousin knock the boys off their feet. Her name was Laura, and she totally impressed me with her skills. She was petite with strawberry blonde hair. She really looked breakable, but I was definitely wrong. Laura took a seat beside me, and she seemed anxious but very sweet. I could tell she wanted to ask me a question but refrained.

"So, is it always that easy for you to get the upper hand with them?"

The roll of her eyes almost made me laugh out loud. "Well, I have more brothers than just those two. Being the only girl in a houseful of men makes one learn how to defend quite quickly. Besides, they all are overprotective and sometimes I need to remind them I can take care of myself. If I didn't, I may never go out with my friends."

She continued to inform me about the rest of her siblings. Evidently they were older and living on their own. I would meet two more of them within the next month. I listened with amazement as she instructed me of each person's weakness. She acted like this was important. They were all trained in Tang Soo Do or something like that, along with a couple other types of combat. I learned that *every* Guardian is trained in hand-to-hand combat. From the sound of it, they had trouble a long time ago and had to be ready for anything. She informed me that eventually I would be required to learn, so I needed to pick up some of their weaknesses.

When we grew bored of watching, Laura and I decided to go for a walk. We walked towards the mountains as she continued telling me stories she had been told about our people. I didn't realize that a Guardian's aging process is different from Mortals. She informed me that every century was like a year to us after our teen years passed. That meant I would stay younger than Heather. If she caught wind of that she would be mad. I really needed to call her.

We finally made it to the base of the mountain when Laura asked me if I wanted to try to learn some Tang Soo Do. Carefully she started showing me the first three forms. It was sort of like ballet, and I liked that there were actual movements to train by. It was finally something I could do easily. Laura promised to teach me so I wouldn't look like an idiot when the time came. We would have to find a place to practice without the boys knowing, though.

She also confessed that when it came to Tyler she had a weak spot for him compared to her other brothers. "He has a very kind soul that others sometimes take advantage of. He wants to help everybody, and he does it without making you feel bad." I understood what she meant. He did seem to try to do things without intimidating you, but he was definitely as mischievous as Mike. His warped sense of humor showed itself when he offered to let the lion eat me.

Softly I revealed to her what I had done to him in the woods and his comeback. Evidently she didn't feel any pity; she acted like it had been a good lesson for him to learn. Suddenly she began chattering on about how she couldn't wait for me to be rejoined with our entire family. She had always wanted a sister, and another female could help defend against all the boys in the family.

Laura hit my side to forewarn me of the boys racing towards us. When they arrived they couldn't believe we were out here by ourselves. I could tell something more was happening with Kirt that was not obvious. Tyler looked to Kirt as he nodded in some silent agreement. Loudly Laura made a frustrated growl, reminding them we were not helpless. All of this made me feel defensive. "Maybe we were trying to get away from all of your roughhousing." All of that testosterone was killing me. Lying back against the rock, I thought of Heather and speculated if I would have a signal out here on my phone.

The wind started picking up, and I thought that possibly one of my cousins could manipulate air too. Laura and Tyler stared at the sky, stating it was looking funny and a storm must be approaching. In a rush I sat up to gaze at the clouds. They were right; it looked like a storm was headed in. We stared with amazement at the darkening clouds as they rolled in. Out in the plains like this, freak storms were known to happen, and most of the time they were life-threatening too. Tyler looked at me as if to inquire if I was doing it. I shook my head no as I realized the mistake I had made. Manipulating air is a Shadow ability, not Guardian. Right away my mind wandered to Shep. "Shep can create storms. Maybe he is doing this to encourage us to return."

Abruptly the storm clouds rattled at the top of the mountain, forcing us to head back to camp immediately. To our astonishment a tidal wave was cascading down the mountain side. It was following the trail, which had evidently been carved out by rain, not hiking. We were directly in its path. Tyler and Kirt tried to push both Laura and I out of the way, but I seemed rooted to the spot. Tyler was having trouble yanking me from this impending doom. Before I realized it, he was practically carrying me out of the way.

After several steps we fell to the ground, gazing back at the rushing water, only to realize it was suddenly splashing closer to us. The water had gained so much momentum that it was still going to pull us into its wake. As I wished for the water to remain in the ravine, it seemed to be diverted from us and continued down the gulch. Tyler wrenched me up and dragged me further away as we were being drenched in its spray. Kirt and Laura looked like they were in shock as they stared at us. Everything slowed down, and I could feel my sides aching as my breathing slowed. When I looked at the others they were afraid and cold. Obviously our troubles weren't over. Off to the side of the mountain where there was darkness entrenched in between a crevice, I could see Billy and Shep appear. They seemed to have walked out directly from the rock wall. Billy continued at normal speed, but Shep didn't.

Wait a minute…I was slowing things down and I was breathing while doing it. Instantly I forced myself to breathe at a normal pace. Just as I did, everything went back to the way it should be. Tyler's sudden yank brought me fully back to reality. He was still pulling me towards the rest of the family, but this time he didn't seem to be hindered at all. Come to think about it, he had still been able to move me some before I released the slowdown. Shep gave me a weak smile as he disappeared back into the crevice. I hadn't seen a cave there earlier—I would have noticed.

Billy jarred my attention back to him, demanding for us to run back to the campsite together. No one was to lag behind. Anxiously I inquired where Shep was going. He shook his head. His children seemed to understand something I didn't, but I wasn't going anywhere until I received an answer. Tyler, sensing my response, whispered to me that I was going back one way or on his back. Immediately I threw him an indignant look as he wrenched me to stand beside him. Billy continued to scour the surrounding area as if we were in danger. With a stern look he motioned for us to take off. Kirt and Laura set a swift, steady pace while Billy was trailing us, as if waiting for something to happen. He snapped at us to keep going and for the boys to keep sharp.

I could see the tension in Kirt's squared jaw. It clamped tightly shut as he seemed to be looking straight ahead, yet not quite. This was the second time I noticed this reaction in him. Did he have an ability I was not aware of?

*"Run like a pack,"* I heard Billy reemphasize in our minds.

We were almost back to the campsite when I spied Betty standing very still, as if listening for someone to scream. Then she spotted us, and I could see she wasn't even blinking as we were nearing. Instead she was concentrating very hard. What was she doing? When we finally arrived, I turned back to Billy, demanding to know what was going on and where Shep went by himself. I could see Billy was not going to take time to answer my questions, especially after he ordered me gruffly into the camper. I heard him say to Betty that he didn't know what happened. He was looking at me like I had done it.

"Didn't Shep create the storm?" His sharp look at me made it quite evident that Shep hadn't. With a look of concern, Billy shoved me in. Then I realized Tyler was being shoved in behind me. Billy commanded him to wait to tell him whatever he thought was important until they were sure this was a natural phenomenon. It was then that my heart plummeted when I realized Billy either thought I had created the storm or worse— that Alexander was here. This thought made me feel guilty; I could place them in jeopardy so easily. This was my family, and I wasn't going to endanger them, and Shep was not going to face Alexander by himself either. Hastily I started back out the door, but Betty stepped in, pushing me back forcefully. She looked stern, like one would expect from a mother, especially as she stated that there would be no thinking like that. We all sat down looking quite miserable.

I could see that Kirt, Laura, and Tyler were shivering uncontrollably, not to mention we were soaking wet. For once I wasn't too cold, and then I remembered why. I was the one who had slowed everything down. It was obvious we all were thinking we might be in danger. I couldn't help but wonder if something really bad was happening. I had lost my parents; I couldn't lose Shep, too.

I jumped as Billy dashed past us to a cabinet and started throwing blankets out. Betty looked at poor Laura and rushed her into a hot shower. Billy ran back outside the camper, opening one of the storage drawers with a bang. From the sound of it, he was rummaging for something. He burst back through the door with a heater, thrust it into its covey and plugged it in. The boys gathered around it quickly.

Then I heard Tyler's voice in my head. *"Dad, she was able to divert the water flowing down the mountain, and I know she didn't cause the storm. She was finally relaxing."*

Billy grabbed Tyler's shoulders and peered at me. "Are you sure?" Billy's stare was unsettling, but Tyler's reaction proved to all it was the truth. Betty looked at me with fear and sympathy in her eyes. I had to get out of here. I had never done well with sympathy, and I couldn't take anymore. Betty offered to make room for me by the heater, but I crunched back into the seat, gazing out the window while crossing my arms. I just wanted to be left alone.

When their attention was back on the two boys, I slipped out of the camper swiftly. I couldn't believe what had just happened. Was Shep all right? With a quick look back at the mountain I could tell the storm was over, and I hoped this meant Shep would arrive soon. Did they think I had wanted to create a storm or hurt my cousins? I was astounded by this thought—I would never hurt anyone.

Billy came out the door and stood underneath the other side of the awning, allowing his thoughts to flow into mine. *"No, we didn't think you would have wanted to hurt any of us, but you are part Shadow and you could have created the storm by accident—that would be one ability we don't need to deal with right now.*

*"When Shep and I saw what was going on, we weren't sure if it was a created storm or a natural weather phenomenon. We had to make sure it wasn't Alexander either. As parents, we have the ability to sense our children, and we could feel*

*everybody's terror. I have to admit, you had great control of the slowing this time. I could tell you had more control than when we were practicing earlier. Later we will all be able to laugh about this. You know you made them feel like they were in the middle of winter without a coat on, don't you? It reminds me of what I did to your father."* His laughter was contagious, and I couldn't help but smile as I glanced back at him with relief.

"Shep will be alright. He is a lot stronger than you know. Alexander would never challenge him in person." Billy wanted me to go in, but I couldn't. Not until I had Shep back with me. He didn't understand how I felt.

*"Little one, I am coming. Everything is fine."* With this announcement I felt a huge amount of relief. In fact, I jumped from the shock of hearing Shep so clearly within my mind. This was something I was going to have to get used to.

A few minutes later we could see Shep's tall, lanky form walking towards us from the forest. Billy came over to me and put his hand up in front to keep me from running out to meet him. When Shep was finally under the awning I wrapped my arms around him so tightly that I am sure he knew I was never going to let him go. He hugged me back and was choking out the words that he still liked breathing. Instantly I released him while remaining as close as I could manage. I imagine he could tell I wasn't going to let him go far without me. "So I can tell you both, the storm was a natural event. But, what is this about Selena diverting water?"

"I guess I can remember the water coming straight for us, and people drown in those freak floods. Remember the flood we witnessed in the Badlands? It was like that. I don't know how I did it." That was all I could think of. Suddenly Shep stood up and announced we were going back to our camper, and wanted to know if we could do anything to help the others shake the effect of my ability. Billy just grabbed his sides and looked back at the camper door, amused. "They will thaw in an hour or two. I'll let you know when the others are about to arrive."

As we made our way to our RV, I asked if we were going to be able to practice any more today. Shep acted stunned at my question. "Wasn't your escapade enough for today?"

"Fine. Then can you tell me how to tell the difference between a natural storm and one that is created?"

Shep sat thoughtfully as he considered my question. "That would take a lot of time and we don't have enough. I would prefer to answer your other question… the one you haven't asked."

"I forgot you can read my mind. So how do you travel?"

"Moving is easy for a Shadow. You travel from shadow to shadow, but it is not a passageway into the Shadow Realm. To pass into the Shadow Realm you must use an access point, which we call a portal. I can take physical things with me—including your uncle—when shadowing. He really has to trust me in order to allow me to transport him, though. You see, when a Guardian travels that way, he has no control. Some think the boogeyman stories were true stories of Shadows who took advantage of people's natural fear of the dark. A lot of myths and folklore are created from true incidents. Makes you really think, doesn't it?"

"So how do you fade in and out?"

"Clearly I have to be in a dark place. The shadow doesn't have to be extreme, but just enough so I can use it. I travel from shadow to shadow no matter what the width. I can never appear magically out in the open, especially if the sun is shining. Rocks have a shadow, trees have lots of shadows. Still, the easiest time for Shadows to travel is at nighttime. Parker used to tell Heather the boogeyman was going to get her, to keep her from wandering the house at night. Do you remember the day you came home from spending the night over there and you were petrified of the shadows in our house? I told you there was nothing to be afraid of and they wouldn't hurt you. We played with shadow hands for the next month before you finally decided it was okay."

"You told me Shadows were beautiful people who helped us to learn different things in life and they could help you if you talk to them. Sort of like an imaginary friend. I did talk to them like a friend from then on. Oh, how embarrassing."

Abruptly a heavy pounding on our door drew our attention. It wasn't much of a surprise to find Tyler standing there with a wide smirk on his face. Shep immediately moved to the kitchenette and started boiling some water. "Sorry, about making you so cold."

"That's alright. If you hadn't slowed the water and moved it we might not be here right now. Although the next time I go anywhere with you, I'm wearing a sweatshirt." We all chuckled at his comment as Shep brought over three piping hot cups of hot chocolate.

We finished our drinks in silence while looking out the window. I don't know what I was expecting to see, but I was suspicious. I was becoming uncomfortable so I had to stand up. Shep inquired what was wrong, but I couldn't put my finger on it. He scooted off of the bench when we heard another knock at our door. This time it was Kirt. He informed us our company was not far off and Shep was needed. Shep looked at me with curious eyes, but I couldn't hear what he was thinking. We hurried out the door and headed straight towards the woods.

"Who's coming this time? Will it be your older brothers?"

Tyler shook his head. "No, this time it is some of our friends from the Shadow Realm. They are very good friends of Shep."

"I think Shep's wife, Sarah, is going to be with them," Kirt surmised. I had never heard Tyler and Kirt sound so serious. As we continued through the woods you could feel a slight breeze. The trees even seemed to be quiet, as if something was about to happen. When we finally came over a hill, I saw Billy and Betty standing in front of a mound. To my surprise this mound was surrounded by trees. This could not be an accident. I remembered how the trees had intertwined together to weave a doorway from my adventure with Heather. I gasped and Shep put his hand on my shoulder, trying to calm me.

"We thought you would like to be here when we open a portal. I am glad you have made the connections. Some mounds are more important than others. When there are seven trees planted around a mound, it is a signal to Guardian or Shadow of an access point to another realm. All the trips I have taken you on through your childhood were important in your education, just not in Mortal things." Shep pushed me back gently towards Tyler and gestured to Kirt to come forward. "You boys know what to do if this is not who we think it is, right?"

"We are to make sure Selena and Laura are taken to the other portal and use it to proceed to our safety zone. There are others there who will instruct us on what to do when we arrive. We know...don't take any chances. Safety is our job this time."

Laura came over and took my hand hesitantly. "You know it's just a precaution. Don't worry so much. We are all well-trained. I know what can happen if something goes wrong and I have confidence everything will be fine." Her voice sounded so sweet, and yet I could feel her fear shaking inside of her.

Billy and Betty closed their eyes and whispered something unintelligible. Laura began clamping her other hand over mine as she looked nervously towards the portal. Gradually it began to wind around, creating a triangular archway. It was just as beautiful as I remembered. My whole body grew tense as Tyler and Kirt backed up against us like a shield. I wanted to see. I heard a loud whooshing sound, and then a glow of sunlight outlining the boys' frames. Was everything all right, or was this a sign of danger?

Laura patted my hand as if to say it was okay. Kirt had his hand reaching behind him as if he was ready to run if need be. At that moment I heard a hiss with an unexplainable noise at the end, and then there was silence. Cautiously I peeked around Tyler and felt his hand come back, pushing on my waist. The silence was more deafening than the horrible hissing noise. Then there was laughter and greeting sounds of people slapping each other on the back saying welcome. Tyler's hand relaxed as he stepped back to press against me. "It's alright Selena...they're friends." Slowly I stepped out from behind him and recognized the woman Shep was holding in a deep embrace. In an instant she looked up, as if she realized I was thinking about her. A simple smile spread across her face as she reached out her hand towards me. For a moment I felt shy, but I found myself walking towards her anxiously. Something inside me knew her and needed her comfort.

Sarah walked over to me with such elegance that one might have mistaken her to be floating, even though I could see her slippers hit the dirt. She must be an angel. When I was standing in front of her I was surprised how close I felt to her. I definitely knew her and knew I loved her very much. Tentatively she leaned over and hugged me so tightly I couldn't breathe. She must have felt my uneasiness because I heard her say, "Mi mon aimee," and I remembered that from somewhere in my past. She had said this to me when I was very little, and I even knew it meant she loved me, or that I was her beloved. I could feel tears coming to my eyes as memories seemed to flood into my thoughts. I remembered my mother sitting on a deck with Sarah as I swung. They must have been cheering me on. Then I had another memory of a birthday party with all of them, including my dad. Seeing my parents happy and with me made my emotions well up so fast I felt my heart would break. To me, emotions were something very private, and showing them was quite embarrassing. Not wanting anybody to see, I hugged her tightly and hid my face in her dark hair. When I pulled away, I knew I hadn't fooled her.

Shep started introducing the others who had traveled with Sarah. They were Brent, Drew, and Tom. Welcoming them was interesting since they were staring a hole through me. Brent and Drew seemed to be the outdoorsy type, and Tom seemed to be highly intellectual. Still, all were very friendly. Finally we all started walking back to the campsite. It became very obvious that Sarah was not going to release Shep anytime soon. Who could blame her?

Quickly I caught up with Tyler and Laura in hopes of easing my anxiousness. All of this was putting me on edge. "Why are they all staring at me?"

"They are amazed that you do not seem to have the dominant features of either family. The Martins have dominant blue eyes and you don't," Laura pointed out. "Since this is the first time they have seen you since you were five, they are having a hard time believing you really are Jared and Analease's daughter."

With some indignation, Tyler chanced a glance around at the newcomers. "Only select groups of people know what you look like. Your appearance has been a secret since you were born." I wondered how many actually knew what I looked like.

Surprisingly Billy answered my thought. "The number of people who could recognize you originally was the number of perfection—seven. You are a well-kept secret. This was the only way we could keep you safe. Your appearance was bound to change since you were so young when the incident happened. As a toddler, everything about you changes from hair color and texture to height. As children grow into adolescence, they develop strong personality traits and may change from time to time.

"The nice thing about you *is* you are such a good mix. You would not automatically be recognized as their daughter if somebody ever saw you, especially with Shep hindering them. You do not have the dominant blue eyes of our family or the auburn hair of your mother's. So the recessive genes helped in your disappearance. Your personality, though, is much the same as both of your parents, and the stubbornness you received a double dose of. Plus, I can see a lot of Shep's personality too. Watching you…I can see Jared's easygoing personality, and you have the elegance of your mother."

"So these people have never seen me before and were looking for family resemblances?"

"Yes, in a way," Sarah explained. "They saw you as a baby, or what you understand to be a toddler. The only consistency between then and now are your big, brown, beautiful eyes." Sarah continued to stumble with every sentence she started. For some reason I knew this wasn't normal for her. "These men have sacrificed trying to make sure of your safety. The men here didn't know until recently that you still lived. They would only know one or two contacts, but for the most part no one knows you exist.

"It is evident you are the granddaughter of Terah Whitlocke. It vibrates all around you. Your grandmother's family has always been well-loved and a moral foundation for our people. Today they thought it a trap.

"Then this past year there were flashes of a great strength, or as some said in our realm, a storm gathering. I knew it was you. I have been one of your main protectors for the past five years, along with Billy and Wayne, but now you need your mother's side of the family."

***

Thinking about everything made me wonder why I was so important. I was nothing special except that my parents were of two worlds. Maybe I was misunderstanding this. I wanted to help bring the killer to justice, but I didn't think they would allow me to help.

While passing through the woods, we came across the training area again. Laura nudged me, offering to practice a little, while the others carried on, oblivious to the two of us remaining behind. Swiftly I agreed with her suggestion and slipped into the square. I watched as Laura went around the square, tapping the stones. She was actually afraid of me, I could tell. When she caught my gaze, she sheepishly agreed she didn't want to be frozen again, which I totally understood.

To begin, Laura showed me ten movements to the first form. Then the first form was made up of fifteen. She was very patient with me as I stumbled through each, and she helped me to acquire the proper stance or turn required to not fall over my own limbs. Maybe out of all of them she was the slave driver of the group. She would bellow out if I didn't do something right and have me start over.

As I glanced around the forest edging, I found myself feeling uncomfortable, like we were being watched. This feeling seemed to be occurring a lot lately, and it was unnerving. I tried to look like I was goofing off as I scanned for the person watching. When looking hard into a corner, it was almost like there was a real solid person in roughage, but it was gone so quickly I wasn't sure if I had seen it properly.

Laura continued on to show me the exact position of the eleventh move when I turned around, suggesting we head back. She asked if I was sick, and softly I muttered I was tired and dinner would be soon. She agreed that her mom didn't like eating cold food after fixing it. I waited impatiently as she retraced the square to deactivate the teaching quad. I rapidly challenged her to a race, with which she agreed. Before I knew it, she was in full sprint. I pretended to run after her but acted like I tripped. As I lay on the ground, I crawled off to the side and tried to circle around to the spot where I had seen the figure. I wouldn't confront anyone, but at least I would have a good description.

My heart felt like it was going to pound out of my chest. I was about to look when I heard Laura hollering for me. Oh, great! She already missed me. This would bring everybody down in a panic. I was going to have to be quicker than I had anticipated. Quickly crawling along, I finally reached the area where I thought I had seen the Shadow, but when I rose, there was no one there. Instead I heard a noise in front of me and saw movement through the brush, which startled me. Suddenly I heard other voices hollering my name as I felt a cold rush in my blood—the type of feeling you get when you are home alone and feel your back is not safe upon entering a room. My automatic reaction was to place my back against the tree as I listened for any unusual noise.

I jumped when I heard Shep next to me. He was chiding me. "This should teach you a good lesson." The wind picked up and I thought I heard a giggle, which totally sent a shiver up my spine. I wasn't even sure if Shep had heard it. He guided me back by my shoulder, asking me what I was doing. I didn't feel like responding, for I knew good and well he could read my thoughts. "Are you going to make things difficult like this for the rest of the time we are here?"

"No," I stated flatly while trying to scan the woods behind us. For some reason I knew the person was still there, but Shep didn't, and that confused me. Why did I know and he didn't? Shep stopped and looked at me. I could feel he was uneasy.

"Selena, anytime you feel that way, call for me. Have I made myself clear?" After a curt nod of my head we headed back to the others in a rushed silence. When we arrived back at the campsite, it was abuzz with the excitement of what was I doing. I smiled weakly. More than likely I was still making more out of things than need be. Shep and Sarah were staring at each other, and I know he was telling her what I had attempted. To my surprise, Sarah walked over to me and patted my back, but I could tell she wanted to chide me too. Thankfully Betty rescued me, hollering for us all to sit at the table.

Betty and Sarah had made a wonderful dinner and brought stuff out for s'mores. Everybody was crowded around the fire, including the three newcomers. The way they kept chancing sneak peeks at me made me very curious to know what they were thinking. Brent and Drew seemed to be ribbing each other about working on a piece of equipment that Billy insisted was a worthless piece of junk. I didn't even recognize what the machine was. I wondered if this was the Drew Uncle Billy had mentioned the other night. Casually I walked over to him and sat down beside him. He grinned as he looked over at me, and then back to Shep.

Not sure how to ask Drew questions myself, Shep interrupted my spiraling, out of control thoughts. "Drew, we told Selena about your exploits with her father the other night, and I think she would like to talk to you." Suddenly I felt totally embarrassed as Drew scooted closer to me, making a funny clicking sound.

"Your dad and I were the best of friends. We couldn't help but play pranks on each other. I have a serious feeling you are just like him—always getting into trouble."

Immediately I shook my head no as I told him I was an angel most of the time… but my halo had a dent. He laughed, throwing his head back. "She sounds just like him!" His comment made me smile. I could see why my dad had been friends with this burly man. He didn't seem to have a care in the world. The fire flickered across his face, but I couldn't see anything but pure joy there. He was a good man, I could tell, and he had a heart of gold, too.

Unexpectedly my attention was drawn towards the edging of trees again. This time I saw no movement except for the wind. Anxiously I excused myself and walked a little ways from the group, leaving Drew with my s'more. I stood there for a few more minutes, wondering if I was spooking myself or if someone was truly there that we couldn't see. Shep stepped up beside me and continued to look at me quizzically. He wanted to know what had drawn me into such a somber mood and what I was looking for. I shook my head with frustration. I wasn't exactly sure how to explain myself. "It's nothing but my imagination." It was clear he didn't believe me.

"I'm being watched. I can feel them and hear them sometimes, but they always disappear quickly. I almost had them when you snuck up on me in the woods. I know I did." Shep tensed up and looked to Billy. Now I could see both men scouring the forest edging. Going back to the fire, I listened to the others talk while I continued to gaze at the forest. A second later Sarah sat down beside me, wanting to know what I was thinking about so intently. Instantly I forced a smile to my face. Drew moved to another corner of the campsite, and I watched as he gazed out into the darkness too.

"I have been practicing on trying to keep my thoughts to myself. I guess I am succeeding. At least that is one thing I can do easily." Sarah smiled at me as she pushed my bangs out of my eyes. For some reason she made me feel like I was a child again, but it was more than that. I was loved dearly. "It's nice to be here. That was all I was thinking." After watching Billy and Betty with their kids, I also wondered if my dad had been anything like Billy. He was a robust, balding man, but from the picture I had of my dad, the only thing they held in common were the blue eyes.

Stepping away from the fire I concentrated on the wind and refreshed the thoughts of what Sarah had been sharing with me earlier. This was the wrong thing to think about. A horrible sadness began to overwhelm me. My eyes welled with tears, forcing me to walk away at a brisk pace back to our RV. I choked out a "goodnight" to everybody as I fumbled a wave to them. Once inside, I went back to the little room and laid down, wondering for the first time in ages about my parents' history. I heard the door open, forcing me to roll over onto my stomach so I could hide my eyes, but Sarah was already in the room touching my shoulder. "I will tell you how your parents met and anything else you want to know about them." Instantly I rolled over to look at her dazzling, grayish dark eyes, and could see she understood that I needed to know everything that had been hidden from me.

"Your father was older than your mother and had never crossed anyone who took his interest. He had never run across a match before." Sarah looked quite amused with this thought. "We were just as surprised when we realized Analease saw him as a match, too. We had been working with volunteer groups in Michigan during the Great Fire near Port Hope. Your dad and his family were doing the same thing. Analease was sweet, but very bullheaded about being self-sufficient. I think they fell in love with each other at first sight. Actually, I know they did. It was the first time your mother ever accepted help. Jared was strong but gentle. His spirit was one of love and endurance. Your parents began helping to start a backfire, and neither one knew when to stop. They became ill from overwork and heat. Your father wouldn't let anyone touch her but him, not even Shep." Sarah actually grabbed her mouth and giggled. "No one denies Shep anything, especially a Guardian." Sarah's eyes were huge and filled with passion as she tucked one of my bangs back behind my ear.

"When our kind finds their spouse, they become inseparable and protective. This can be very dangerous for any who would cross them. Anyhow, we all worked together and convinced them they could rest with each other and no one would separate them. It was a dark time; relations between Shadow and Guardian were strained and none of us knew what was really going on. There were people who couldn't tolerate mixed relationships, and one of these people was very close to your mother's family…someone they would need to be leery of." Sarah took a deep breath, and for a moment I saw pain cross her expression as her fingers began to play with the zipper on my bag.

"We all feared for them because it looked like there was a conspiracy to ruin relations between our people, but your parents persisted. After a while there was a beautiful ceremony in the backwoods of Michigan near what you would know now as Mackinaw Island. It had been a mix of both cultures and the partying carried on for days. Your parents' gifts to each other were very special. Guardians wear wrist bands often, and your mom had a special one made for him with what she called their emblem. Your father gave your mom a beautiful antique locket with their pictures inside it.

"After a week, the elders issued their blessing for your parents' life together. This was very important for our two realms to see unity. They had waited all that time patiently on the Guardian laws for such bindingsI mean marriages. Your parents spent the next fifty years alongside us, helping wherever we were needed, whether in the Shadow Realm or here. Your mother was like a daughter to us. Did I mention your dad is a couple centuries her senior?

"In any case, our families mixed very well. Your dad's families were even helping with the mysterious murders that were happening, until a threat was issued against him. Needless to say, we hid for a good two years, and then the announcement of their pregnancy came. When you started showing signs of having mixed abilities we became very excited with the possibilities. Your mother enjoyed this. For once she was able to understand the ability of a Guardian. It scared your dad to death. Strong abilities for children of Guardian and Shadow don't show up until around the age of fourteen, but not with special ones like you.

"News reached Terah—that's your grandmother—that you were going to be extra special, and she raced to Analease's side and confirmed what we already knew. When she returned to the Shadow Realm she received a threat against you, and your mother and sent warning. Our hiding became your dad's paramount focus. His protectiveness became as strong as Shep's. Not to mention, your parents appointed Shep as your Protector in every legal sense that existed before you were born.

"When you finally arrived, we all were in high spirits. Shep and your dad couldn't stop smiling. Your dad was still concerned for safety and wanted to keep you both in hiding. It worked for the first couple years, but you know what happened when you were five, and your life took a new course with us. We knew we would have time on our side before your abilities would establish. They were so happy to have you, little one." In silence I sat while listening about my life with my genetic parents. I truly didn't remember much from then—just one bad nightmare. In many ways they never seemed real to me until tonight.

"Well it is time for you to go to sleep, or Shep will have my head." Softly I expressed my thanks to Sarah as she left. Not bothering to change, I rolled over and tried to find a comfy spot. Unfortunately, sleep never found me like I needed. A little while later I could hear only silence, aside from the small crackle of the extinguishing fire. Everybody must have gone to bed. I was probably the only one still awake. Thoughts of today started to make me wonder what could go wrong.

After tossing and turning the whole night I gave up on sleep around five-thirty. By this time I was totally flustered and decided to can it all. I was going to go practice without any onlookers. Quietly sneaking down the hall, I made it through the door without waking anybody. I had to admit it was a bit awkward to see Shep's bare chest holding Sarah in his arms. I didn't take too long to look, for I was sure she didn't even have a gown on.

The sun was rising over the mountain and it looked beautiful. Glancing towards the woods, I scoured the area for anyone who didn't belong. Once I decided there was no movement I began a swift jog. Upon entering the trees, the area was still dark and a cool breeze was blowing. I was sure I would find the quad with no problem.

Hearing the sound of a breaking branch, I jumped. I was being watched, and this time I was determined to find them. Quickly I slipped down against a tree and closed my eyes to listen. It felt like they were circling around to my left, so I scooted to another tree. Suddenly I found myself engulfed in a mist and panic slowly rose through my senses. Out of nowhere a hand clamped over my mouth, and when I looked up, Shep was making a shushing motion. He grabbed my hand and pulled me back to the open area, ordering me to return to the camper. I was shocked as a Shadow appeared next to me. It was Drew, and he didn't look friendly by any means. He motioned for me to take off as he kept pace with me.

Once we were back to the RV he opened the door, shoving me in. It was funny how he just stood there in the open door, staring at me like I was crazy. His hair was in disarray, and for the first time I noticed he was wearing pj's. "What were you doing out there by yourself?" Hastily I began to explain how I couldn't sleep. He fumbled with his hand as he tightened the string to his pants. When he glanced back at me, his eyes held steel. "How do you know you were being watched?" His question only proved to frustrate me more.

How did I do or know anything? By instinct. "I have always been aware when something isn't right. I just know." Without reason I jumped. Drew took hold of my hand and asked why. Slowly I pulled away from him and went to the door. Without an excuse he effortlessly pulled me back. I had the horrible feeling Shep had found someone.

Just then the sky thundered, causing us both to jump. It was odd how the clouds were rolling menacingly over each other as lightning screamed from the sky like rockets. When the sky suddenly stilled, it became very unnerving. Nervously I glanced towards the table. I needed to shake this guy in order to make sure Shep was fine. Drew grinned at me as he shook his head. At that moment I didn't care how I escaped him, so I insisted I needed to go to the restroom. I sure hoped he hadn't been listening in on my thoughts like everyone seemed to do.

Drew nodded, and I went into the restroom to slowly open the window. I jumped to the ground, only to find Drew standing there with his arms crossed. He looked so cocky I wanted to scream out my desperation. "The apple doesn't fall far from the forbidden tree. Your mom used to pull that with me, but I am well-seasoned at preventing such hare-brained schemes. You will have to do better than that." I had to continue to guard my thoughts if I was going to shake this guy. He was good, but I was better.

Like a ton of bricks I suddenly had the strong feeling that Shep was fine and the threat was gone, leaving me relieved and tired. Maybe now I could sleep. It hadn't been ten minutes when Shep threw the door open and looked amused, but ticked at me. He commented that I was very much like my mother, especially when it came to challenges. "Drew, I would be careful with her. I worry about how she has a drive to protect us. She seems to have no regard for her own well-being. I have noticed all her life how she takes care of me and her friends, but very rarely herself. Drew, you are going to have to forge your Protector bond with her quickly. I need you at full strength. You need to be able to sense any impending danger. You are her first defense against our enemy." My eyes grew heavy as sleep overtook me. I felt happy at being able to be compared to my mom.

# CHAPTER 7.
# TRAINING

**When I woke**, I didn't want to disturb anybody after what I had put them through at sunrise. Still, today was the day I would truly start some hard training from the Shadow Realm. At least that was what I was led to believe. Quietly slipping out the door, I went to the quad. I totally expected for Drew or Shep to follow me; thankfully, no one did.

As I entered the quad, I proceeded to touch each of the stone columns. To my amazement I saw a diamond center glow bright green before it dulled. I had never noticed this before. Going back to the center of the training area, I sat down, knowing today I could slow things down with no problem.

Throwing grass and dirt into the air, I concentrated on my breathing and found I was able to slow their descent to the earth. I had succeeded doing what I wanted, but now I wanted to do it gracefully like Billy. I needed larger objects to work with. Quickly I made my way to the edge of the clearing to collect several differently weighted objects from leaves to small limbs. As I was walking back to the square, I threw a couple of the leaves and a few twigs high into the air in front of me. Cautiously I listened to my heart slow down and realized I was walking in front of my falling objects. As I concentrated harder, they floated gracefully to the ground. Once they hit, I drew in a deep breath and picked my items up again and became startled by someone clearing their voice. When I glanced back over my shoulder, I was shocked to find Tom sitting on the ground within the dark confines of a shadow. "Very good. I see you are controlling the slowing of atoms quite nicely."

As he stood up I noticed how tall he truly was—taller than I had remembered from the night before. His sandy burr hair and clear eyes were beautiful. He had kept his distance since he arrived, yet still conversed with me mildly. The whole time he seemed to be studying me, and for some reason I hadn't minded. I figured he was examining me like Laura had. The only difference I felt from him was a deep sadness every time I caught him staring. At times he also looked to be enjoying a secret joke. He shivered a little as he remarked that next time he would prefer to be in the training quad, if I didn't mind. A small smile spread across my lips as he moved.

"So how long have you been here?"

"I was here before you arrived. I wanted to meditate on this beautiful morning. I am surprised no one has taught you to check an area before you enter. You must be vigilant in protecting yourself in case no one is around to do it for you. I understand your abilities are of Guardian and Shadow. I envy you in many ways;

your gifts could be uncountable. Your grandmother believed you will be a new, stronger beginning for our house. Some look at you as a threat while others, including myself, know you are a blessing. What we do as two you will do as one.

"You know, there has always been a natural mistrust of each other. And it has been proven a Shadow ability is what was used to murder your grandmother and Lovie. Guardians seem to be a nonaggressive species while Shadows are very much like Mortals. Many Shadows have problems with Guardians because they can control most portals. There are Shadow portals. Not to mention some of the ancient Shadow portals are not known to any that are not of the sanctuary or of high rank and security. There is a portal outside of our home, but it is a Shadow portal created by our originator. Thank Zeus we have the Martins to aid us. They are the only Guardians who may access any of our Shadow portals due to Analease's provision.

"All that I have mentioned are minor things to me, and I have never encountered any problems. If you ask me, when we work in harmony the benefits are beyond belief. I was thrilled at your parents' bonding, not to mention your unexpected arrival. I believe Jared and Shep were more surprised than any of us, though. You were unexpected but very much wanted by many.

"But for the matter at hand…I have the privilege that Terah would have had to teach you. She asked if I loved her enough to teach her dear little one if she was not able to do so. There was nothing I would deny her. When I look into your eyes, I see her. I don't mean the color, but your spirit. Your eyes have a gentle spirit that will have to toughen up, but I hope you will never lose it. She never did. She could teach, be tough, but yet she always showed mercy, and I know you will do the same."

For a moment he seemed lost in his thoughts, almost like he was listening to a whisper. "Heavens! Life is full of challenges and is not fair at times. I am sure you already know that, but I also see you consider yourself blessed with others. Good for you. Now continue, and when you are ready, I will teach you what I came to teach you." He simply resumed his cross-legged meditation, which made me curious as to what he wanted to teach me. Again I threw the objects up only to watch them slow down, but the wind picked up, interfering with the way I wanted them to float gracefully. This time I concentrated harder on my breathing. Gradually my objects began to float just the way I wanted until a gust whistled by my ears. I needed a barrier like a wall to protect my practice because I wanted to create the effect Billy had made with his. At this thought the wind was still whistling but my objects were swirling like I wanted. When I saw them on the ground, I realized I was not breathing appropriately and had to bend over to catch my breath.

When I straightened back up the wind was gone. That was strange. Then I thought of Tom behind me and wondered if he had created the wind. With great caution I threw the objects into the air again. This time, as I concentrated on my breathing, the wind picked up. Again I resumed my thoughts for sheltering my leaves. My breathing became shallow, but at least I was breathing. Then the wind really picked up. I dropped my concentration and spun around to see if Tom was interrupting my practice. With a wide grin, I knew I had caught him.

The wind started picking up around the square. It seemed that the trees didn't like what was happening. They were creaking loudly as they swayed. "You were successful in stopping me from interrupting your practice, so why don't you stop the wind that I have started?" He sat there reading his book as if he was an aged monk. I couldn't believe he hadn't even looked up long enough to meet my eyes. A quick glance around my surroundings proved the wind was strong outside the quad. I realized that not more than thirty feet away the forest seemed calm and unaffected. The sky didn't even look to be foul. Suddenly a tree sounded like it was going break, drawing my attention to its bowed form. I wasn't sure where to begin. Tom simply shrugged his shoulders as I looked back at the trees. There was nothing I could isolate to stop the wind. That was when I heard his mind touch mine softly: *"You are thinking like a normal person. You are not normal. You are not bound by those rules. There is a part of you that knows what to do, so listen. You know Shadows block light, so what is air? Don't hold yourself to the physical realm or the rules you have lived by all your life."*

In a rush my thoughts began to scan all that I had learned thus far. The day that Shep and I had practiced with wind I remembered I felt it cross my skin. Maybe if I thought the reverse it would end. That wasn't working. Suddenly I realized that someone was coming up towards the square, and to my horror I saw it was Tyler. The tree I had heard was now swaying dangerously like it would break. Just as Tyler started dashing for the square it snapped. The only thing I could do was to slow the area down and start my own wind in the opposite direction. I could feel a cold sweat on my brow and my legs felt weak. Luckily the broken tree did not fall as fast as it should have. The wind stopped as the branch floated to the ground. Only it wasn't a branch—it was the top trunk of a tree.

"That was amazing," Tom commended, but I shook my head at his assessment. My face was coated with sweat as my temperature began to rise. Tyler's concern made it even worse. Tom proceeded to tell me that he would not have allowed Tyler to be hurt. He would have intervened if I had not.

"Glad to hear that," I said through broken breaths while clutching my side to stop the dull ache. "Although next time, don't have so much confidence in me." I continued to stare at him with disbelief. He acted so self-assured and cocky. This made me wonder how old Tom truly was. When Shep entered the clearing, he and Sarah were holding hands like a new couple would. They were awfully cute.

"What happened here?" Shep asked as he assisted Sarah over the tree trunk. Tom replied with a simple word: "test." One thing I realized now was that Tom McIntosh was a definite prankster. Tom and Tyler proceeded to tell the events and how I had combined both types of abilities to avoid Tyler being injured. Shep and Sarah both looked impressed. I couldn't believe they weren't going to chide him.

The rest of the morning, similar tests were being thrown at me until I had to admit I needed a break. I was a sweaty mess. Heather would have screamed at my thought and would have corrected me with "Girls do not sweat, we glisten." Yeah, right. I was missing her terribly.

As I glanced back, Tyler and Shep were sparring outside the square. Tyler had been trying to get Shep to change into his Shadow form, and he seemed to be doing pretty good with following Shep's movements in the shadows. Sarah smiled at me while inquiring if I could discern Shep's movements from the rest of the shadows. Of course I could. His form moved differently from the trees and foliage. "The more you know a person, the easier it is for you pick them out when they are in Shadow form. Tyler can't see that separation yet. I imagine you have always noticed us watching but could not identify us. Now you are aware you should always be able to differentiate between natural shadow and one of our kind."

Acting like I was really interested in Tyler's approach to finding Shep, I tried to avoid the thought from the previous night: every time I think my imagination is taking over, maybe it is someone. I still did not want to share this with everybody.

I left the square and started telling Tyler he was getting warmer, when Tom suggested I try to catch Shep myself. I wasn't completely convinced I knew how to do that. It would be easy if he had physical form, but how could you catch a Shadow?

"You're thinking too physical again." As I stepped towards the direction of Shep, I noticed he seemed to fade from one shadow to the next. I would need to box him in with light to trap him. A Shadow cannot pass through a clear light path. He would have to be in physical form to do so.

The sun was very bright in the powder blue sky, and if the trees were parted a little bit more, there would be no shadow for him to pass to; he wouldn't have anywhere to go. Shep was moving towards the area where the tree had fallen, and that was where I would trap him. Seeing the trees inside my mind, I kept an eye on Shep while walking in the wrong direction. Tyler was scoffing at me as I stuck my tongue out at him in defiance.

When Shep was close to the fallen tree, I imagined the wind blowing hard enough to move the trees apart. This forced Shep to appear in his human form trapped in the daylight. Sarah hollered her pleasure with, "Girls rule!"

Tyler was displeased with my capture. "We will see how she is in the classes we will be attending after lunch." He grinned at me with an evil grin, and that was when I knew he must be an "A" student. Great.

Tom then gestured for the two of us to sit down in the square. Laura and Kirt arrived as if this had been planned. We all sat down together in front of Tom in the moist grass. We could hear total silence. No breeze, no birds. I did not even hear anyone's thoughts. That was strange, but I had also realized there had been no planes in the sky or anything. Shep had said this would be a safe training ground.

Were we in one of the other realms?

Tom's mind came in very clear and gentle. He began going over how important it was to check the area you are in for any dangers before you proceed. *"You are not always in danger of others hurting you, but there could be weather, animals, accidents, or who knows what you could encounter, and this will help you to avoid those situations. Guardians and Shadows both can communicate telepathically, and this ability can be used to listen for problems that could expose us or could alert us to a situation we could render help in. You all realize now that everything is calm, so close your eyes and think of darkness. As you are sensing, you will need to clear your mind of all thoughts. I want you to listen to your own heart-beat...That's right. Now relax every part of your body. Start with your farthest extremity and relax each joint one at a time. Continue each at your own pace. Listen to your heartbeat and relax on each beat. Good. Your heart is beating steadily. Continue. Now listen to the world around you. What do you hear?"*

I felt extremely relaxed and I could hear insects moving, which made me cringe, but I ignored the sounds and continued to listen. Voices were talking about fixing something. They were ribbing each other about it. That was Brent and Drew talking. I could hear their whole conversation. Tom's soothing voice encouraged us to look farther away. Suddenly I was aware of fear, but from what? An animal was being hunted...I could hear a mountain lion hunting—the one that Tyler had summoned earlier. The mountain lion was stalking its prey, and even further from him I could hear cars riding down a gravel road.

My attention became distracted and I was back in the square. Wait a minute—I had never left here. Everything seemed so real. Tom smiled at me as I closed my eyes again in order to explore in a different direction. I don't know how much time had passed, but Shep tapped me on my shoulder, drawing me back to the square, whispering it was time for lunch. When I stood I realized my legs had fallen asleep and the needles were shooting through my feet. Quickly I began to shake the feeling from my legs. I walked with Shep and Sarah and the others back to the site. To my surprise, there were two more campers there. Shep beat me to the table and pulled Sarah down on one side and me on his other. This felt nice, like we were finally complete with Sarah acting as my mother. She smiled at me from across Shep's body and nodded her appreciation at my thought.

Tyler and Laura were sitting across from us when I heard Kirt teasing two new arrivals—Shane and Dillon. They were apparently responsible for bringing us two more campers for us to use. One was to act as a classroom, and the other would be extra sleeping space. Gazing at them, I noticed they had the looks of the Martins, and it was unmistakable they had to be their older brothers. Our table was quite full with twelve of us. The conversation started with all that we had been working on and led to news that seemed to be from all the different realms.

When I was totally full from Betty's excellent lunch, I excused myself to call Heather. By now she was probably ticked I hadn't called earlier. Once across the clearing, I sat down in the shade and leaned against a tree. Nervously I dialed her number and waited to hear her cheery voice. When she answered, I could tell she was at the beach. "Hey girl, how are things going? Are you seeing a lot of boring historical sites?"

"No, we are doing a lot of hiking and stuff this time. How are things there?" I didn't hear her verbal answer. Instead I heard her mind thinking how annoyed she was with Mike.

"We are having a lot of fun. You know how Mike is into doing a ton of outdoor stuff." *He's driving me nuts. I wish you were here. At least we could listen to music or watch TV a little, or talk about guys.* I couldn't help but laugh, which was the wrong thing to do.

"What are you laughing about?"

"Sorry, Heather. I just know you would prefer to not be so active all the time. Maybe..."

She cut me off. "Well, Dad is going to take me to Michigan Adventure and we are going to spend a week doing some shopping and stuff."

Shep sat down beside me. "Selena, you are going to have to get off the phone." We said our goodbyes. I could tell by her thoughts that as soon as she was out of Empire she would be ecstatic and not so lonely. She was an awfully good friend for not trying to make me feel guilty. It really had caught me by surprise to hear Heather's thoughts for the first time, though.

Hearing my thoughts, Shep responded, "Remember, if you know somebody really well, then their mind is really loud. Since you think of Heather as a sister, she will be the hardest to block out. You have to put everybody's thoughts into the background and eventually you will be able to block what you want. While you are here, you will not have problems, for the others are able to control their minds better than Mortals. They have dealt with this a lot longer than you, and that is why you can't hear them. They can already shield their minds." For the first time I really was concerned about this telepathy thing. I had never considered this complication before I left. How would I be able to act normal?

Shep sighed heavily as he patted my hand. "When you were a baby, your telepathy was already taking off. But when we moved away together, I immediately stopped teaching this ability. I kept your mind shielded from Heather and Mike and all those around you. Eventually you forgot it ever existed, and you didn't access it anymore. It won't be as difficult as you think. You are latent in basic skills and advanced in others. We will assist you and you will learn. Speaking of which, it's time for classes, so get going." I knew arguing would be of no avail. I couldn't believe that with everything I had to deal with, I now had classes to attend. What were we going to study anyway...math?

When I arrived, Betty and Sarah were already there with my cousins, patiently waiting on me. Betty began with the lore and history of the Guardian. She acted very pleased and comfortable in this setting. She was a natural frontier woman in many ways. "Our people had been around for centuries. When enough of us had discovered each other, we were approached by a scientific group of Shadows. They were fascinated that maybe the human species had developed better brain functions. Working together, we found that we were using more of our brain than a normal Mortal. Indeed, we all know that our two species use more brainpower than the Mortal species.

"Our people ran across an older Indian man who claimed to have been aware of our kind for a long time. He spoke of legends of Tracespers, Shadow, Seheirenel, and of course Guardian. He was amazed this group of Guardians was still roaming among his kind without leadership from an elder. This group was the largest group of newborns he had seen in ages. He spoke of Tracespers who protected both realms. He claimed this group would send newborns to a great gate of ages so they would find more of their kind to teach them.

"This aged gentlemen seemed to know more than the Shadow how we were connected to the earth, and that our people had been waiting for a rebirth. This was how the friendship between our people began, though as with all species, there was a natural distrust. But our true origins were way before this man's knowledge. Our realm was actually started by three main families—our family being the leader in the beginning. But it was hard for us to maintain our secrecy, and this is part of our beginnings with the Shadow Realm."

Sarah interjected as she walked gracefully forward to join Betty at the front. "Some were frightened that this group of people could go undetected. A rumor was started that the Guardians did not welcome us Shadows as friends. My people felt the Guardians had way too much control. They considered it a danger. You see, Guardians can hold any portal closed that they have made, and Shadows can't even access their realm, just as the Shadow Realm is only controlled by Shadow. Both Shadow and Guardian have influence in the Mortal Realm, for it is the common passage between the two realms. You see the problem this could cause."

Betty moved with amusement as she looked at me. "Our plain had been established by our forefathers as a place of safety from Mortals, among others. Many of us had been charged with dealing with evil and our talents had to be hidden. We can only go by word of mouth handed down from each generation, and by memories that have been shared through the ages. Each family has their own historian, and each historian is sure to deliver our history to each new member. Some say we are descended from the Shadow Realm beginnings. Zeus, being our father, took many Mortal women as his own. There were many children born from Zeus and other Shadows. These half-Shadow, half-Mortal children went on to develop into the Guardian species. Many of us stay in the Mortal Realm so we can help our friends. You remember the turbulent history through the ages: Greek and Roman gods were prevalent, but no Mortal can prove their existence. What if these gods were actually Shadow, or even Guardian? Our elders took it upon themselves to protect the Mortal from domination of that possible threat."

Sarah smiled as she sat upon the desk. "Some of my people are not a good influence on humans. The Greeks were wonderful forerunners, but back then we did have depraved ones who went along with Hitler, sorry to say. We tried to purge ourselves of this but have never totally succeeded in this effort. Good always exists with its counterpart of bad. Many cultures have references to that in their history and lore."

I felt totally spellbound by this twist of influence on the human culture. Maybe we were the first to be taught history with both species teaching at the same time. Betty grinned as she moved around the room. "We know that all of us are human but no Guardian has ever influenced war. Our counterparts from the Shadow Realm are the Mortal muses. We help maintain a healthy balance so that no one thing could cause total annihilation of our planet. Our intelligence is helpful too.

"We exist here easily now without drawing much attention, and that allows us to be vigilant with monitoring the portals since one of our own was murdered by a rogue group of Shadow, which brings us to where we are now. You all know what happened so long ago. Your grandfather was one of the three that were there that night and watched Jonathan die, and to our horror and disappointment, Matron Lovie too. She was a bridge between our two people. Many were misled into believing a Guardian had a hand in her death, but I know this is not true. This rogue group messed up when they killed Terah. It was their own world that was able to recognize the bacterium that was infecting them. Nevertheless, not knowing who is a part of the infection is hard to deal with. Many from both sides resumed their friendships, but for others the trust must be rebuilt. A way to help bring this into fruition is by bringing Alexander to justice. We have lost and sacrificed much to bring back our unity."

Sarah and Betty both seemed to be studying me as they continued. It was hard to avoid their gazes because I knew what they were thinking; I didn't even have to hear their thoughts to know.

We spent the next several hours continuing our journey into the past. Sarah and Betty released us, but only after we had studied a lot of science, anatomy, chemistry, and math of all types. It looked like there would be no end in sight. Guardians and Shadow had to be of above average intelligence. This thought frightened me.

In hope of finding some peace and quiet, I headed towards the woods. Luckily I found a place that looked to be far enough away to study my notes. What was funny to me was that I really didn't seem to have as hard of a time as I usually did in school. My reading had always been a challenge to me, mainly because I found it to be boring. But today it seemed I couldn't get enough stashed in my head. When I leaned back against the tree, I noticed Brent coming towards me.

He seemed to be full of joy. As he took a seat beside me, he wanted to know how everything went. Reluctantly I admitted that I felt overwhelmed. He could see I was leery of what my next challenge would be with him. Immediately he laughed. "One might say I am here to see what type of artistic skills you have. Some things you might think are purely for enjoyment can be used as a weapon." He was dead serious. Well, at least this would be something I could do.

I proceeded to explain to him that I play piano and love music. My artistic ability wasn't awesome, but I could look at things and be able to do a decent job. His smile broadened as he proceeded to tell me he didn't expect any less than what I had already informed him of. He felt I was going to make his job a breeze. His only problem was how to hear me play the piano. To my surprise he asked me to think about anything I had done in the past weeks with music. Slowly I remembered my last practice. It felt too real, almost like it was happening all over again. I didn't like this feeling at all and it ended abruptly.

Brent let out a little wail and grabbed his head. He looked at me with surprise. "I see you are very defensive of your memories." Brent continued to rub his head as if someone had hit him. When I questioned why, he explained that he was watching what I already knew by sharing my memory with me, and evidently I had kicked him out with a slight shock. "I thought you didn't know any defensive art forms," he teased.

He continued to inform me of how sound could be used defensively. As Brent began to walk away, he looked mischievously at me while commenting on how the area was abnormally quiet. There was no noise of any kind, including the sounds of the trees. Lazily I leaned back and closed my eyes, straining to hear something, anything…but there was nothing. Then I began to think how it should sound with so many pines and deciduous trees around. The wind started picking up and I could hear the pines barely making a noise. I concentrated a little harder, and as the wind grew faster, the pines began talking like they did at home. Abruptly I felt someone's hand touch mine and found Brent kneeling in front of me. "Now see, I knew you would make the music that you liked in your own way. I can tell you understand sounds and know what can soothe and what can scare a person. I love the sounds you created with the wind. Just continue doing things to help with moods. Such a gift is counted a prize."

We closed our eyes and I heard the happy sounds of the forest—his "theme" as he called it. Then the wind took on an eerie sound, and he told me if I ever heard this sound then I would know there was danger and to be careful. He taught me how sounds could cause pain and discussed Cronos' theory on how noise could be used as weapon. The entire time he was teaching me he continued to look around nervously. I could tell that this was something he wasn't comfortable with doing, but it was valuable. We played around with sounds for quite a bit until he admitted I had worn him out. Still, I didn't see the need to know how to use this ability. I didn't want to hurt anyone. Brent smiled broadly.

"I can see this is a natural ability you have always had. We will have to create more music later. Our next lesson will be why we might need to use sound as a weapon. My people feel that those who have this type of control of sound barriers are far more dangerous than we ever should be. At one point in our history, a major battle was won by those who are able to feel the effects that sounds have on one's body. You probably have always been aware of vibrations within your body and soul, and those feelings can be as sharp as any lightning."

As Brent left, I couldn't help but think this was the easiest test. Some of what he taught me was fascinating and deserved more study when I went to the Shadow Realm. He explained there was a library there that was bigger than the Empire State building.

Without thought I left all my paperwork behind to explore. I sensed into the woods and could feel Tyler and Kirt practicing sparring with Drew and Shep in their Shadow form. I didn't want to be bothered by everyone, so I headed towards the river to relax. Once at the riverside, I kept looking at the water, trying to figure out how I had diverted the cascade from the torrential downpour the other day. Cautiously I slowed things down. As I watched the water lap slower, I concentrated on its fluid movement. Then I tried to push the lap before it hit and it worked. Beginning to breathe normally again, I felt someone coming towards me at an alarming rate of speed. No one should be able to move that fast.

Instantly I turned around to face whoever it was. Immediately I slowed things down. I could feel I stopped their progress. When I released the slowdown, I could feel others coming from a different direction. I hoped I could keep this up if I had to. I bent over and grabbed my legs as I tried to control my breathing.

The two who had been charging for me slowed but were joined by someone who my ability didn't seem to affect. Quickly I moved to a different area. I kept a steady pace while creating a high wind at the same time. I stopped suddenly when I saw the shape of a man in the shadows. I slowed things down again and went straight to him, but I had to release it to catch my breath. *Hold the slowdown longer*, I thought to myself. When I looked back up, he was gone, and a heavy mist was in his place. I heard Billy hollering for me and I started to head towards his voice. It was then that I spotted the stranger again off to the side. He saw me and another heavy mist formed. Out of pure desperation I slowed the mist, only to find I was exhausted, and it released.

Seconds later I fell to my knees as the mist rolled towards me. Slowly I felt my body force itself to lay back, only to feel the heat rise from my feet to my shoulders until I could no longer hear anything but a loud buzzing. As I called out to Shep I could feel his terror as my vision swirled when the heat crossed my eyes. And then I lost consciousness.

***

Gradually I became aware of the dampness and cool mist surrounding me. There was a whispering, almost like I could feel someone's hand caress my face, but nothing was clear. I couldn't even understand the whisper. When I tried to lift my head once again, it felt too heavy to move. I couldn't remain awake either. Suddenly a feeling of peace came over me, and I allowed the sickening darkness to take me.

Billy continued hollering my name as he pulled me into his arms. My eyes fluttered and I looked around to find there was no mist and no stranger around. Shep came running from the edging of the woods and fell down beside me with a wild look in his eyes that made me feel guilty. My eyelids were still heavy, and I didn't feel like I could keep them open. He rubbed my cheek, calling my name softly, demanding to know what had happened. I felt so far away. My eyelashes felt like lead as I tried to force them open. Billy kept demanding for me to respond, but I couldn't. "*I can hear you. Where is the stranger*?" Finally I managed to hold my eyes open long enough to catch all their concerned gazes. Their expressions made it clear that there had been no stranger near when they found me. Immediately my mind rushed back to the memory of the man's figure. I could see they saw my thoughts too.

When I woke next, I was in bed, with Betty and Sarah watching me very carefully. Sarah rushed over and asked how I felt. "*I'm fine but tired. Where's Shep?*" They both looked at me and were smiling. What was it with all this smiling stuff?

"*Selena, you are using telepathy and you prevented the others from helping you when you used your abilities. The only one who could make it to your side was Billy.*" I tried to pull myself off the bed, but they weren't going to allow me.

I heard the heavy thud of Shep's rushing feet as he entered the RV. He quickly forced me to lie back down, but he still had not lost that wild look in his eyes. Billy moved swiftly into the room to sit at my other side. He seemed to be studying my face, knowing that I was concerned about the intruder. "I saw the mist too. It was definitely a Shadow form," Billy kept saying to Shep. Neither man would look to the others' eyes, almost like this was an argument.

Shep looked flustered, growling that he had found no one. Shep rarely sounded so stressed. Billy's temper began rising, and I could feel tension flying through the roof. Billy began yelling that something wasn't right, and he knew the difference between a Shadow form and a Guardian. My head began to pound like it was going to burst if they didn't stop arguing. Sarah and Betty pushed the two men out, telling them they had to take it outside until I felt better.

The women remained outside trying to quiet the two men, but nothing was working. I had to stop the arguing. Even if I couldn't hear it, I could still feel it. The hall of the RV felt like it was leaning, but I knew it had to be me; I hadn't yet regained my balance. Once I stepped outside the door I clung to it, trying to make my body stabilize. My cousins were sparring and the adults were all sitting at the picnic table. By their looks, they were in a heated debate. Everything stopped when Tyler ran to my side.

"Are you feeling better, Selena?" I could barely nod my head to say "yes" because of the dizziness. Slowly I headed to the table with his help. The fresh air was helping me with the vertigo, but the weakness was unbelievable. Shep rushed to my side and scooped me up into his arms as he finished bringing me back to the table.

The discussion began again, but this time their tones only showed the strain they were under from the possibility of having an intruder. I listened intently to them and filled in the empty spots that I hadn't been privy to. The conversation finally changed as they started going over what abilities I had discovered in the past twenty-four hours. Brent was nervous as he asked Shep if he had been working on any defensive abilities with me that were similar to his. Shep and Sarah looked at him inquisitively. "When I was working with Selena earlier," he explained, "I began sharing her memories without permission. It was accidental, but I received a shock. In fact, it was quite an impressive one. She felt me invading her space and didn't like it. I could tell."

Shep became very nervous and started stuttering. "Selena, go to bed. You have a lot to practice tomorrow." For once Shep looked nervous.

We spent the next two weeks learning math, history, combat, wind, and slowing, but no one was able to teach me anything about water. To my dismay Brent, had to leave and return to the Shadow Realm. I knew I was going to miss him. He had become a great companion. The stranger I had seen never showed again. Even Billy had seen a mist form.

Tyler came to the RV, telling me it was my turn to spar with Kirt. Unfortunately Kirt was too cocky for my mood, and today I wanted to knock his confidence. He hadn't been leaving me alone with his teasing, and I was fed up. As soon as I walked out, Kirt began again. "Well, are you ready to fall on your butt some more?" I began to growl softly. I wasn't in the mood. He just winked at his dad as he came near.

Before I knew what was happening, he came at me and I blocked. Instead of following the rules, I fell to the ground, sweeping his legs, and jumped back up and slowed things down. Billy started laughing and said it was about time. I felt amazed as I looked to my uncle. Here I thought that would have been considered cheating. I thought for sure it wasn't fair to use our abilities. Billy shook his head no and then looked to Kirt. "You'd better ask him if what he is doing is fair then."

When Kirt stood up he was smirking. "You surprise me with how long it took you to cheat."

I watched as the boys tried to drag Shep and Drew to the quad for practice. This was my chance to go for a jog. Thankfully everybody was busy when I left, so they didn't notice when I disappeared into the woods.

After a while I came to a stop, only to realize I had been jogging for a good hour. Hopefully I hadn't upset anyone. Surely they wouldn't even notice since dinner was at least a good two hours away. Before I turned around I felt cool air blowing across me. It made me wonder where the source could be originating from. My curiosity got the best of me and I began to search the area. Finally I discovered a cave at the base of the hill. It wasn't huge, but it had to be deep, for it felt like air conditioning. Not daring to go all the way in, I sat down at the entrance to enjoy the coolness. Today had been very humid and the cool air helped to soothe me. Gradually I began to think about my experiences here. They all had been good. In some ways too good; I had become very close to all my family and friends.

These thoughts about leaving them weren't settling well with me. I would miss their banter, and I would miss Billy, for I felt he had to be a little like Jared would have been if he had lived. All of this made me wonder more about my parents, and today it hurt. It was easier when I didn't wonder what it would have been like to have them around. Everybody continued to spout off stories about Billy and my dad and how they had been inseparable as kids, along with another sibling called Barry. It was also interesting to hear other stories about Drew and my dad. It sounded like they had a love-hate relationship going on with the physical pranks they continued to play on each other.

Being startled by noises above me, I began sensing the area only to find two teenage boys climbing. One dropped down in front of me and hollered to the other that they had seen a girl. Politely I smiled at him as we both said hi. Shyly they introduced themselves. "We haven't seen you around here before." At the time, admitting I was visiting family didn't seem like a bad thing for it was true. Besides, this area was supposed to be void of interference from outsiders, but evidently I was wrong. They both joined me in the cave asking a ton of questions. It was difficult to avoid answering them, especially since I didn't have the details that a normal traveler would have. There were a lot of things that I couldn't share either.

"I'm not alone. I just decided to rest here." Both of their minds were screaming at me. Carefully pushing myself back up, I knew I couldn't head back to the campsite without drawing suspicion. My only hope was not to be followed once I left the cave. Unfortunately, it became evident that they intended on guiding me back to the road. Quickly I surveyed my surrounding to discover where the boys had climbed down. It looked like I needed to pretend to be heading back the way they had come. This way I wouldn't lead them to our camp. Later when I was out of sight, I would circle back around and return home. To my surprise, the embankment was quite steep and looked unstable, but that was the way the boys had come and I would have to act like I knew what I was doing.

The clouds were darkening overhead which concerned us all. One of the boys suggested we stay put until it passed. There was no way I could deal with the building pressure of their screams. "You don't have to be concerned with me. I can take care of myself." Regrettably they didn't see it that way. They felt obligated to play the knight in shining armor to make sure I made it back to town safely. Great. All I needed was to travel further away from where I needed to go. The pressure, however, took on a new feature—a stabbing pain that made me groan from the shock. Instantly the boys thought I was not feeling well and proceeded to touch my hand to offer support. Unfortunately, this was the worst possible thing they could have done, for the pain shot right through me even harder as he squeezed my hand. Their thoughts were escalating with their emotions, and it wasn't going to be long before I would not be able to function. Instinctively I stumbled back. The poor guy quickly apologized for scaring me.

I blew it off and started to climb up the steep embankment, only to find them following. I couldn't believe they weren't leaving. The storm cracked above and began to look menacing. There was a sudden downpour and the clouds rolled in menacingly. Great. This was just my luck. I prayed for a reprieve but knew that wouldn't happen anytime soon, so I focused on the climb.

The boy named Anthony continued to fret over the storm, but I wasn't having it. He could stay if he wanted. I couldn't. When I glanced back, I saw him begin to slip due to the sudden downpour. His fingers began digging into the muddy earth fruitlessly. By instinct I reached down and grabbed his hand while slowing the area around us. This helped me to ensure a good hold on my hand as the water rushed over us. The other boy immediately jumped out of the way to land safely below us. Still Anthony was dangling, unable to pull his feet back onto solid earth. To my dismay, I began to slip but heard myself yelling for him to hang on and to try not to swing so much. If I could stop Tom's wind, then maybe I could stop this storm, especially if it was natural. Anthony hollered for his friend to help, but I could see the boy was unable to maneuver the pouring mudslide. Eventually he hollered that he would try a different path and left my field of vision as he darted through the trees. This alarmed me even more. What if I couldn't hang on? I began concentrating on stopping the feel of the storm as I forced my mind and body to calm. This was key.

Anthony continued to dangle around, causing me trouble with keeping a hold on him. Again I slowed things down and concentrated harder on the storm. I prayed that I was strong enough to continue. The rain suddenly stopped, but when I looked up, I could see that the clouds were still rolling. At that moment I braced myself carefully as I reached down with my other hand. Anthony grabbed it, which helped to steady his body. We both were relieved when he was able to pull his leg onto the embankment and started to make progress to safety. Suddenly, I felt hands grabbing my shoulders as someone else grabbed Anthony's arms. When I looked back I found Shep and Drew glaring at me. Without a word they quickly pulled Anthony up. The other boy had found another route up and was thanking us for the assist. The whole time I felt pressure building and began to feel weaker. As I watched the boys walk away, I knelt down from the weakness I was feeling.

I looked at the sky to see the clouds, but there was no storm, no noise. Shep quickly sat down and demanded for me to stop guarding my mind from him. I didn't understand what he meant. I wasn't guarding except from the boys.

My energy was draining faster and Shep was becoming panicked. He grabbed my face in his hands and asked what I was doing. "I think I stopped the storm. I had to, so Anthony wouldn't fall." I was struggling with even forming my thoughts, let alone words. Drew and Shep looked up and I heard them both gasp.

"Selena, release the storm. Everybody is safe. Release the storm." When I admitted I didn't know how, I felt Shep enter my thoughts. He was helping me release the storm. My eyes closed from the heaviness as a feeling of peace encapsulated me. I felt safe again. I had Shep with me and he would take care of me. Suddenly there was a clap of thunder and I felt a downpour of rain. When I opened my eyes, Shep was brushing the rain from my face, trying to look closer at me. It was like he was looking into my soul.

*"Sarah, I could use your help. Are you near?"* Sarah appeared a few minutes later, and somehow I found myself in the mouth of the cave again. Sarah was sitting by me, but I had no idea how we had gotten here. I heard Shep telling her that I had stopped the storm to save a boy and how I had no regard for myself. He was angry but proud I was willing to help.

"What am I going to do with her? These abilities are coming faster than she can control. We need to work on the basics first before working on the harder ones. She is not ready for it." Sarah couldn't believe it either. When she spied my eyes open, she asked how I felt. I admitted I felt tired and confused. Shep smiled but continued to rub my head.

"Selena, how did you stop the storm?"

"I didn't feel it anymore. I just pushed it back, sort of. I thought my slowdown might help me gain control of our bodies. *"Sarah, I have a headache and I need to rest for a moment. Could we please talk about this later?"*

*"It's alright, Selena. We want you to rest."*

# CHAPTER 8.
# GUARDIAN COUNCIL

**When I woke** I could hear a storm raging outside and found I was safely in bed again. This time Tyler was sitting with me, looking quite shaken. When he discovered I was awake, he wanted to know if I needed anything. As I shook my head I found I had a tremendous headache and every little movement hurt. *"You gave everyone a scare. I could have come with you. In fact, next time I will go with you. Don't ever go off without me again."*

A second later I could hear Tyler informing everyone I was awake. Shep and Sarah both faded into view as Tyler moved out into the hall. Sarah inquired if I felt better. Trying to convince them I was fine didn't work. Shep bent down and kissed my forehead. "Selena, you are not to scare me like that anymore."

*"I didn't mean to scare you. I went for a jog and stumbled across the boys, and then the storm happened suddenly. I was trying to come back but they wouldn't let me. Anthony was following me and it would have been my fault if he was hurt. I knew I could stop the storm since I could stop Tom from interfering with my practice."* Shep smiled, still rubbing my cheek.

"Selena, you cannot put yourself in danger. This is very dangerous. For now I don't want you to stop any weather phenomenon." Hearing his voice aloud made my head hurt worse.

*"I think we need to use telepathy, Shep. Your voice is hurting her."* Tyler came back into the room and handed Sarah a bottle of water and some Tylenol for me. After I took the pills, Shep leaned back over and kissed my head. I could feel he was nervous, but I didn't understand why.

The next day, I woke up and felt fine. Quietly dressing, I opened my door to find Shep waiting on me. He had breakfast already on the table while Sarah had remained in bed. *"What do you think you are doing, Selena?"*

*"I thought I would get an early start and do some practicing."* He motioned for me to sit as he pushed my plate towards me.

*"I am glad you helped him, but you didn't call for me when the real danger occurred. In fact, you began guarding your mind from me and you can't' do that. If I have to I will know what I need to know whether you want me to or not. When you thought you were Mortal, I knew you were very good at hiding your emotions most of the time. But with your abilities, you can no longer do that. As your father I can always force you to let me hear your thoughts, but I respect you enough to know you will try hard not to hide them. Okay?"*

As I nodded I tried to explain to him that I didn't realize I was doing it. He relaxed as he watched me eat. *"You will get used to guarding your mind. I imagine the two boys probably triggered the defense. Mortals scream when they are excited, and it would be natural for you to have to guard your mind. Try not to do it with me."*

He cleared the table and opened the door for me to go outside. To my surprise I found Tom meditating on the ground. When I stepped out, he wanted to know how I felt. Hastily I assured him I was fine. I continued to feel guilty about not sensing around me while I jogged. That was the first thing he had insisted on during my training, and he had been correct. When I tried to apologize for neglecting this task, he didn't try to make it any easier on me. "I will try to remember to sense from now on."

"Today you will spend your time with me and Tyler." Drew was smirking behind his coffee cup and I could only imagine what he was thinking. Tom stood up and started walking towards the woods. Shep gave me a shove and nodded for me to follow. Instantly I frowned back at Shep. I figured this was going to be a challenging day and not one I was anxious about starting. You would think they might take it easy on me since I hadn't been well. As I passed the table I chanced a glare over at Drew. He merely grinned as he nodded in the direction that Tom was taking us.

"By the way Selena, people who are close to me call me Tommy, and I wouldn't mind if you called me that." He had stopped and was waiting patiently on me. He had the look of innocence, but was far from it, I was sure. "Why do you consider me a challenge?"

I almost snorted when he ask me this question. "Because as my best friend Heather says, the quiet ones are the ones you always have to keep your eyes on. You never know what they will do."

He nodded. "Why do you try to hide your emotions so much?" Suddenly I felt uncomfortable with his question and began to guard my mind. Tommy smiled and looked at me complacently. "You have now started guarding your mind and I might add, you are very good at that, but you need not be today. Try giving me an honest answer."

As we resumed our walk I picked up our pace but Tommy, being extremely tall, matched it with no problem. He continued to wait on my answer. Today felt really hot and muggy, so I created a breeze and stopped at the edge of the woods to consider his question. Suddenly the breeze stopped, but not on my whim. *"Little one, I stopped your breeze because you are not cooperating with Tommy. Cooperate and I will allow you to use your abilities."*

With a nervous look back to the campground, I knew Drew was getting a kick out of what Shep was doing. I could see today was going to be a very irritating day. Why would Shep think I would talk about anything personal with Tommy? Tommy was standing next to me now, but I didn't have to have a breeze to help me. "Listen, I know you think it is important for me to answer your question, but I don't know you and I don't share easily. Now, if this is a lesson on how to control my abilities, then let's work on that. But my personal life is off limits."

Tommy turned, walking into the forest before shadowing on ahead. I watched him carefully without trying to follow. I would arrive when I arrived. When I found the quad, I was shocked to see Tyler waiting on us. "Tyler, what is Selena's biggest problem?"

Tyler smirked at me. "She doesn't want to rely on anybody except Shep, Heather, and Mike." There was a rumble above us, forcing us all to look to the sky. Tommy became nervous and immediately had us start sensing exercises instead of pressing the issue. As I sat still, I had a hard time calming down enough to sense. Shep entered the quad in a rush to join us. It was almost as if he was frightened. As I sensed around I could feel Tommy was uncomfortable. Finally I gave up and opened my eyes.

"I am aware you are uncomfortable," I commented snidely.

"I am uncomfortable because of a different reason than you."

Cautiously Shep interjected and wanted to know why I wouldn't answer the question.

"Listen, it has always just been us and nobody else. We take care of each other and that is all I need." Pointedly Shep asked a question. "What if I am not around to take care of you?"

My face was growing with heat as I answered, for this was not something I was expecting. "Selena, I am not going anywhere, but if for some reason I die, I would want to know you were all right." Thunder clapped above our heads again, and Shep closed his eyes. Tommy fidgeted nervously and stood to pace in front of us. The minute Shep opened his eyes, I knew I would have to find an answer to put him at ease.

This time he shook his head. "I don't want you to find an answer to put me at ease, Selena." Again I felt flustered since nobody was giving me my privacy. A second later I found myself standing. I needed a walk, now! Tyler grabbed my hand and informed the others that we were going for a jog. Tommy looked up into the sky and said it looked like that would be all right, but to stay close to the campers this time. In a rush I gave Shep a kiss on the top of his head as I began to leave, almost at a dead run. I didn't want to think about his questioning, let alone give an answer. Besides, nothing I could say would be any good.

Tyler stayed with me as we jogged towards the mountain range. We weren't talking, but I really needed a challenge to help put my mind at ease. Tyler grabbed my arm, demanding to rest. This was frustrating. We had only been running for a little bit of time when I encouraged him to remain behind. He jerked to grab my arm and wouldn't let go. "Selena, why is it so hard for you to answer that question? I am not trying to push, but today's lesson is to help you control your yelling at me. I would appreciate some quiet." I hadn't realized how much pain I had been causing him. Probably like those boys from the day before.

Suddenly today's lesson became very clear. "That is why you are being included in the training." He nodded in agreement. Slowly my mind scrambled through a fact list as the simple truth became clear.

"I have always taken care of myself and others, like Heather, and I really wouldn't want to have to worry about taking care of many more because it hurts too much when I can't help or if they leave. It makes me feel helpless and I can't stand drama. I don't like disappointing people either."

Tyler stood up and reached down to help me. Instead of jogging, we continued to talk. He wanted to know why I had chosen him as the special family member with whom to share my thoughts with. I didn't have an answer for that. I hadn't intentionally picked him; it was just instinct that chose him. My laughter escaped me. I figured it was because he was a lot like me. He smiled and asked if it was that obvious. I did see him as more of a brother, just like I felt about Mike. Ever since we had met, he was the one I depended on, and it didn't hurt when he was honest with me.

"The closest thing I have ever had to family is Heather and Mike. They are my best friends and we take care of each other. Now Mike, he has always been our protector and he shares what it is like to have two parents who are really in love with each other. His family is what I imagine your family is like. You all love each other and do things together all the time. Your mom and dad are always being affectionate even though it's embarrassing. I am glad to have family and I love all of you, but its suffocating and really pushing me to share my feelings will only make things worse. I can share with Shep, Heather, and you but no one else has to know my private business. Can you understand that?"

He grabbed my hand. "Since you have been talking you have stopped screaming. Trust me, I appreciate the quiet."

Roughly I shoved him away from me as I informed him what a pain he was. He scoffed, adding that was what brothers were for. A few seconds later he began jogging and I followed through the rocky terrain. This area was beaming with heat. We had reached the base of the mountain. The sun was shining bright now, and I felt at peace for once. We decided to rest and lay back on the rocks to try to catch our breath.

Tyler jumped suddenly as I saw two forms fade into the crevice of a rock formation. It was Shep and Tommy. The sight of them just irritated me for the moment. I wasn't exactly ready to face them, even if their intentions were good. Tommy held up his hands, announcing the lesson was ended. Lying back against the rock, Shep came and sat down beside me.

"Guess you were listening?" I accused sarcastically to both of them.

"Yes, we were. But we agreed that if you feel comfortable with Tyler and I, then as long as you talk to us, everything is fine. You know you can't talk to Heather about your abilities and stuff. We can't guard her mind yet." I had already figured Heather wouldn't be allowed in on this secret. Still, she knew me too well and would figure it out eventually.

Tyler came over with something in his hand. He knew I was concerned about the souvenir I needed to buy for her. How was I going to explain I hadn't been shopping?

"Selena, here. Kirt and I make these. We give all the women of our family one, and this one is for you and the other is for your sister Heather." He held up a prism necklace, causing rainbows to bounce all over the place. The neck strap was an intricate braid and looked absolutely beautiful. Very carefully Tyler slipped it over my head and dropped Heather's into my hand.

Shep smiled. "I think she will really like this a lot, Tyler." I could tell he was impressed with the detailed design of the necklaces. One thing they needed to understand about my dad was that he didn't hand out compliments easily. I jumped up to give Tyler a hug and heard him mutter that was why I had a big brother.

A moment later Shep informed us that Betty was holding lunch for us and wanted to know if we wanted to shadow with them. "No thanks. I have had enough new stuff happen to me lately and I prefer the jog."

At quick pace we began the jog back and arrived thirty minutes later. Upon spying Kirt sparring with Shane, I made a beeline for him. I heard Tyler cackling that he better watch out, but Kirt didn't know what he was talking about until it was too late. Immediately I threw my arms around his neck and gave him a big hug. Everybody was laughing, especially when I discovered how embarrassed he looked. Kirt continued to pat my back, asking what he had done to deserve such a wonderful hug. Quickly I produced the necklace. Shane slapped him on the back and teased that he needed to find someone special to give one of those to, too. It was funny how lighthearted they all were. A second later I slowed things down out of meanness. Billy hooted as I came to sit at the table. Once I released the slowdown, Billy told them they deserved it as he took his seat. Tyler disagreed fervently, requesting next time to leave him out of my punishment for Kirt and the others. Laughter roared from all who surrounded us.

We filled our plates and ate. I tried to enjoy the conversation, but couldn't because Drew kept staring at me. When he had finished eating he continued to stare, almost like he was puzzled by something. His actions, however, were making me more uncomfortable by the minute.

Finally when lunch was over, Tyler had grown annoyed by my mind and glared at Drew. "Why are you staring? You are making her upset." Everybody was surprised by Tyler's curt voice, but Drew straightened up in his chair as if being jarred from his thoughts.

"Sorry, I didn't realize I was staring. I see some of Analease and Jared in Selena, but not enough. I want to know why we were left out of helping until now, and why she doesn't have a stronger resemblance to her genetic parents. Nevertheless, being with her this past month, I have no doubt she is one of us."

All eyes fell on Shep and I could tell he wasn't surprised by Drew's question. In fact, I had wonder about this question myself. Why now were others being called into help?

"You're right it is a good question. There is a lot I can't explain yet, although I will soon. What I can tell you is that Jared and Analease made sure in their will for me to be able to take care of Selena properly. I don't know if you realize, but I adopted Selena at five years and seven months in the Mortal Realm. She is legally my daughter. Moreover, she is mine completely. Nothing can ever change that she is Sarah's and my daughter."

I could tell nobody knew this piece of information. Billy then asked the obvious, but I interjected. "My name is Selena Marie Goodwin. I mean, on legal papers it shows my name as Selena Marie Martin-Goodwin." I could feel everybody's surprise at this piece of information. Shep stiffened in his seat and was saddened at Billy's shock.

"Jared insisted that if anything happened, he wanted me to be Selena's father in every sense of the word. I don't know why it was important to him, but he was adamant on this point, as was Analease. Now I am very happy for it to be this way. Still, I understand this is a shock to all of you. There was no harm in what we have done, and Selena only knows her name as Goodwin. This made it easier to hide her. If any of our kind ran across her, then her mind would only register Goodwin.

"We did run across our kind, too, but on those occasions I would keep her home with me to assure myself of her safety. It was more for my own comfort than anything else. What you have to understand is that Selena is right. We are a family and I am the only family she has known, so all of this is hard on both of us. I have protected our identities up until now, but with her abilities smashing down on us I need extra help. We knew this day would come, and I knew I would have to share our life with others. It is hard.

"I will do anything to ensure her safety. Jared and Analease covered every possible avenue and tied our hands tightly. What I have done we all agreed on after the first incident took place when Selena was two. Sarah has known all these years, but we weren't even able to stay in contact until five years ago."

Drew and Tommy both looked at Sarah. "You have known since the day of the crash that Shep and Selena were alive?" asked Billy. "You and dad knew? I can't believe you two. How...I thought this was a recent revelation." Billy moved in disbelief from the table. His frustration and hurt was obvious.

Sarah nodded and took over their explanation of the past. "As Shep said Jared and Analease tied our hands. Our priority was to keep Selena safe and it meant I couldn't be with them. The first two years were the hardest for me. I knew every day I was protecting not only my charge, but also my daughter. She is worth the world to us. I assure you no harm will come to her, not with us around. She is not just a charge—she is my child. I have helped keep an eye on her here in the Mortal Realm these past five years. Drew, you wear proof she belongs to us."

Somehow I knew she was telling the truth. I had never felt like a stranger with Sarah. In fact, I looked at her as my mom, and this surprised me the first time I saw her. Sarah looked at me and smiled. Shep reached over and was holding both of our hands.

"There isn't any more we can tell you right now. I need you to trust Jared and Analease. Their plan is very detailed and you know I am bound to what they have declared." Billy nodded his head, but Betty didn't like not knowing more.

As she began a fuss, Shep tugged us from the table. Swiftly he began walking us towards the forest, and I could tell he wanted to give them all time to talk about what he had said. He grabbed us both around the waist and we hugged him back. When we finally reached the woods, Sarah embraced him like a wife would when giving comfort. Upon catching sight of me, she motioned for us to have our first family hug. I had to laugh a little, for Heather would gag at this type of display, but to me it made me happy. Shep admitted I was right: she *would.* We all laughed.

We took a hike and I found it fun to have another female to antagonize Shep with. Softly I told Sarah she was going to have problems when we went home because a lot of women were interested in Shep, even if he did have a daughter. What was fun was watching how they used their Shadow abilities to tease each other. I could see why Sarah was Shep's.

Finally they both asked if I wanted to shadow, but my answer hadn't changed. I was a little leery of it, and besides I didn't know how. Shep then inquired if I was sure I didn't know, especially since he hoped I would be able to. He felt it would be a good way for me to escape if the need ever arose. "I prefer to run."

Shep looked back towards the campsite, and I could feel he was concerned. "Don't worry, they would have found out sooner or later. I mean, I have always looked at you as my dad. My name doesn't mean anything. I am thankful for what my parents did." Shep ruffled my hair as I told him one of these days I would have to find a way to get even, but I wondered if he was ever going to grow hair back. We all laughed, but Shep pulled us both up and said it was time to face the music.

With a look behind me, I felt something was wrong. Sarah came around and grabbed my hand as the mist encircled us. I was a little surprised to find a misty wall around us. Softly Sarah informed me that when our hands were in complete contact with each other, people outside of the mist couldn't hear what we were thinking or saying. She seemed to be concerned about something.

"I want you two to know that whatever happens back at the site, we have done things right. Jared and Analease wanted this, and you and Selena are a definite father and daughter team. I know you both love me, but your bond is stronger, as it should be. We knew this wasn't going to make anybody happy, but we can't help what has been done. I know Selena doesn't regret it."

I didn't. Why would I?

"Shep, would you have done anything differently?" He had a look of confidence as he shook his head. "Then do what you do best and take care of this family. We are your immediate family and no one—I mean no one—has any right to us. You understand what they want to do?" He shook his head with dismay as he glanced back towards the campsite.

"I have everything I need with me, Sarah. I will take care of the problem. I was certain they would make demands since I now need assistance." Sarah released my hand and told me I better stay here and she would send the others to me.

"No, I am staying with you. I can tell they don't like that I am yours, but I don't care. It won't change anything." Shep grabbed my shoulder and patted my back.

"She's right; it wouldn't change anything. Our bond is too strong now. I couldn't give you up if I wanted to." Abruptly I felt frightened by what he had admitted. I wondered who would want to take me from him. Again he looked at me, uttering I had nothing to worry about. "Everything is going to be fine."

We began walking back to the campsite and I could see from afar that others had joined the table—people I had never met before. Sarah whispered they were elders from the Guardian Realm. I could feel a division between the groups. It looked to be a group of six had joined us, but it felt like more.

"Sarah, would you go find my box in the RV? I am going to need it." Sarah shadowed off as Drew joined us. We stopped a good two hundred feet away from the group and watched them carefully.

"Shep, I hope you are right about everything being legal, because Old Wise Bones wants to take Selena to the Guardian Realm. We won't let him. If we have to fight to keep her, we will. You know I will." Tommy was standing with us, acting very guarded as he kept glancing nervously back at the new grouping of strangers. I could sense he was distressed.

"Shep, I think Selena should go with me to the portal. It's not safe." Shep gripped my hand tighter as he bounced our hands against his leg.

"No, she stays with me. Nobody will be taking her anywhere, I assure you." I was beginning to feel stressed when Shep gripped my shoulders to assure me all would be fine. "Selena, I need you to stay calm. You have an ability I haven't explained yet, and it is very dangerous. No matter what, you hold my hand so I can control it." This scared me even more. Why would anyone try to take me from Shep? "They won't Selena, I promise." Shep's eyes changed and it frightened me. I had never seen eyes that swirled, not in reality. I heard Drew whistle and could tell he felt more confident with Shep's change. Sarah had shadowed back to us, holding Shep's old wooden box.

Shep began to scrutinize the group ahead of us as he spoke without moving. "Sarah, there is a leather pouch with all the important documents from all three realms. Could you find it please?" Tommy sounded aghast and grabbed the box so Sarah could rummage through it to find the documents requested. Nervously, Sarah looked at how he had my hand and gazed to the sky. I tried to see what she was looking for, but I only saw storm clouds rolling above, which seemed to happen daily around here. Tommy began questioning if he meant two realms, but when Sarah found the pouch it was stuffed with a bunch of documents including a large feather. Drew came round and took the box from Tommy as Sarah handed the pouch to him. Drew immediately pulled the documents out and started thumbing through them while mumbling to himself with disbelief. Whatever he was looking at he couldn't believe. "Oh my goodness, Shep. How did you ever do this without anyone knowing in the Shadow Realm?" "I told you, we did it when Selena was two." Shep was truly agitated as he took a moment to glance down at Tommy. "Her adoption was set and would happen if anything occurred. The adoption would take immediate effect in the other two realms secretly. Old Wise Bones doesn't have a leg to stand on. If you had ever checked, there were no death certificates ever issued with mine or Selena's name in any realm, not even the Mortal. We have friends in high places, and they helped with our secret."

Drew chuckled, saying he wasn't sure Old Bones would see it that way. Tommy looked at Drew with relief as he stated that Old Wise Bones didn't have a choice. The sound of Tommy's confidence made me feel better.

"Glad to see you have confidence in me, little one." With a glance to Shep I reminded him I never doubted. Tommy suddenly looked puzzled as he held up a parchment with my parents' signatures on them with very large print. He acted startled as he continued to read the document.

"Shep, have you ever looked at all of these documents?" Shep shook his head no.

"I have had no need. I only looked at the official adoption papers."

"This one is signed by both parents relinquishing their rights to Selena; it even has their seals." Shep looked puzzled, stating he didn't even recognize that one. Without thinking, I took Sarah's hand in mine. I felt very much like a kid, but for some reason it felt right.

Drew came back around and promised Shep he would do whatever was needed. Tommy threw Drew the pouch and told him to put it back in the box. He looked as if the battle was already over. Then it happened again: I was being watched.

Shep jerked me towards the campsite as I turned to look behind us.

An older man was arguing with Billy, and I could tell it was over me. As we drew closer, I heard Billy stating that the council had no right to interfere with his brother's decision, and it was staying as far as he was concerned. I was glad to see Uncle Billy wasn't against us. Tyler came running over as Sarah moved to Shep's other side so Tyler could take my hand. "*They want to take you away to the Guardian Realm, and Dad is really mad that Elder Craddic is trying to interfere with our family. I have never seen Dad so mad. Shane and Dillon are ready to take you all to the portal and will keep you all safe if need be.*"

Shep and Drew grunted their approval, and I could tell it made Shep feel better knowing Billy wasn't against us. *"Shep, Dad said if we do have to leave, I am to go with you and stay until he comes for me.*" Shep looked over at Tyler and winked.

"Fine, Tyler, hopefully we won't have to do that." When we approached the table, everybody turned to stare. Shep stopped and addressed the new group of men. "What can I help you with today?"

The older man stood where he was at, and I watched as his fingers tightened around the tie string he had begun to fiddle with. "We hear Selena has come into her abilities, and we wanted to check up on you. If I understand correctly, the young lady can slow things down."

"She can."

The man threw his arms behind his back and held them there as he raised his chin to glare at Shep. "That is a Guardian ability, which you are not immune to."

Shep was very calm—almost too calm. "It is, and you are right. I am not immune to it, but that is why we called for Billy here to help with his niece. She does have other abilities as well, and they are of the Shadow Realm. If I understand correctly, you are not immune to those."

The man barely shuffled a few steps before throwing his pointed chin up with resolve. "The young lady has abilities of both realms?"

"Yes." There was a murmur among his whole company. I could feel Shep rubbing my fingers, and I knew he was telling me to stay calm. I continued to listen to the banter between Shep and this old guy, but it was very hard not to feel angered by his rudeness. Tyler snickered, but no one else must have heard my thoughts. "We were thinking Selena's best interest now…would be to bring her to the Guardian Realm where no one can intrude with her studies."

"Her studies would need to be of Shadow Realm as well. You have no knowledge in their control."

Elder Craddic nodded, but then continued. "Selena was Jared Martin's daughter, and he was Guardian. I am sure she needs her family and better protection. No Shadow enters the Guardian Realm without permission."

Shep stepped forward in a bit of agitation. It was funny to see Craddic back up, even though we didn't go anywhere near him. Shep stood tall as he glared at the old grump. "Selena was also Analease Whitlocke's daughter and she was Shadow, Lady of the House of Zeus. You are right; she does need her family, and that is why we are all gathered here. As far as her protection, she is very well cared for."

"Yes, but some of us feel differently. An individual with gifts from both worlds needs special attention and security." Drew was growing angry. One could see his temper was above simmering and about to boil over. Sarah warned him to keep it in check. Billy came around in a hurry and told them all to settle down.

"Selena is a Martin and is well taken care of, and any of her training will be addressed by our personal family plus anyone else we deem necessary. Guardians have taken care of their own families for centuries, and I don't see any need for change now just because my niece has two worlds of abilities."

Many of the men nodded to Billy with their approval, but I could see the man who had been arguing must be important.

"Yes, I understand. But her parents are no longer alive. They say this matter falls to the Council in her upbringing, especially since her father was Guardian. We have allowed Shep here to take care of her because it was deemed to be important in her protection when discovered. She needs Guardians with her training. With no immediate family…"

Shep interrupted the snooty old jerk. Had to admit the man was beginning to chew on my last nerve. "I beg to differ. She has immediate family, and you have no say with her. You forget who this child is." The man looked eagerly at Shep. "I know of nothing which gives you the right to say you are immediate family, Shep Goodwin. You merely are staff."

Tommy stepped forward producing a document proudly. Drew stood next to him as Tommy handed over the rest of documents. "This document shows the Guardian Realm issued an adoption of Selena Marie Martin-Goodwin upon her parents being declared deceased."

Craddic grabbed for the document but Tommy faded in and out too quickly for him to grab it. Billy came over and requested the document. Tommy handed it to him graciously. Billy smiled as he stated the date had been certified three years before his brother's death, and Jared's signature was present with his personal seal. Old Bones, as Drew referred to him, was squirming. The man truly looked furious. Billy handed the document back to Tommy as others of the council came to look at it, but if anybody tried to touch it Tommy faded in and out.

"How did this document come into existence?" Old Bones began growling.

"We knew our lives were in danger. Jared and Analease made all of these decisions. I have to admit, they had to convince me to follow what they had declared. I have been Selena's dad for ten years, and legally I might add, in all three realms.

She is *mine*. I regret nothing. Selena will always be my daughter. Our bond is stronger than any document. The document, which Drew has, shows the adoption and everything it entails in every realm and they are completely legal. You have no rights to make any decisions without my consent. Furthermore, I have my own legal documents to see to her protection."

Tommy handed Drew the paper he held and selected another, showing it to every person present. "As you see, this document has all the appropriate signatures and seals from your own realm." He then handed Drew the paper back and pulled out another, more ornate document and proceeded to show every person this one. "This is her adoption paper from the Shadow Realm, and once again, every signature and seal is present. He then grabbed another and these I knew were from the Mortal Realm. Showing these papers once again he proved they were correct.

Old Bones grew flustered, and in some ways he seemed desperate. "Why did they go to the extreme of having papers drawn up in every realm?"

Billy was being cocky as he pressed forward. "Probably because they were sure someone like you would try to interfere. I admit I don't understand everything they were thinking, but what I do know is they were taking care of their most precious gift. They wanted Shep to be her father and I have no doubt they were right. We have been here almost a month and their relationship is totally what one would expect of a father and daughter. If you had tried to destroy their family because of having no documentation, then you would be no better than this Alexander. Legally you have no rights."

Billy was beyond ecstatic with all of Shep's documentation. I could feel Old Wise Bones was not. He began to come towards me, causing Shep to pull me behind him while still holding my hand. Drew and Tommy blocked his approach. It must have taken him by surprise, for he stepped back abruptly. As he did Shane, Dillon, and Billy fell in front of him too.

Two men from the council came forward and inquired if they could see me better, but I heard Shep say my identity was for only family to know. I didn't understand what he meant; I was right here in front of them. As usual, Tyler answered my thought. *"Shep is holding your appearance from them. They can't see you the way you are. He is holding you in Shadow form."*

Old Wise Bones was irritated, and I could tell he didn't like Shep. In fact, I wasn't so sure he liked anybody. Again he tried to approach, but this time I heard a clap of thunder accompanied by lightning above me. "I suggest you stay your distance. I will take care of my daughter how I see fit." Shep's tone was deadly. Shep didn't have to yell to make his point; even Cassidy back home understood his voice. To my horror, the standoff didn't seem to be falling to the wayside like I hoped. In fact, none of my family or friends were standing down, and this was making me very tense. To add to the situation, it looked like the Council was frightened by what was taking place.

Finally a taller gentleman with tan skin stood from the back of the screen tent. "Shep, we now have established to the satisfaction of the Council, that you *are* Selena's father. But as the Council of Elders, we did promise to help in her protection and training, for she is Guardian as well as Shadow. We stand by our oath. We will protect your entire family if a need should ever arise. Some on the Council feel she would be better served by the protection of our realm, but for now it is not called for. I personally believe we would not be able to separate the two of you for any reason. I can sense Selena is in every respect your daughter, and speaking as a father, I would feel outraged by what has happened here today. Your bond has been established. I can feel it within Selena. I apologize for our misjudgment and the intrusion into the Martin family affairs. Please understand we only want to protect her. Jonathan's death—and now Jared's—have devastated our trust. We must protect our own, and Selena is one of us. Her essence is one of innocence, and I cannot believe how that has been so well- maintained by you. I can also sense she holds great abilities and will surprise us all. It matters not how the documentation was acquired, for it was done so legally three years prior to the final act. There is no question in my mind of any legality, Craddic. Stand down."

The man who was speaking evidently held the ultimate authority for the group, and so far it sounded like they were going to leave us alone. "She does need to be around our kind to learn and to find a match." Drew and Tommy both grunted at this.

Uncle Billy spoke up. "Do not forget her mother was Shadow and was also lost that day. Her sacrifice to their family was just as great. Selena will be around Guardians as well as Shadow, and as far as a match, only time holds the answer. We will not overwhelm her with all that is a part of us yet. She has lived in the Mortal Realm and only knows their rules, and in time she will understand the other two. Until then, I request you remove the other possibilities when you leave." Shep let out a guttural sound with Uncle Billy's last words.

*"What are they talking about?"*

"*You don't want to know,*" Tyler said in a disgusted tone. Shep pulled me in front of him. He was very careful as he placed both his hands on my shoulders, and I could feel it was important for me not to move. The Council began leaving, and I was surprised to hear one of them holler a word. To my great horror, many more men appeared and began to follow them out. Billy and the others watched them leave, but Shep didn't move and neither did I. I could feel Shep reach down and kiss the top of my head as relief flooded his body. The final council member who had spoken approached us cautiously.

"Shep, you are a wonderful father. I know Jared chose wisely and I am thrilled you all had the foresight to protect yourselves legally. Please keep this treasure safe. She is the first mix in a long time that has these gifts of both worlds, and I sense she has even rarer gifts, too. You may not even be aware of them yet. In fact, two of the young men who came with us today are like her. Granted they are centuries older, but I wish you would allow them to meet her. I guarantee Billy trusts them, and one counseled Jared about a mixed child. Should that be possible, they are awaiting my signal."

"I need a minute to talk to my family." The man walked off graciously, but Shep still did not release me. Everybody came over to us except Drew who continued to watch the forest boundary.

"Billy..." Shep was feeling confused, I could tell. "I think you should let the men meet her especially since they hold both abilities. We don't know. They could help her deal with what she will have to face in the future. If they are not a m...." Shep cut him off.

"You are right. We shouldn't turn them away without a chance. She won't understand. You know that don't you?" Sarah came over to me and took my hand.

"Selena would you like to meet the others who are of mixed abilities like yours? We call them Seheirenel." Nervously looking to Shep, I didn't know what was going on and I really did want to understand what this meant.

Tommy piped up, saying he would want the others to leave but the two should stay. Even if I didn't understand, Shep and the men would. Shep shook his head in solemn agreement. Billy told Dillon to inform Moses and the Seheirenel to remain, but the rest were to leave. Dillon ran off as Laura began looking very pale. I wish I knew what she was thinking.

Dillon came back and said they would see to it the others left, especially Old Wise Bones. He snickered as he chanced a glance towards Drew's immobile form. We all laughed at the nickname we had given him. Tyler was still holding my hand, and I could feel that same annoying presence somewhere near. He was closer this time.

Shep turned me around and asked if I was all right. "You're guarding your thoughts again." Quickly I apologized as I chanced a look over his shoulder. I wanted him to be aware of what I felt. Thankfully he understood what I wanted him to know. He pulled me into his strong embrace as he whispered all was well. Sarah placed a hand on Shep's shoulder, asking what was wrong. I could feel he gave her an answer, for she started scouring the area with her eyes, too.

The councilman and three others came into view a moment later, but still they were not the presence I felt. Shep relaxed a little and looked to the four men. Betty started hollering for help with dinner, but Shep was looking at the ground, rubbing his toes in the dirt. Tommy slapped him on the back, saying everything would be all right. "If at any time you become uncomfortable at all, I will end the meeting." I understood and he released my shoulders. All four men jerked to a stop and stared at me for several minutes. Drew circled around and I could feel he was standing right behind me. He was being very protective, and I appreciated that.

"Who is the third man?" Shep demanded of the leader. "This is Japeth, the head of the Seheirenel. He comes purely as an observer."

"She is an absolute mix of both her parents. She has no dominant trait of either family. She is amazing. I don't know how the Mortals haven't noticed the difference." My cheeks heated, forcing me to seek the comfort of Shep's hand. He stood up straight, holding my hand tightly.

"I would like you to meet my Selena." All four men nodded as they began to introduce themselves.

"My name is Moses and these three young men are Japeth, Adrian, and Ellis. They are of mix abilities too—Seheirenel." Immediately I shook their hands, only to feel totally awkward. Tommy let out a sigh of relief. I could feel his whole demeanor relax. Drew clapped my back, and I could feel relief run through all of my family, but the three were disappointed about something. Tyler pulled me aside and asked if I didn't hear or feel anything at all about these two men.

"No, why would I? I don't hear anything either. I have never liked any guy, not even at school. I know one day I will, but not today. Is that what they were talking about?" I was floored as Tyler smirked at me.

"Matches happen easily and you evidently feel nothing towards them." As I shook my head, the two men approached me.

"Hi Selena, I imagine this all is very strange to you." They had no idea how strange this all seemed. Shep and Tyler both laughed. I elbowed Tyler. The others probably already knew what I was thinking.

We spent the rest of the night talking to our four new friends who gave me pointers on how to deal with both realms. They were very excited to have a new "sister" as they called me. I couldn't believe all the information they gave me about others like us. Japeth and Adrian had known my dad and had discussed it would be funny if one of them would be a match for me. Luckily Adrian said I was not. I couldn't help but tell the whole group that love at first sight wouldn't happen with me, and to let me find my own love. Shep's mouth dropped as he asked if I was looking. "Of course, but I haven't found him yet. But when I do, I'll let you know."

Shep pulled me into the seat with him and told me he had to approve of any guys I was interested in. We all were laughing at how possessive he seemed all of a sudden. That was Shep's fatherly instinct taking over. Unfortunately, this aging thing was confusing. I was really beginning to understand it meant something totally different in the other two realms. Carefully I looked at my two older cousins. I figured they were between two and three centuries old. You wouldn't believe by their looks that they were that old. According to the council leader and my family, a match can happen from the age of fourteen up.

When the three left Shep began to tease me. "Maybe I should call them back. If

I leave it to you, you may never find a spouse." When I told him I didn't care if I married, he actually blushed. "All that matters to me is having you and my family." Slowly I drew closer to the edge of the awning to look toward the tree edge. I could see a small mist rise and the familiar presence was there again. That mist was strange.

Billy gingerly joined me as he draped his arm around my shoulders to pull me back into the hub of our family. "Selena, that mist bothers you doesn't it?" With a slight nod I agreed softly. Without hesitation Billy signaled his boys and they took off in a dead run. Shep looked up and took note of what Billy was doing and shadowed off quickly, as did Drew and Tommy. We could see them progress to the mist, which evaporated before they arrived.

Swiftly Sarah ushered me to our camper while Billy followed closely behind. All were sent to their campers to wait for my cousins and the others to return. When they did, they all admitted there had been at least two other presences in the woods, but they were unable to catch them. Billy didn't like that at all. He thought maybe we should leave tomorrow. Shep reminded him we had very little time left in the summer to practice. Once I was home, it would be difficult to train.

It was decided that they would up security for the rest of the stay and make preparations of a second site. After Shep sent me to bed, Sarah followed. She asked if it bothered me what the Council had done with bringing possible matches today. I had to admit it did. She agreed it would have bothered her, too. I didn't like that they had tried to take me from Shep. She tried to soothe away all my concerns, but that wasn't going to happen easily.

"You have nothing to worry about. Nobody will take you away from us—ever." This statement made me feel better. She actually cuddled up to me and wanted to explain why I was important to both realms. It was all because of being a mix with active abilities, not to mention my rank.

"You are rare. They were hoping if you found one of theirs to be a match, then you would have no desire to go to the Shadow Realm. They are unaware of the other influences there will be in finding your match. There will be no match among them." To me this sounded archaic, like they were trying to buy me. Sarah laughed at my analysis of what had happened. Softly she stated matches sometimes take centuries to find, and they were trying to help.

I felt exasperated at her statement. "I'm fifteen. I don't think I will be interested in anybody anytime soon." We both were laughing hysterically at this when Shep hollered that we were having too much fun and I was supposed to be sleeping.

Shep walked heavily down the hall, only to cause us both to act innocent when he entered. "Alright, what is all this laughing about?" He grinned. Sarah started explaining to Shep how I thought the match thing was archaic and I didn't like the Council. "You don't have to worry. I will be taking care of you. But the match thing will happen one day, but it will be in its own time." We all stayed up much longer than we should have. By the time Shep finally convinced us to go to bed, it was almost too late to even worry about it.

# CHAPTER 9.
# ENEMY

**The next morning** I walked out and could sense Drew trying to sneak up on me, so I changed my exit. Shep's curiosity got the best of him and he inquired what I was doing. With a brisk shush I slipped the window open as Sarah knocked his shoulder and waved me on. I climbed out the window and began guarding my mind while sensing around. Instantly Drew noticed my mind was guarded and began trying to find where I had disappeared to. I couldn't shadow like he could, so I used the storage bin. After he asked Shep where I was, I felt him shadow to the woods. Thankfully Shep didn't give me away. I waited a few minutes to be certain he was gone before I sneaked over to Drew's RV and short-sheeted his bed for the third time. This was just like my dad used to do, or at least that was what I understood from Billy and some of the other adults.

This time when I sensed my surroundings, I found Drew was still searching and hadn't returned yet. Immediately I flew to the table and sat down beside Shep, who asked why I was sitting so close. He knew why, but still insisted on acting like he didn't. Tommy's dry tone of voice indicating that he didn't want to know was met by several amused grins. Once Drew returned to the campsite, he accused Tommy or Sarah of helping me disappear. Of course both denied it, acting as if they were insulted by the implication. Even if Tommy wasn't mischievous outwardly, he was inwardly. He enjoyed our games as much as we did—I could sense it.

Nevertheless, Kirt's snickering made it obvious that I had been up to no good. Thankfully Laura gave him a swift kick to divert his attention to his ankle. Drew became very suspicious of why so many had silenced their excited minds. Billy was practically roaring with laughter, evidenced by how red his face was becoming. "I remember this feeling with both of your parents. What have you done?" I shrugged my shoulders and began shoving food into my mouth.

When it was suggested we do some hide and seek with sensing, I took advantage by slowing our surroundings down in hopes of making a clean escape. I jumped from the table and took off for the quad while Billy encouraged me to run. Lately I had been able to control my slowing without any ill effects. Luckily Billy kept my effect contained. That was one thing he kept repeating to every adult who suffered at the hands of our ability: proudly he would charge that I was a true Martin because of it. Still, he made it clear that I had a lot of maturing to do with this ability, and each step would be a doozy. My ability to slow things down was becoming easier.

When I finally released my hold, I heard everybody laugh, all except poor

Tommy. Instead he was complaining that I was going to have to give him warning if I was going to do that all the time. Tyler and Kirt raced after me, shouting they really were going to have to figure out some sort of defense against my slowdown. Billy reminded them there was no defense to my ability unless someone had the reverse effect.

Once in the woods I scrambled for a good, dark hiding place. Cautiously I guarded my thoughts as the boys entered and passed. Laura and Drew quickly followed them. Being careful not to move until I had sensed they were at the quad, I carefully made my way to the river. When I felt someone trying to sense, I dropped and guarded my thoughts and feelings again. No one was going to get the drop on me today. I wanted to be the winner and besides, a bit of quiet time would be a blessing right now. I remained still for a bit longer until I decided it was safe to move. Again I checked the surrounding area before charging towards my goal.

Upon reaching the riverbank, I found the heat of the day was starting to set in, which made this an even better choice of recreation. Hastily I removed my shoes. I couldn't help but put my feet in when I found a small hole at the base of a tree. I placed my shoes there behind the overgrown vegetation in case I had to hide suddenly. I then slipped into the water and found it to be warm and refreshing. Suddenly I sensed someone approaching, and whoever it was, they weren't family. Quickly I hid within the brush near the bank. As I slid into the brush, I only left my head among the reeds. To my amazement a mist was forming. It continued to take shape, forcing me to rub my eyes in hopes of being able to make out if somebody was there or not. Then my mind registered someone else approaching. The mist disappeared as suddenly as it had appeared. I remained hidden in order to see who was coming, only to find it was Drew. He continued to look around, and when he looked in my direction, I went under the water. Thankfully I didn't have to stay submerged long. When I surfaced I could sense him leaving. Swimming back out, I floated on my back. It was so peaceful here.

"*Selena, there you are!*" Practically drowning I realized Shep was on the riverbank. He was smiling and said I was doing a very good job on guarding, for I had even beaten Drew for the time being. Drew had found the others and they had even tried to find me. Shep figured I had to be somewhere near water on a day like today. Quickly I pleaded with him to let me continue to evade Drew. He conceded by shadowing back to the campsite. I sensed someone nearing again and dove back under, only to surface in the brush at the shadow of the bank. This time it was Laura. To my disappointment, I had another feeling there was someone else too. It was making me anxious. With a quick survey of the area, I didn't see anyone at first glance. Then to my horror I found a mist with the shape of a man in it again. Without thought I jumped from the water and slowed things down as I ran to Laura. After I released my hold, I yelled for her to run. For a short distance I ran with her until I realized the mist was rolling in faster. I needed to delay him so Laura could escape. It was almost like the sun was trying to invade the mist, outlining his form even more. Instantly I created a strong wind that bent the trees as it ripped around us. Suddenly the sound of wood splitting drew our attention as the top part of a tree snapped. The man looked above his head as a tree tumbled to the ground in front of him. Hopefully he was as surprised as I was by my strength. "STAY WHERE YOU ARE!"

Even though I felt certain my message was clear, he continued to draw closer. The mist billowed around him while growing thicker than ever before. A second later I couldn't see anything but smoke around me. My heart was racing as I tried to get an idea of where this man was. With my wind I tried to blow it away from my person. Nothing was working. My hearing sharpened as I listened for any sign of where he could be. I couldn't slow things down this time, for I wanted help. Suddenly I felt hands grabbing my shoulders, and I was whipped from the fog to the camper.

I found I was screaming from the shock of being grabbed and felt extremely nauseous. Shep was holding me tight while griping under his breath. His eyes had changed again. Shep turned me around and held me against his chest, telling me to breathe slower and the motion sickness would go away. His heartbeat was soothing as I closed my eyes, trying to stop the sickness. Drew faded in a second later with Sarah at his side. Both were agreeing it was definitely a Shadow, but they were unable to track them. Shep growled with frustration just as banging began on the door and Billy shouting that he needed to see me.

"Is Laura safe?" I gasped. "Billy and Betty felt her fear and took off after her. She is fine," Sarah whispered as she opened the door. Billy stepped inside the camper and grabbed me from Shep who was hugging me tight.

"We have to leave, Shep. That was too close. Both of the girls were at risk this time. Betty and I feel we are no longer safe here."

Shep nodded in agreement. "But we still need to send Tommy and Drew back to the Shadow Realm." Drew grunted that he was staying. His determination was clear.

I felt extremely dizzy and stumbled back to my bed and draped my shivering body across it. Sarah ran in, throwing a blanket on me while rubbing a towel through my wet hair. "We need a heater, NOW!" Suddenly Billy went crashing through the door, hollering for Tyler or Kirt to help. A second later I heard banging and could hear Shep opening a cabinet out in the main part of the RV. After Billy returned, I knew they were installing the camper's heater. Drew's burly form bounced the RV as he came in and began pulling me from the bed. The movements made my head spin again. He laughed a little, telling me next time maybe I would know better. Gently he placed me down in front of the heater, which was blowing full force.

"How did she get so wet?" Drew asked. A smirk twitched into place as I confessed to hiding in the brush of the river from him. He looked wickedly at me, but

I could see his appreciation of my cleverness. He appreciated how I had evaded him.

Shep sat down and began rubbing the blanket against me, trying to warm me faster. "She has always loved the water."

Unfortunately I felt my feet freezing, only to realize that my shoes were back at the riverbank. Then there was another soft knock on the door, only to present Betty.

Billy laughed nervously. "She's fine, love. She is a little sick to her stomach from shadowing, but fine all the same." Peering through the door, she smiled weakly as she watched Sarah rubbing me down with the towel.

"Laura is alright." Everybody was looking at Betty nervously. Unfortunately Sarah asked for Betty to tell them what Laura had revealed. I wished she hadn't. "She said Selena jumped onto the riverbank, and when she turned to see what had Selena so upset, she saw a man and a mist very close to her. She felt things slow down and Selena grabbed her, pulling her further away, and then released the slowdown. She told Laura to run—and she did—but when she realized Selena wasn't with her, she turned around and saw Selena using her wind to drop a tree on the attacker.

"Selena, she said you stood there and never moved and that you kept fighting back. Then the mist came in so heavy she couldn't see you anymore. We arrived by that time. Selena, she was right. We couldn't see you or sense you. It scared me. What were you thinking? Thanks for taking care of Laura, but next time run with her and don't go back to the attacker, please." The silence was deadly as Shep's arms pulled me to him.

Softly Shep whispered with a tone that would scare the dead. "Is that what you did?"

"Shep, I don't know. There is something about this Shadow. I didn't want anybody getting hurt and from what I understand, they want me, not Laura. I was protecting her. That was all." His hug tightened around me as I felt Sarah rubbing my forehead.

"Selena, you will not surrender yourself to them for anybody." Billy's tone was harsh. "We are working hard on keeping you with us, and you have to help by not sacrificing your own safety. You had a chance to run and didn't, and if this ever happens again you are to run. Have I made myself clear?" I tried to focus on the blow of the heater.

Drew began whistling as he went out the door with Betty following closely behind. A storm erupted outside, causing me to jump at the clash of thunder and lightning. "Billy, keep your family indoors. DREW!" His head popped back in as Shep began to stand. I had a bad feeling about this. In a complete rush of horror I grabbed his hand in hopes of stopping him.

"I'm going with you. You are not going to leave me here."

He grabbed my arms and pushed me into Billy's waiting grasp. "Little one, you are staying here. I am going to take care of this, and you do not have to worry about me. I am quite capable of taking care of myself. Sarah, can you deal with her Shadow abilities?" She nodded with assent.

"Drew, I need your help to hunt these forms down. Billy, make sure nobody goes away from the campers. You two don't let her out of your sight. She is resourceful and she hides in the storage cabinets and waits until it's clear to make a run for it."

Suddenly I felt funny, like I was very light. Shep quickly grabbed me while smiling down at me. "No, not today, little one." Then I felt drained as he shoved me back into Billy's grasp. Immediately Sarah came over, trying to calm me down. "Sarah, I can take care of the slowdown, but you are going to have to stop the other."

Abruptly I felt very cold again. Loudly pleading with them didn't help. I even promised next time I would run, but they didn't release me. There was another knock on the door, and this time it was Tyler. He looked shocked at what he saw. "Tyler, tell your dad to let me go. I'm fine. I won't do anything." Tyler shook his head and Billy knew I had been lying. "You are supposed to help me not betray me." We all jumped at a huge bolt of lightning that struck. Tommy rushed to the door before looking back at me with a worried expression.

"Selena, you need to calm down," Tyler pleaded. Another lightning strike and I suddenly felt too tired to struggle anymore. Sarah went to the door with Tommy to look out. Billy asked if I would behave when I slumped in his arms.

"I have no choice." I felt defeated as he let me go. Gradually I scooted onto the bench to lean against the table. I concentrated on the memory of the man I had seen. It seemed to be the only way. Tyler reached over and took my hand and asked why I was focusing on the man. "He'll come for me," I stated blankly while staring back at him. "If I think about him, he will come." Everybody heard me loud and clear.

Sarah pushed into the seat beside me with a worried expression on her face. "Selena, why will he come for you?"

"I don't know. He knows me, though, and he won't leave." Somehow I knew deep down in my heart he wouldn't leave if he felt me searching for him. I patted my hands on the table, trying to control my search for him. It was almost like I was pleading into the nothingness of the atmosphere. Somehow I knew he would sense me.

"Why would you want him to come, Selena?" This question irritated me, for I felt it was obvious why. "That way we could trap him and Shep will be back when he senses he is coming. The man won't leave. I can feel that. He has been near ever since my abilities showed up. I don't know why, but he is still near. I could track him now. I know I could. I have become familiar with his presence. I can sense him all the time lately. I just didn't understand till now. I…I…don't think he means any harm."

I began concentrating again. We heard the storm take a turn for the worse, and I could feel a huge amount of anger, to the point that my head began to feel like it was going to burst. The panic in Tyler's voice became loud as people began scrambling around us. Suddenly I felt something very cold as I closed my eyes, trying to stop the pain. The room became deadly silent. My head was killing me. Sarah was all in mist form again. When I pulled away she faded back into her human form. "Selena, I need to block your mind right now. It will help with the pain, at least some." Another sudden clap of thunder shook the whole camper, and I knew Shep was angry. A searing pain went through my head, causing me to cry out. Sarah grabbed my head and entered my mind. It felt like she was trying to close some door that held a room full of pain.

Thankfully the pain lightened. "Sarah?" Tyler sounded frightened.

"She is going to be fine, Tyler. I need to concentrate." The storm outside was growing worse, and I could feel everybody's fear grow. Finally an abnormal quiet met our ears and I could feel Sarah still protecting my mind. The pain had lasted a good forty minutes according to Billy.

A moment later Shep faded in. He looked sick when he stared at me. Shep took ahold of me as he studied my eyes again, demanding to know what had gone wrong. "Selena's mind was being torn apart, Shep. Whatever was going on out there I had to block. There wasn't much I could do though. I'm afraid…" Sarah trailed off. "I think she is alright now, but the pain she endured was the worst I have ever felt."

Shep began rocking me back and forth. Swiftly he kissed my head as he kept repeating that I would be all right. He would take care of me. Nobody moved until Tommy suggested that maybe I be put to bed. Instantly I clung tighter to Shep. That was the last thing I needed. "No, I am taking Selena somewhere else tonight. Drew, Tommy, if you could bring the others to the other safety, that is where we will be. Everybody started moving, and I could feel Billy's panic as he began calling for Shane and Dillon.

"Selena, I'm sorry. So sorry you were hurt today." I cried softly into Shep's shoulder as he kept patting me. "Keep your eyes closed, little one. I will take care of us…I promise." For an awkward moment Shep's voice sounded full of tears. "Go to sleep." I wasn't sure if I should. He must have read my thoughts, for he assured me wholeheartedly that he wasn't leaving me—ever. I had his word on that. Shep never breaks his promise. Of that I had no doubt. I rested.

When I woke, I was still in Shep's arms, cradled like a baby. To my surprise we were in a log cabin, and the wall I was facing was mainly a large window so you could see the terrain around us. I could see we were high up on a mountaintop. The ground was filled with all kinds of trees, and they were large. A picnic area stood to the side, and red dirt was pounded almost into pavement.

A gentle kiss to my forehead brought my immediate attention back to Shep. He wanted to know if my head still hurt. "No," I told him.

Slowly I began to move, but realized I still had no shoes. "Drew brought your shoes, they're at the door." He must have been listening in on my thoughts.

"Where is everybody else?" Shep muttered they were out practicing.

"We're safe now, but I don't think you will be doing much today." Curiously I looked at him, while asking what had happened those last forty minutes. He looked miserable as he glanced out at the sundrenched patio. "It is a bit complicated. What I can promise is you is that you have nothing to worry about." It was obvious he didn't want to talk, so I let it go.

Tommy faded in with water and Tylenol for me. For a moment I felt unsure of moving as I cuddled back against Shep's shoulder. "She is exhausted from the experience, I see." Tommy's voice sounded concerned.

"Yes."

Tommy thrust his hand forward while staring at Shep instead of me. "Shep you know how I feel about Ale…"

"Yes, I know." As I reached to take the pills, I realized how shaky my hands were. Tommy immediately assisted by steadying the water bottle as I swallowed. Just that little effort seemed massive. Slowly I leaned back against Shep's sheltering embrace.

Tommy still looked upset. "This is his style of warfare. I would like to address him personally. I have wanted to for a long time but didn't because of Terah's wish. Selena could have died back there."

Shep's whole body shook, forcing my immediate attention to him. His eyes looked sorrowful as he glanced down at me. "I know, and it won't happen again. It was me. I became so angry and you forget I have never had a child of my own to shield when I battle. We are so tied together that she felt my pain. I can't lose control like that again and I won't. Sarah is going to help me. The bond between us is stronger than most because she is not only my charge, but my daughter. I had no idea it would happen with us. She was genetically not mine…I thought it wouldn't. But it looks like fates have changed that. No one would ever be able to take her from me because it would kill us both. Sarah confirmed that last night after she arrived. It looks like Selena and I are bound for eternity as father and daughter." Tommy sighed heavily as he glanced down at me with sympathy shining brightly in his eyes. "Good. That was what Jared and Analease wanted."

Billy growled as he and Drew came in and plopped down on the couch beside us. "Tommy had a letter for me from Jared when he arrived. He gave it to me privately. In it, Jared said he wanted you and Selena to be father and daughter if he died. He wanted me to support you like I would him. Did you know he thought you would be a much better father than he would? I remember back to that first incident and we talked for days after about that. He would have been a good dad, but you are too. I know right now you doubt your abilities after what happened yesterday, but don't."

Billy shuffled over to a chair and sat down so we both could see him plainly. He looked hot and sweaty, but that sweet smile that all his children seemed to have was back in place. "I have to admit I had heard Protectors who are parents have to shield their children when in extreme circumstances. I never understood what it truly meant. Then when Sarah checked the DNA and found you had connected in such a way, I was shocked. I had always understood when Guardian or Shadow adopted, the DNA *did* transform to include the adoptive parents genes too." I could feel Shep's amazement about this fact, but I was shocked.

"What DNA test?" My voice was as shaky as my hands. Tommy sat down across from me with a self-satisfied look as he did what he did best—share his knowledge.

"It is just like Billy said. Adoptive parents' genes adapt in adoptee's genetics when a bond is formed.

"'Bond' in our world is eternal, literally," Billy continued. "When you started doubling over in pain, Sarah suspected Shep was in pain and your bond was transferring between the two of you. This means when Shep is battling, hurt, or his emotions are out of control, you can feel it and you did. It is clear he had no idea he needed to shield you. When the testing was done, it proved your genes have adapted with his gene markers now. Your bond is unbreakable; not even the Guardian elders can do anything about that. This is considered the final stage of the adoption process, and it is limited to Protectors for some reason." It was official. Billy stated proudly that Shep was another brother. Drew laughed heartily at that one.

This made me laugh because I was very happy to know Shep was a part of my "gene pool" as they called it. Shep leaned over and kissed my head. "I'm glad you are happy, but I feel rotten over the pain you experienced yesterday. Now we will have to be extra careful and I have some practicing of my own to do." He would have to practice with dealing with pain so he could shield me. We all heard Betty calling lunch as Shep asked if I was up to moving or if he needed to bring something to me. My pride was taking a beating today. I needed to prove to all I was fine, so I stood up.

"By the way Shep, who were you dealing with yesterday?" Drew inquired while passing the food. "A stranger. He escaped…barely. I don't expect to have any more problems either. Let's just eat—I need to eat."

The next morning I was shocked to find I had slept since yesterday. Laura said Shep was in all night checking on me, so she hadn't been able to sleep. I didn't think my weak "sorry" was enough, but as usual Laura brushed it off with a smile. Once I walked out to breakfast, Kirt and Drew kept calling me "Sleeping Beauty." When I started to slow things down to get back at them, Billy grabbed my shoulders in order to restrain me. "No slowing of things for a while. Shep's practice is going to take all of your energy, little one." Instantly I cringed at his soft reminder of what I would be facing.

# CHAPTER 10.
# SHEP'S TRAINING

**Slowly** we made our way towards the training quad. Tommy draped his arms around my shoulders protectively as we walked. "Dear little one, this is going to be very hard today. I think I owe it to Shep to tell you why he and Sarah have never had any children. Shep's biggest fear has always been not being able to shield a child from his pain. He is a Protector after all, and his abilities are magnificent. For example, if a war broke out, he is the military and his pain would be transferred to his children, and his need to protect becomes stronger. He had no idea when he adopted you that this could happen. He admitted that to us last night. It wouldn't have changed anything, but today he will be facing his worst fear."

When we arrived at the top of the small mountain, I could see everything in the area. The sight presented to me was breathtaking. I could see flat bluffs all the way across. Some seemed to be barren while others were full of life. Hastily I took note of my own surroundings and found there were four large, medieval cornerstones that lit with a green eye at Drew's every touch.

A small tent had been erected and it appeared to have a ton of pillows. This bluff was barren in the quad area. Tommy took my hand as we settled down in the tent. Shep came over and sat with me. "Selena, I'm so sorry for this." Out of pure instinct I hit his shoulder, trying to change his somber mood.

"We can handle this. Trust me."

His sigh was heavy as we were joined by Sarah and Drew. Sarah cupped my face as she knelt down to look deeply into my eyes. "Selena, if at any time it becomes too much, tell Tommy and we will stop, okay? She looks well today. We should begin. I am going to start, and Drew might help later, but for now he is going to be guarding the two of you." A second later she stood up and crossed the square. The wind was blowing quite hard and Sarah looked at peace with what she was about to do.

Drew knelt down and pulled my head forward as he kissed me. "Little one, be strong." He quickly jerked up and I saw him pass to the entrance of the quad, taking Shadow form as a guard. The feeling that surrounded me was one of total agony. Shep pulled his shirt off and entered the flat, rocky quad. This place reminded me of Stonehenge, with rocks that stood almost as in protection of this training ground. Tommy stood and reminded Shep he was to deflect but not use any lightning. He nodded in affirmation. Abruptly Sarah burst into a dark circle with a form in the middle. This form terrified me as much as it amazed me. Shep changed into Shadow form, causing the air to fill with electricity, so much so that my hair stood on end. Sarah's form moved towards Shep's, and they both seemed to be circling. In a sudden flash, lightning struck the rock behind Shep and several pieces sheared off. As they flew his shadow jumped. I felt a scratching sensation across my shoulder. Unfortunately I could feel the pressure already building.

Tommy leaned over and placed his arm around me while whispering, "You are not actually cut but you can feel what has happened to Shep. The pressure in your head is what we must be concerned about. You can help by guarding your mind." Gently he released my shoulder as I bit my lip. I could feel a pressure building. I quickly closed my eyes and concentrated on guarding my mind. Yet I heard another explosion, which caused the pressure to rise.

Tommy shuffled closer to hold me tight. With a shove I pushed him away. "I'm fine."

Silently I concentrated on anything but what was going on in front of me. More horrifying sights and sounds continued as they sparred, carving chunks out of the boulders. I could feel the pressure building as I sat watching, not allowing myself to feel anything. Shep called for the sparring to stop as he ran back to me. "Selena, don't cut your mind off from me."

He knelt down in front of me, demanding for me to speak to him. If I did I was afraid I would scream. "Sarah!" Shep was close to hysterics as he patted my face, trying to jar me from my hold. Sarah changed back into human form and ran towards me. She dropped to her knees and I could see her concern as her eyes darted frantically to Tommy. "Selena, answer me!" Rapidly my heart jumped, helping me to push them both away from me as I rose. The pressure was leaving. "I am fine!"

Sarah cupped my face and announced what I already knew—that I was fine. This only proved to agitate Shep as I shuffled away. "You need to go practice. I will relax here in the back of the tent on these comfy pillows. No worries… really." Slowly I began to move to the back of the tent while creating a comfortable spot to lie on. Reluctantly Shep returned to the quad. It was amazing how this quad hosted both shadow and sunlight. It basically was a challenge in its use. Tommy's voice rose as he reminded them of the rules. Without looking I could hear and feel it begin again. They continued on for a while. This time the pressure became blinding as I laid there with a pillow clenched in my mouth to keep from screaming. The pain was almost unbearable. My face was soaked from my tears, but I didn't dare let Shep see me. He had to concentrate on this new skill in order to learn.

The noises were becoming worse and I could feel debris blowing across my own body. Finally the pain felt like it did the other day and I heard Tommy hollering for them to stop. Everything became unearthly quiet as I heard the approach of running footsteps towards the tent.

Once I managed to open my eyes I became frightened since I could see nothing. Shep grabbed my head and pressed my face into the curve of his neck. I was blind. Shep began to rock me with a wail of despair. "I can't do this. I don't know how."

Again I tried to focus my eyes. Light started appearing in small specks across my line of sight. Finally I could see his blurry image. *"Dad, I'm fine but you look a mess. Take the water now please."* He looked at me and pulled my head up to his lips as he released me into Drew's strong arms.

Drew's arms encompassed me protectively as I laid heavily against his chest. A small kiss to the top of my head startled me. Drew had never kissed me before, but for some reason today he felt like family to me. Cautiously he positioned me into a seated position as Tommy checked me. Sarah looked just as bad as Shep. This was perfectly miserable to have to learn. I hadn't realized it until now how Drew was rocking me. I was feeling like a rag doll.

Finding some strength I pushed my body to the outside of the tent to stand. Thankfully, I didn't waver like I thought I would. "I will not be your weakness, Shep Goodwin!" With haste I walked to the entrance of the quad and left their sight. Drew shadowed to my side, asking if I wanted any company. Gently I took his hand and walked around the outside of the training area to a small running stream down the mountainside. It was cool and refreshing. This would give Shep time to gain control. For once in my short life I was praying for strength. Heavily I leaned against a small boulder.

"Drew, do you think Shep is making any improvement?"

Drew frowned as he shook his head. "Selena are you cold? I can get a blanket or jacket…"

"No Drew, I'm not cold, just tired." I took a couple of steadying breaths as I walked back to the quad where it looked like the three of them were having a heated discussion.

Before I knew what was happening, we were suddenly back outside the log cabin, to everybody's surprise. Shep kicked the door open. With a quick glance over his shoulder I could see Tyler sitting at the table holding his head. Dillon was patting him while watching us curiously.

Shep took me to the couch. He sat down heavily only to cover his eyes with his arm as he held a drink in his lap. He was flustered. Sarah was watching us warily from outside. I went to the door, dismissing his orders to sit. "Where's that first aid kit?" I hollered. Shane waved it as I began to walk towards him until the dizziness swept over me. I grabbed the door hard and remained very still until it passed, while Tyler ordered everybody to freeze. He grabbed the first aid kit and glared. Tyler understood. Softly he rubbed my cheek, stating my face was tearstained.

I climbed onto the couch beside Shep. "Alcohol swabs." Shep jumped at my touch as I began to administer some first aid. Wincing, he tried to move only to find Tyler jerking him back into place so I could work. "What do you think you are doing young lady?"

"I'm taking care of you like we always have done, and when I'm done a kiss will make it all better." He couldn't help but smile. Again I looked out the window only to see how miserable Sarah was. Tyler, registering my thought, stood up and excused himself quickly. With a nod she straightened her shoulders and approached. "Sarah, can you hand me some ointment?" Sarah rushed over and scrambled through the box for the ointment. "I'll check you next."

Sarah's laugh was weak. "When did you become the parent, little one?" I had to smirk at her comment. "I have always acted older than I really am. That is what Chelsea, Cassidy, Shep, and Parker have always said."

Shep opened his eyes while looking at Sarah and I. He took both of our hands and held them to his chest. "I am not as good as the two of you thought. I am not sure how to shield. I don't understand it." Sarah looked like she could cry, and I felt like it too. Yet, we both knew we had to be strong.

"You always say control comes with practice." This was a phrase Shep was known for.

"Selena, this practice hurts you. When I say that, I know you will become tired and sore, but most of the time there is no blinding pain."

With a shrug of my shoulders, I repeated another saying he has used ever since I could remember: "No pain no gain." He was amazed at how I could mimic him in this situation.

"Shep, she's right. You have taught her well. You have to continue to practice."

"I will practice, but we may not be able to return when we planned. I will not weaken her." Going over I hugged him as he held me tight.

"Shep, I'm strong. Stronger than you think; I can handle this." Sarah joined our hug.

***

Upon feeling a hand rubbing my forehead, I awoke to Shep's smile. "Dinner is ready and it is time to eat, little one." It was nice to see him smiling. Carefully I climbed down from the bed as Shep offered a steadying hand. He was worried. In a determined fashion I walked out as if nothing had happened this morning. Once at the table, I didn't feel like eating either. Shep knocked my plate and nodded for me to eat. I nibbled at it, trying to make it look like I was eating. When I finally felt I had stayed long enough, I started to get up until I felt Shep's firm grasp pull me back down. He wasn't going to let me away. Shep finally seemed satisfied when I cleared half of the food he had served me.

"I think I would like to go explore. I won't go far." No one seemed to stop me, so I started walking down the paved path with Dillon, Shane and Tyler.

"So what exactly are you learning up there? I…I mean," Dillon clamped his mouth shut as Tyler let out a growl. Without intending to, I cringed at the reminder of what had taken place earlier. None of it was pleasant. I was certain they were curious, but I wasn't so sure I wanted to think about it either.

"You guys are jerks. Do you think she wants to talk about the training?" Tyler's loss of temper caught me off guard. He always seemed so in control.

"It's alright, Tyler. They are just curious." I wasn't up to listening to their sibling squabble. "It is painful. Shep has to allow his body to endure pain when he could easily defend himself. Every time he is hit or injured I feel it. I don't receive the injury, but there is a pressure that builds up into a searing pain. Today my eyes were so blurred I couldn't see. Luckily Shep is making progress. He will have it down before long. I know he will. Now it is your turn to tell me about you."

Shane had found his match, and it was hard for him to be away from her. Still, he felt he needed to be here. Besides, he wanted to meet me since the last time he had seen me I was only four. Dillon was the younger of the two, and he was working mainly in the western states right now and was enjoying a break from fire control.

Then I remembered the question I wanted to ask Tyler. "Do you feel my pain, Tyler?" Tyler's face saddened. He shook his head, which made me feel a whole lot better. "I don't feel your pain, but I know you are in pain. I feel absolutely helpless."

Dillon commented, "You better just be thankful you didn't meet your match the other night, because he will feel your pain and he wouldn't be able to deal with this training, I know. It makes me wonder if finding my match would be a good thing or not." Shane punched him and Tyler started to haul off to hit him.

I stopped him by becoming a dead weight as I grabbed his arm. "It's alright, we will be fine. Now walk me back to the quad. Dillon, tell Shep and the others I am waiting." They both gulped as Tyler tucked me safely against his strong body. "You don't have to, Selena. Give yourself a break, and Shep." Adamantly I refused. Slowly we made our way back up the blacktop path where we passed the abnormal quiet of the house. We continued on up the mountainside. Tyler didn't try to stop me.

"Selena, before the pain becomes blinding you need to stop them so you can recuperate. This way he will be able to practice more effectively. Your tears and sleeping all the time is hindering him."

"I will try." To our surprise, Tommy was standing at the entrance. Gesturing for us to enter, Tyler followed reluctantly.

"I knew you would be back. You are bullheaded and this time that is a good thing. Shep is going to need all the encouragement you can give him, but remember what Tyler just said."

Drew appeared and walked towards us. Tyler jumped to his feet to leave as Tommy offered for him to stay and support me. "I can't. It hurts too much just sensing what is happening. I couldn't bear to watch it. Sorry..." Drew patted his back as he crossed paths with Sarah and Shep. Sarah took her position as Drew touched all the cornerstones of the sparring area. Then it began again.

Shep was hit several times by small surges of energy, and these snaps hurt more than any cut. At one point I let out a scream accidentally and lost consciousness. When I looked up, Shep was on his knees. I had totally distracted him. Tommy gave in and helped me to walk to Shep's side. I fell to my knees apologizing for distracting him. When Tommy started to interject he jumped like he had been shocked with electricity. Shep quickly rose to his feet and grabbed my face.

Drew began grinning with amusement at Tommy's shocked expression. The sun was high and outlining his beautifully chiseled face. Softly I insisted for Shep to try again. We spent the next half hour with no success.

Somehow I would have to hide my weakness. *"Drew."* He looked over from the entrance and I knew he could hear me. *"I need you to help me back to the cabin. I don't want Shep to know I need help. Can you?"* He nodded stiffly. Sarah looked defeated as she leaned against the wooden rail. Shep shook his head with disgust as he gritted his teeth.

"She thought she knew me well enough to be able to draw this natural instinct out faster. But I have tried and I can't find it." Swiftly I pressed my fingers to his lips to shush him. "You will figure it out." It about broke my heart to see her hug him so tight. Drew approached and pulled me up. When I sensed Shep was about to look, I pushed all hands away from me in order to be able to stand on my own.

"Goodnight, I love you both." Sarah drew his attention back to her, but peeked as Drew grabbed my arms when my legs gave out. Drew hastily carried me to the cabin, placing light kisses on the top of my head all the way.

That night, I had so many nightmares that Shep insisted I sleep with Sarah in their bed. From the look of things, this would be a permanent change in quarters. I felt bad that Shep slept in a chair in our room.

The next couple days and nights went the same way to the point that the pain had become excruciating. I didn't know how much more I could handle. We had to practice in shorter intervals due to my tolerance level, but Shep was finally making some improvements. Before we began our practice, I called Heather. Fortunately I was only able to get her voicemail. This was a lucky break because she would be able to tell something was wrong by my voice.

As I walked up to the quad, I was hoping Drew would take over the sparring because Sarah's emotions were close to the breaking point. She didn't like hurting us, and I felt sorry for her. Once at the quad I went and stood close to the edge, only to realize we were much higher than I thought. The other cliffs were flat tops on most of the mountains. We had to be out west, for I remembered a place in the Badlands that looked like this.

It was absolutely beautiful until a downpour of rain hit. Quickly stepping back I went to my tent to lie down. As I laid there I continued to enjoy the breeze as it whipped across my body. Hopefully today Shep would gain complete control of guarding me, because if he didn't soon, summer break would be over. Even though he had time coming from the clinic, he couldn't stay much longer.

According to Shep we would not be able to return home until he had mastered this skill for both our sakes. It was obvious that Alexander—or any enemy—could use this against us. Why not kill two birds with one stone? It became painfully obvious we couldn't be without protection until he had control. As I sensed someone approaching, I realized it was Tommy. When he entered the quad he smiled his big smile and asked if I was ready for more pain. Immediately I moaned before admitting that I wasn't sure how much more I could handle. I felt like a jerk for admitting this to him, but he understood. He sat down and tried to convince me that I was doing an outstanding job as a daughter. This made me feel better, yet I had caused Shep to have bruises and cuts all over.

Tommy registered my thoughts. "Selena, this is the only way Shep can learn this type of guarding. If he had the child naturally with Sarah, the instinct would seem to manifest without encouragement. But when a child is adopted, the instinct is much like an ability and must be taught in this barbaric way. For that I am sorry." He winced as he muttered that there had been improvement but not enough. I watched as Tommy slowly turned his back on me and reminded me this was Shep's worse fear from way before I had ever come into his life. Tommy looked to the entrance as I turned over on my stomach, not wanting to acknowledge another day of sporadic pain.

When I felt Shep near, I quickly sat up next to Tommy and pasted on my smile, covering my fear of the pain with the beauty of the day. Shep started to pull off his shirt. That was when Sarah announced that Drew was taking her place today. He looked grim. "You know I didn't want to do this. Nonetheless, Sarah is tired and she is weakening in her determination for you to learn. I will not. Selena has been through enough, and you need to gain control today Shep." Drew's determined face and speech caught us both off guard. "I am not going to take it easy on you. Selena, I apologize in advance but it is for the best. I think you better lay back. This is going to be rough."

I know fear crossed my mind, but I quickly did as I was instructed. Before I knew it, I felt a searing pain with the first blow. They continued to bounce between human form and Shadow forms, fighting like there was no tomorrow. Drew got in a horrible double kick to Shep and I had to moan with tears sliding down my face. The next thing I heard was a huge bang and Tommy yelling for Shep to stand down. It was obvious that Shep had been pressed to his limit, for Tommy didn't cease in his order to desist. A second later I heard Shep running to the tent. He looked in horrible shape. Quickly he cradled me in his arms and said we were done for the day. He couldn't control his abilities.

Shep was angry—angrier than I had ever seen him. I began to feel hot spikes jabbing into my head with each breath I took. Suddenly Shep realized his anger was hurting me worse than any blow had, and I felt his mind calm, allowing the pain to cease. Being able to feel nothing was wonderful. Shep grasped what had just happened and asked if I could feel anything. Weakly I shook my head. He started whispering to me how he thought he understood what to do.

Shep began walking quickly away with me back to the cabin as Drew followed closely on our heels, stating that Shep would have to refine his new skill. Sarah ran ahead opening the doors, and when he set me down on the bed, I felt totally at peace for the first time in a long time. I hadn't realized I hadn't felt this good in a while. Shep continued smiling and I could tell he was excited. He truly felt he had learned the skill, but I wasn't sure he could do it when fighting yet. Our little group was filled with hope.

The next day Drew and Shep squared off, remaining in human form. I could see Shep take a blow and I didn't feel anything. They changed into Shadow form, and I still didn't feel anything. Tommy told them both to stand down excitedly. By this point I couldn't help but run out to hug Shep. We both were laughing. We were so excited, nothing could ruin our celebration. Drew began clapping Shep on the back as Tommy looked totally relieved, but where was Sarah? Hastily I looked over at the gate and found her weeping. It didn't even take a second for Shep to lead me to her. She threw herself into his arms in a pure fit of sobs. Suddenly I felt awkward. I started back towards Drew and Tommy but was quickly absorbed into their hug.

During our final week we continued to work on guarding, not allowing forms to change, and by the end, Shep's instinct to guard me. He never messed up. In fact, he no longer had any cuts and his bruises were healing. We also spent our time working on our sensing, trying to distinguish when there was danger, because everybody was jumping us at anytime whether day or night. Sometimes they would get a real treat when we retaliated. It turned out to be a lot of fun. Still, I was tired and wished to go home. I had become very close to my family and the others who had been training me, but I missed just being us.

The last night at the cabin, Shep and I went for a hike together. When we reached the gorge, I could tell Shep had something he needed to say but wasn't sure how to. It was rare for Shep to be so unsure of himself. "Selena, I have a friend who is helping keep watch over you now. I trust him and I need you to trust him, too. Do you remember the man in the mist?"

Nodding that I did, he continued. "If you are ever in need of assistance or are in danger that I can't help with, I want you to do whatever he says. I need to be clear on that point. He was a friend of the family and I trust him with my life. He will always let me know whenever he has helped you. He doesn't like for people to see him so you must not try to learn his identity. It will be safer for you. Can you do this?"

"Of course I can." A smile of relief crossed his face as he patted my hand.

# CHAPTER 11.
# RETURNING HOME

**Grateful** to finally be home, I started to track back to my room. Before I knew it, Shep was at my side. He grabbed my arm as he pulled me behind him protectively. Sarah moved in front of me too. Ever since our training to seal our family bond, I felt like we had truly grown.

I hadn't sensed any presence, but now with both of them acting like there was danger, I froze. If someone was here I would be able to surprise them with my abilities to protect myself and others. Out of instinct I began to guard my thoughts. This instinct had become second nature over the past couple weeks, making life a lot easier for all of us, especially Tyler. Shep faded into his Shadow form and entered my room while Sarah stayed poised protectively in front of me. When my door sprang open, he came out carrying a package with Heather's style stamped all over it. We all grinned in relief as Shep allowed me to enter my room. He threw the package at me with a snort.

I found a small letter written from her that she had gone to her nana's for a couple days and would be back before the weekend so we could have time together before school started. The thought of having to go back to school made me cringe. I wasn't ready for that. I hadn't really had a break this summer with all my training, and I deserved one.

Upon opening the present I found a Snoopy shirt from Michigan Adventure. This was one of my favorite cartoon characters, along with Scooby Doo. Shep threw my stuff into my room, causing Sarah and I to jump. Sarah rolled her eyes as I told her she would get used to him being annoying. We all laughed and then Shep burst out he had something he needed to show me.

Rapidly we walked out the back door, only to be greeted by a beautiful sight. The sun was setting, and the most beautiful hues of red and purple were announcing its end. We proceeded to our pine trees at the back of our yard. Once there we climbed over the fence and continued on into the forest. Shep was acting awfully strange, making me wonder what this great mystery could be. I had grown accustomed to them surprising me with new information every day, but why were they both acting so nervous this time?

When we came to a stop I saw a mound surrounded by seven trees. Complete amazement ran through my whole body as I recognized the makings of a portal. This portal had been in my backyard all this time and I didn't even know it. Boy, how dumb could I be. This must have been how Tyler and Billy had come so many times before. This meant there were two portals near us.

"You remember how to open it, correct?" Shaking my head yes, I started to repeat the phrasing I had learned to open and close a portal. I felt very pleased with myself as I watch the portal work its beauty. Once it was open, Sarah took my hand and walked me to the entrance. I could tell she was very emphatic that I remember to follow their directions very closely.

"If any danger should happen, you come to the entrance and say "agape," which means love eternal." I was excited with this turn of events.

"Alright, are we going to do this for real?" I was hoping we would. Nevertheless, I could tell the answer was a "no."

"No. When you enter the portal you will be taken to a safe place, and if you knew now where that is, your thoughts could be compromised, making the safety unusable. We know you want to visit your homeland, but things are safer here, understand?" Sarah stated emphatically.

Slowly I turned around and repeated the phrase to close the portal. The sunset was practically gone now, and Sarah and Shep seemed to be cuddling. It was definitely time for me to get lost. Hastily I walked back to the house as they began to make lovie-dovie sounds. I wondered if this was what Mike was talking about with his parents.

Climbing back over the fence seemed too easy, so I tried to vault it, which was stupid. I had forgotten there was a small incline on the other side. Luckily I landed and jogged down to a stop. I had to admit that my physical abilities were becoming well-coordinated.

Without realizing it, I had shut my eyes for a brief moment and checked the area ahead of me like Tommy had taught. Just the thought of that man made me smile. He would be proud of me.

Once inside the house I shut the back door, knowing Shep and Sarah would not be along soon. Quickly I made a beeline to the front of the house in order to peek out the window to see if the house next to us was still up for sale. To my surprise it had been sold, but it still looked vacant. I hoped the new neighbors weren't nosy. Before we left there were three houses on our block for sale this summer, and houses in this economy weren't selling well. Going into the kitchen I was able to scrounge up some chips and a pop from the cooler. I would have to do the grocery shopping tomorrow.

How were we going to explain Sarah to everybody? We couldn't tell them they have been married forever. Oh, I couldn't wait to see Shep wiggle his way out of this one. I smiled to myself as I went back to my room and closed the door before unpacking. As I looked out the window I could only see a reddish-purple line left on the horizon, and I knew that meant tomorrow would be a good day according to folklore. These days folklore meant more to me than anything. With one last glance back at my clothes, I knew I didn't want to deal with them tonight and threw them into the corner. Sleep won out.

When I woke the next morning I was surprised to smell eggs being cooked. In the kitchen Sarah was in a purple silk gown looking absolutely at peace with the world. It truly seemed like she belonged with us. How had Shep handled not finding her every morning in his bed?

"We heard what you were thinking, and you're right—Cassidy is going to be on my back until she gets every bit of information out of me about Sarah. So we are going to stick to the truth, mainly," Shep stated with a huge grin.

"Okay. This is going to be good. Let's see…you and Sarah met how many centuries ago?"

"Not that truth, but when we were with your parents back in Indiana. They can know we lived together for a while. Her job dictated she had to move. Due to the circumstances things didn't work out for us at that time, but now we are sure things can be managed. She knew your parents and was there when you were born. She came back when the accident happened, but her job was so precarious she was unable to commit to a life with a child and husband in another state. We kept in touch and had decided to meet over vacation to see if we could pick up the pieces of our relationship. Not to mention if you would be able to accept her as a part of our life here. She now has a partnership in the company and she feels secure in being able to fulfill her responsibilities as well as being a part of the family. Of course she will have to take business trips from time to time. Still, we know we can no longer put our lives on hold. She doesn't want any children and feels very comfortable with you being our only daughter. If they ask how you feel about her, you can answer truthfully."

"I love Sarah. You know that." It made me giggle to think how she filled the void of a companion to him. My face was going to break if I kept smiling like this all the time. Now it was clear why he was never interested in anyone; he already had everything he wanted in Sarah. Boy, wouldn't that blow people's minds to think some stay together for centuries. Hmmm…I never did find out how long they had been married or how old they were.

"Anyway, Sarah and I get along great and I am looking forward to being able to have boy talks with her." Sarah and I both giggled at that as Shep's head drooped.

Then to my amusement, Sarah chimed in with her two cents. "Shep, we are going to go clothes shopping and while we are out we will pick up some groceries." This would give us some time to bond the way women like to bond—shopping and food.

Twenty minutes later I was ready and waiting on them to get into the car. When we entered the garage I was surprised to see a sporty red Trans Am sitting there. "Is this yours, Sarah?" Sarah followed the plane of the front of the car with her fingers, caressing it like a lover. Her eyes were bright with excitement as she continued to look fondly at her vehicle.

"Of course. This has always been my favorite style of car. I like fast and something classy. Shep's friends have to think that I am well-off to believe the story. The rest of my belongings will arrive later tonight. Besides, how was I supposed to meet you guys on your trip? Just magically appear there? Now you have a little more for your story." She smirked sarcastically. She really does have class, and I love how she fits so easily into our family. It is almost like I have known her all my life. I guess I had.

When we pulled in to Shep's clinic, sure enough Cassidy and a couple others were just walking in as we entered. Shep parked and proceeded over to us as Sarah rolled down her window. He wanted to know when to expect us for lunch. Sarah stated we would pick him up at noon. She wanted to go check out the lay of land and get the groceries before she and I had fun. He laughed and leaned down to kiss her. I thought Cassidy was going to faint. I waved to them as Sarah pulled back out to the road.

"Slow down, I want to watch!" Sarah muffled a soft laugh as I turned to watch Shep walk to the doors and give Cassidy a "so what" look. "Oh, she is going to kill him."

As we entered the city limits of our small town, one could see the hills rising behind the stores with the powder light blue sky hanging behind them. I loved the sky here in Michigan. It always felt like you were closer to heaven than anywhere else in the world. Well, I don't know about the world, but when you travel down south the sky did look to be further away. Today the clouds even looked like cotton balls floating by.

Sarah nudged me, wanting to know what I was thinking. I told her I felt the beauty here was awesome even if we were a small community. It wasn't like we were some big city. When you go further into the U.P. some areas aren't even developed.

"Your mother loved this area, too. Both your parents enjoyed the natural beauty of this state. I think that's why Shep brought you here to live. Years before you were born your parents lived close to this county. They knew these hills and waterways like the back of their hands. Hiking was second nature to both of them. They did do work in this area too. There had been a catastrophic fire and it was the largest in Michigan's history somewhere near Port Hope, I think. Anyway, Michigan was in the lumber and shipping business during that age. You do know your parents worked with many volunteer groups in disaster situations, and their abilities helped many to survive. In fact, that was how they met."

Amusement lit in Sarah's eyes, almost like she was watching some event. I liked how she had been sharing stories about them as a couple. It truly did make them seem real to me. Hearing their stories gave me new insight into some of my own personality.

I hadn't been paying attention and found we were almost to Cox's. Sarah commented that our little town was exactly that—little. Where were we going to do clothes shopping? My giggles escaped me as I explained to her we had few stores including Wal-Mart and Kmart. She couldn't believe we survived here.

Once inside the grocery we both were grabbing things and putting them into the cart. It seemed we both knew what was needed and would have to make sure we didn't duplicate. Many people were looking hard at Sarah, wondering who she was. When you live in a small town a stranger is always news, even to the youngest of us. Unfortunately I had a slight problem keeping their minds at bay, so Sarah kept encouraging me to relax and block them. At times, if someone was distraught, it sounded like they had a megaphone blasting at me. Sarah, sensing my distress, helped me to relax and reminded me their voices would eventually sound like background noise.

"Before long you won't even notice." After ten minutes I was able to guard my mind, except every once in a while someone would break out of the background and I would have to start over. By the time we made it over to the curio section, I stood with the cart watching the ladies whispering amongst themselves. I loved eavesdropping on their conversation. I was pretty sure they were interested in Shep, and it would be interesting to hear what they thought of Sarah. It wasn't much of a surprise to find out I was right.

***

Jeremy Baker was a bag boy at Cox's and helped us out to Sarah's car with the groceries. He was totally impressed as we walked back to her sporty car. He looked it over and wanted to know if Shep had bought it. "No it is Shep's girlfriend's car." He looked dumbfounded at me. He couldn't believe Shep had a girlfriend, let alone that she would be living with us for the duration of Shep's life.

Sarah tipped him, which was not always common for the bag boys. It was obvious she had tipped him big as he looked at the money and then excitedly waved to her. Sarah hinted that she thought he liked me. I rolled my eyes as I told her we had been friends since pre-K, and I would never think of him in that way, not even if he was the last man on earth. Sarah threw her head back and laughed as she stated that someday some guy was going to walk into my life and I was going to fall head over heels for him.

Sarah drove back to the house with no problem while discussing all we had learned from our curio ladies. They had been totally amusing. Mike was in his drive practicing basketball with his brother. They both looked to us with a great amount of amusement and curiosity as we drove past. Sarah blushed as her eyes darted to the outside. "I am going to be the gossip around town for a long time."

Once inside, we realized we did not have much time to put everything away, so we threw all the cold stuff in the fridge and left the rest on the table. Sarah rushed to pull us out of the garage and spun out down the road, causing everyone to notice. I was sure she had done that on purpose. Going towards the end of our subdivision, we spotted a moving truck turning in. It must be some new neighbors. The driver seemed to stare a hole through us. I figured he must be appreciating Sarah's taste in cars as much as everyone else was. Our last neighbor had been a yard freak. He mowed two or three times a week, putting chemicals on it to make it greener. He didn't care what it was actually doing to the earth. He was making it dependent on drugs in a way.

We returned to the vet's office. Sarah held such elegance as she walked into the lion's den. They were none too happy he had never told them about her. Cassidy pulled me aside and wanted to know if I had known anything before our trip. "No," I answered honestly. "Sarah and I are becoming great friends." When Shep came out, Sarah greeted him with a kiss, and his dark cheeks actually blushed as he embraced her tightly. Lunch with Shep was short since he had to catch up on some of his paperwork that the state required.

As we drove back to town, we picked up paper products for school and other things I would need. It was close to three p.m. when we decided to head home. The sky was still clear and a lake breeze was blowing. This was one thing I loved to feel on humid days. When we turned onto our street I saw Tyler standing out in the drive next to my house, talking to Mike. Wait, that was not supposed to be happening. What was Tyler doing here, and out in the open, no less?

Sarah told me to calm down because obviously Billy and his family would be our new neighbors. They also had a surprise for me before Heather would get home. Once we pulled into our drive we went in to put away what was left of the groceries and my school supplies. Then Sarah led me out to our neighbor's house under the pretense of introducing ourselves. Mike was back at his house with Kirt and Laura, playing basketball with Andy.

Anxiously I risked a glance toward Mike's drive and found Laura looking impatiently my way. After making our way up to the door, Sarah rang the doorbell. It was obvious Tyler had been waiting on the other side since the door opened before the first bell finished ringing. He reached out, greeting us as Billy and Betty did the same. Tyler looked overly excited and made me wonder if my surprise was inside.

"Okay, now we're inside what is going on?" I begged. "What is this surprise? You all are making me anxious."

Billy took my hand and guided me into the living room where I could see another couple sitting in chairs facing away from me. Who were they? "Selena, I want you to meet your grandparents, Clark and Eloise Martin. They have waited a long time to see you. Granddad here was driving the moving truck earlier. He almost had an accident trying to get a closer look at you when we passed."

As they rose up out of the chairs, they turned around and I could definitely see my father in both of them. The family blue eyes and the gentle smile were present in every Martin I had met so far.

Eloise came around first, with tears running down her face as she hugged me. Clark followed and hugged me when she finally released me from our embrace. These two people were my grandparents, and I had wasted time out buying school supplies. There were so many questions I wanted to ask them, but I didn't know where to start. So Billy started answering some of the questions he knew I had.

"Your granddad here has been the one who helped with hiding you. That meant he would not be able to help keep watch over you when you were finally safe. Alexander would be expecting him to lead them to anyone who might have survived. Since he never came near you, Alexander presumed you were dead."

Granddad began speaking as he walked over to the hearth and grabbed at it as if it was there to hold him up. "Alexander and his group kept close tabs on us for a while. I knew if I let any of the family know you were alive we would have a full out war on our hands with Alexander. He did a lot of sneaking around then. I couldn't even tell Eloise her grandchild was alive. This was a secret I couldn't chance thinking about. I tried pouring myself into my work. I did more work in one decade than I had in a century. Everybody thought the work was my way of dealing with my grief. They had no idea it was pure torture driving me.

"I had to stay far away, no slips on my knowledge. It was the hardest thing I have ever done. Hiding the truth is not easy when your emotions are trying to scream everything out for you. Shep was smart by not giving Sarah and me too much information or keeping in contact with us. I knew I had to wait five years, which would be the anniversary of the car accident before I could have any news on you. If I suspected I was still being watched, I would not show up at the meeting place.

"By the fifth anniversary of the accident, Alexander had stopped following us, and I was able to take a peek at you every now and then. Shep and I both knew I couldn't be one of the main protectors. We decided on Billy, here. I am sure you are tired of hearing this, but now that your abilities are active, we have had to involve more individuals in the knowledge of your whereabouts in order to help in teaching and protecting your identity. With Billy's family living here, we will be able to see you occasionally and be involved in your life like we should have if none of this had ever come to pass. This will also make us feel better knowing there will be more of us around.

"Eloise will be able to give you all the cuddling she has grieved about these past ten years. Prepare yourself. That is a lot of years to make up for." He smiled down at my grandmother, but I noticed his white-knuckled hand was clenching the fireplace mantle still. His hands told the real story of how hard it had been for him.

By this time we were all seated around on boxes or on the floor while hanging on his every word. Somehow Laura and Kirt had come into the house unnoticed and were leaning against the door frame next to each other with sadness in their eyes. Going over to my grandfather, I hugged him and found myself being hugged back fiercely. I knew this was exactly what he needed. Like me, he would never be able to hug my dad again, but we would have each other.

Suddenly my phone rang, startling me from my morbid thoughts. I hadn't even realized it was almost four o'clock. I panicked because Heather would be home soon. To my surprise it was Heather informing me she wasn't going to make it home tonight. They were stuck in a traffic jam, and to my relief, I heard Parker say they were going to stay at a hotel. She assured me they would be home in the morning in time for us to have our normal school shopping spree. When I hung up my phone, I noticed Sarah coming back into the room with Shep hanging on her arm. This sight still tickled me. Shep quickly greeted my grandparents and ruffled up my hair as he passed. I smiled back at him as I informed him Heather wasn't going to make it tonight. He acted like he already knew this bit of information. "How do you know? Did you do something to make sure they wouldn't make it tonight?" The only answer I got was a sly "maybe." We all laughed, but I knew I didn't want to leave my grandparents right now, and I was happy I wouldn't have to.

Eloise walked over to me and looked me up and down. Neither one of us knew what to say. Finally she blurted out that she could see Analease in my face a little, and she could tell Shep had been a good father for me. I knew she was probably looking for my dad's looks.

"You have your father's smile and his tenderness. I can already tell. I will be here a while and will enjoy hearing and seeing you for the next couple of months. You probably don't remember any of the time with your parents. Someday I would like to share my memories of them with you and answer the many questions I know you have. In the meantime, you and I can make some memories of our own."

Eloise was definitely the picture of the perfect grandma. She was so sweet. "Most of the grandchildren call me Gramms or Grandma. You can call me whatever you feel comfortable with."

Billy slapped his hands, stating we were losing daylight and still needed to unpack his family. We had already lost some time with our reunion. It was decided the boys would work on the big stuff while the girls would organize each room as we unpacked the boxes. Of course Gramms and Sarah stayed with me while Laura and Betty worked in other rooms. As I looked around I realized I was surrounded by a large group of people who were family. I had never really thought about how my life would have been different if they had been in it always. I imagine my dad would have been a prankster like Shep always said, and my mother always happy but mischievous. I began to feel sentimental as I watched everybody interacting with each other. Shep placed his arm around my shoulder. "So this must be a surprise for you to have family living next door to us. You and I used to be the only family each other had. Now we have an extension to that family."

Everything seemed right with the world as Shep, Sarah, and I walked home for bed. I couldn't wait to see Heather in the morning. Then I would be able to introduce her to my family. Technically, I wouldn't be able to tell her.

I slept well through the night and woke at nine a.m. When I went into the kitchen, I found breakfast waiting. Gratefully I ate while wondering where Sarah and Shep were. You would think they would have left some kind of note. Cautiously I began to sense the area around our home and then further out. It wasn't much of a surprise to find them already at Billy and Betty's helping.

Quickly I rushed through the morning rituals. As soon as I walked out the door my grandparents were beaming at me. I picked up a box and walked into the house to help unpack. This box had Tyler's name on it. Upon reaching his room I bumped into a wall of boxes while trying to squeeze in. "Hey what are you trying to do? Cause an avalanche?" Tyler teased. Gramms was caught by surprise when I growled that he wouldn't be talking right now if I had. Her smirk proved she enjoyed the banter of all her children no matter what they were doing.

"Well, I guess I could slow the avalanche down if you wanted." Tyler's involuntary shiver caught my attention and that of my grandparents. I hadn't realized they both were present until Granddad began to laugh while trying to smother it. Forcefully he pushed into the room, informing Tyler that he could see I was definitely one of his since he was all the time stopping Billy from doing the same thing to my dad.

The sound of a car door slamming jerked my attention to the outside. This could only mean Heather was home. I raced out the front door and peeked around the truck to see her making a beeline to my house. Suddenly Shep appeared at my side, reminding me to be careful of what I said to her. It hadn't taken Heather long to reach our door. She was already there, waiting impatiently for me to answer, which made it easy to sneak up on her. Her squeal of surprise changed to glee when she found me standing behind her. As we hugged she began to bubble on about her vacation while eyeing Sarah suspiciously. Hastily I proceeded to avoid the issue as Shep opened the door for us.

Shep began introducing Sarah to her as she gave me the look like "what's going on." We all could hear her mind automatically begin assessing if Sarah even looked trustworthy. In a rush I took her back to my room to explain. "Sarah is Shep's old girlfriend. She knew my parents. This past vacation we spent with her." For a moment I felt speechless as Heather's mind continued to make comments. "She came home with us to see if we could be a family. Anyway, when we got home we found we had new neighbors. They are great." Heather acted shocked with us already helping absolute strangers move in, let alone having Sarah living with us. My explanation sounded weak.

"Our new neighbors have a lot of kids. I thought I would try to make things easier for them before they had to attend school with us." Heather's long dark curls bounced as she gritted her teeth in a sarcastic smile. "I'll be the judge of that. We don't even know if they are really nice." No one walked into her life easily. Not after what her mother had done to them. For a somber moment I considered all the times other women had tried to enter our lives. There hadn't been any that stuck around, especially since we had Chelsea and Cassidy to back us up.

"Heather, I have a present for you." Clumsily I fumbled through my bag to find the small box that held the special necklace Tyler and Kirt made. Her gasp made me sure it was the perfect item for missing the rest of our summer vacation together.

"Selena, it's beautiful," she said. Absentmindedly I began to rub my head as I felt a new hum enter, and I knew it wasn't Heather. I wasn't sure who it was, especially when I didn't sense anyone near.

"I'm glad you like it. I have one too, see?" I produced the chain from underneath my shirt and I showed her my matching necklace. She pulled hers out of the box as I offered to show her how it would produce rainbows if you caught the sun through the prism. As we glanced to where the rainbows were, I noticed a fleeting shadow that moved in a way it shouldn't. In horror I pushed Heather out the door as Shep and Sarah came walking down the hall. I tried to warn Shep, but nothing seemed to stop him from entering my room. Heather's protests became loud as I continued to push her towards the door.

"Wait! What are you doing?" Once in the backyard I took a calming breath as I tried to come up with an excuse for my odd behavior.

"I thought the sun would be better out here. We should be able to see it real well." Luckily the rainbow was showing brightly against the house.

A minute later Granddad and Betty made noises in their backyard, proving I had support if there was someone around that shouldn't be. To my surprise I heard Billy's voice in the house as he shouted that he needed to borrow a screwdriver if we didn't mind. Heather merely rolled her eyes in disgust as she mouthed he was being rude by just marching into my house without being invited.

I excused myself from Heather and went in to give the lowdown on what I saw. Once back in the house, Sarah rushed out of my room and grabbed my arm, shaking her head. Hastily, we went to the garage and found a screwdriver for our cover. Sarah mumbled I had been right. The shadow was not normal.

Without hesitation I began to drag Heather out to the front. Once there I noticed Tyler, Kirt, and Laura were pulling things out of boxes while Grandma was scouring the neighborhood suspiciously. It was obvious by her stern look that she wasn't about to let anybody hurt her again. Parker was still unloading their luggage as he eyed Sarah up and down. A moment later his own thoughts sounded as suspicious as Heather's had been. Cautiously I looked around the neighborhood, trying to sense if there was danger. At least I did until my eyes fell upon two dark-haired teenagers our age lugging suitcases into the house next to Mike's. With a nudge to Heather, I pointed to the house at an angle to hers that had obviously just sold, too.

She noticed the two teenagers. "Looks like our neighborhood has grown. The school bus is going to be overflowing. I hope they add a second bus or something." Abruptly the front door of the house across the street opened and a tall, slender, olive-tone woman with dark hair called for Matthew and Meg to come in. Evidently she needed help unpacking the last boxes. They obediently started towards the door, but the boy looked back at me. His eyes were abnormally blue, almost as if they were shimmering liquid. Heather poked me in the side and giggled that he must have seen something he liked.

Grandma's arms were crossed in front of her as she watched the new neighbors as well. Nothing was getting past her. My cousins were walking towards us as Shep, Sarah, and Billy came out of the house and looked in the direction of our new neighbors. Unfortunately the lady had already closed the door, not allowing anyone else to see them. Both Shep and Billy nodded towards each other as Billy scurried back over to his house. I wasn't sure what he was up to, but I knew they had decided on something.

Hastily Shep jogged over to our side while greeting Parker with a man hug. "Why don't we send the girls on their shopping trip? Sarah wants to spend some time with them, if you don't mind. I think it would be a good idea." It was obvious what he was playing at. To my surprise, Betty had joined her children as we began introducing the whole motley crew to Heather and her dad. I was surprised to see Heather blush as Tyler shook her hand. I couldn't resist asking if she saw something she liked.

Parker teased Betty about having three kids, so her interjection that she had older boys too shocked him. He grinned at Heather. I knew she and Parker always thought large families were ridiculous.

When I remembered I didn't have my purse I ran back to the house, but was intercepted by Granddad hollering for me instead. Cautiously I walked over to him. I could see he didn't want me to go back into the house. Shep came out of the house with my purse like he already knew what I was going for. I had forgotten my mind was probably screaming at them. Swiftly I closed my eyes as I tried to relax, but was surprised to hear my grandparents advising me not to worry. Granddad tapped my shoulder with his pointer finger and warned me to stay with Sarah. He looked very stern as he emphasized each word. Shep hugged me and pulled me towards the Rendezvous that Sarah was pulling out of the garage.

We all piled inside, and somehow Kirt managed to acquire the front seat while Laura and Tyler were in the very back, leaving Heather and I in the middle. We noticed that our new neighbors across the street had shut all their curtains since entering the house. That was suspicious since most people take all the sun they can get here in Michigan. Once winter hits we rarely see the sun for about eight months. Winter always starts off fun, but after a while all the snow gets me down.

Once we were on the main road, Sarah asked for directions as we pointed her to the state road. The drive would take forty minutes. Heather seemed to be getting along with everybody, which pleased me. My concerns, however, were wearing on my nerves. I wanted to talk to Shep but was uncertain if I could. Then I remembered distance didn't matter unless a portal was involved. So I closed my eyes as I tried to relax enough to reach Shep. Surprisingly I could hear Shep in my mind actually sounding very pleased I had managed to reach him.

"*What's up?*" I asked. The reply was simple: everything was fine but they still had not found who had been in my room.

*"How is that fine?"*

*"We have other Shadows in the area that are still protecting you, so we will have to find out if anyone else has peeked in to make sure you were okay."*

Tyler's mind interjected. "*Don't worry. You'll get wrinkles before you're old. We're on top of it.*"

I still felt suspicious of all those new families who were moving into our neighborhood. "*What about the family across the street?*" They were already aware of them, and for right now they seemed to be what they were supposed to be—a Mortal family. I was glad Tyler had noticed them too.

Sarah announced we had arrived as the car filled with cheers. Unfortunately poor Laura seemed to be getting car sick in the back. Before long we were able to pile out of the car while Heather continued to grill my cousins on where they were from. I had to admit I was impressed with how easily they answered her questions. Hopefully I would do as well as they were when Heather had me by myself.

Upon entering the mall we immediately headed to the clothing store as the boys demanded to go to the gaming ones. Sarah didn't allow us to separate up, so the boys had to endure girly shopping for a while. While browsing I felt the pressure of minds pushing against mine. Thankfully Kirt and Laura came up on either side of me as Tyler distracted Heather from my inability to cope with the pain. It had been hard enough to hear Heather constantly, but with so many I wasn't sure if I could do it. Laura whispered after a while it would be as easy as riding my bike. Kirt touched my shoulder and commented that with a friend like Heather, learning this would be easy. "Her mind never lowers with excitement. She is head over heels for Tyler."

Laura elbowed him for me. I appreciated her camaraderie. Finally I was able to force everything to the back of my mind, but it made me leery of what Monday at school would bring. Laura, sensing my thoughts, encouraged me that they would be there to support me. She reminded me a lot of her mom right now. Sarah, seeing I had things back in check, hollered for us to come on and she would buy everybody a cookie from Mrs. Fields first. None of us were going to turn down a cookie.

Walking to the teen stores with our chocolate rush seemed to make everyone fit together quite well. By the end of the day we all seemed well-stocked in new garments. I had been able to put together two outfits that I could intermix with clothes I already had. Of course Heather, on the other hand, was rebuilding her closet. Laura, Sarah, and I had the fun of trying on things that we would never buy, and it turned out to be a blast.

Tyler and Kirt finally were allowed to go to the gaming store when it was apparent they were done clothes shopping. Since it was very close to where we were, Sarah allowed them to go without her. Heather had been giving us the rundown of her summer. I had forgotten how fast she could talk. This was a common Michigander trait that we both had acquired. When we went to pick up the boys we found they had purchased some new games and were excited to try them out on the new system they had purchased before moving here. I thought it funny how Tyler kept telling Kirt how to work it like Kirt had no idea how to play. Every guy knew how to play most systems nowadays.

As we drew close to the doors I noticed Tyler bending over to tie his shoes. It was obvious to me he had purposely untied it so Kirt could check ahead of us. Kirt stood at the door with that dazed look he gets when he is checking the safety of the darkness around us. This was his special ability that he shared only with his mother. Kirt nodded to Tyler and we proceeded out to the parking lot while continuing to bubble over with the events of the day. Once at the car, we piled in. Sarah didn't ask for directions but we still made it back to the highway with no problem. She had a good memory.

Later, we pulled into my garage in record time. Before getting out, she informed us she had called Shep and had him make fresh brownies for a snack along with some pizzas. She was pretty cool. Bailing from the car we went in and found all of the adults were there, already chowing down. We all showed off our stuff and to our relief, all items were acceptable to the parents. After about an hour and a half, Parker decided to go home. Luckily he had already brought Heather's overnight bag over so we wouldn't have to run to her house for it. We offered for Laura to stay, but Betty insisted there was still too much to do before Monday. Once everyone had said their goodbyes Heather and I finally had the house to ourselves.

Back in my room, I was reminded of Shep at the vet's office. This is how he must have felt. I couldn't tell her the truth, but I wasn't good at keeping anything from her either. Heather's mind continued shouting at me. There was no way to avoid having to tell as much of the truth as I could and convince her of the lie when I had to. I gave the explanation of Shep and Sarah's previous relationship and how Sarah had been around through the accident. Unfortunately this backfired on me, for she assumed Sarah couldn't handle having a child around and that was why she left. When I assured her Sarah wanted a career, it seemed to put

Sarah in a better light. Heather respected that.

We continued on through the night, sneaking out to get more pizza and brownies around midnight. By then my head was splitting and I was beginning to hope Heather would fall asleep so I could nurse the headache she had created with her screaming. Kirt was right. Her mind stays excited all the time. Sarah and Shep were sleeping in each other's arms on the couch in the family room, and it was one of those "aww" moments. Heather giggled before whispering that she was glad for Shep and me.

"Although, Sarah had better not hurt either one of you or she will answer to me." Her voice was so deadpan I couldn't find a bit of doubt in her voice or mind. I appreciated her protection of us, and I could tell even Shep had a hard time not smiling. Minutes later we returned to my room where our conversation took a strange turn, to what I thought of Tyler. Shoot, he was my cousin. That was gross. She looked at me and was gushing on since she was glad to see I wasn't interested in him. Then she turned the conversation over to the boy across the street. To my dismay, my mind did wander to his beautiful blue eyes, but I stopped that thought immediately. No boys for me. It was going to be hard enough to keep this secret from Mike and Heather. Suddenly I felt as if someone was listening. It must be Shep checking on me. It was time to change the subject. "What about Mike?"

Heather rolled her eyes with the usual fashion of droll amusement. "What *about* Mike? We have told you a million times we are more like siblings than anything your wishful thinking can imagine." Okay maybe I was wrong—they were never going to be boyfriend, girlfriend. Heather proceeded to tell me the other house down the street had sold, and the new owners had already moved in a week before I came home. She began updating me on all the new news of a Super Wal-Mart being built in town and all that had happened socially with our friends.

I felt very tired as my mind wondered if Shep realized we had more new neighbors. As I dozed off, I received a punch in my side as Heather asked if I could help her with ideas on how to get Tyler to notice her. "Go to sleep, Heather," I scowled. Then I heard a snicker in my thoughts that woke me completely up. Instantly I made sure to close my mind so no one could hear my thoughts. I tried to return to the comfort I had just a moment ago.

I don't know what time it was when Shep came in, but I know he did. He turned my lights down to the nightlight. Slowly I opened my eyes, just enough to see him peering out my window. As he walked past me he winked, and I knew everything was all right with the world.

Sunday went by quickly. It was seven p.m. before I knew it. Heather had to return home in order to prepare for school tomorrow. As she left I couldn't help to think of what she was about to put poor Tyler through. Oh well, he deserved it.

# CHAPTER 12.
# STARTING SCHOOL

**I woke up** late for the first day of school. In a rush I grabbed my school junk and headed for the bus. A second later Sarah called for me to stop as my hand hit the handle. For some reason she seemed a bit nervous as she rushed into the hall. She almost acted like we had never been apart. "I want you to remember to be vigilant in keeping a check around you. If at any time you feel uncomfortable or in question, you ring out and I will answer. Now relax so you don't give yourself away. Oh, and Billy said to remind you your cousins should be waiting for you at the end of the drive."

I didn't have time for this. "Well, they better already be there because I am late." At once I could feel the surprise that ran through her. Maybe I had been a little sharp.

Her head poked back out from the kitchen with an amused look. "I'd say we already have this routine down, now go." I couldn't help but to smile at how true her underlying statement was. We were already acting like family.

The first day of school always made me tense. Yet this year would be even worse. I had a secret to keep. One little slip and I would endanger everyone that was important to me. This thought didn't settle well with me at all. The burden seemed heavier than I could bear. For now we were to live here like normal and as far as we all knew, we were safe.

With a quick turn of the knob I proceeded out to a beautiful day. Sure enough, Tyler, Kirt, and Laura were waiting in the drive for me while Heather and Mike were already at the bus stop along with our other classmates. There were four new kids walking slowly to the group, and they didn't look happy at all. Our bus was going to be packed to the gills this year. Hopefully they had divided our route up between two buses. I rushed to Heather's side as she let out a scream of excitement at seeing Tyler with me. Of course this made me laugh as her mind took off.

A minute later our school bus showed up with Debbie at the helm. She had been my bus driver since elementary school, and every day she played the same Prince album. Debbie greeted us with her Prince music blaring like always. She was really stuck in the eighties. Kirt, like usual led our party onto the bus since his ability was more of a defensive kind. It just seemed to be the natural progression of things. As I stepped on, I was overwhelmed once again with everyone's minds screaming at me. Laura's hands touched the small of my back and pushed me forward as I stopped on the step. Swiftly I tried to relax but found it almost impossible to do. With so many out-of-control minds—not to mention the close proximity I was to each—nothing I tried was working. I was thankful that Tyler had Heather's attention. I could see the concern on his face.

Finally finding a seat, I leaned back trying to remember how to relax, when the new boy with the jet black hair bumped me back to reality. He was trying to squeeze his legs into the seat behind me. Mike didn't care for his carelessness and growled for him to watch it. Unfortunately Mike's brother Andy shoved him.

"Hey, Selena you don't look good. Are you okay?"

I could barely utter anything aloud. "I just have a headache." This was the truest statement I had made all morning. The thought of going to school was bad enough. Evidently there were too many kids for me to tolerate. Maybe I needed to get off and go home.

Laura and Kirt had managed to sit beside each other, and I could see they were sensing my pure desperation. Laura shook her head slightly to tell me to hold out. It would be a short ride. The question of how I was supposed to manage was repeating over and over in my head. Again I leaned back against the seat as the bus started moving only to make panic my next stop. Suddenly I felt Mike's arm snake around my shoulders, trying to offer me comfort as he muttered I always did let the first week of school get to me.

When our bus hit a huge chuck hole in the road, I decided we no longer had any shocks and I was going to break very soon. I remembered enjoying this usually, but today everything was causing discomfort: the music, the noise of voices in my ears—let alone the noise in my head—were killing me. Again I squeezed my eyes tight and concentrated on my breathing. Still, nothing helped. As we made our final two stops, Tyler put his leg out in the aisle at the last one. I know it was to make sure I didn't run off the bus. Heather may have had him cornered, but he was aware of my mind.

It struck me odd when no one tried to comfort me. I had forgotten we were supposed to avoid communication by telepathy until we were sure of our safety unless we had an emergency.

Within a few minutes we arrived at the school, driving my panic even higher at the massive pouring of bodies from the other buses. I had to get off the bus fast. Maybe I could find some solace outside. As soon as Debbie pulled into our usual spot, I hopped up and was the first to leave. Unfortunately, the new girl with the jet black hair bumped into me and started to speak. Instead of listening I rushed passed her out of pure desperation. I didn't mean to be rude, but I couldn't do this. Not yet.

With a look in every direction I found crowds of teenagers, and the drone in my head was getting worse, not better. With my items clutched tightly to my chest I began to walk towards the nature center, even as Mike hollered a reminder to me that I needed to obtain my schedule since I hadn't been here on registration day. I feigned a wave as the panic built inside of me. I wanted to run. No, I needed to run.

The brick corner of the school finally came into focus as did the smell of wet dirt and vegetation from the nature center. As soon as I passed the corner of the high school I began to jog towards the edge of the trees, dropping everything I had in my arms. Once in the woods I went further in, trying to drown out the oppressive noise. I hadn't realized Kirt and Laura had managed to follow me. I knew my way, but they didn't. I was heading to the creek, which ran through our little sanctuary here. Water always did help comfort me.

Kirt's continued hollers for me to stop didn't register. I couldn't stop. I felt like my head was going to explode. Finally Kirt caught me and grabbed my shoulders. His encouragement to breathe was hard to handle as I struggled to leave the area. Finally Kirt demanded for me to look him in the face, which gave me a brief moment of relief when I saw how concerned he was.

When Kirt saw that I had gained some control, he loosened his grip on my arms, slowly warning me not to move. The only option I had left was to cover my head and ears. Maybe that would help drown out the noise that was left. When I bent over, I heard Kirt ask Laura if maybe this did qualify as an emergency so she could inform the adults.

"Fine…but be short. We don't want to draw any attention from any travelers from our realms. It is enough that we are here and near portals, especially the one behind our house." I shook my head vigorously as I swatted a hand towards her and growled for her to hang on. I just needed a moment in order to gain control. It wasn't like I truly had any other choice. If I couldn't pretend to be normal, everything everyone had sacrificed through the years would be in vain. To my dismay, this thought made everything worse. Not only was I trying to shield my mind from teenage minds, I needed to get a grip on my own situation. There were so many factors in this one loss of control that I felt beaten.

I felt Laura's hand patting my back, while muttering it was hard for her to handle too. I looked over her shoulder and could see a mist behind her. There was a form of a man in it. Who was this person? If it was one of Shep's friends, I usually knew. This was all I needed…to endanger my cousins further. With a quick intake of air I pushed Laura out of the way and began slowing things down. This time I was going to catch whoever was spying on me. Abruptly my senses began to warn that the man in the mist was with another. For one brief moment I lowered my eyes when I realized the other person had disappeared into the swirl of the mist. With a glance to my side, I found the man in the mist standing firmly beside a tree. He seemed to be searching for something…maybe a friend. Shep had said to trust him. When I glanced to the man, I found he had shrunk down beside the same tree. This time he surprised me by signing the "I love you" again just before the mist enveloped him heavily. All of this was done in a matter of seconds. This surprised me enough that I had stopped the slowing effect.

With a sharp turn back to Kirt and Laura, I found them rubbing their shoulders vigorously in effort to warm up. Hastily I apologized, but Kirt wasn't having it.

He knew I had seen something and it made him nervous that he hadn't. "I…uh… saw a mist again, and I thought I saw someone, but I was mistaken." I felt stupid and miserable. "Maybe you should go back to the school or you will be late for first class. I will follow shortly. I just need a moment to gain my control…I hope."

Kirt chuckled loudly. "We aren't worried about school. Tyler is stuck with Heather. He couldn't draw attention to your panic run so he stayed behind."

I began to pace as I tried to assure them I just needed a few minutes to try to prepare my mind for the bombardment of the other people who surrounded us. Finally I convinced them everything would be fine. Besides, I wouldn't be that far away and would only need to holler for help to have them return. Reluctantly, they left me. As I watched them return, I wondered if I would muster up the courage to try again.

When I felt hands on my shoulders, I jumped. Luckily I found myself looking into Tyler's worried eyes. "How are you doing, Selena? Where are Kirt and Laura?"

As I explained, he became disgusted that they had fallen for that gibberish. "If you could, you would run home from here. No! I won't be leaving you. I am not that naïve, Selena."

This statement infuriated me. "You are not helping." All of a sudden we heard a noise in the woods like that of an animal. After all, it was not uncommon in Michigan to have coyotes making their annual dash to the U.P. at this time of year. My breathing quickened as Tyler closed his eyes to concentrate. After a few minutes a wild dog appeared close to us, and I knew Tyler was using his influence with it. With a grin down at me, Tyler informed me the dog was going to circle around us until I was ready to try again. I tried to argue with him to go get his schedule, but of course it fell on deaf ears. Sharply he reminded me to concentrate on keeping the voices in the back of my mind and not let them get out of control. He would wait all day if need be. Then a wicked thought crossed my mind, and he read it before I could say it. Heather. To my surprise Tyler looked dazed.

"I can see how Heather is your best friend. She is loyal and very nice. Give me a break though." His eyes began to twinkle as the crow's feet at the side of his eyes grew. "I am really here doing a job, and I have to keep up appearances after all. Besides, taking care of my little cousin is a lot of hard work," he snorted. Appearances was an excuse, I felt. Maybe he was interested in Heather after all. I wondered if Mortals ever dated or married Guardians or Shadows. Again I leaned back against the tree. I heard the first bell of the day ring as I continued to concentrate. Gradually I began to feel calmer. When I glanced up I expected to find Tyler in front of me. Instead I was surprised when I found him over to the side, petting the wild dog that he had called earlier. I tried to hold the sounds of everyone's minds in quarantine. "Nothing" was his sharp reply, but I knew better than that, and by his face I would say something was upsetting him. Swiftly Tyler sat down and drew my hands into his cold ones. He looked so serious.

"You can do this, Selena. I know you can. After what you and Shep had to deal with in the past weeks I can't see any reason you can't manage this. You have to know it will get better. Trust me, if you can't handle it we'll call home, okay? But for now I want you to relax and remember what you have been taught. Are you ready? We are not too far away now." His voice sounded serious and protective.

As we walked in the main entrance we heard a group of students being released from gym early as we headed to the office. Tyler continued looking over his shoulder nervously, drawing my attention to where he was staring. The new boy with the jet black hair was at the corner, seeming nonchalant as he stared at me with those electric blue eyes. Carefully I tried to study his face a little closer. He seemed familiar somehow. In fact, he reminded me of someone, but who? I wasn't sure. Tyler pushed me forward as he growled for me to focus.

Miss Anne was the school secretary and greeted me with her normal enthusiasm. She was always a sweetheart. "Where have you been?"

Tyler piped up, "She lost an earring outside and I was helping her find it." Rapidly I agreed while asking for my schedule. Miss Anne went to the box that held our schedules and pulled them out. On our way back into the hall, the bell rang for first period to be over. It was now passing time. Instantly I prepared myself for the hustle and bustle of those around me. I stood very still, waiting for the screaming in my head to start. I knew this time I had to control it. Tyler patted my shoulder as I closed my eyes and focused. I was to hold their thoughts in the back of my mind. That was what I had been told to do. Their thoughts were to be background noise only, not surround sound. I had to admit I felt a little giddy as I felt bodies passing by but not knocking me in the slightest.

As soon as I opened my eyes, I was shocked to find Laura was beside me while Kirt and Tyler stood in front like they were shielding me from something. When I peered around them, it wasn't a surprise to find the two kids with jet black hair talking to each other, but looking our way occasionally. They were definitely siblings by the similarity of their eyes and black hair. Yet the girl wasn't tall like her brother. She had a small frame with her hair falling far down her back. She looked so pale in the sun, and yet the light didn't seem to touch the darkness of their hair. There was something odd about that. Kirt and Tyler turned back to me, demanding to know how I was doing. Their questioning drew my attention away from the duo. "Everything is under wraps for now." Again the boy looked directly at me and smiled as Heather and Mike came crashing in on me.

In a rush of excitement I made the excuse I had a hard time with getting my schedule. Mike jerked my schedule from hand and began comparing them loudly. It looked like Mike and I had geometry next and only had two or three minutes to make it to the third floor of the high school. We said our goodbyes and started off towards our class together. When we arrived in class, we found Mr. Cain was our teacher. This was the one math teacher whose voice could put every member of the high school to sleep, including the staff. I had even heard some of the teachers state that if one had trouble sleeping, just have Mr. Cain come over to talk and that would do it.

The bell rang just as the new boy from across the street entered the classroom. He brightened with a huge smile as he took a seat behind me. Right away Mr. Cain started putting us in alphabetical order, which was so kindergarten. I wound up with Mike behind me anyhow. The boy from our neighborhood was seated to the right of me. I found out his name was Matthew Sturley.

It was a long period, and thanks to Mr. Cain's monotone voice, most of the class slept. When the bell rang Matthew introduced himself boldly. Mike did the same but was not as friendly as he usually was. Matthew must have taken the hint and immediately apologized for hitting me on the bus. "It was no big deal," I replied. "I need to head off to biology, though so I won't be late." Mike hesitated before leaving me. In fact I had to encourage him to go on to gym.

Once in biology I found Tyler and Kirt had the same class. They both looked anxious. Without any warning they pointed to a seat next to them. They had saved it for me. This time we had Miss Donnelson. She had been my environmental science teacher last year and was very cool. She wasn't going to treat us like kindergartners as long as the class was well-behaved.

To my cousins' unhappiness, the new girl from our neighborhood came in with her black hair flying gracefully around her face. There was something eerie about her manner. Everybody had taken note of her presence as she sat down, acting as if she hadn't noticed one person. Both Tyler and Kirt stared at her intently. What was up with them? I could tell they didn't trust her, or like her for that matter. I wished I could rib them about not making judgments of others without cause. Abruptly a mind broke through my barrier. I grimaced at the sudden burst of noise and leaned my head against my hand while allowing a slight moan to escape my lips.

Once class was over I found Kirt and Tyler waiting on me anxiously out in the hallway. This time I put my hand up to prevent the barrage of how I was. "I am holding my own. Thank you for your help. Nevertheless, I have to do this alone. You aren't going to be with me all the time. Give me some room, please. We have one more class then lunch." Both scowled but gave in without a word.

Fourth period presented another set of voices, although I managed. The boys met me outside of the cafeteria because they wanted to be sure to eat together. As usual I could hear Heather and our usual crowd being obnoxiously loud, trying to attract our attention as we entered. Without hesitation Kirt and Tyler followed me over as I introduced them to my friends. To my relief Laura was already there with Heather. I volunteered to hold the table as everyone rushed to the lines to gather their food. Heather stayed behind to voice her concern. Fortunately I was able to confess I wasn't feeling well today. At least that was part of the truth. Thankfully she accepted my answer as she offered to pick me up some fries to share. She felt maybe some food might help my ailing disposition.

I laid my head down on the table and could feel it throbbing through my arms. The tabletop felt cool against my hot skin and I was glad school was almost over for the day. Suddenly my thoughts were interrupted by a voice, which could only belong to Matthew. "Mind if I join your table?" With a shrug of my shoulders he sat down. I knew if Kirt or Tyler caught sight of this they wouldn't like it. I wasn't sure what they would do…hopefully nothing. With a troubled expression he inquired if I was all right since I had my head down. This question had been asked too many times today. I could barely confess I had a headache. The white noise in my head was edging up the volume control, and not only did I have a headache, but my stomach had a sick feeling too. It was hard to carry on a conversation, for my concentration wasn't what it should be.

When I inquired about his family, he volunteered that his dad had received a job transfer. Evidently his father was the head of a security alarm company for the area, or something like that. At that moment, Tyler and Kirt dropped their trays on the table quite loudly, almost as if in warning—not to me, but to Matthew. I frowned at both, for they were acting mean.

Rapidly our table became full with the chatter of all of my friends. Heather had been right about the suggestion of eating some fries. It seemed to help my disposition. Matthew's twin sister Meg had joined the table and was sitting with Mike, while Heather was totally blown away by the fact that Tyler and Kirt were twins too. They looked like brothers, but their personalities and hairstyles made them look totally different from each other. Meg commented that being a twin meant you were never lonely. I wasn't sure if that was a slam. What I did know was that my two best friends were definitely not interested in each other like I had always suspected.

It seemed our mysterious bands of new friends were mixing well with the old. The only thing was that both sets of twins seemed to glare at each other when they thought no one was looking. Matthew kept asking questions, and I kept hedging most of them, trying to change the subject back to him. When lunch was over I was grateful. Hedging wasn't in my book of skills yet.

The rest of the day continued to be the same struggle. Still, I managed. When it came time to go home, I knew I wasn't getting back on the bus. I would walk before trying that again. My last class of the day had none of my family or close friends in it, and it would make it easy for me to escape. Glad for this reprieve, I decided that when the bell rang I would head to the environmental science center outside and stay there until the buses had left.

Right on the dot the bell rang, and as I had planned I headed to the gym doors and made a beeline to the woods. I felt a little guilty for ditching everybody, but I really needed some time alone. Boy, I never thought I would want that. After the buses left I would call Shep and have him come get me. He would understand. I pulled my cell phone out on my lap and leaned back against the tree, praying this one was well out of sight of the building and rest of the parking lot.

When I woke up I found Shep sitting beside me and knew I was in trouble. Had I been asleep long? He was not amused, and I didn't know where to begin. "Feel better?" His curt voice caused my nerves to spike.

"Yes, I didn't mean to fall asleep, but I couldn't get back on the bus." Instantly he held his hand up for me to stop, which caused me to hold my breath. Shep never really became mad at me, but then again I really never broke the rules either.

"Listen, I know today was hard on you, but Tyler, Kirt, and Laura were frantic when you didn't get on the bus. Billy and Betty could feel their panic. Luckily Tyler figured you had decided you couldn't handle the bus situation. Lucky for you I was able to trace you here and found you sound asleep. I let everybody know you were alright and that we would be home later. We hadn't thought about who you would be riding with. Teenagers and hormones make Mortals even louder than the norm.

"Selena, you should have involved your cousins in this scheme. You placed yourself in danger. Four of you are stronger than one. This is why your cousins are here going to school. They don't need Mortal education. You know that. If you needed to rest then they could have kept watch while you did so and made arrangements to get you home safely. Next time at least keep the boys with you, okay?" I felt like a total goofball. All I could do was apologize. We stayed a while longer. Not meaning to, I fell asleep again. This time when I woke, Shep was not next to me.

Right away I began scouring the woods, only to find his form a little ways off. Sensing me, he came back and wanted to know if I was up to traveling by shadow. Intrigued, I slowly stood. Carefully Shep walked me further into the forest until we found a pretty dark spot. He had me stand in front of him and warned me that no matter how I felt or what I heard or saw, not to pull away from him. After his instructions, he placed his arms protectively around me as the darkness enveloped us. Even though I couldn't see anything but dark shapes, I could feel I was moving, and moving fast.

As I looked up, I could hear the familiar sounds of machinery and animals. We were at Shep's vet office. "You didn't think I could leave my car at work without anyone in the office noticing, did you? Go get in the car and lay down in the back. I will be out in a minute and we will go home."

When we finally pulled into the garage, we were met by Sarah who looked relieved as she opened my door. She shook her head as she muttered that she would head over to Billy's and let them know I was safely home. Before leaving she kissed my forehead like a worried mother hen as she faded into the darkness that enveloped her. This was becoming a normal sight to me. Once in my room I laid across my soft comforter, thankful to be home. I didn't feel like moving or changing my clothes, for my head felt like a lead balloon.

A little while later, I heard my grandparents talking with Shep. They were suggesting I stay home tomorrow. Granddad sounded upset as he continued to talk. "Tyler and Kirt felt suspicious of the family across the street, especially since none of us have been able to catch a peek at the adults. Shep, the boy and his twin seem too familiar to me. I just can't place from where. We never are able to see the children clearly, which is a sign to me they aren't Mortal, and more than likely than not they are Shadow. In spite of this, our children have been able to see them clearly but are never able to transfer the memories to us. It is beginning to add up."

Shep and Billy both agreed it would take some serious investigating. Somehow I knew the boy was not my enemy, no matter how suspicious they were acting. Maybe they were like us.

Later, I woke to find my grandmother sitting in my room. When she noticed I was awake, she smiled at me as she gently caressed my cheek. "How's your head?"

"It feels heavy. Sorry I scared you today." I felt so guilty about how I had acted. Her eyes were full of compassion as she leaned over and brushed my hair away from my eyes. "It's alright. We all misjudged the day. We won't make the same mistake twice. You don't have to go to school tomorrow. We decided you overexerted yourself today. You're so much like Jared."

It was funny how she looked so adoringly at me. One thing was clear: she loved me without even knowing me. "No, I have to go. It will draw attention if I'm not there, especially if there is anybody watching for me. I can do this. I really can." Briefly I felt petrified with the thought of riding the bus. I could tell Gramms was very aware of my thoughts, too. She patted my shoulder and simply whispered that we would see tomorrow. As I turned towards the door, I found Shep staring at me as my head began to pound again. My only escape was to fall asleep. To be honest, I was grateful for the peace and quiet of my own mind.

When I woke, my grandmother was no longer in my room. With a glance at the clock I was surprised to see that it was morning and I still had time to get ready for school. Promptly I made sure I had my thoughts protected against anyone listening as I dressed quietly. When I ventured to the kitchen, I didn't see or hear anyone in the house. I grabbed some oatmeal and ate it while keeping an eye on the time. I had to make it to my torture chamber.

As I sneaked out the door I could see my cousins and friends already at the bus stop. If I made a mad dash I was sure no one would be able to prevent me from leaving. To my dismay, I was startled by my granddad clearing his throat. He had been waiting at the corner of my house to catch me. His semi-bald head was red from where the sun had been resting as he waited. Unquestionably his smile was soft, with that beautiful twinkle that all of the Martins seem to carry. "You didn't think I would know what you were planning, did you?" Granddad said sourly.

He grinned at me as I shook my head. "You are definitely like your father and mother. Shep said he had a terrible time with your mother trying to sneak out with your father. It had to be passed on to you. We figured you would try this. I will drive you to school instead of taking the bus. The others will meet you there. If you have problems like yesterday, call home on that phone of yours. Someone will be there to get you. I must warn you, though: the boys will be tough on you today after ditching them yesterday. You won't be able to escape them easily again." He chuckled and I watched his mustache twitch with his amusement.

Granddad pulled the car out and headed to the high school without much guidance. He didn't ask for any directions. Therefore I figured he had scouted the area so well he knew where everything was. With a wave goodbye I walked to the main entrance of the school, only to find the pain to be excruciating. I took a moment to stand where I was as I worked on the screaming voices. I succeeded on pulling them into the drone. I figured I would have to get used to the noise. Hopefully nobody had noticed my stillness.

Heather came running over to me and was all excited since I had missed the bus twice now. Tyler and the others waited patiently for me at the doors and were teasing me about being late for everything. Once in the hallway I could feel my heartbeat in my head as we drew closer to the crowds. Rapidly Heather walked ahead to save us a seat in our history class together. A minute later Tyler asked how I was doing, only to have Kirt mimic my response from yesterday. "I have it under wraps," he teased.

Even when I apologized, it became painfully clear how difficult it was going to be in order to make up with them. For the first time in a long time I felt uncomfortable as I shuffled through my locker, trying to figure out my best defense. *"Listen, I should have confided in you guys yesterday, but my head hurt so badly and I was so tired I couldn't think straight. I couldn't even really think at all. Please forgive me and I promise I will let you know when I might do something stupid."* It was apparent that Laura appreciated the apology, but the boys seemed to reserve judgment. I could see I wasn't going to gain any favor with them today.

Thankfully Laura interrupted their glares by reminding us that if we didn't hurry we all were going to miss our first period. I walked towards Mr. Jensen's class with Tyler remaining right at my side. We saw Heather racing towards us, waving. She picked up the pace beside Tyler as I rushed on ahead. I didn't exactly want to be a third wheel. Once in our class I found a seat while Heather dawdled at the door with Tyler, acting as if she was having the time of her life. What happened to getting here in order to save us a seat together? When she finally took her seat at the desk beside me she was beaming from head to toe. I had to admit it was a little odd to see her so enamored with a guy. Tyler waved and swiftly crossed to his classroom across the hall, but his stiffness hadn't changed when he chanced a glare back at me.

Mr. Jensen's buff form seemed to glide to the front of the room. Not only was he my favorite history teacher, but he was good-looking, too, and fresh out of college. This year I would be taking U.S. history with him. What was unusual about him was his heritage. He was originally from England, and I loved listening to his heavy accent, which made it easy to learn. I think every girl loved his classes. However, because I— like my cousins—were also taught history from the other two realms, this would make things a bit difficult in class. The drone in the back of my mind was obvious, but at least I was relaxing a little better today. By the end of period, I prepared myself to grovel before Tyler if I could ever get him alone.

The bell rang, causing the pressure in my temples to skyrocket. Fortunately Heather had to go to her other class, so she couldn't wait around to flirt with Tyler. When I came out of the class, Tyler kept a close eye on my every move. This was not the time to have a conversation, I decided, for I was having a time keeping the drone in quarantine. Still looking back, I started walking towards the stairs and accidentally bumped into somebody.

I could see Tyler stiffen even more and when I jerked my attention around I found Matthew picking up my books. He helped me up carefully as I felt the heat hit my face. I couldn't believe I was blushing so. Without warning, I lost my concentration and everyone seemed to be screaming at me again. This truly was not the time to lose it. Next thing I knew, Tyler was at my side, glaring at Matthew. He jerked my books from him while growling for him to get lost. I was shocked at how mean he sounded. Matthew's retort was just as deadly as he growled for Tyler to chill. In the next moment I found myself closing my eyes in hopes of gaining some of my control back. I tried to restrain the voices that were screaming.

The next thing I knew, Kirt was at my side, pressing me back against the wall. To everyone's surprise a clap of thunder made us all jump as a storm roared to life outside. When I turned back around from gazing out the large window, I found Matthew grudgingly going up the stairs. He took a moment to glare back down at us before continuing on. Again the thunder clapped. This time I heard lightning make contact with a tree or something. Even our school lights flickered from the jolt. Boy, I hadn't seen such a sudden shower in a long time.

When Tyler turned his attention back to me I couldn't believe how red his face was. He truly was angry. Even his Martin blues were filled with his dislike for the new boy. Why was he a mystery? I really didn't feel like he or his sister meant me any harm, or anyone else for that matter.

I struggled with my books until I realized both boys were following me. Tyler moved to my side. *"You haven't figured this out yet.* ***We*** *are family and* ***we*** *take care of each other. You are going to have to learn to accept that."* His eyes were flashing flames and I knew we couldn't have this conversation here.

Rapidly I rushed up the stairs to math as I tried to keep my mind relaxed. Relaxing was the key. After I entered the classroom, Tyler and Kirt headed to their classes. Luckily Mr. Cain wasn't there and class hadn't yet started. Mr. Cain's wife was also a math teacher, and they sometimes talked to one another during passing, so I was lucky today. Hastily I took my assigned seat as Matthew asked if I was all right. "Yes, and thanks for helping me with my books." Mike's face contorted in a funny way and his eyes darted to Matthew as he inquired what had happened. Matthew informed him of my clumsiness, once again drawing a laugh from Mike, who was obviously amused. Mike offered that I had a magnet on me, and it was drawing me to Matthew. Totally embarrassed by his remark, I wanted to kick him in the pants but couldn't.

Matthew then asked me the funniest question: he wanted to know if Tyler and I were boyfriend, girlfriend. I guess my startled reaction and almost shout of "no" made him relax. My reply must have been too quick too, for Matthew began to laugh. Abruptly a lump rose in my throat when I offered that Tyler seemed more interested in my best friend than me. Still, Matthew disagreed vehemently. In the next moment Mr. Cain entered promptly, ending the conversation.

The rest of the period was heaven with everybody sleeping behind their books until the bell rang. As all rushed out trying to catch their friends, I made my way to biology while maintaining the monotony in my head. Seconds later I found myself flanked on both sides by Kirt and Tyler. We arrived in biology without any incidents, and to me this was a good sign, even if I did feel a vein throbbing in my temples. Unluckily I struggled through the period. When class was over I promptly reminded them that I was capable of walking by myself so they could take care of their own needs.

Going on to my art class, things went without any interference from the peanut gallery in my mind, making this my favorite class of the day so far. Sadly, it couldn't last forever. When class was over I waited for the main stream of people to find their way to the lunchroom while I took my time following. As I made my way through the halls, Heather caught up with me and demanded to know if I still was suffering from yesterday's headache. I told her I was fine, but she knew me too well and didn't believe me. Quietly I muttered it was a minor migraine again.

Regrettably, her mind shifted directions to my incident with Matthew. It took me biting my tongue to not say anything before she informed me that everybody was talking about me bumping into Matthew. Her eyes looked devious as she giggled, wanting to know if I was flirting with him. "No, I wasn't looking where I was going, that was all."

I tried to change the subject as I asked how things were going with Tyler. This time she brightened up to a painful point. I had done the wrong thing by changing her focus. Her mind was racing into mine, which made me feel woozy. I began to sway and I felt someone steady me. This time it wasn't Tyler or Kirt grabbing me; it was Matthew. When I offered to the two of them that I had tripped again, neither acted convinced. Heather left, stating she would save us a seat at our usual table. I knew what she was doing. She thought I wanted to be alone with Matthew. Matthew looked at my eyes and commented that he didn't believe I had tripped. His forthrightness caught me off guard.

Instantly I pulled away and I leaned back against the wall. Before long, Tyler and Kirt would be looking for me. Suddenly Matthew interrupted my thoughts by wanting to know if he could help with my books. He began mumbling that he understood what it was like to get bad headaches, especially at school. I allowed him to take my books as I stood there for a moment, wondering why his eyes looked so blue. A person could become totally lost in them.

Matthew was grumbling under his breath that Tyler and Kirt would be looking for me before long, so we needed to move. Matthew seemed concerned, which made me feel certain he would never hurt me. He was so kind. I would have liked for him to hold me. I couldn't believe how he made me feel or why. My head had stopped hurting, and everything was locked in place once again as I continued to be lost in his eyes. Finally Matthew encouraged me to walk to the lunchroom before the boys hunted us both down.

We started walking towards the cafeteria, talking about our math teacher, until my heart stopped beating upon seeing Tyler and Kirt headed towards us. Matthew mumbled that Kirt and Tyler seemed more like older brothers than neighbors. This was exactly what I had been concerned with. Seeing me with Matthew didn't make them happy by any means. Casually Matthew placed his hand on the small of my back as we walked past them. It wasn't much of a surprise when I heard a small growl erupt from both of my cousins as we passed.

As we entered the cafeteria and approached our table, Laura's mouth dropped as Heather whispered something into her ear. Laura's cheeks were tinged red as she looked towards me with embarrassment. Tyler and Kirt followed us in as we all sat down.

It was funny to find that Mike and Meg were talking like yesterday, but even she blushed as she saw her twin sit down next to me. Great, now I was in trouble. Finally I decided to purchase my fries and headed to the line, only to be followed by Matthew. This time Tyler and Kirt remained at the table while staring a hole through me. One thing Laura had been right about was that having a family full of boys was trying. Matthew and I made small talk while in line until the sound of everything around me created the same feeling I had when I was on the bus yesterday. This made it clear that I couldn't stay in this little room. Anxiously I excused myself and darted for the door that led to the outside picnic tables. Matthew continued to follow. It was funny how strong his voice was as he demanded to know if I was sick again.

"You are not all right. I can tell. Let me help you," Matthew mouthed. At least that was what I thought he was saying. Before I knew it, I was walking towards the nature center with Matthew tagging along, matching my fast pace. Finally I was at the edge of the woods and grabbed a tree to help steady myself. My breathing was becoming ragged, and I didn't know what to do. I really needed him to leave, but he wouldn't. My family had been concerned about his family and I would have to stay on guard until it was proven he was not our enemy. What story could I make up to get him to leave? I couldn't guard my own mind right now, let alone block everybody else's.

Unexpectedly I felt the light pressure of Matthew's hand on my shoulder and the voices lightened again. With a startled look at him, I grew suspicious when I saw he had his eyes closed, as if he were concentrating on something. At least the small amount of peace helped me to gain enough control so I could function properly. When I looked back at the door, I saw Tyler and Kirt standing there with their arms folded. This all was making me nervous. Why couldn't they give him a break? With a whisper to Matthew I thanked him, but he looked unconvinced as he glared at my cousins. "The air has done the job. You'd better go back in and eat." When we turned to walk back to the cafeteria, I felt Matthew's hand once again against my back. This felt nice. Nonetheless, I couldn't allow it, not with my cousins looking like they were going to clobber the guy.

With regret I knocked his hand down and told him I decided to stay out since I needed a little space. Matthew grinned as he glanced between me and my cousins before walking back into the cafeteria. He didn't look the least bit intimidated by my cousins as he moved between them. In fact, I wasn't exactly sure there hadn't been an exchange of words. My body became overwhelmed with the pain of today's events, causing me to stumble as my cousins came over to me. "Can you make it to the nurse's office? Lunch is about over," Tyler asked anxiously.

"Sure, no problem." Too bad I wasn't a better liar. They stayed in the woods as I started walking back to the building at a slow pace. The bell rang, causing everyone to rush from the lunchroom. Unfortunately there were a couple of stragglers, which was usual for high school, but to my pleasant surprise Matthew was waiting at the corner. I could tell by his cocky smile that he had planned on catching me.

"I thought you might need somebody to walk you back to the office. Here are your books." He continued to stare at my eyes. I couldn't help but feel close to him. I wouldn't even mind if he held me again. Matthew draped his arm around my waist as he blushed slightly. "You know I know, so let's stop playing." This caught me off guard. "Listen, I happen to be the same as you." At this I played dumb, which was not my strong point. He grinned and begged me not to look at him like I was scared. "I want you to trust me and give me a chance to talk with you privately without your family around. Maybe we could go on a date." Instantly I stopped where we were and turned to face him while resting my hand on his chest to give me support. Again I looked deeply into his eyes and felt dumbfounded.

"Matthew, why do you want to talk to with me by myself, and what do you mean we are the same?"

He acted like he hadn't heard my last statement as he continued on with his own explanation of things. "I know you don't know me real well. Nevertheless, I understand people. It is a rare ability, and I know you understand. We are probably doing the same things. Please, I know you share the same ability as me. You read people pretty accurately. By the way, don't mention this to Meg. She would be mad at me. Although I know I am right. We present no danger to each other, I promise."

We arrived at the nurse's office, and Miss Anne gave Matthew a pass back to class. She felt I had the flu instead of a migraine, since it was very common at the start of every year for a number of students to become ill. As she began to write in my folder, she muttered that I wouldn't be missing anything of importance since this was the first week.

When Shep arrived to sign me out of school, he acted agitated by something. What it was, I wasn't sure. While walking to the car he demanded to know what Matthew had been saying to me on the way to the nurse's office. My mind had remained silent during that time, and he didn't sense any kind of fear from me, so he didn't invade my privacy. Not wanting to tell too much, I asked Shep if we could talk later, because I truly was feeling sick. I figured it was obvious to him that I didn't want to talk, but he gently reminded me that I couldn't keep secrets either.

After we arrived home, I found my head was pulsating from everything I had dealt with. How was I ever going to make it through a day without getting deathly sick? I felt disgusted with myself as I darted to my room and quickly closed the door. The last thing I wanted was to have to talk to anybody. I just needed to rest. Why couldn't things be easier, and why didn't anybody else sense how Matthew cared for me? The sky had darkened as a light rainstorm began. The window felt cool to the touch as I placed my head against the pane. I needed to be able to think clearly about everything that had happened today, and I didn't need anyone else listening in.

How long I stayed there I wasn't sure, but when my knees felt like Jell-O I took a seat on the floor. I continued to watch the small drizzle as I propped myself against the side of my bed. It was interesting how the raindrops would make a stream and run down the window. As I thought about Matthew I still felt like a wreck and what was strange was how he made me feel. I wanted to cuddle up with him right now so I could feel the solace of not having anything to concern myself with.

This time when I looked out the window I found the rain had stopped, but no sun had appeared. The clouds were still gray. There was no noise in the house, which helped me to decide to go outside. I needed to find some place to think without anyone interfering. As I walked to our back fence, I had the feeling I needed to continue on into the woods. I wasn't sure why. Sometimes one's feet have a way of taking a person to a place where they need to be. At least that was what an old wives' tale had said. Sometimes when you really think about those little sayings you could totally understand what they meant. Your feet always did take you to where you needed to go, so why did some act like it was some kind of proverb of great wisdom?

As I proceeded on into the woods I could feel the dampness begin to cling to my clothes. The coolness felt good, even though my body was still hurting and my emotions were a total wreck. After climbing over the fence, I headed towards the portal. I didn't know what had brought me here. Before long my mind began thinking about the past two days. It made me wonder if I would ever manage to keep everybody's mind from attacking my own. Maybe being a mix of Guardian and Shadow was the problem. Maybe I wouldn't be able to ever control the sound completely. Wow, that was a horrible thought. Surely it was just of matter of practicing. Again I thought back to my other problem of Matthew and felt conflicted. I was certain he meant no harm towards me. In fact, he seemed more interested in me in a different way. Matthew had been right when he pointed out how good of a judge of character I was. It was rare when my true feelings were ever wrong, even though my mind wanted to believe the opposite of my intuition, or what some prefer to call your instincts. I definitely trusted him and I wasn't sure if he hadn't helped with the voices somehow. I would even like him if I wasn't concerned about his intentions. Everything was so confusing now. I just wished I was normal. For once I was listening to my own thoughts and no one else's, which was pleasant.

The sound of crunching on the ground under someone's feet drew my immediate attention. To my relief it was only Tyler. It was still raining, and by now I was drenched. Tyler sat down beside me, and with a touch of concern he pressed our hands together as he asked what was I doing all the way out here alone.

"Really, I don't know. I just wanted to be alone and think." I could even hear the frustration in my own voice. This irritated me. I hated to be that transparent to people. "Do you mind if I stay with you?" A small, uncontrollable smile spread across my face at his question. "I wouldn't have it any other way."

We both started apologizing at the same time, causing us both to laugh at the absurdity of our closeness. We knew we had come to an understanding of one another; we just needed to set the ground rules. "Sorry, Selena, if I was hard on you today. See…you are important to me. You're not just a cousin, but more like a sister. Everybody in our family was overjoyed when they found out Jared's daughter was alive." He fell back on his butt with an exaggerated look passing across his face. "They had a celebration in a way. Granddad finally had some color back in his skin and was happy. Then the decisions had to be made about who would help in protecting and teaching you. See, if I mess up at school, then I wouldn't be able to live with myself. You are so strong and smart, but naïve to our world. I need to be able to protect you, and I need to know you trust me to do so." I knew he was bearing his heart to me. I couldn't help but take his hand in my cold one. The rain was coming down lightly as he started shivering.

"Tyler, I know I don't understand everything about our worlds. You have to understand I have never had anyone but Shep to depend on. It is hard for me to trust, but I know I love and trust you. In fact, I have some questions I want to ask... and yet, I'm afraid to. Please don't tell anyone. I really need someone to confide in." After a silent agreement was reached, I asked my first question. "Would you consider it an ability if you are able to understand people really well most of the time, almost like you know them?" His reply didn't surprise me when he said it could be an ability both Shadow and Guardian could possess. He also added that it was a rare gift and one that most believed had not existed. Still, he didn't ask the question I knew he had.

Going on to my next question, I asked if he would trust me enough to let me do something I knew the adults wouldn't. This time I got a response. "What are you going to do?"

"I want to go out with Matthew. I think I could figure out if he is a danger to me." Tyler was aghast. Hastily I reminded him of my ability to slow things and how that would stop Shadows. This was an ability Shadows didn't have. "Plus, I am pretty sure I can read people. At first, I thought I had just been reading people's minds when I first found out about my heritage, but now I am sure it is this rare ability to read people. I know I am not always right..."

Tyler stared at me for a while and started asking his own questions. "So you want me to give you some space at school to get to know him? If I did, would you keep me informed anytime you are alone with him?" Carefully considering this, I knew he had to be thinking about earlier today. "Yes, I will try to keep you totally informed, but I have the feeling, Matthew shares the same ability to read people. He knows we're family."

# CHAPTER 13.
# MATTHEW

**Tyler was** being unbelievably patient with me. My body still ached, and I didn't know where to begin with what Matthew had told me in our brief walk to the nurse's office. Tyler was trying to figure out how Matthew could have known we were family. To me that was obvious. It had to be how we were acting at school, and if Matthew was a Shadow, then he would have heard some of my outburst when everybody was screaming out of control. It wouldn't be a coincidence for my cousins to keep popping up every time I was in trouble. "Tyler, I think he helped the voices to lighten for me. When he touched me, they died down." Tyler shook his head. "You probably had diverted your concentration onto something else."

"You think I like him."

Tyler's expression showed his pure determination. "You do, Selena. I can see that you love his eyes and his dark hair. That is the way falling in love always begins. You have to be attracted to the person first."

"He suggested he and I should go out and be by ourselves so we could talk. I really don't feel like he intends to hurt me."

Tyler leaned back with disgust. "Well, we know that is not going to happen. Selena, if his family is Shadow, then you would be putting yourself in harm's way. We will give you some space at school, but you will not go anywhere with him unless you are on a double date with me, understand?"

After what I had done to him yesterday, I didn't want to tick him off again. I had been wrong and he was right. I was naïve about these other realms. Trusting my instincts was valuable, and I needed to make myself trust his, too. Tyler snickered as I realized he had heard my thoughts.

At that particular moment, my stomach started growling. "When learning to use major abilities, it usually requires a lot of energy. In order to have that energy, you have to eat. Come on, let's get you something from your kitchen. My house barely has food with all of us around. By now you should be starved."

I did feel awkward as we began to walk hand-in-hand back to the house. For some reason I needed his support as we trudged through the forest. When we climbed the fence I could smell Shep's pizza. It smelled wonderful. Rapidly we made our way to the kitchen.

The eating did help my stomach, but not my head. It still felt like I had been smacked a couple hundred times. Truly, this had been one of the most trying days emotionally. Nothing was the same. Our conversation continued on about light matters, which made me wonder when Shep would demand the real conversation he wanted to have.

I preferred to get the challenge over with. Softly I informed Shep that Matthew had wanted to ask me out on a date, and I thought I might go. Then I quickly added how this would help us to decide if his family was a threat. Shep didn't seem too convinced. Why couldn't he understand that I knew Matthew didn't want to harm me? It was just the opposite. I was certain he liked me.

Tyler leaned forward with a goofy grin on his face as his elbows supported him so he could stare at me. I didn't exactly appreciate his smirk. His mind was almost challenging me to figure out how to change Shep's mind. Evidently he didn't think it was possible. I knew I would have to divulge more, but one thing I wanted to keep private was my own attraction to Matthew. I still didn't understand that myself.

"Matthew seems to realize that Tyler, Kirt, and Laura aren't just friends." I couldn't believe it, but Shep actually flung himself from the table. I pleaded with Shep to let Tyler help me deal with this, and if we felt there was anything to tell, we would do so immediately. We continued to talk for some time as Sarah tried to help. Why she had, I wasn't sure, but I appreciated it. For once she was on my side.

Finally by early evening we convinced Shep that I wouldn't be by myself with Matthew, but Tyler could give us space at school to talk. Not liking that he was outnumbered three to one, he begrudgingly gave his consent. My head was still aching. Nonetheless, I was holding my mind back from exposing my private thoughts. Tyler started clearing the table and I assisted, while Shep and Sarah continued discussing how they could monitor me at school to ensure my safety from every possible point of vulnerability. Boy, tomorrow would be another agonizing day.

At this thought I was informed that I would not be attending school, and there would be no negotiating on that point. This time I didn't really mind their authority. What shocked them even more was when I voluntarily went to bed at eight o'clock. The sun was still out, so I closed the blinds in my room and fell on top of my covers, not caring to change. Carefully I looked around my room, half expecting to see Matthew appear from some dark corner. His looks kept running through my mind and made me want to kick myself for allowing this. I had never been infatuated by any guy, so why now when nothing in my life was easy? I tried to clear my thoughts so I could keep control by sensing around the house. Cautiously I enlarged the circumference of my sensing exercise to outside my house. I sensed Heather fantasizing about Tyler. I sure hoped Tyler wasn't intruding on her privacy. I cringed at how embarrassed she would be if he was. I was going to have to make sure he was giving her privacy. It had become clear to me that he was more interested in her than he wanted to admit, even to himself. He was as confused as I was. As my sensing reached further, I could sense Meggan reading a book, and Matthew was thinking about…

It was then that I realized I had intruded into a stranger's home. Instantly I pulled back and sat up. One rule of telepathy was to not intrude on others, and this was one of those times. It was hard to divert my thoughts from the glimpse I had of Matthew, and yet I had to. Gradually my mind began to tire and turned to the fact that I wouldn't be going to school tomorrow to deal with anything that had been giving me problems recently. That was a blessing.

Sometime during my thoughts I had fallen blissfully asleep and everything became quiet. When I woke in the morning, I didn't hear anyone in the house. Eyeing my clock, I was astonished I had slept past ten. The night had been soundless. I crossed the hall to the bathroom, and I was surprised to find Sarah sitting quietly in her bed reading. Immediately she looked to me in question. "I'm fine, but my head is sore."

She felt this was to be expected and returned her attention to her book. To me this was interesting to see a scantily-clothed woman in my dad's bed. Definitely not something I ever expected. This was still going to take some adjustment, even if I did love her.

I headed to the kitchen, only to pass the family room, and noticed my grandparents drinking coffee while reading different sections of the newspaper. It was obvious they were here to keep an eye on me too. My home was brimming over with people these days. After saying good morning, they followed me into the kitchen where Sarah was now microwaving some water for my oatmeal. It hadn't taken her and Betty long to learn that oatmeal with peaches 'n cream was my favorite breakfast, for it was quick and filling. Being mischievous, Granddad broke the silence. "We wanted to make sure one young lady didn't try to sneak out again." Immediately I pretended to be appalled at his suggestion. They all began to snicker. I guess it was obvious I was a poor actor.

Throughout the day, Grandma proceeded to tell me stories about my dad as I sat there enjoying her memories of him. It seemed to do them good to talk about him. At one point I offered to share my father's journals with them, explaining how I had recently just read them. They seemed to appreciate the offer, but declined. They wanted to remember him through their own eyes. For a brief moment I could feel a bit of sadness drift from them, but Granddad clutched Gramms' hands, almost as if trying to comfort her.

This all made me feel uncomfortable, so I excused myself. Since I had the whole day ahead of me, I wondered what I was allowed to do since so many were keeping tabs on me. Finally I decided to take my book and go for a walk in the woods, in order to relax without being under everybody's observation. This way I would be free to have some fun of my own. Not to mention, I could de-stress by doing some activities I enjoyed. When I hollered out my intentions, I received an okay, but with the understanding to use telepathy if I needed assistance with anything. Hastily I headed straight to the fence and climbed over. Tommy would be proud with the way I checked ahead before even leaving the house. I sensed no cognitive presence ahead and proceeded on with my book in hand.

Luckily the sunshine was warm, while not being overwhelming with its brightness. When I found the portal where Tyler and I had sat the night before, I sat down. This place was becoming a true sanctuary for me. Lately I felt the need to be here. It was almost like I was being drawn; the temptation was great. In many ways I wanted to explore these other realms. My imagination had a way of conjuring up magical lands far beyond anything we had here. Yet with all of that excitement, a good dose of fear made its presence well-known, always helping me to obey. The trees around this portal were young—so young that I bet Shep had created this one after we moved in. I wondered if that was possible. I imagined the trees weaving their branches around until it made the beautiful door. Another thing to consider was that the earth had to have natural characteristics to create a portal. To my surprise, I sensed someone approaching, and it wasn't a member of the family.

Abruptly his voice softly broke the silence. "Hi, don't be afraid." The sound of his voice made the blood rush through my body. I wasn't scared, but I should have been. With a quick glance, Matthew stepped out from the shadow of the trees, grinning. He looked pleased. "I guess we both are playing hooky today. Mind if I sit?" Without hesitation he took a seat across from me. Nervously he picked up some of the ground debris and tossed it in the air in front of me. I wondered why he had done that. Could he know I could slow things down and wanted to tempt me to show off my ability? That was not going to happen. I didn't trust him yet, not completely. We looked awkwardly at each other, and he finally broke the uncomfortable silence.

"I figured you wouldn't be at school today. You were too sick to go back. So I thought this might be a good chance for us to get to know each other. Meg helped me out. She figured you and I would never be alone with your family always hovering around. She's a pretty good sister." This wouldn't have happened this soon if he hadn't been so daring. "Meg wasn't going to miss school today. She likes that guy, Mike. He is interesting to her, maybe too much. He is a pretty normal guy to me, but to each his own, I guess. So why are you sitting out here?"

Carefully I considered my answer. With a flutter of my hand, I looked around at the forest that sheltered us. "I like the peace of the woods, and reading is my favorite pastime…outside of hiking." Matthew surprised me by picking up my book. He shook it playfully at me. "You weren't reading when I found you."

"Well, the headache from yesterday was pretty bad and I didn't want it to return…" I couldn't believe I was stuttering while trying not to stare at his beautiful eyes. I could tell by the way he was playing with the ground that he didn't believe me. So I decided to turn the tables on him and ask what he had against poor Mike. He grinned at my question. I could tell his answer was going to be an interesting one.

"Alright, he is into sports, but Meg is only into basketball. He is a prankster and a showoff, but overall a nice guy, maybe too cocky for my liking. But…I get a kick out of his fear of things, particularly the dark." He continued to look at the ground as he told his story. "The other day when we were at school, the lights went off and he became angry, almost panicked if you ask me. I know it was to hide his fear. They came back on a few minutes later, and he started teasing another boy about being frightened." Knowing Mike, that sounded about right, but I didn't remember any major electrical problems the other day. When that thought crossed my mind, Matthew looked directly at me.

"Selena, answer me honestly. Are you and Tyler a thing, or is there something else that none of us know? I have to admit the twins are always around you. They don't let anybody have a chance with you." I liked where this was heading. He wanted a chance with me. I phrased my answer carefully. "We have been friends for a long time, and they are just protective of me, like Mike."

He realized what I had done and scooted closer. "Alright, we can play games all day or talk about your book, or we could answer one question honestly with each other." Matthew's challenge made my heart skip a beat. Again I caught myself staring at his beautiful eyes. There was one question I wanted to ask him so badly: are you from another realm? But I knew then that he would be able to ask me any question, and I would have to answer honestly, too.

"I choose to talk about my book." This disappointed him, I could tell, but he wasn't volunteering the truth either. We both reached for my book at the same time, causing his hand to brush mine. My face flushed and I relinquished it to him immediately.

We discussed the part of my book where Hawkins sneaked back onto the ship and fought the pirates, resulting in him being pinned to the mast with a knife in his shoulder. That was my favorite part. He agreed. Then added he would earn my trust over time, and one day we would ask each other the question we both wanted the answer to.

Once again I found us both staring deeply into each other's eyes. It was then that I knew beyond a shadow of a doubt that he would never harm me. Matthew looked to his wristwatch and tapped the glass as he muttered it was about time for the bus to arrive. I could tell he was reluctant, but he stood to leave. "My mom will be home soon. I shouldn't be out here." We had been having so much fun just talking. I hadn't realized how much time had passed. I wished we could talk a bit longer. Nevertheless, we didn't want to get into trouble. As I stood, I bumped into him again. Could I really be doing it on purpose like Tyler suggested? Softly he chuckled at my embarrassment as I tried to apologize. He didn't want to leave either. Gradually I began to walk back to the house, only to remember my promise to Tyler. I would have to admit this to him. Otherwise my guilt would betray me through my telepathy. I hadn't done it on purpose.

Once back in the house, I found nobody inside. Thankful for that, I waited to hear the bus pull up, knowing Heather would be calling to check on me. Sure enough the phone rang, and it was Heather. She was all excited about Tyler and how they had walked through the halls together, and had even sat alone at lunch. She also noted he had become edgy after lunch and thought maybe he was coming down with the flu, too. When I explained to her that I didn't know when I would be returning to school, she instantly volunteered that they had already procured my homework for me. She had given Tyler the job of bringing my homework over today. Like usual, she had choir rehearsal tonight and would have to rush off. When we hung up I knew I would be receiving a visit from Tyler very soon, which made me uptight.

I waited for the knock on the door as Sarah walked into the room, looking a bit anxious. "I have to go out for a while, but Shep and I will be back at six. You don't have to worry about fixing anything. We will bring something home." That was strange. When I had entered the house I thought it was empty. I must have been wrong with my sensing, or maybe she had just appeared to check on me. Things weren't exactly clear with how shadowing actually worked.

That was when the dreaded knock on the door came. I found Tyler with my books in hand. Hesitantly I invited him in, while taking my books into the kitchen. My throat went dry as I tried to force my confession out. Nothing was coming easily to my mind. "Tyler, I told you I would be totally honest with you." His stony silence was making things harder. Nervously I glanced at him as I began explaining how I had been at the portal, and Matthew had been there, too. Still looking at Tyler for some response, I asked what he thought. Finally he spoke, but I could tell he was almost gritting his teeth together as he did.

"I figured he might try something like this today, but I didn't feel anything out of the ordinary. I even had Kirt scanning things out. He said everything was fine. We knew since Matthew wasn't at school he might try to get you alone. How long were you with him by yourself?" I wanted to make sure I didn't lie. "For a short time after lunch hour. I didn't give anything away when we were speaking." Tyler frowned.

"I'm sure you have been careful, but next time you should leave if it happens again." Next time…next time I thought I would like to talk longer. Tyler punched my arm, which brought me back to reality really fast.

"Stop that, he could be the danger we are watching for. On the other hand, you could be right, too. If you still feel he is not our enemy, I will try to trust your judgment…for now. Although you must continue to keep me informed and try not to be alone with him." A few minutes later Betty called Tyler home for dinner and offered for me to join them. As delicately as possible I declined. Sarah had been clear that they would bring something, and besides, I needed some time alone to think.

When Tyler left, I realized I had the whole house to myself. I might as well make the most of my solitude. After walking through the house, I found myself in the backyard. The sun was starting to go down and it still felt pretty warm. Carefully I created a small breeze to cool myself by. The breeze was very small and felt good blowing across my skin.

While I was enjoying this, my mind wandered to my parents and to this new family that surrounded me. Since I had grown up with only knowing Shep as my dad, I wondered if my parents would be unhappy with me feeling happy with my life. To be honest with myself, I felt guilty about everything—from surviving to being happy.

"No, I know Jared would have been thrilled with that thought, Selena." Somehow my grandfather had found his way into our backyard without causing any major disturbance.

"I thought you all were having dinner." His swift nod proved I was correct.

"I ran across your thoughts when the breeze picked up. You realize if the family across the street is of the Shadow Realm they will recognize this is not a natural phenomenon." His small reprimand brought my attention to my lapse in judgment. I needed to be careful. I wouldn't be the only one in danger if I did draw attention. Little by little I began to dissipate the soft breeze. Granddad waved a dismissive hand as he muttered to leave it. As I sat down beside him, I felt a bit sentimental as I looked at him. He was my grandfather, and he needed me to see him this way. He loved me.

"So what has you so deep in thought, little one? Are you having a hard time adjusting, or is another ability trying to break free?" He genuinely was concerned, and it was evident that he merely wanted to help. He wanted me to confide in him, too. I wondered if I could trust him, or if he would he just blow it out of proportion.

"Sorry, I didn't mean to intrude, but you haven't been shielding your mind from me. I figure you really do want to talk." I did. I explained to him that before I knew anything about the other realms, I felt I was always able to understand people better than most people could.

"I can read their emotions. If they are tense, I know. I know no matter what emotion it is, even if they look like it is nothing, I can feel it. Once I found out we all have the ability of telepathy, I figured I had been reading everybody's mind. Now I know the difference between a thought and what they are feeling. It actually drives me nuts."

As I awaited his answer, I held my breath. "Some say such an ability exists. Eloise fears some of our children have it." At that moment, Granddad turned gray. "Maybe we can test it somehow." His answered ticked me. Why did he seem grieved to discover this ability might truly exist? My concentration became focused on those members of my family next door; not on their thoughts; but the way the air felt around them. What most people didn't realize was that the air around them or their personal space is charged with their emotions, no matter how good of an actor they were. This should prove it. Granddad looked to me with concern as he demanded to know what I was up to.

"Betty is ticked, Billy is concerned, Laura is mad, you are still worried, and you're hiding something which makes you feel guilty." Instantly Granddad backed away while holding his hands up.

"You can stop. I don't need a rundown on my emotional state. Shoot. You and Moses are more than enough to deal with. Give me your phone." There was no request in his voice, only pure demand. "Billy…No, no…she's fine. I need for everyone in the house to state truthfully what their emotional state is right before I called, and I mean the truth." A couple of seconds passed as Billy questioned our family and confirmed that I had been correct. Granddad motioned for me to follow as he headed towards the back fence after handing me my phone. With a note of frustration, he warned me not to think about him hiding anything. He was sure I would understand later. Not knowing why, I agreed—I wouldn't tell anybody. Once over the fence, we climbed into Billy's yard.

Billy said they had set up a test and he wanted me to tell him what I sensed now. Feeling around in my mind, I felt someone was worried. That had to be Grandma. There was confusion, and someone was pretending to be mad but was really happy." This knocked Billy off his feet. Betty had been listening and said Kirt was trying to act mad but wasn't, Grandma was worried of course, but she didn't know if anybody was confused. Tyler piped up that he was the one confused and didn't feel like sharing. Granddad snickered, and I couldn't help but grin since Tyler's confusion was more than likely Heather. Without announcement, Shep came walking through the back door and asked what was going on. He was quickly informed of the discovery of my new ability, or what I thought was an ability. Shep didn't seem surprised and told everyone he had always suspected I was more sensitive than most at understanding people. Defiantly he stated it wasn't an ability, either. It was just an insight. Besides, he didn't feel it could be helpful since I only knew the information at the moment. In spite of everything, Betty thought it was an excellent skill to have, and she was sure it was in relation to a forbidden ability once used in ancient times.

She began to ramble on about an old Zeus legend. Evidently Zeus had ordered for people to not practice mind warfare, which stemmed from what one used to call an emotional gift. Shep huffed that it was all lore, but Betty had peaked my interest. I wanted to understand how mind warfare worked in conjunction with this…skill. It was clear I would have to study on my own or find some private time to question Betty. Shep hustled us towards the back fence, acting grumpy. "Sarah is waiting on us for dinner. Come on."

We had dinner and discussed Shep's day at the office, but when I asked what he and Sarah had done after work, neither one gave a straight answer. Instead I was told not to inquire about their activities over the next several days, for what they were dealing with was very sensitive and about more than just our safety. By the looks that they kept giving to one another, I could tell something was truly bothering them, and they felt protective.

Not wanting them to question me about my afternoon, I grabbed my schoolwork and started working on it. It didn't take long for me to finish. For English 10 I had to write an essay on what I did over the summer. Teasingly, I wrote what I had really done, and then I wrote the fake one that I would turn in. Shep appreciated my sense of humor in the first one I handed him, but stated clearly I was to use the second and burn the first one out in our small fire pit immediately.

The rest of the night we did our usual things as the sun descended below the horizon. Sunsets were always beautiful to me. I truly did love the deep purples and reds that announced the ending of a day. The overwhelming feeling of being watched consumed me. Hastily I looked across the street to see Matthew looking out his second story bedroom window, too. I was sure he was staring right at me. Not feeling the least bit scared, I smiled. My mind had had time to relax today, and I didn't feel any pressure or pain from anything. I felt totally at peace with the world. Shyly, my mind began to taunt me. Maybe I did find Matthew attractive. Still, I couldn't allow myself to think about him. My life was too complicated to involve another person.

The curtains fell back into place as my somber mood took seed. Quietly I prepared for bed as my feelings deepened. How could I continue on normally if I couldn't even be truthful with those I cared for? I called into the study and asked if I was going to go to school tomorrow. This drew everyone's attention. Shep poked his head out of the study as Sarah entered the hallway, each questioning me on how I felt. "I feel better. My head may be sore, but it is barely noticeable. I could try." They all agreed that I should be allowed to attend, the biggest stipulation being I would not be riding the bus.

The next morning I did exactly as we had planned the night before. Billy took me and the others to school by car and dropped us off ten minutes early so no one on the bus would see how we arrived. At first when I looked at the school building, I felt overwhelmed. Things weren't going well here for me, and I wasn't sure if I would ever get this telepathy thing under control. With a pat to my back, Kirt reminded me that I was not alone. His whisper was soft. I was able to keep the few minds at bay that were already there. I grew more and more anxious as we waited for the first busload to enter the building. Tyler and Kirt stood behind me as Laura and I talked about taking a trip to the beach this weekend. The buses started arriving, but before the doors even opened, I could feel the pressure of everybody's mind flowing against mine.

Laura questioned how I was doing as I opened my eyes to give her a weak smile. “It does seem a little better today,” I lied. Tyler knew better. “You need acting lessons.” We turned to enter the building and head to our lockers while Tyler waited at the entrance for Heather.

We dropped off our books, and we all headed to our separate classes. Tyler and Heather lingered at the door to our history class, and I was happy to see things going so well for them. They would be a cute couple. As people started piling into the room, my head began swimming, but I was still in control. This was a good sign that I was doing better today.

First period was a struggle, and yet I made it without a hiccup. The first person I met in the hallway afterwards was Kirt. He had to have rushed to meet me at the door. His concern was clear. “How’d it go?” My response of having it “under wraps” actually drew a chuckle. “You’re getting better. Still, you need work on the delivery.” Mike dropped into stride beside me as we went up to geometry.

Matthew was already in the classroom, and I was grateful to see Mr. Cain busy at the chalkboard. Matthew said hi shyly as I sat down. “Glad to see you are feeling better…are you sure you should be here so soon after having the flu?” I couldn’t resist asking him the same. Mike knew he had missed something. Luckily he didn’t have a chance to ask since class was called to order. Suddenly I felt a stabbing pain in my temple as one of the girls in front of me became upset. She was practically in tears over her boyfriend. She felt he was giving another girl too much attention. With her mind yelling, it was giving me a serious run for my money to keep everything as background noise.

When the bell rang, Matthew’s sister was at the door, and I watched as Mike seemed overjoyed at her appearance. He immediately skipped asking Matthew and me about our comments before class to run to her side. Matthew asked if he could walk me to my next class. “So how is your head this morning?” I hated to admit that I was still having some trouble, but I was fine. Then he reminded me he knew better because he could read people, too. When we had finally reached the door to biology, I felt Matthew become angry. It became obvious why when I saw who he was staring at. Tyler and Kirt didn’t seem the least bit affected by my realization since their heated stares looked deadly. It almost looked like they wanted to hurt him. Matthew excused himself, stating he would see me at lunch as he added a pat to my back. I was sure that infuriated my cousins even more.

When lunch came, I once again found Matthew at the door of my classroom, waiting for me. He looked very satisfied as he winked at me. We walked slowly towards the lunchroom. It was pleasant, even if he did ask if we had to sit at our usual table. It was obvious he wanted to be alone and had even suggested sitting outside in the commons area where it might not be so crowded. For a moment I considered the option, but my promise to Tyler came back to bite me.

As we entered the lunchroom, it was buzzing with excitement and my head started throbbing, causing me to panic. To my surprise, Matthew’s hands steadied me as he called for Laura. Immediately Laura rushed to aid me. She frowned at Matthew as she inquired what was wrong. He didn't reply, but Laura knew the look in my eyes and started pushing me towards the nearest exit with Matthew's help.

Once we were in the courtyard, things calmed down in my mind thankfully. It was funny to hear Laura order Matthew to go ahead and have lunch while she took care of me. A moment later, Kirt appeared at our side, looking nervous as he bit his lips like I did. When he knelt down in front of me I realized Matthew was still standing beside us. Kirt cleared his throat and muttered his thanks, but he was firm in pointing out that he was no longer needed. Matthew took the hint and left as he reminded me he would be inside if I needed him.

As soon as the door closed behind Matthew, Kirt suggested we call home. Laura, however, was insistent to give me a chance to find control. Firmly Laura ordered Kirt to retrieve their lunches, suggesting we eat outside where there weren't so many others to deal with. Once he returned, Tyler and Heather had joined him. The rest of our lunch period was peaceful compared to the enclosed building. Matthew never returned. I wished in a way I could just ask him if he was a Shadow employed by Alexander. I knew I would be able to tell if he was telling the truth. To my surprise, Mike never came out either. I figured he wasn't willing to leave Meggan. Lunch was about over as Heather grumbled that she had to go to her locker early so she could pick up a book she had forgotten. Hopefully Tyler realized she had forgotten it on purpose in order to be alone with him for a few minutes.

The lunch bell rang, and it was time for the last half of the day. If I continued on the way the morning had gone, I would finally make it through one whole day in school.

Fifth and sixth period came and went. By the end my head was in severe pain, but I had made it. I felt rather proud of myself. Going to the locker, I didn't know what to do. We hadn't discussed how we would be getting home if I made it. Tyler and Heather were wandering down the hall, and there was no sign of Kirt or Laura.

As Mike was walking by with Meggan, he asked if I would be riding the bus home. Reluctantly I explained that I had to stay after for makeup work. Mike and Meggan chatted on for a bit longer on the school policies, and how I needed to get over these migraines or I would find myself in the same boat as Andy. Mike even suggested I go to the clinic where Andy had gone last year for pneumonia. He had confidence that they could help. Then I noticed Meggan acting a bit demure as she commented on how everybody seemed to be getting sick this first week of school. Finally they left for the bus, with still no sign of Kirt or Laura. Knowing the buses were leaving any minute, I wandered to the front office section to see if I could find them. To my relief, they were waiting at the front steps. "Shep is going to pick us up." We discussed how I had made it through the day, but it still had been a struggle, especially when the girl from math was having a breakdown over her boyfriend. When I commented on Tyler being missing, they both laughed hysterically as Laura struggled to inform me that he had ridden home on the bus with Heather. This brought up my number one question: "Do you think Tyler really likes Heather?" They both rolled their eyes and doubled over as they snorted out that there was no doubt. Minutes passed before Shep pulled up in his car.

The ride home was enjoyable since everyone around me was in control of their minds. I never had realized how valuable it was not to hear things constantly.

Once home, Kirt and Laura went to do their chores and homework while I decided to rest. Shep had to return to work where Sarah was going to join him later. Again they reminded me that they would be back at six. I waved goodbye to him and decided to see if Heather wanted to go for a walk on the lighthouse trail.

It was a surprise to walk over to Heather's house to find her doing homework with Tyler in the backyard. Parker wouldn't allow her to have anybody in the house but me or Mike if he wasn't home. Not wanting to intrude, I told them I would go see if Mike wanted to go for walk. I figured Mike was probably with Meggan, so I decided skipping his house and going it alone.

At a leisurely pace I headed towards the end of the cul-de-sac to the planked sidewalk. The sky was clear, and today there was a breeze blowing that I hadn't created. Before long I came to the sand hills where I had slowed things down for the first time. It seemed like it had been a long time ago. Carefully looking around, I sort of half expected Shep to appear out of the shadows, but he didn't.

With one last check of the time, I calculated how long it would take to be sure I was home by six. I hadn't seen the lighthouse in a long time, and I did love to look out over the horizon and see ships floating past. I walked on down the path and made it to the lighthouse in record time. All the exercising I had been doing in the past couple of months was paying off. Slowly I made my way out onto the beach to sit while watching a barge float by. It didn't seem to be moving at all. Quickly checking the time, I was disappointed to see I barely had enough time to make it back by six.

When I turned to go back to the planks, I found Matthew leaning against the lighthouse watching me. Startled by his presence, I walked slowly towards him and asked how long he had been there. He admitted it had been a while, but he didn't want to interrupt my enjoyment of the peace and quiet. Awkwardly I stepped up onto the planks and removed my shoe to get the sand out. I almost fell over. My balance was still off from trying to control all the noise in my head. It hit me like a ton of bricks. That was exactly why I was stumbling so much. It was affecting my balance like an inner ear infection does. Matthew continued to hold my hand while I shook the sand out of my shoe and slipped it back on. Slowly he released me as I turned around to sit on the edge to remove my other shoe. He sat down beside me as he gingerly lifted up my foot and began to brush it gently of all of the sand. At first he acted hesitant, but he swiftly lost his inhibitions with helping me.

"So how did you get away with walking all the way out here by yourself?" Matthew asked coyly as his eyes twinkled like the sun had hit them.

"I do it all the time. I like hiking." He gazed back out at the barge and I watched him grin as the wind blew his dark bangs back from his face.

"I figured you did. But still, how did you get away from your bodyguards?" This sounded right, and I couldn't think of what to say. He bounced into my shoulder, snorting as he caught my expression. "How is your headache? At lunchtime you looked like you weren't going to make it again today."

"I almost didn't, but being outside helped a lot. Thanks for calling Laura over." He smiled and told me being outside is what he liked best, and he figured he would make points by calling one of my family members over. With this point I couldn't help but ask him why he kept calling them family. To my shock, he wanted to know if we were to the point of asking questions and answering truthfully. I cringed at this thought and began to stutter. "Don't people always try to ask each other questions when they are trying to learn more about one another? I mean it is only natural when you…" An awkward silence swept between us. Finally remembering I needed to leave in order to make it home in time, I stood up. We walked together in silence for a while. "Selena, is that what we are doing? Trying to learn more about each other, I mean would you like to get to know me…I mean for real?" I held my breath, wishing time would stand still, only to accidentally start a slowdown. While grabbing my sides, I quickly stopped it from happening. Shoot, I hope no one caught that. Matthew seemed to shiver, but he continued to stare at me seriously. I knew I couldn't lie when answering his question. This was too important.

"I wouldn't mind learning more about you, but there is a lot going on in my life. Besides, I'm a pretty boring person."

He snorted at my answer while taking my hand. "I doubt there is anything boring about you." We both laughed and started walking again. As we continued down the path, I spotted Billy and the entire clan minus Betty, Laura and Grandma walking toward us. Oh brother, what now? Billy had to have felt the slowdown.

Softly groaning to myself, Matthew leaned over. "I enjoyed our walk. We should do it again sometime." Rapidly I agreed as my family continued to walk closer and the tension began to beam. Matthew's swift wink made me smile. "Don't you love having such close family?" Again I didn't know how to respond. He grinned at me as he excused himself till tomorrow. Quickly he passed my family, but he seemed to intentionally knock Tyler.

Billy asked me what was I doing out here by myself with that boy. It was a struggle not to seem angry. "I have been taking walks out here since I was little. I am perfectly fine." Then the question happened that I didn't want to hear.

"Well, if you were fine, why did you start to slow things down?" Billy was practically yelling between his gritted teeth. The blood rushed to my cheeks as I tried to explain that it was an accident. I didn't know what to say. This was partially the truth. I definitely was not going to tell him the reason. At that moment, I wished I was normal and didn't have to worry about anything. Not wanting to get on anyone's bad side, I settled down to explain.

"I had wanted to clear my mind by taking a walk. I met Matthew on my way home and we were just talking. It was nothing dangerous. I would know."

Billy started going on about responsibility and as he did, I was getting madder and madder. Shep and I had always worked well with each other, and I couldn't believe Billy was yelling at me. For some reason my head was beginning to throb and I needed something to lean against. My eyes dimmed and I noticed Billy turn pale as I leaned against the tree. What was he so concerned about? I wasn't yelling back like I wanted to.

Then it happened. I felt everything go black and I was moving fast. But moving fast where? I felt frightened and tried to grab something to stop. I abruptly did and found myself flat on my face in the middle of the woods. I didn't know where I was. I heaved, but luckily I had nothing in my stomach. When I rolled over I tried to breathe normally, only to feel completely terrified as I started crying. For the first time in my life I was angry, scared, and totally out of control. The wind picked up and I could hear the trees creak as I laid there. After pulling myself into a seated position, I tried to get up but was too dizzy to do so. That was when I felt a hand rubbing my back.

"Are you alright?" Matthew's voice sounded shaky. "Yeah, I'm…" I couldn't really answer. Matthew didn't ask any questions. Instead he helped me up. The trees started sounding with raindrops and I couldn't stop crying, no matter how hard I tried. Somehow I had traveled through the shadows. I must have done it myself. Matthew continued to help me walk, and we quickly found the plank path. I thanked him, trying to assure him I was all right. He just looked at me, and then back down the path to where my family was probably in hysterics by now.

We started to head out of the woods when I spied Shep walking towards me. Not asking what happened, he came over and lifted my chin to look into his eyes. I knew he had felt what had happened and didn't know what to do about Matthew. "Thanks for helping her back, er…" Shep looked puzzled at Matthew and I watched him squint to look closer at him.

"Matthew, sir. I would help her with anything," Matthew stated quite frankly.

"I'm…sure…you would, Matthew. What is your last name?"

"Sturley, sir." Shep's sharp intake of air took me by surprise. Hastily Matthew left without another word, leaving Shep to stare after him. Unfortunately I felt extremely nauseous. I was going to vomit again. Shep picked me up and took me back into the woods where we faded into the darkness, winding up inside my home somehow.

"Billy had pushed you into using the ability to move through shadows. I was wondering when that would happen again. I am glad to see you can. It wasn't the perfect situation, but I am glad it happened. Matthew seems to be a nice kid. Did he see you travel?"

"No, I don't think so. I was far enough off the path he wouldn't have seen. What happened to me?"

"You became mad, from what I felt, and you were very conflicted. I think you wanted to get away, and you did. I can't wait to find out how you looked when you shadowed." Shep was totally overjoyed with my new experience, but I wasn't.

"You're not mad at me?"

"No, should I be? The way I see it, we haven't set down the new rules well enough yet. You and I have been on our own for a long time and now we have to deal with more than ourselves. We are going to have to remember to involve Billy in our everyday decision-making until we are certain you're safe. It is for your own good, but I know something Billy doesn't, and I think he needs to know now." As I looked at Shep with questioning eyes, I already knew the answer to my question.

"I will know when the time is right," I chimed. Shep nicked my chin as he nodded in agreement.

"Yes, and I promise—one day I will tell you." Sarah faded into the room with a huge smile pasted on her face. I bet Billy wasn't smiling.

Shep instructed Sarah to turn on every light possible so I wouldn't accidentally travel by shadow easily. Suddenly the front door burst, open only to reveal Tyler rushing in.

"Good grief, Selena, how did you do that?" At least Tyler was happy I could travel by shadow. I was still reserving judgment on that myself. The front door opened again, and this time Granddad and Billy entered. Shep stepped in front of me like he was trying to defend me.

"Billy, your dad and I have something we need to discuss with you out by the portal." At this point Shep ushered him to the back door, with Granddad following closely behind. Granddad didn't look happy at all.

Once they left, I wasn't sure what to think or do. Tyler sat there for a long time and started asking me questions about Matthew. At least I knew he was guarding our conversation as I explained most of what had happened, leaving out my personal attraction to Matthew. If I knew Tyler, he already knew that part anyhow. Sarah left the room, and I had no idea where she went. When I headed towards the kitchen, Tyler suggested he should make sure there was no place for me to disappear into. We both laughed but knew he was right.

Shep, Billy, and Granddad returned a bit later, finding Tyler and I drinking some hot cocoa. "Looks like you two need something to eat," Shep stated. Tyler agreed wholeheartedly. Then I noticed Billy was paler than ever and had to look as bad as I did. Billy excused himself and shook Shep's hand with an unusual vigor, and I wondered what had happened out there.

"Billy, I really am trying. I will try not to break the rules anymore. Please know I didn't mean to hurt you."

Billy came over to me with tears in his eyes this time, and gave me a huge hug. Gently kissing my forehead he left without saying a word.

"What's up with him?" Tyler asked with concern.

"Nothing," Granddad replied dryly while slapping Tyler on the back. "He'll be fine."

# CHAPTER 14.
# FRIENDSHIP

**When I woke** the next morning, I was hoping to return to school without a fuss. I needed to do this without everybody complicating my life. I understood my own body was against me, but it was time to fight for the right to be normal. Most kids try to get out of school, and here I was trying to go. I really was screwed up.

"Watch your language," Shep hollered in to me. What was he doing home?

"I thought you had to work, today." I found Shep shaking his head as I entered the kitchen. "I decided I would be late so I could drive you in personally. We haven't had a lot of time alone lately." I was shocked he was allowing me to go to school. This is exactly why I loved Shep. Since he was my dad, we always understood each other, even when at odds.

"I'm glad you see things that way, but here's the rub: not only do you have to deal with telepathy today, you have to be aware you could escape easily and can't allow anything to happen. If you don't think you can resist the urge, call and I will come for you. Besides, we will need to teach you how to control shadowing. We wouldn't want you to wind up on some island." I had never thought about that possibility.

Rapidly I gathered up my belongings and grabbed a cake roll with some milk before heading out to the car. When Shep opened the garage door I was surprised to find my cousins walking in. They had uncanny timing. It helped to be telepathic. A second later Laura came over and gave me a big hug before she climbed into the car. Kirt crawled into the car quietly. "How did you wind up with that Matthew character anyhow?" he asked.

With exasperation I repeated my story for the tenth time since last night. Finally Kirt had to push the limit. "Selena, I want to know why you slowed the area down too…is it because you like the jerk?" He was lucky I was nowhere near him because I wanted to beat him. Shep called us to order and reminded Kirt not to push my buttons before I had started the school day. I froze. I had to control my emotions.

Once we arrived at school I could see the sky was cloudy, and that wouldn't help with my particular shadowing problem if it rained. I winked at Tyler when I saw he was escorting Heather to our class. He was definitely not doing that for my benefit. When he left, Heather started asking my opinion on how I thought things were going with her "conquest" as she called him. When I told her he really liked her, she began to bubble over with her excitement.

Then, with a sly smile on her face, she demanded to know how I was doing with Matthew. At that instant my mind jerked with hesitation. Anything I told her Tyler would know, so I played around, saying he was nice and maybe I could become interested in him some day. Satisfied with my answer, she looked at me incredulously. "I know you like him. Stop trying to fool me. I have known you since I was little and you know you can't fool me. Or maybe you are trying to convince yourself." Then she stunned me with her insightfulness. Carefully she stared at me. "Why don't you trust him?"

"No! He didn't do anything yet. I..." Heather slapped her notebook shut bringing my excuse to an abrupt end.

"Then give him a chance. You both like each other. Listen, I have been thinking about this a lot, and we are not my mom. When we fall in love we can make sure it is the right thing before we commit or have a kid." It was obvious Heather's mind was thinking back on her mom's abandoning them. This always made me feel sorry for her.

"Listen, you weren't Sarah's to start with. You weren't abandoned. Your mom died. Sarah wasn't ready, and I think she is now. Give her a chance, but if she screws up, then we both will deck her and I am sure Chelsea and Cassidy will help us." Avoiding an answer, I looked in my backpack for a pencil until Mr. Jensen called the class to order as the bell sounded.

History went slow, but I wasn't able to concentrate on the lesson anyhow. Instead I kept looking out the window at how cloudy the sky was. I was worried I might accidentally shadow in front of someone, and I didn't want to draw any attention to my weirdness.

The bell rang and I found Matthew waiting for me at the door. Lightly he traced his finger down my arm, sending goose bumps behind its trail. It was then that I felt like somebody was watching me. When I started to turn, Matthew took my hand and politely told me not to look. It was my big brother Tyler watching. Matthew then smirked, saying his touching me had infuriated Tyler.

Mike noticed Matthew holding my hand as we walked into geometry. He leaned forward with a look of sarcasm beginning to crease his face. "You'd better watch out because many of the guys won't like you if you truly are...becoming an item. She and a couple of the other girls have been a paramount goal for too long for someone like you to just walk in and sweep her out from under them."

"Tradeoff is worth it. Trust me, I know what I've found." Matthew's bold statement took me a bit by surprise. Suddenly I realized I had never heard Matthew's thoughts. Questioningly I looked over at him. I couldn't help but stare. This was proof he wasn't of this realm. Why hadn't I noticed it before? I tried to lower my guard a little. I wanted to see if he would acknowledge the fact. It would be hard to maintain everybody's mind in the background, and still I wanted him to hear what I had just realized. Gradually I lowered the guard on my mind as I thought, "*I can't hear your mind.*"

In the next instant he saluted me with his pencil. A feeling of excitement arose in me that almost had me jumping with my elation. Then reality stepped in, cooling the water. I had to make sure I kept this under wraps since in the process of revealing my thoughts I had allowed some voices out of quarantine. Gingerly I rubbed my head while concentrating hard on closing the door to those around me.

Before the end of my next class, Mr. Cain had everybody asleep and I was back in control. After the bell rang I found Matthew at my side as I headed to biology. Out of nowhere, Meg appeared beside us without one sign of rushing. She looked straight ahead as if she was speaking to the air. "Do you want me to get rid of my brother for you?"

Matthew gave her a slight push. "No thank you, I enjoy his company. Truthfully I would like to spend more time with him than I am allowed." A small smirk twisted the side of her mouth but was caught before it became a full-fledged grin.

"Mike and Heather are planning to go to the beach tomorrow. Are you planning to join?"

Of course I was. This was a tradition I hadn't missed since I was allowed to attend. "I always come as do most of the kids in the area." I stopped at the door to tell Matthew goodbye. It wasn't much of a surprise when Kirt pushed in between of us pretty hard.

The thunder with lightning outside finally broke into a huge storm. The raindrops on the window were huge and pounding fiercely, drawing everyone's attention to the sudden downpour. I knew Kirt was ticked as I walked to our usual spot and sat down. I hoped maybe he would lighten up, but that wasn't going to happen. "So what are you doing holding hands with that guy? You know…he might just be using you." His vicious warning caught me totally off guard.

"I am going to find out if we really have anything to fear from Matthew and his family…" Before I could finish, the bell rang and class began. *"...And if we don't, you will need to lighten up."*

Fortunately the class went by quickly. Before I left for art, I made sure Tyler was going with Heather to the beach tomorrow. His quirk of a smile assured me he was. "I'm already on board."

Kirt shoved through while griping that we were here to do a job, not to be lovesick puppies. I wondered if he knew there was a rock band with that name. Tyler reminded me not to worry about Kirt, for he was suffering from protective brother syndrome, too.

Fourth period passed swiftly, announcing it was time for lunch. When I went outside, our whole table seemed to be filled with our usual guests, including Mike. He began teasing me about having a boyfriend as we approached.

"You don't have much to say. Look at who you are with." Matthew gestured towards his sister, Meggan. Mike's face flushed since Matthew had trumped him.

It was nice to see that Mike did like someone. When I sat down, the table cleared, leaving just Mike and me. Our discussion took off as we watched the last of our table go inside to make some purchases.

"Our lives are changing, Selena. Who would have thought our trio would have grown?" Reluctantly, I bumped against his leg playfully. "Here I thought you and Heather would wind up an item."

Unexpectedly Mike looked a bit somber. "I knew no guy here was ever going to win your heart. You grew up with them. To be honest, I didn't think anyone would be able to even get a flutter from your heart…but I was wrong. You like him…Matthew. He seems to be a nice guy. You know, this year there are at least four new ones for you to pick from." I couldn't help but groan at the options he felt were set before me. Softly I muttered I didn't have a boyfriend yet. He bumped me hard. "Sure," he said. With a quick glance back to stare at him, I added firmly that I was exploring my options. He grinned as his long bangs covered his eyes. "No, you may be able to fool yourself but you have already made a decision. No guy has ever held your hand or traced your bare skin before."

Without being able to respond, Tyler and Heather came back and were chattering on about the beach party. Heather was hoping for a bonfire at the beach tomorrow, but we all knew someone would have had to pull the permit long ago for that to even be a probability. Mike jerked his head as he waved a dismissing finger at me. "Dad already pulled the permit. The coast guard will be by around two a.m. to be sure all fires are out in case we miss any."

Matthew sat down beside me. "So, are we having a party tomorrow?" Mike explained that we were nailing down the details. By the time lunch was over, our plans for tomorrow were pretty well made. We all walked to our classes in pairs, separating up as we dropped off one person at a time. It was nice to see all my friends actually finding someone to date. It was a miracle for me to make it through the rest of the day.

Betty picked us up after school and was happy to see I had made it through the day unscathed. As we were driving home, our discussion led to the beach party. Unfortunately Betty wasn't too thrilled with the prospect of us being out there alone, and added that Billy would want supervision. She seemed to think it was a good idea to have some fun so that I might relax a bit more while around others my own age. According to Betty, part of my problem was being penned up inside of a building and not being able to relax.

We arrived home before the bus. "Betty, I want to go sit by the portal and read, if you don't mind." At least I had remembered part of my job was to keep them informed of my whereabouts when either Shep or Sarah wasn't home. Going into the house, I grabbed some Tylenol and proceeded out the back door, going to the spot that was becoming my favorite place to think.

When I arrived the ground was still wet, but I didn't care. Instead my mind was going over the beauty that each of these portals made, and where I might go if I was ever allowed to enter one. I felt a strange need to open it. I figured it was my own curiosity trying to kill the cat, so I refused to allow myself the temptation. This was becoming a real obsession with me. The overwhelming desire to go sometimes took my breath away. I felt there was something important about entering, but turning down the idea, I walked back home.

When I entered the backyard, I heard the bus pull up to our normal spot. Wonder what Heather was up to today? Hastily I made my way to the front door and caught sight of Heather and Tyler strolling to her house like it was the most natural thing in the world. It was clear they were going to do homework together again. My best friend would not want any company this time, not that I could blame her. It would be nice if Matthew were here with me. I continued to watch others tumble out of the overcrowded bus. A second later I spied Mike walking with Meggan, while Maymie Jean and Karen were walking to their house. It seemed like everybody was doing something with somebody else but me. The thought of this made me feel lonely.

Suddenly Matthew stepped off the bus. For some reason he was last. He saluted me in such a corny way I decided I would see if he wanted to do our geometry together. As I opened the front door, I waved to him as he started running up the hill. Upon reaching each other, I invited him into my backyard to work on homework. It was obvious he liked the idea of being invited, not to mention alone with me. We sat down at the picnic table and pulled out our books to do our assignment. It was a surprise to see how quickly we had accomplished our task. It only took fifteen minutes.

"So, are you going to be able to go to the beach tomorrow?" Matthew inquired.

"Of course, why wouldn't I?" Suddenly my thoughts flew back to earlier in the day. I explained how Mike, Heather, and I had a secret clubhouse where we had stashed some beach supplies long ago. This pleased him.

"You never share the place, huh?"

"No, we never have, but I would like to share it with you." Slowly I began to explain all we had done there and what we had established as our clubhouse. He couldn't believe we had been using an old wolf den since we were in elementary. Unfortunately, we heard someone coming in the back gate, and I was surprised to see Meggan. She looked curiously at him, almost as if she was enjoying every minute of his irritation.

"Mom needs you to find those batteries she gave you to put away the other day." He asked her if she couldn't find them for him, but was flat out denied. It was interesting how she tipped up on her toes and almost laughed at his frustration. Swiftly he gathered up his books as he whispered he would see me tomorrow, and walked off in an irritated rush. After he left, Meggan came over and sat down without being invited. She truly was enjoying her brother's misery too much.

Their relationship reminded me a lot of the Muir boys. Carefully she turned around and placed her clutched hands out on the table as she seemed engrossed in my back door.

"So…how long have you known Mike?" Her calmness was eerie; she continued to remind me of Wednesday from the Addams Family.

"I have known him since I was a toddler." She didn't act surprised. In truth, she had figured we had been friends for a long time. Then she began asking me different questions, like what were my favorite subjects, and other junk. I could tell, however, that there was something bothering her, and I wanted her to just ask.

Finally she looked directly at me as she blurted out that she needed to know if I liked her brother. Taken off guard by her bluntness, I didn't know how to answer her. Of course I liked her brother, even though I wasn't sure if I should. She then proceeded to tell me that Mike told her I had never gone out with anyone, and he was surprised I was even interested in Matthew so quickly.

Immediately I tried to change the subject back to her and asked if she liked Mike. She smiled at me and stated firmly she liked him. I liked how she didn't beat around the bush. She looked at me as she reiterated her question. Hesitantly, I confessed I was very interested in him, but only time would tell. I was grateful when she accepted my answer.

We continued to chat for a long time. I found out she preferred to be called Meg. She loved the theater and had joined the drama club. The way she was cool one minute and so reserved the next was unsettling. There would be this small spark of excitement that would dash out of control and then disappear almost as quickly as it had appeared. I knew somewhere beneath this cool demeanor was an excitable teenage girl wanting to burst out.

We seemed to be getting along well until she brought up that Mike had mentioned Shep was actually my legal guardian, and she wanted to know what happened to my parents. My sharp intake of air didn't seem to draw any apology. I wondered how I should answer. Shep had said stick to the basic truth.

"My parents were killed in a car accident when I was five. Shep had always been my legal guardian whenever they went on business trips. His final act of that guardianship was adopting me after their deaths. I don't remember much. It is not something we talk about either." She dropped the subject and apologized if the question had bothered me. When I realized it was close to six, I needed her to leave so Shep and Sarah could arrive without any surprises. "Um…I need to do some chores. If you don't mind I need to go inside. I am not allowed to have company in the house." After waving goodbye, she said she would see me tomorrow.

When Shep and Sarah arrived home, I didn't ask them where they had been. I had dinner ready and sitting on the table. We spent the rest of the night like a normal family would, if there *is* any family that is normal. I asked Shep if he and

Sarah were going to come to the beach for the bonfire. His response was a resounding, "I'll be there with bells on." That drew groans from both Sarah and me. His phrases were sometimes over the top.

When I woke the next morning, I found Heather had already called two times since seven a.m. She must have had a problem of some kind to have started so early. After breakfast I called her back to find I was right. She was in the middle of one of her first crises over what she should wear to impress Tyler. From the sounds of it, Parker was having a meltdown over Tyler while she was having one over what swimsuit she should wear. Now that sounded like my normal old life.

While walking to Heather's house, I looked at Matthew's. His house didn't seem to have any life stirring. This struck me as odd. As I looked to the sky I could see it was going to be a pretty day, and the sun was shining bright. There were very few clouds in the sky and no sign of rain. After ringing the doorbell, I could hear Heather race to answer it. Roughly she dragged me inside. Her mind began to click off all she wanted to ask, making it hard for me not to answer before she had verbalized it. My head was still sore from school, and Heather really needed to relax.

Going by the living room, it was funny to see Parker pretending to read his newspaper. He didn't seem to notice me, but his thoughts were running a million miles per minute. He couldn't believe his little girl was interested in a boy. He was trying to figure out if he had done the right thing by letting her even go to the beach today.

Being pulled into Heather's room, she had all her swimsuits lying out. We were deciding on which one would look best on her when Parker came in and told her she would have to wear a one-piece today. We both giggled.

"Yeah, I know. He has been trying to go over the birds and bees with me, but I told him I already had health and we had Chelsea and Cassidy to help us. You know, he hasn't really met Tyler except for the weekend he moved in." I picked a tan one-piece swimsuit with a dark blue design. This choice seemed to please Heather.

She then started asking me how I was progressing with Matthew. My voice shook as I told her I could see myself dating him if he ever asked. She was absolutely thrilled with my answer. It had been so long since we had talked boys, I almost had forgotten how fun it was. This was turning out to be a great day. Before I left, I reminded her I would meet her in at the end of the cul-de-sac after I had my supplies and had put on my swimsuit.

Once I arrived home, Shep and I were laughing at Parker's misery. He sort of understood. It wasn't often Shep looked so deep in thought. "Look, Selena, I know you like this boy Matthew, and I agree I don't think he would hurt you. We haven't found anything showing they have any dealings with Alexander. But..they are not Mortal. Matthew definitely was able to guard his thoughts with me the other night. This only means he is from one of the other realms. I think we will know more about him when his father arrives.

"On the other hand, I do agree he does seem to be right for you. If you weren't in danger from Alexander I don't think I would be concerned at all. I am pretty sure I know his family, and if I am right, he is safe." I was so glad to hear Shep say this I could have hugged him to death. Like I had always known he trusted me, most kids wished their parents would trust them.

I had just finished dressing when the doorbell rang. Not knowing who it was, I was surprised to hear Matthew asking Shep if I was ready to go to the beach since Mike and his sister were waiting on us. Shep invited him in and came back to my room to get me. When Shep entered my room, I could have died by the expression he wore on his face, for it was similar to Parker's. *"Did you know he was going to pick you up?"*

*"No, but I may have implied it by accident."* Shep reminded me to be careful as he glared back down the hall. Then he added for me to have fun. We walked to the foyer together, only to find Matthew twitching restlessly in his spot, which made Shep smile. Shep's deep voice boomed without him even trying. Matthew jerked to attention as Shep informed us he would see us at the bonfire.

The next moment Sarah was rushing out with my cooler of supplies for the day. I noticed how she seemed to be staring a hole through Matthew. I was glad she had remembered the cooler, and yet I had the feeling she had an underlying motive. When we reached Mike and Meg, I was grateful that Mike had brought a wagon for our coolers. I didn't know what we were waiting on because Heather was with Tyler. When I inquired, Mike reminded me sarcastically, "Who do we always wait on?" Sure enough, Tyler was carrying his and Heather's coolers as they approached. Heather looked like she was beyond happy. Our group was finally complete and we were ready to start walking to the beach.

The sky was clear, and the temperature was still hot. Fall would be coming soon, and here in Michigan it is winter by the end of October. I even remembered on occasions wearing a winter coat over my Halloween costume. The winters in this area seem to last forever.

Heather had come up beside me and reminded me of the last time we had gone to the beach together, and to be honest, it wasn't a memory I liked to remember. In so many ways my life ended that day. I was no longer unaware of the dangers that seemed to encircle me, and my new life began soon after. The route I was on right now, I wasn't even sure I would be able to manage. I still hadn't had a peaceful day at school, and now I could travel through the shadows by accident. I sometimes wondered if I wouldn't have been better off if I had never had my abilities.

Heather knocked me out of my daydream as she let the group in on the events of our big adventure. Tyler piped up that maybe they didn't need to know anything about it. But Heather was in one of her hyper moods and nothing seemed to stop her from telling them how we had stayed out too long and the weather turned into one of the worst storms this area had seen in a long time. She ribbed Mike about leaving us behind and looked at me to see if I would join in on the conversation as she continued.

As we were passing the hill where she had slid down on her butt, she stopped everybody and asked if they wanted to see it. Shyly I looked over the edge of the hill and could still remember the night clearly. It was wet, musty, and so dark. Matthew sidled up beside me and asked if I was all right as I continued to look over the edge. I tried to convince him I was fine, but I could barely paste a smile on. By now everybody had gone down the side of the hill but me. Mike hollered up to come down. Reluctantly I walked down the side of the hill. It was like walking back into the memories. The man in the mist still bothered me, even if I was supposed to trust him. This place where I had seen him held a lot of emotions. I remembered the mound off to the side. This made me anxious as I started to hear other minds crashing in on me again, and today I didn't want the noise to drive me home. Taking a deep breath, I pushed them back into the background as I searched for what might have been a portal. Tyler came over and asked what I was looking for so urgently. I so wanted to tell him, but I couldn't with so many around.

Heather then piped up that maybe I was looking for the ghost I had seen that morning. Without intending to, I found myself cringing at her statement. I wasn't sure how to react. Everything that happened here was personal, and Heather had no idea how personal it was. I tried to brush it off as a joke as I reminded her of how misty things had been. "The shadows make scary shapes when your best friend conks out on you for the night." I tried to sound sarcastic, but I knew I hadn't convinced Tyler or Matthew. Mike still couldn't believe she had slept through the storm. He hadn't been able to sleep that night, even in his own bed.

Anxiously I continued to search. Finally I found what I was looking for. It had to be a portal, and an old one. As I stepped, I found Matthew was nearer to me than I thought. I felt his firm body pressed against my back. "What do you see, Selena?" he inquired. Tyler, hearing the question, came over and recognized what I was looking at. Immediately he scoffed as he said it looked like a bunch of trees to him. That was when he found one of my socks laying on the ground. This discovery made me amused. Swiftly I picked the sock up and asked Heather if she needed any help. She gagged at remembering how I had kept the swelling down on her ankle. Mike started laughing before informing everybody of our inside joke.

They all headed back up the hill while I remained behind to look around. Tyler stood beside me and said I would have to tell him everything later. Not acknowledging his sentence, I turned to walk up to the path but wound up wandering over to our little shelter. Shakily I put my hand out and pushed the ferns back to look inside. Matthew was there beside me in an instant and asked if I wanted to go in. "No, that night was a rough one. This place doesn't exactly hold fond memories for me." He took my hand swiftly as he led me back up the hill, stating that sometimes our past experiences prepare us for what tomorrow may bring. He sounded like Shep. "You remind me of that Yoda character. Shep resembles him from time to time too." Matthew chuckled as he said he would take it as a compliment.

When we made it to the beach Mike ran to our clubhouse and brought our beach tents and towels. Everybody was having a good time, and I couldn't help but enjoy all their kidding. Meg asked Mike where he had gone to get our things, only to be informed it was a spot where we all used to play. It was our secret clubhouse. The water looked calm and I couldn't resist putting my feet in. Mike began being mischievous as usual and came running over to splash water on me but I didn't feel much like chasing him right now. Matthew inched closer to the water acting hesitant. Before placing his feet into the tide, he questioned if the water was warm. Evidently he didn't like the cold any better than I did. Heather and Tyler were setting up the beach tent with Tyler's watchful eyes keeping track of me. I was going to ruin his day if I didn't get in a better mood.

After I splashed into the water, Matthew followed me in promptly. I couldn't help but choke back my laughter at the sounds he was making with the first splash of water. "If you aren't used to Michigan weather the water will be cold to you." At this time of year the water was always colder. He didn't seem to mind it, though. Finally he couldn't keep his question back anymore and wanted to know what I had seen when I was in the woods. I tried to avoid his question by diving under the water, but when I popped up for air, Matthew was swimming straight for me.

Immediately I yelled that he couldn't catch me, and it turned into a game of tag. I was a good swimmer after all, and to my surprise, so was he. Tyler seemed to be trying to get Heather into the water while worrying about me, I could tell. Surely he understood that Heather was not a water person by any means. Her mind should have given that secret away long ago. Meg and Mike were playing their own game of tag, too. Swimming further out than normal I finally stopped to tread water. To my surprise Matthew had dived under. I couldn't see where he was until I felt myself being pulled under too. We both popped up laughing while I vowed next time I would get him. A moment later I launched myself at him, only to find myself locked tightly against his body. He felt warm, causing my body to surge with excitement at his touch.

After he let me go I started swimming back towards the shore so I could stand on the sand shelf, but the water would still be above my shoulders. Matthew seemed to be racing me and I accepted the challenge. We both were pretty equal in our abilities, but I was sure he could have beaten me if he had wanted to. He was a lot taller and stronger than me. Finally standing on the wet sand, I could feel the tide hitting. It wasn't rough, just relaxing. Matthew was laughing while pointing out how Heather was holding Tyler captive on the beach.

"Heather always stays on the beach. It will be pure luck to get her in."

Matthew's smile grew. "Tyler will have to go in first and she'll follow since she wants to be with him." Matthew thought this was great. Then he could have me all to himself. We swam around, sticking to where I could stand for a while. Suddenly I found myself being dragged underneath the water again, but this time it was Mike. When I popped up spewing water out, Matthew was at my side in no time asking if I hadn't known better than to not keep an eye on Mike. Softly I admitted I had forgotten to watch him.

"I should never turn my back on him!" I splashed as hard as I could to give Mike a face full. Instead, poor Meg was my victim. This started a splash war.

When I became tired, I dove under and swam out to where Mike usually wouldn't follow. Out of all my friends, I was the strongest swimmer. Floating on my back felt wonderful. Matthew seemed to be sticking right with me. He was good at floating, too. It was nice to have someone who wasn't afraid to swim and could do it without help. We talked about his family for once, and he admitted his father was away on business a lot lately. He couldn't wait for him to get back because he had something he needed to talk to him about. It seemed important by the way Matthew reacted. Without thought I admitted how Shep and I had always been able to talk. I understood how hard it would be to have to wait for him to come home from a trip. "Do you have any family in the area?"

Matthew acted thoughtful as he swam around me. "We mainly keep to ourselves. My family doesn't live in Michigan, anyway. My grandmother was murdered before I was born, and because of what happened, my parents don't keep in touch with anyone. It's safer that way."

I felt bad I had brought it up. Swiftly I flipped over and tried to knock him back to the here and now. "Sorry, I didn't mean to remind you of something so unpleasant." He smiled a weak smile but told me he thought we were supposed to ask questions in order to get to know one another. "Ha-ha," I glared.

Again we started to play around as he pulled me under, but this time he held me close to him as our heads bobbed back into the air. I had the funny feeling he enjoyed the race of my heart. Pushing away I turned back towards shore to see Tyler was already in the water swimming our way. This could only mean he didn't like me being so far out with Matthew by myself for so long. "He can't give us a minute's peace."

This time I needed to defend Tyler because Matthew didn't understand. "It is only natural."

Matthew's response caught me off guard. "Why would he care about you if he wasn't your boyfriend? I can understand Mike. He is like a brother, but you didn't grow up with Tyler." He knew he had caught me this time, but I didn't care. I met his eyes with an intentional hope that he could read me. I had given something away. Reluctantly I swam towards Tyler. We met him before he left the shelf area. We realized Heather was inching her way into the cold water like a scared cat. She didn't want to be left behind. Tyler grimaced and swam back to her after asking if I shouldn't come in and rest a little.

For once Matthew agreed we should. We all swam back to shore together. Once back, I was surprised to see Heather staying in the water while playing around with Tyler. We both took a seat in the beach tent while drinking some water. The beach was starting to get crowded with other teenagers slowly showing up for the afternoon. Not to mention that Laura and Kirt had joined our little party too. It wasn't much of a surprise to find Mike and Meg were setting up the volleyball net while several others were doing the same with the supplies they had toted along. Laura loved to play, so they challenged Mike and Meg to a game. Meg was smart. She knew Kirt would pummel her if he had a chance, so when dividing up into teams Meg chose to play on Kirt's team while Mike and Laura would play the opposite.

We enjoyed watching for a while until Heather interrupted us by asking if I would mind getting our boards to float on. "I can in a bit." Heather lazily stated I didn't need to hurry. She didn't mind Tyler trying to teach her how to float on her own. I knew she never had been able to, and Tyler was wasting his time. For some reason I felt Tyler had heard my thought, because he frowned at me. More teenagers began arriving and the pressure in my head began building. This encouraged me to go get those kickboards now. A slow acclimation to the others arriving might help.

For once I felt bashful. "Matthew, would you help me to bring the rafts and stuff back?" Matthew's smile broadened and his cheeks reddened as he stared at me. We decided to pull on our jeans over our suits since we were going into the woods for a small part of the trip. I pulled on my T-shirt as we began to walk away from the tent. I was hoping Tyler would keep his word and give me some space. I wanted to give Matthew a chance to talk to me. To be honest, I just wanted to be alone with him. Matthew followed and took every chance to help me over any obstacle. He was such a gentleman. The last time he helped me down from the fence I couldn't help but to stare at his beautiful eyes as he pulled me tighter against him. He was taking my breath away. Matthew was astonished when we arrived at the wolf's den. He couldn't believe that no animal had ever come back. Softly I agreed we were lucky.

We went inside. Roughly I pulled out the blow-up loungers and threw them outside. I then picked up our three kickboards only to find myself colliding with Matthew. He grabbed my elbows to steady me while asking if I was always this clumsy, or was I doing it intentionally. As I looked into his deep blue eyes, my body felt the electricity flowing through it again. I tried to steady myself as I stepped back, feeling totally mortified. My body was working against me.

We exited the wolf den and started pumping the lounger up with the bike pump when he interrupted our work. He sat back on his legs, staring a hole through me. "I would like an answer." Immediately I squirmed at the determination in his voice. When I looked up at his blue eyes I wondered if he really was someone I could trust, and that seemed to ignite a fire in him. "The other night when we were walking back on the plank path and your family showed up, didn't you accidentally travel by shadow?" he pressed. I watched as his hands fumbled with the lounger as he tried to calm down.

A gasp escaped me at his question. I could tell he knew he had hit it the nail right on the head. "I thought so. It had to be the first time you did it. I could sense you were out of control and I wanted to help. Admittedly I didn't mean to throw you to the ground though. Sorry about that. But you were so scared and upset I knew you could have wound up far away if I hadn't grabbed you." I continued to stare at him with absolute disbelief at what I was hearing. I couldn't tell if I should feel relief or if I should run. Finally I found my mind sliding down my guard and allowed my thoughts to enter his.

*"Yes that was the first time I had traveled by shadow alone and it was accidental. It is not something I think I will ever get used to or enjoy."*

Softly he smiled as he pulled me up by my hand. "You're wrong about traveling. It can be absolutely fun and sometimes beneficial if you control it properly." He opened his arms wide as he asked if he could show me. I knew this could be dangerous and I was going to get in trouble if anyone found out, but I wanted to trust him. I wanted to let him prove to me how nice shadowing could be. For a moment I hesitated as I fumbled forward.

Matthew then answered my thought. *"I can help you guard this memory and our little adventure if you will let me do so."* Slowly walking towards his open arms I started to turn around, but he stopped me, saying he would prefer to see my pretty face. Bashfully I leaned against his chest. I could feel his heart pounding. "Lay your head against my chest." His arms outlined my sides finding their way to the small of my back. He pressed me tightly to him, and I closed my eyes to feel the movement around us. But his shadowing seemed controlled, and I could still hear his heart pounding in my ear.

When we finally stopped, the noise around us was different with the sound of water falling on itself. I opened my eyes and was shocked to see a beautiful waterfall with exotic wildlife around us. As I leaned back a little, I realized he still hadn't let go of me. *"How was that?"* he asked, smiling down at me. As I turned to face him, I noticed his tan skin and well-built abs. My cheeks lit like they were on fire.

Hastily I turned back to the waterfall and asked him where we were. His answer was interesting. "I discovered this place by accident. I needed space from Meg.

Ever since then, whenever I need time alone, this is where I come. It took a while to understand where this place was, but with some help from my dad and books, I now understand this is a part of the shadows of my heart, a safe haven. Selena, I am pretty sure I know who you are, and what you have to understand is I am in the same boat as you."

He knew I needed to understand so he continued. "See, my grandmother's name was Lovie." My heart jumped. "My dad was one of her sons. In fact, he was the one who found her. He tried to convince the authorities that my grandmother was working on a problem they were having with a new discovery. They had planned to work out the problem when he arrived home. This piece of technology had a deadline on it in the Mortal Realm. My dad couldn't get anybody to believe him when he stated that no Guardians were at our home that night. Alexander and others kept saying my dad did not have any understanding of the situation the Shadow Realm was facing.

"My dad says it's a silent war but won't be much longer. He feels it in his blood. The night my grandmother was murdered, others were killed including someone named Jonathan Martin. That was a big issue since he was Guardian. Not long after that, my dad received threats on his and my mother's lives. Meg and I hadn't been born yet or weren't even thought of. He says that was good since they have no idea he has any children. My dad and mom came into the Mortal Realm and have lived in secrecy ever since.

"As you can see we are as much at risk as you are. My dad has been looking for Shep and had no idea you were across the street. He felt Shep had to be alive, and then my parents discovered disturbances of sorts in this area. My dad was all excited, saying it would be Analease's child causing the disturbances, especially if they had been able to hide the child's abilities. He felt that would be the way to hide you, but when the child reached a certain age, then your abilities would show no matter what. I figured the disturbances were you. Your family has strong abilities according to what my parents have told us. My dad wants to help in bringing Alexander down. He should be returning this week sometime. He has to keep up appearances with his job like you all do, too."

A glance at the waterfall reminded me of what Shep had said: my abilities would be a beacon to our kind. Matthew was now smiling at me. "You are Analease's daughter aren't you?" Matthew touched my face gently. "For a time the disturbances disappeared, and I imagine this was when you were gone over vacation. My dad was very disappointed. Where did you go?"

"I don't know. We went to a safe zone so I could be trained. But I still have abilities appearing and they are frustrating, like the other night."

Matthew smirked. "You don't need to concern yourself. My mom hasn't found any disturbances related to you. My dad is still searching the area too. They didn't believe me when I told them I could hear you and feel you. Meg is the only one who believes me. We will help with your protection when Shep and my dad talk. I won't let anything happen to you, I promise." As I gazed into his eyes, I knew he would always be here for me.

Gently reaching up to his face I rubbed his cheek. "I'm glad we've talked." Before long we sat down at the side of the water. It hit me we had been gone too long for Tyler not to be concerned. I hastily stood as Matthew agreed with my thought. He opened his arms again in offering. Swiftly I went over and leaned against his chest gratefully. He looked down at me with a grin. "So finally you trust me, don't you?"

"Of course, I do…since you explained. Remember, I can read people too." We both laughed as he asked what I was going to tell Tyler. "I'm not going to tell him anything until Shep and your dad talk. Just to put your mind at ease, Tyler is my cousin, but he seems more like a big brother."

"Good. I knew you had to be related somehow. He always knew when you were stressed, and that type of relationship only happens with close family members. So you are free and clear to date." Matthew grinned. With a quick look into his vibrant blue eyes, I smiled as Matthew's hand traced my jaw line while his other hand pulled the small of my back against him. My heart was pounding as I realized he was leaning down, pressing his full soft lips gently against mine. It felt wonderful. As he pulled back he grinned at my reaction and asked if this was my first kiss. My answer was simple as I leaned my head against his pounding heart. "Yes." His hands rubbed my back, causing the peaceful feeling to fill me. Being in his arms was where I belonged.

The light faded around us as we slid through the shadows back into the shade of the trees beside the wolf den. I continued to stand in his embrace before I heard Tyler and Heather walking towards the clubhouse. We both recognized how close they were and jumped into action, pretending we had been pumping the lounger up.

When they arrived, I knew my cheeks still had to be red, and I didn't dare look at them. Matthew's thought was flowing into mine, telling me he could keep this our little secret. I chanced a glance at him and grinned, knowing I would love to feel his lips against mine again. Tyler dropped to his knees, stating it was taking us an awfully long time to do nothing.

"We are enjoying our own conversation. Besides, I had to show him the inside of the clubhouse." Heather, taking the hint, asked Tyler if he would like to see how childish we had been when we were little. At this Matthew and I couldn't stop smiling at each other.

We finally succeeded in getting the rafts blown up and the four of us carried everything back to the beach. When I drew closer to the tree line, all of the people there were causing my head to throb. Matthew and Tyler both noticed, but Matthew being faster, caught me as I withdrew to the trees. He whispered in my ear this wouldn't be a good time to practice and kissed my cheek. Shock ran rapid as I looked into his blue eyes. He knew this had made all the difference in the world. My mind closed all the pressure off and I focused on Matthew's touch. Tyler caught the peck on the cheek and was totally infuriated. Wonderful, but Matthew had helped me not to accidentally disappear in front of Heather. That would be very easy to do with the forest right behind me.

Heather challenged us to beat her to the water's edge. Maybe going in the water would help things out. After I pulled my jeans off and threw them on the sand, I started towards the water. Without thinking I reached back and grabbed Matthew's hand to drag him into the water behind me. Once we were deep enough, we both dove in. We had made it past the shelf point, leaving Tyler to deal with Heather back at the water's edge. I could tell he was growing frustrated, but he would understand soon that there was nothing to fear. Matthew swam around me, totally enjoying how he had ticked Tyler off. For a moment I felt a bit unnerved by what my poor cousin was dealing with today.

"Maybe we shouldn't make things harder on him. If it wasn't for him I wouldn't be out here with you." Then I remembered Kirt would be able to hear us. "We need to be careful. I do have others around me who are sensitive." Matthew understood, but claimed he wouldn't mind making Tyler a little madder. Before I could see what he was up to, he dove back under the water, pulling me down. When we rose to the surface, he continued to hold me to him while kissing my cheek. I could feel that we had not gone unobserved.

As we swam back to shore, Matthew kept up with me as we joined Tyler and Heather for a while in the shallow water. Once out of the water, we decided to lie out on the beach while we still had a little light left to dry by. Today had been a good day. I was doing pretty well with protecting my mind thanks to Matthew's presence. As dusk began, bonfires popped up all along the edge of the beach. It was a beautiful sight. We had music playing, and kids were dancing. As we looked towards the sunset, Matthew placed his arm behind me, sending shivers down my spine. He must have noticed my shiver. "Do you need my sweatshirt?" I took it happily. He said it was his favorite so he would need it back, but I knew it would never happen.

The horizon showed half of the flaming sun with the deep colors it brought. It was like an artist's palette at sunset, and I loved to watch it fade into the night. The breeze picked up, allowing the seagulls to glide higher. I scooted closer to Matthew, noticing Shep and Sarah coming down the path. I couldn't tell if Shep was bothered by what he saw or not. I was pretty sure he would let me know later. Shep introduced Sarah to Matthew. Since we had rushed out of the house so quickly earlier, they hadn't been properly introduced. As they greeted each other, Sarah studied his face closely. With a small nod to Shep I could tell she had agreed on something with him, but I wasn't sure what. I could tell this was even unsettling to Matthew.

Shep and Billy started another bonfire and we all enjoyed hot dogs and chips. The seagulls glided in, landing on the beachfront as the tide washed food up for them to eat. Matthew took my hand and wanted to know if I would take a walk with him. Softly I explained to Shep that we wouldn't go far and maybe he and Sarah would join us. Sarah motioned for us to go on without them. She was fine where she was. Thank heavens for Sarah.

We walked down the beachfront, watching the waves bubble up with white caps as the surf hit. I loved hearing the waves. Matthew commented he liked it too. I hadn't realized he was still hearing my thoughts. I would have to be more careful, especially around my family. Cautiously I glanced back to Shep. I could tell he was keeping a close eye on us, causing me to feel a little nervous. Matthew took both my hands in his, turning me away from their view, reminding me he would prefer for us to share our thoughts with each other. He also reminded me our thoughts could be private if we wanted.

His eyes gleamed in the light of the moon. I knew I wouldn't be able to deny his request. Happy with my agreement, we continued to walk further down the shore. This had been the happiest I felt in a long time. Heavily I leaned against his shoulder, which felt natural. When we walked back to our group we joined in the fun.

Around eleven o'clock the adults felt it was time to head home, so we grabbed our belongings. It was then that Mike and I realized too late that we would have to take our junk back to the clubhouse. Shep volunteered to help us with the stuff as John shouted he would start back with some of the stragglers from the community. He and Chelsea were making sure all fires were extinguished as we passed them. Shep looked at me as he asked the three of us if we really thought he didn't know about the clubhouse. As we walked back down the dark path, the area took on a whole new meaning to me, and I felt uneasy. The last time I had been in these woods in the dark was the worst night of my life. Matthew, sensing my tension, placed his hand on the small of my back as he whispered he was here this time. I felt a new energy flowing through my body as we entered the darkness together. Shep and Sarah were walking behind us as well. They seemed to be affected by the night in a romantic way, too. I could hear them cuddling and kissing. For once I felt like I had a mother, one who was very much in love with my dad. It was so nice to see Shep act this way.

We all eventually made it back to the cul-de-sac and slowly started going our own separate ways. Watching each of my friends, I was hit by how our little group had paired itself off and I was happy. Shep and Sarah went on into the house as Matthew walked me to the door. I was glad they were giving me some privacy. Matthew stuttered through saying he had enjoyed the day, and maybe we could do it again sometime. Slowly I leaned over and gave him a peck on the cheek and told him goodnight before I went inside.

To my surprise, I had no inquisition upon entry. I walked back to my room as Sarah and Shep both hollered goodnight and they loved me. We were really becoming a family. Once in my room I switched on my night light and dressed in pj's before cuddling into my fortress of pillows. It had been a very good day. So good I couldn't stop going over it in my head.

# CHAPTER 15.
# SCHOOL FIGHT

**I woke up** the next morning feeling refreshed and excited. Last night had been what my dreams were made of when I read my highland books, maybe even better since it was real.

Going through the morning chores I was ready to face a new challenge. Shep came out of his room and teased me, wanting to know what had put me into the best mood since we returned home. Instantly I glared at him without answering. Hopefully he was giving me the privacy that I had been used to before this mess started.

I was hoping to skip breakfast when Shep came bustling in, inquiring if my head would be up to practice shadowing. I know my jaw dropped as I stared at him. "How can we do that?" Shep's smile widened as he said arrangements had already been made if I was up to it. Then the thought hit me like a block wall. I didn't relish the idea of traveling by shadow alone. My first trip had been out of control and horrifying. Shep sensed my anxiety and he said I would be traveling with him under his close supervision, and Sarah would be helping us. I figured I could try. I had to learn eventually. Otherwise those freakish accidents would continue to happen until I learned from pure desperation.

Sarah flipped her hair behind her shoulders. "You will need a sweatshirt on, in case you wind up somewhere cold." I couldn't help but flinch at that possibility. I hated the cold worse than anything. Shep's huge chuckle was louder than I had heard in a long time.

An hour later we were walking out the back door and I knew we were heading to the woods. What a great place to practice. Tyler came climbing over his own fence wanting to know what was scheduled for the day. Shep challenged him to join my training on shadowing, but he had to have permission from his parents first. To my surprise, he jumped on the chance to join us. He was thrilled with the prospect. He felt it would be a good idea for him to learn how to relax if he ever needed to be shadowed to a safety.

Tyler returned shortly with a sweatshirt in hand, stating his parents had warned him we might wind up somewhere cold. I shivered at the thought. I could sense Sarah and Shep's amusement at my involuntary reaction. We continued to walk further into the woods near the portal. When we finally came to a stop, I knew what was expected. I went straight to Shep and turned around, but in my peripheral vision I spotted Matthew not too far off. He was in his Shadow form behind a tree. My heart skipped a few beats, wondering why he was being so daring. I wondered if he would be able to follow.

I felt Shep wrap his arms tightly around me as he asked Tyler to do the same with Sarah. Hesitantly Tyler went over to Sarah and turned around as she wrapped her arms around him. Shep began going over basic rules and warnings, including that inexperienced shadowers could cause things to be bumpy, but no one was to ever panic, for their partner would be able to manage the difficulty. He then added that some become sick from the motion of the travel so it might be best if we closed our eyes until we adjusted.

"Remember, do not let go, no matter what you hear or feel." Tyler looked a little scared, but he wasn't closing his eyes, and I knew that would be a huge mistake for him. Hastily I shut mine tight. Then I thought I heard Matthew in my thoughts, whispering that I wouldn't have to close my eyes with him. His presence put me at ease. Suddenly Shep leaned down to remind me not to block my thoughts. He had noticed the brief moment of silence, though it couldn't have lasted more than a couple of seconds.

In the next minute we were sliding through the shadows with small bumps here and there, but not as bad as the first time I had traveled with him. When we came to a stop, I heard Tyler gasping for air. When I opened my eyes, I found Tyler on the ground throwing up, with Sarah patting his back with amusement. "We told you some first timers experience motion sickness." Tyler seemed to nod as he heaved another ounce of his breakfast.

Shep held me tight as he asked how I felt this time. "I'm a little queasy but fine." With this announcement he felt I was already improving. Shep snickered as he caught me looking around. I spied Matthew peeking out from behind the tree, smiling as he thankfully ducked for cover when Shep followed my gaze. I was sure he was enjoying Tyler's misery.

Shep began explaining we were in a forest area still in Michigan, and they had already placed boundaries to make sure I could travel by shadow but wouldn't be able to leave the training quad. "So Selena, do you remember how you felt the first time you did it alone? It was pure desperation that drove you. We don't want that to happen here. Many precautions have been taken and I will always be able to keep up with you. When traveling by shadow it must be as controlled as walking. The only thing is, you are driven by your emotions. It seems the keyword as usual is control. You find a shadow and you think about your desired destination. Since you are just beginning, we chose a pretty dark place filled with plenty of shadows. As you become better at it, you can see how to maneuver from shadow to shadow even when there is light breaking the stream a little. There is as much thinking in this as there is maneuvering around a group of people when walking. You will be able to hear and smell different things. Always remember not to stop because you hear voices, unless that is what you are intending to do." The only thing his explaining did was make me tense. I wasn't sure if I was going to enjoy this experience after all. At least Tyler seemed to be feeling a little better as he sat over against a tree. Shep came over beside me and told me to close my eyes while clearing my mind as I sensed around. Shep whispered I was to figure out what direction I wanted to go. As I did, I stumbled over to where Matthew's heart was beating. Comforted by the sound I wished I could be near him. That was when the funny dizzying feeling hit me. Suddenly Matthew was moving. I was giving him away and tried to change my direction. This was successful until I stopped with a thud and found myself on my back, breaking into a cold sweat, and to top it off I was nauseous.

Shep appeared and helped me sit up. He was amused. "You did well. You need to slow things down so you don't get sick every time you shadow." With a steady breath I pushed the sick feeling from me, and without realizing it I wished I was back home.

When I stopped this time it was like I had hit a brick wall. That meant I must have hit one of those boundaries Shep had put in place for my safety. Immediately I touched my face. I thought for sure I had busted my lip, but there was no blood. This time Shep appeared laughing. He took me in his arms so we could travel back to Sarah and Tyler.

Tyler looked much better than before and now it was his turn to laugh, but he didn't. Instead he came over and offered his presence in comfort. "So how's it going?"

"Miserably," was the only response I could muster. "I will never get this down without breaking my neck." He hit my shoulder lightly to encourage me to try again.

Overcoming the motion sickness I tried again, and this time the bumping was worse than ever. Every time I stopped I would always find myself on the ground. I wished I could land on my feet. Back at our base I told them maybe I needed to quit for the day. It was clear this wasn't going to work. They all disagreed, stating I needed to keep trying so if I ever lost control again I could stop myself. I laughed dryly. "That would be no problem," I teased. When they all looked at me funny, I clarified. "I always stop abruptly by landing on my butt somewhere."

I sat down against a tree and wondered if Matthew was getting a kick out of my dismal performance. Sarah gingerly encouraged me to try again, and then they would practice with Tyler so he could get used to it. When I started to ask why, I received the look that indicated they would tell me later.

Again I tried to concentrate on moving smoothly. Still it became bumpier than ever. Suddenly I felt the warmth of someone holding me and everything smoothed out. I recognized the heartbeat and the feel of Matthew's arms. His embrace was the most comforting thing in the world to me. We were sliding along smoothly and I could hear his mind telling me to think about feeling peaceful as the breeze passed across our bodies. I felt a kiss on my forehead before he let go, and I did as he said, landing on my feet. With this triumph I looked around and saw Matthew in his Shadow form. His eyes were full of excitement and approval at what had taken place, until Shep appeared. Then I noticed the oddest thing: Matthew's eyes dimmed out as does the flame in a lit lantern, and then he was gone. Shep peered over to where Matthew had been, but he didn't act like he saw him. Hopefully Matthew had been unnoticed.

"That was the longest ride you have done all day. You must be getting better at it," Shep stated with approval. Instantly I searched his face to see if he knew Matthew had helped me. Not saying anything I slinked back into the shadows, traveling back to what I hoped was our base. When I stopped I was pretty close. Still, I practically fell over as I stumbled over the roots in the ground.

Tyler grinned before teasing me. "I don't understand…Matthew isn't around, so you don't need to act clumsy." At that statement I was tempted to slow things down, but I heard Shep interject it wouldn't be wise.

"It would make me feel better, though." Shep chuckled at my cynicism. Tyler went and stood in front of Shep as they faded into the shadows. Sarah and I both heard Tyler holler, causing Sarah to excuse herself quickly to find out what had happened. I could feel Tyler was in pain and I figured he must have pulled away from Shep during travel. Upon spying Matthew I headed towards him. "What are you doing here, Matthew? Aren't you afraid Shep will catch you?"

"No, not really. I figure he is allowing me to be here anyhow. I think he has already figured my family out and is just waiting to approach until my father returns. For some reason, I feel I can trust him. My dad has talked about him so much. Back to your traveling though. You need to relax." Abruptly we heard a noise back at the base, forcing us to separate. Matthew faded into the shadows as I retook my seat. I felt him breeze pass me, making me want to follow. Stopping for a moment to clear my thoughts, I tried to concentrate on Tyler.

Back in the clearing Tyler limped towards Sarah this time and they faded into the darkness together. "Well, are you ready to try some more?" I felt like saying no but I didn't. I really was disgusted with my ability, but decided if I kept it up maybe Matthew would butt in again. I tried several more times.

This time I heard someone passing by me, and I could sense it was Tyler with Sarah. My travel became dizzying this time, and I felt like I was falling. I knew I had taken too much time concentrating on who else was in the darkness. It was bound to hurt when I hit. Pleasantly I felt the warmth of Matthew's body slide against me. I leaned my exhausted head against his chest as his arms wrapped around my body. I felt a tremble run the length of my body. We slowly came to a stop, bringing everything back into focus. This time I didn't move away and he seemed content holding me. "Why did you help this time?"

"I can't stand for you to get hurt. Besides, it gives me a chance to hold you. I could get use to this. Couldn't you?"

"You already know the answer." His lips kissed the top of my head, making me tingle all over. With a shy glance up I wondered if he would kiss me if I gave him the chance. Of course my heart jumped when his hands cupped my face as he leaned down and kissed me gently before fading away. That could only mean Shep was near.

"So did you enjoy yourself this time?" Shep asked with his arms crossed as he leaned against a tree. I couldn't deny I had totally enjoyed myself. Even my toes felt like they were on fire. I tried not to let my thoughts betray me. "Come on, it's time for us to get something to eat. We are going to shadow into town and eat at a restaurant, but first we need to go back to base camp to meet up with Sarah and Tyler." Shep's arms encircled me as I smiled at the thought of how I would much prefer it to be Matthew. I was sure I heard someone chuckle.

Tyler looked like he was weathering the shadowing a little better. As we arrived in town, we both wondered where exactly we were and wondered if we wouldn't draw attention to ourselves by appearing. Shep heard us and said, "You both should know that Shadows have been traveling in this realm for centuries and we use our sensing skill to make sure we arrive unobserved. A Shadow literally could be the fly on the wall and wait for a group to leave before appearing."

We were in the small town of Gaylord, Michigan where we did a little souvenir shopping and went into a mom-and-pop deli for lunch. They had the most wonderful food including pasties indigenous to the U.P. area. Shep loved beef pasties. Tyler had a pizza while Sarah and I enjoyed our subs. Tyler asked Shep if anyone or anything else could travel in a shadow at the same time.

"Sure. Many Shadows can travel close to each other in this form. Sometimes you can even physically feel them. Right, Selena?" Matthew was right. Shep knew he was here. Instantly I tried to bring the attention back to what happened with Tyler.

"Are you sure you didn't feel me shadowing?"

Tyler looked defiantly at me. "It wasn't you. You were unwinding. I felt someone near us. I was fighting vertigo when I sensed the person. When I reached to grab them I dropped to the ground. I swear I felt something." I tried not to snicker. I bet it was Matthew trying to freak him out.

We spent the rest of the evening practicing. When dusk was showing itself I tried one more time to travel the length of the boundary without hitting it. By now I could sense forms of the physical world mixed in with the shadows. I knew I was getting close, but I hadn't decided to stop yet. When I felt Matthew joining me he brought us safely to a smooth stop in the middle of a grassy meadow. While staying in his embrace I told him I thought he had left for the day. He grinned at me saying he had to allow me to concentrate on one thing at a time. Now he just wanted to wish me sweet dreams for the night. I wanted him to stay but I knew Shep would be along soon. In a rush I reached up on my tiptoes and took the initiative to give him a kiss. Gently he rubbed my cheek. I could tell he didn't want to leave either. It was unusual for Shep not to have interrupted yet.

Matthew pecked the top of my head and faded away, leaving me feeling the desire to follow him home. Suddenly Shep's hand felt firm on my shoulder as I froze. "How long have you been there?" I knew my voice sounded shaky.

"Long enough, Selena. I have known all day he was here. Besides, his dad and I have already talked. Victor and I agreed we would talk to the rest of the family when he returns from his business trip. That is why I have been letting you be with Matthew. I have a strong feeling he is very important to us. We have nothing to fear from them. Victor even released a bit of his security for us to verify who they are. They want to put things right as much as I do. Sarah and I recognized Matthew's looks right away. The only thing that surprised me was his last name. I couldn't believe Victor would have allowed it to be used. It is a dead giveaway to our enemy. He had used false identities off and on, but he wanted his children to have their true name. Victor has been a friend for a long time. Besides, I am glad you are attracted to Matthew." I rolled my eyes. This was too much from my own father. I thought every father was supposed to have a problem with their daughters dating or falling in love. Shep informed me that he had always trusted my judgment and this would be no different. Then he turned with an amused look on his face as he raised his eyebrows. "By the way, it was Matthew who spooked Tyler. Have to admit I enjoyed the trick."

We traveled back to the quad and then home, where we faded in right where we had left earlier this morning. I was exhausted. I took a hot bath to remove the soreness from my body. With a sigh of relief I slid into the hot bubbles and settled into the soothing warmth. My body was aching all over and the scent of lavender helped ease the tension. When the water finally went cold, I climbed out. As I glanced into the mirror I realized I had many bruises, which made me wonder if I was ever going to get a handle on shadowing. This traveling by shadow was actually a little more dangerous than I had ever realized. My lip hadn't cracked open, but it felt swollen from hitting the boundary this morning.

When I left the bathroom I peeked into Shep and Sarah's room to find them cuddled in each other's arms. I couldn't resist but to walk in and sit down at the end of their bed. Totally amused by this, Sarah asked what was up. "When I was little…I didn't have a mom. I just wanted to say I love having you around. Thanks for being my mom." Sarah, catching Shep's eye, moved down next to me and gave me the largest hug she had ever given me.

"So is it time for you and I to talk about Matthew, yet?" she whispered.

"Maybe later," I replied, walking nervously from the room. Rapidly I crossed the hall and found my bed unmade from this morning. I figured my pillows were just right as I settled in before checking my alarm. I couldn't help but wonder what Matthew was doing. It had been a good day with him around.

The next morning my alarm hadn't gone off, and Sarah came rushing into the room to wake me. Our electricity had gone out during the night and we were all late. I grabbed the first thing I touched and pulled on an outfit. We all piled into the Rendezvous quickly as Sarah threw the car into gear. When I inquired where Shep was, I was informed he was away on a trip and would not be back until dusk.

When we pulled up to school, the buses had already left and most of the students were in the building. We all ran towards the doors, and even though I could feel the pressure of everybody around me, I had succeeded in keeping them as background noise. For once I didn't have an issue. Maybe this week would be better.

We all ran to our classes without anyone giving thought to following me. Thankfully everything was going fine. When Mr. Jensen started his lecture, I had time to wonder when Victor would be arriving and if Matthew knew Shep and his dad had already talked. He would be happy.

The bell for second hour seemed like it would never ring, but it finally did. Matthew met me at the door under Tyler's watchful eyes. Matthew smirked. The crowd was pushing in around me and many of them seemed to be in rotten moods. For a moment I stopped to scan my path ahead to make sure I wouldn't accidently fade into a wall or something, and then proceeded. Matthew draped his arm over my shoulder, probably sensing I was concerned about the pressure I was feeling. As I leaned heavily against him I could feel his heartbeat, almost like it was intended to comfort me. When I entered the classroom, the girl from the previous week was arguing with her boyfriend. Unfortunately this meant I was in for a rough period.

Biology and art both went off without any major hitches. The knowledge of knowing I would be seeing Matthew made things easier than the previous days in school had been. Out of the blue, I felt someone grab my hand. I knew his touch without even looking. Matthew had matched stride with me, and he knew there would be no lunchroom in my future today. "Does Tyler know?" I had to admit, I hadn't thought to tell him. Matthew definitely liked the idea of us having a table to ourselves for once, but knew Tyler and Kirt wouldn't allow that and would eventually come searching for me. Upon entering the courtyard, we sat down, pulling out our lunches. True to form, the boys and our other friends joined us in the great outdoors. Matthew's comment made me giggle when he suggested that he needed to find his happy place away from everybody. I knew where he meant, and it reminded me of how special our time had been there. This made me wish to do it again.

Immediately Tyler plopped down across from Matthew to glare. "Today would be a great day for traveling." I wasn't exactly certain of what Tyler meant, but evidently Matthew did, for he merely met Tyler's glare. At just that moment Meg made the comment of preferring to travel at night. Matthew looked at her almost as if he was chiding her. To everyone's surprise we heard Meg giggle profusely. Then her serious disposition took over again. "Does anybody know what is up with the boys on the football team? I heard some of the players were mad about how driven the coach was during practices and after the games." We did have a new coach, and Jeremy was on the team this year. He had said the guy needed to get a life.

"He treats you like you're in the military or something. 'Drop and give me twenty' or 'Run a lap' is all he can say," Mike mimicked. At that moment part of the football team burst into the courtyard. Meg had been right: the tension they were carrying was like a keg of dynamite. Laura's face showed the panic I felt. Both Tyler and Kirt exchanged glances as they began to move. Matthew instantly joined by taking my hand and giving me a slight tug towards the door. At this moment I didn't care where Matthew was leading me, just as long as it was far away. There was no place to run. Nestling in beside a locker I felt Matthew push me against the wall, and without thinking I laid my head on his chest.

"Feeling better yet?" The concern in his voice was touching as his breath felt warm against my neck. My mind was racing, figuring out how to shut the noise down when I felt Matthew lean over and let his lips linger on my forehead. "A kiss will make it all better," he whispered, and he was right. I looked at Matthew and could tell he was pleased with himself. Kirt looked disgusted as he walked off.

Matthew could sense I was concerned and demanded to know what had me upset. "Do you think Kirt, Tyler, and you will ever get along? I would like for you to."

"For you, anything is possible."

***

Walking towards my English class I noticed a little more pressure, but I adjusted. When I hit the door of the classroom, my head swam out of control with pain. I couldn't believe I had to grab the doorframe so tight to remain standing. There were boys from the football team inside throwing punches. I had rarely seen fights at our school, let alone a full-out brawl in a classroom. Desks were being thrown out of the way and my head started bursting as their violent thoughts echoed. Suddenly I felt a warming sensation climbing up my body from my feet. Instinct took over, forcing me to back up until I found someone blocking my exit. When I turned to push through, I was shocked to see Matthew's concerned face. He firmly grabbed me around the waist and began to pull me out of the way as a teacher came charging in.

We could hear shouts for help as some teachers rushed towards the room and others were calling the office for security. Some of the faculty were urging students to go to the auditorium. Matthew continued to pull me by my waist towards the exit and pushed me through the doors that led to the sunny tennis court.

The sun shone brightly all around. There was no easy escape for me. To my surprise, I was knocked to the ground as Kirt rushed Matthew. Pain shot through me. What was he thinking? They both looked like they could kill, when I was able to gain my bearings. My head started smashing even worse.

Suddenly Tyler had me by the shoulders, telling me to calm down and then yelling for Kirt to cool it since we didn't want to draw attention. Matthew came around and knelt in front of me while calling Kirt a jerk as he pointed to my knees. Evidently I had scraped them up when I fell. To my dismay, Matthew was even having problems with his control. He seemed to be struggling—almost fighting—something, which made me concerned.

Kirt took off his shirt as Laura and Meg entered the tennis courts. This looked like it was turning into a bad show. Everybody's emotions were making things worse, and before long I wouldn't have any control left. Thankfully they all sensed the thought and immediately tried to refocus their minds into silence.

Carefully Kirt began dabbing my knees with his shirt. I was bleeding like a faucet. I had bled easily ever since I could remember. Laura pulled out a package of Kleenex from her backpack and handed them to Kirt, insisting he put his shirt back on. To my dismay my head continued to ripple with pain, and I couldn't even feel how my legs should have been stinging because of it.

Sensing the tension in the air I glared at all of them, shouting for them to get a grip. It seemed like being mad was to my advantage. I was able to control the noise a little better. In as calm of a voice that I could manage I asked if they would put aside their mistrust of each other and be nice, at least until I could go back into the building. Matthew sat beside me while Tyler remained on my other side. Matthew continued to murmur to me when a teacher burst out onto the courts. It didn't take long for Mr. Flores to spot my knees. His approach was hesitant as disgust filled his face. Quickly he assumed I had been hurt in the classroom. Softly I muttered I hadn't been quick enough to get out of the way. He took another look at my knees and cringed at the sight of the blood.

"You all need to report to your own classes. We are going to have to take a head count due to this incident. Matthew, you can take Selena to the nurse's station." Quickly Tyler volunteered to help me, but Mr. Flores denied his offer. With a nervous glance towards the exit I knew I couldn't go back down the hall yet. To top it all off, I couldn't exit the courts either since I might fade into the shadows.

We heard more crashing inside, causing Mr. Flores to run back in, leaving us to squabble amongst ourselves. Matthew glared at Tyler and offered that he had an idea but they would have to work together to do it. Sensing what Matthew was about to do, I moaned. Without hesitation Matthew lifted me up and carried me towards the shadow. Suddenly Tyler blocked his path, demanding to know what he thought he was doing. Then I heard Kirt calling to his parents that there was trouble. It was evident this was going to get worse before it got better. I had no idea where Laura and Meg had moved to, but I was praying they weren't squaring off like the boys. Surely being girls they would act more levelheaded, I hoped.

The wind started picking up and I could tell it was not a normal wind. My voice was soft and one could barely hear me as I begged for them to work together. I was feeling sicker by the minute. "I trust all of you." Luckily Tyler seemed to relinquish a little but demanded to know what Matthew intended on doing before he did it.

"I am going to shadow her to a safe zone where she can gain control. I know you don't trust me, but if I don't help her she could wind up who knows where and we both know the situation inside is not getting any better. Besides, I am pretty sure Shep would approve of my help." Matthew's voice sounded authoritative as he practically dared Kirt to say another word to him.

"Fine, but you have to take me with you. She is not going to be out of my sight," Tyler growled defiantly. Kirt didn't like his suggestion and started to argue with Tyler until they sensed I couldn't handle anymore.

"Alright, you can come with us, but don't let go. I don't have the patience to try to take care of you. No freaking out while I shadow; it is hard enough with one let alone two." My vision began spinning and they both felt my desperation at the situation. Objections were being made loudly from Laura and Kirt, and that was when I noticed the thunder rumbling above us.

"Thanks Meg," Matthew said in a coy voice, and I knew she must be creating the wind, but the darkening clouds with thunder seemed to be Matthew. The three of us moved to where the shadows were darkening. Meg followed with no sign of distress on her beautiful face as her dark long hair blew across her. Anxiously I grabbed Tyler's hand. I was determined he would not fall with me around. Matthew whispered in my ear it would be just like the other day when we had been by ourselves. Matthew's reassurance that he wouldn't let anything happen to Tyler either made me feel better. Matthew continued holding me firmly in his arms as Tyler continued to hold my hand. He placed his other arm on Matthew's shoulder as we stepped back into the shadow. Suddenly I heard Laura and Kirt yelling in panic as Tyler tensed up. Matthew let out a curse but confirmed he had everything under control.

Our trip smoothed out, but we were definitely moving fast. It did seem we were going quite a distance, too. Our movement was slowing down as we faded into a lightly lit forest. We landed on our feet and Tyler was still standing, to my relief. A maniacal laugh came from Matthew as he told Tyler he could open his eyes now. Just as he did Meg faded into sight, barely bracing Tyler as he relaxed. Carefully Matthew bent down and set me on the ground while Tyler grabbed his knees, trying to fight the motion sickness. I felt too weak to keep my eyes open.

"She's fainted." Meg's voice resounded as the darkness enveloped me without movement this time. I felt Matthew's hand rubbing my face with something cold and when I opened my eyes, I could hear Meg humming happily off to the side, which was too weird for me. With a great effort I struggled to sit. I recognized the feeling of overdoing it. Tyler was whispering through his totally pale lips that we were all right, and yet I wasn't hearing his voice properly. It was garbled. "I would not hurt either of you. We are on the same side Tyler Martin. I happen to be Lovie Sturley's grandson of Embers Greene."

Astonishment reflected in Tyler's eyes. He still didn't know Matthew's family didn't even go to the Shadow Realm because of the threats against his parents' lives. I could not build up enough energy to speak. Thankfully Tyler was looking at Matthew with new understanding.

Matthew helped me lean against him as Tyler's pale lips started mouthing something. The ringing in my ears was too loud to understand. The sound was fading like my ears were no longer able to hear. To my shock, three Shadows started taking form in front of us. Luckily it was Shep and Sarah, but the third man I did not know. Meg did, however, for she hopped off her rock and ran to give him a hug. Matthew didn't move, even though I could sense he knew the man too. Sarah had Tyler move out of the way as she fell into a mist form beside me. I had only seen her in her mist form once before when she was checking on Heather the night we were stuck in the woods. The buzzing in my ears was becoming fainter by the minute. I couldn't understand what they were saying, but I could feel Sarah's coolness as she brushed her hands around my face.

I continued to depend on Matthew as I leaned against him heavily. I could hear his heart pounding but it wasn't like before. It sounded different. It could be stress. When I closed my eyes I began to feel like I was floating and could no longer feel my limbs. Matthew's mind was all that made any sense to me. He wanted to know if the buzzing in my ears was gone yet. I forced my mind to respond as I told him it was going away, but I didn't feel right. I felt something cool against my cheek and then his heart started pounding fast like it did when he held me, especially when we were alone.

This made me smile. Slowly I opened my eyes and what I saw was a heavy mist crossing my vision. This sight frightened me a little. Thankfully I could see Shep, Tyler, and the stranger looking at us like they had never seen me before. Then I could feel Matthew telling me not to be afraid and to listen to his heart. It would guide me. I strained to hear him as my own heart began to beat louder. Seconds later I could still feel Matthew beside me. His heart sounded wonderful and he was warm. When I turned my head towards his face I saw his beautiful eyes leaning towards me as he pecked my cheek. At that moment I knew everything was all right. Sarah reminded me that she was there, too, as she forced me to look at her. She acted like a doctor, checking my pulse and looking into my eyes. When she was satisfied, she announced I was back to normal but would require a lot of pampering.

Shep bent down on one knee and checked my face. "Thanks Matthew, I knew you would be of help." His voice cracked as he tried to bring it back under control.

For the next several minutes or seconds I felt confused. I didn't know what they were going on about. For some reason Tyler and Meg had started a fire behind Shep, and the stranger was looking very pleased with…Matthew.

"Selena, I would like you to meet my dad, Victor."

I tried to lift up, only to have Sarah push me back down, repeating over and over to rest. Matthew wasn't moving and I figured he would want to be with his dad, but his mind said he was right where he wanted to be.

Shep turned to Tyler and asked if he had contacted his parents yet. "I need to. I haven't found the chance since this happened. We had to work so hard to keep her safe." I could see the strain on his face as he rocked nervously. Shep moaned they had better go back and let them know everything was all right. Tyler refused flat out. "I am staying right here."

Shep froze as he studied Tyler's determined form. "Fine, son. You stay. I will take care of this." Gradually he faded from sight with one last glance at me.

"When are we going home?" I asked in a weak voice. I could tell by the way the light was filtering through the trees that dusk would be soon. Sarah piped up we were not going home tonight, for I was still too weak. What is up with all this weak crap? Both the boys chuckled as I realized I was not guarding my mind appropriately. "Sarah, how did the day go by so fast? I thought you all had just arrived."

"Your mind and senses were overloaded. Thankfully the Sturleys had placed this safe zone for their children. Victor was able to help us access it."

Tyler came over and sat beside me. "We needed to allow your senses to calm down, and the only way to do this was to help you leave your physical body. This is done very rarely. Most of the time we allow our body to transform totally into mist. In this case we needed to separate the two halves so your physical form could mend. In other words, using your mist form allows your brain to relax and heal. Since you have a strong connection to Matthew he was able to separate his mist form from his physical body, and you followed."

Sarah looked down as she took a deep breath. "I was able to help your physical body repair itself while Matthew kept watch over your mist form. He actually is well-trained from what I have observed, well beyond someone his age."

Tyler continued. "When you moved into your mist form it scared me. I couldn't sense you like I usually do, and what was worse was that yours and Matthew's bodies lay lifeless on the ground. I couldn't see either one of you breathe. Every once in a while I could feel both of you. I don't want to ever go through that again. Shep told me you could be away from your bodies up to twelve hours but if you don't return, the physical body dies. Trust me, I was watching the clock."

Matthew punched Tyler on the shoulder, stating he didn't think he really cared. Tyler didn't respond as he looked at his hands. Suddenly Shep reappeared and dropped a whole bunch of supplies, as did Victor. I hadn't even realized that Victor left. Tyler asked what the damage was back at home.

"Well, your brother and sister are totally freaked out. They felt they let you down since they couldn't follow. It was even worse when Meg followed you all off and smiled at them when she left. Laura said it was like watching something from a horror film. I gather Meg has an artistic ability." Matthew and Victor both made snorting sounds of agreement. "She really hammed it up, but to top it all off, she waved as she faded out too. Neither Kirt nor Laura tried to stop them by preventing her change in form. Kirt says it was Meg who had an impact on the environment." Shep was looking squarely at Matthew as he spoke but no one else seemed to notice. Victor sounded irritated. "Neither of my children have that ability."

Shep continued. "Your parents now understand and have been filled in with the Sturleys here. They are willing for you to stay with us until we can manage to go back home. They will also take care of the school. It seems like the three of you have come down with the chicken pox." I couldn't help but utter an "ouch" as I moved my legs. Immediately Sarah looked at my knees, wanting to know how they had been injured. Sheepishly Tyler explained what Kirt had done.

"Kirt is going to need a lot of consoling," Tyler agreed loudly as Sarah was handed a first aid kit and began to put new bandages on the minor cuts, but they were sore. Matthew was helping her and seemed to be overly concerned with how much pain it might be causing. Gently I assured them I felt very much in control and I didn't even have the pain in my head. Sarah uttered that it was going to stay like that for a while. She looked totally cross at Shep. Victor had been sitting by, listening to our whole conversation while holding the first aid kit. I watched as he kept biting his lip. Finally he couldn't hold back any longer.

"You're right, Sarah, they can't keep driving her like this. I would like to check her if I may?" Sarah motioned towards me as he slipped over next to me. I watched as his mist hand roamed around my head several times and then over my chest. He then tilted my head back and looked deep into my eyes. "She is strong, but not so strong that you can keep this up. The next time she might not survive the overload. To be honest, I can't understand how she lasted this long without an episode."

When they were finished with my legs, Shep laid out a tarp and several sleeping bags near the fire. To my surprise he also had my pillows I liked to bunch up around me at night. Matthew picked me up and carried me over and ever so gently set me down. Tyler had followed with a blanket and laid it on my legs as Sarah followed and sat down beside me. She wasn't going to allow herself to be too far from me, I could tell.

As I looked around, Tyler and Matthew were working on building a canopy over our heads, which impressed me. They were actually joking with each other. Both of them looked abnormally pale though, especially in the flickering of the firelight. Sarah leaned over and whispered that Matthew would definitely make one's heart flutter. When I giggled, they both looked at us like they knew what we were talking about.

"You're right. He does make my heart flutter." In truth, I had never felt this way about anybody before, and it was sort of confusing. She smiled and brushed my cheek.

We continued to watch the boys work while Victor and Shep seemed to be laying another boundary around the camp. They all would be taking turns on watch. Even Billy and Granddad would be here later. Speak of the devil, the two of them appeared as if on cue. Mrs. Sturley had shadowed them to us. Billy went directly to Tyler and hugged him. I was sure they were carrying on a conversation. Tyler was probably thankful for the privacy. Matthew tried to give them space by sitting down beside me. "So how are your legs?"

"Fine. Thanks for all your help today. I don't know how you were able to manage it all. I hope I didn't cause you any pain." Matthew's reply didn't surprise me as he said keeping me safe would always be his priority. I laid down on my pillows, and he laid his head on the opposite side and continued to smile at me.

"What are you smiling at?" I asked.

"I will get to see you sleep tonight, and I always wondered what that was like." Carefully I placed my hand on the pillow only to have his warm large hand cover mine. I fell asleep smiling with him beside me.

# CHAPTER 16.
# FALL

**We all had** survived the night, and Matthew was still holding my hand as if he hadn't moved. The cool air hit my warm skin, causing my whole body to shiver as I took in our surroundings. The area was covered in mist and our clothes were damp from the night. There looked to be others farther away from us, almost as if they were guarding us. I was disappointed not to see Shep, but Mr. and Mrs. Sturley were here, along with several members of my family. As I looked around my circle of friends and family, I wondered how anyone could deliberately hurt any of us. Matthew stirred as if on cue and cracked a silly grin. When I sat up he jumped like I couldn't even do *that* by myself.

Sarah informed me Shep had to keep up appearances at work but would return in the afternoon. She was wrong. Shep faded into sight still in his lab coat and knelt down next to me. His hand cupped my chin as he looked sternly into my eyes. Gradually he relaxed until he found everybody had taken note of his surprise appearance. "What? I'm her father and I felt her wake. I needed to check on her."

"Shep, you have taken care of her alone for over ten years. It is only natural that you feel you are the only capable person of doing so. But I assure you, we are here to help you now. You have two of the best-known healers in the Shadow Realm here taking care of her, let alone that one of them is her own mother." Shep glanced around, but he never did agree. His hand automatically went to his bald head, which always meant he didn't feel comfortable. Sarah came over and hugged him from behind, teasingly.

"We are the most sought after Protectors in our realm, and Selena only has to know how to escape. We will do the rest." Sarah kissed his bald head and shoved him forward with her soft laugh. "I need some time alone to nurse my child. You have taken care of all the scrapes—and bumps and bruises and hurt feelings. Now…let me have a memory of taking care of her this time. I have five years that I lost with both of you, and I need to fill that void."

Shep patted her arm, agreeing loudly. He looked over at Mr. Sturley, Billy, and Granddad. "You won't leave her alone for any reason while I am at work, right?" His question was more of a command.

"Shep, I lost you two once. I won't ever let her out of my life again. I couldn't bear it. I don't think Matthew or Tyler are going anywhere either. Now you need to go back before you are missed. Tell them you are taking the rest of the day off—and possibly the week— to stay with Selena if you need to, but you can't keep this up."

After Shep faded from sight I saw Wayne and another big man walking through the mist. "Time for a change of guard." Mr. Sturley started up, but Billy grabbed his arm.

"No, I will do it. You have been away from your son long enough, and I think he needs your attention."

Mr. Sturley grinned as he glanced over at us. His eyes were dancing with the same deep blue color of Matthew's. Matthew hadn't let me out of his arms all morning. "Yes, I can see that, thank you."

The trees were dark behind them, and I was surprised to see a heavy mist enveloping the area. Billy and Granddad took off as Wayne introduced yet another uncle to me. "This is Kenny. He is more brain than brawn, but he wanted to help this time." Kenny swatted Wayne in the breadbasket, forcing him to double over.

"Hi Selena, I am the baby brother of this motley crew." I watched as he studied me from head to toe. Kenny actually wore gold frame glasses, but yet had those Martin blue eyes. They were a different blue from Matthew's vibrant sky blue, for they looked clearer—almost like they were barely tinted.

Mr. Sturley held his hand out towards Matthew. "Come on son, I believe you have wanted to talk to me and I wasn't listening." Matthew seemed uncomfortable as he leaned over and kissed my temple.

"I won't be far if you need me." I nodded with understanding as he took his father's hand, but I watched as he closed his eyes. I felt him sensing all around us.

Matthew looked over at Misty, his mom, and then left with his father. Their forms seemed to fade into mist as it swirled around them, covering them from sight. As soon as he was gone, I felt a little anxious but chided myself that it was all due to circumstances from yesterday. Softly Sarah and Misty chuckled, causing me to ask what they found so funny. "Absolutely nothing," Sarah muffled out through her amusement.

Misty and Sarah chatted about how the Sturleys had been surviving in the Mortal Realm. I was shocked with all they had done to keep Matthew and Meg undetected by the Shadow Realm, especially by their own people or family.

Matthew and Mr. Sturley returned shortly with a look of deep satisfaction on their faces. Matthew immediately reclaimed his spot back beside me, forcing Sarah to move. Happily I leaned back over into his embrace, feeling safe and loved. I even allowed my eyes to rest as I listened to Mr. Sturley demand to know how Sarah was going to deal with the onslaught of my abilities.

"These abilities are like a cascade, and Shep is going to have to take care of one at a time." Mr. Sturley's voice didn't sound kind. Instead he sounded like he was demanding for Sarah to listen. He held an authority like no other. "The child may be latent in receiving these abilities, but you all held them off far too long. Did you know this would happen?"

Sarah's voice sounded weak. "No, I have never done research into the effects of holding off children's natural abilities. I see that was an error. We were completely focused on keeping her off the radar." The "tsk-tsk" sound I heard sounded disgusted. Poor Granddad then asked what they should have done.

"Shep should have trained her with the minor abilities to keep them pacified, for now even the smallest ability is going to feel major to her. Her telepathy alone is a challenge from what Matthew has shared. I know she had to have it before Analease died, so why didn't you continue at least with that?"

"Shep needed her to not give herself away if any from the other realms happened upon her, and from what I have learned, we are fortunate it has been that way."

Mr. Sturley remained quiet while listening to Sarah's explanation, but he soon interrupted. "When I started feeling her abilities show, I began trying to shield the area the closer I came. When I found Empire, I found Shep's traps that surround the general region but realized I would be safe as long as I didn't use my Shadow abilities, and we wore no markers. We were lucky. Our two families have a lot to protect with our current situation, and I need to make some hard decisions soon." Mr. Sturley sounded distant, and when I looked, Mrs. Sturley was kissing his cheek while holding his arm. I could see how hard this had been for them. What Matthew had said about his father was true. He really was afraid of his home, and he wanted nothing more than to keep his family safe.

During our time in the forest, we were visited by Kirt and Laura. They really were miserable and there didn't seem to be any way to help them feel better about things. They kept us updated on what was going on at school and how Heather was calling so much Betty told her their phone was broken. Betty had become adamant that she needed to concentrate on taking care of Tyler instead of answering the phone. Poor Heather had to be totally miserable. Shep, knowing how Heather would react, had already told her he had turned the ringers off on our phones so I could rest. The way she received her information about me was to run to Shep's car every day when he pulled in from work. Several days had passed before we returned home. To Shep's dismay, it had been much later than planned.

Mr. Sturley seemed to be taking over my care, and from what I understood, he was much sought after in Shadow Medicine when he lived in the Shadow Realm. From all I had learned, he was renowned. We would be returning to school the next week, which happened to be the first of October.

"Are you ready for a dry run? I want to see if you handle things better, especially teenagers. If you can't, then it will be another week off." Over the past week, Sarah hadn't allowed me to do any practicing, to the point that being home was more like being in prison. A person can only watch so much TV or listen to music. I was becoming bored fast. I would be thankful to be back in school.

Tonight we were going to go to the mall, and Meg was joining us. I hadn't really gotten a chance to get to know her since she spent most of her time with Mike, even when her family was over. A couple hours later I was dressed and waiting on Meg to show up. When Sarah came into the room announcing Meg would be arriving shortly, I ran to the door and peeked out the side window to let her in. To my surprise, I didn't see her or anyone on the street. Sarah must have been wrong. Sarah's giggle brought my attention back to the family room. I could see she was facing the darkest corner of the room as I rushed back in. I watched the darkened space and could see small movement. This particular corner had always creeped me out when I was alone, and now I wondered if it was the natural place that Sarah and other Shadows had watched over me from. It would be the perfect place to hide, especially if you weren't aware of the other realms. Shep had said Sarah had been here a lot. I imagine that was why he spent so much time in solitude in this room. He wouldn't have to use his speech; they would have used their telepathy.

We waited patiently as Meg faded in. Her dark hair really did seem to stay in the shadows even though I could tell she was no longer in Shadow form. Every time I saw her fade, I could see what had freaked my cousins out. She had the attitude of one of those people in the mall that gravitates towards Hot Topic, although she wasn't Goth. Meg moved slowly as she inquired what our destination was.

"We are going to the mall," Sarah informed. "I understand you are good at following in Shadow if I keep a slow pace." Meg's curt nod proved she was unsettled by something, but what, I didn't understand.

Sarah squared her shoulders as she studied Meg closely. I was taken by surprise that we would be shadowing such a distance, let alone with Meg following. "Don't worry, I won't lose you."

A few minutes later we faded in beside a wall in one of the dark alcoves. Sarah had made me travel with her since I still didn't have shadowing down, and she didn't want me to tax my abilities yet. This made me feel like a dweeb with Meg doing it by herself.

We walked to the mall entrance, only to be accosted by the business of people all around. I could hear a light buzzing in my ears, although I was containing it fine. This was a good sign. Going further in I could see the mall wasn't too busy, and everything was aglow with twinkling orange lights. Meg acted curious about our habits of celebrating Halloween. I couldn't help but look at her like she had asked the stupidest question.

"Shep transforms our house every year into a dilapidated, noisy haunted house." Sarah just rolled her eyes, mouthing that sounded like him. It wasn't much of a surprise when Meg proceeded to request going to Hot Topic and Spencer's. When she said, "Hot Topic," I had to smile. We visited the stores and were not impressed with any of the costumes this year. Then Meg piped up that maybe we should just go in Shadow form and see if anybody would know the difference. Sarah thought that would be real helpful in keeping us hidden. Sarah really needed to work on her sarcasm. "Matthew and I did that one year and it was fine for the most part. It was the most entertaining Halloween we ever had."

"So how did you pull it off?" With this question a quick smile appeared and disappeared on Meg's face. She took in a deep breath as if gaining some control.

"You remember the boogeyman movie? Someone is always making a remake of it along with way too many others. We hid in the shadows and gave our friends the night of their lives. We scared them to death, but they wanted to be scared. They never realized it was us completely, especially since they don't even know about our realm. Unfortunately, Dad reacted just like Sarah, and of course we paid the consequences by having to move."

This brought up one of Meg's concerns with Mike being afraid of the dark. She felt he would be easy to scare. That made me think. "Do Shadows or Guardians ever marry Mortals?" Her smile was genuine as her eerie laugh sent shivers down my spine.

"Of course we do, and I know Guardians have too. There are two major problems with this, though. Mortals are exactly that—mortal. We, on the other hand, live for very long periods of time, and their life span is so short most of us choose not to make that choice. The second problem is that most stay with their mate until they die, but in rare cases there have been breakups, your grandmother being one of them. Once you have chosen who you want to be with, it doesn't change. Mom says we have people who were made just for us and we are drawn to them. For most, they find their true love, which we call matches…"

Suddenly Meg became very quiet, almost upset if you asked me. Her voice even quivered as I took note that she wasn't even looking at us anymore. Instead she was looking at her shoes. "Mike is a nice guy and all, but he is not Shadow. I don't even know if he can get over being afraid of the boogeyman. Moreover, if he ever found out I was like the boogeyman he wouldn't want anything to do with me. So I guess I'll enjoy his company for now. Anyway, we never live in one place long enough to get serious about anybody."

This made me feel sad for Meg more than anything. "I like Mike but I'm too young to even consider settling down yet," she crooned in her abnormally happy voice. I could accept that at least she was giving Mike a chance. We went into a dress shop where my head gave a little pound, but nothing like what I had felt before. I was able to push it to the back of my mind.

When we arrived back at the house, I found Tyler playing video games with Shep. They both stopped in mid battle to inquire how I had done. Sarah answered, "I don't understand how anyone could want to go back to school so badly to learn so quickly. She did a very good job. There were a couple of difficult situations happening around us, but she adjusted without trying. It is safe for her to return. I believe she is gaining the control she needs." Tyler hollered out his praise, but wanted to know if he had to go back, too. With a punch to his arm, I reminded him how disappointed Heather would be if he didn't return.

To my surprise, I watched as a look of panic cross his face. He had forgotten she was calling tonight at bedtime, and if Kirt answered the phone he would cause problems. Hastily Shep offered to shadow him home, which Tyler accepted uncharacteristically fast. All of us were laughing at Tyler's dilemma. "I know he is becoming serious about her I can feel it. He is confused though. Until tonight, I never realized how complicated a relationship would be with a Mortal due to the longevity thing."

Shep faded back in and spoke as gently as he could. "This is the way our life is here. You will see the ending of many Mortal lives. You need to accept that and live on. Heather and Mike…neither one would want you to end yours because they weren't around. Who knows, by the time it comes you may not be as close as you are now. I have many Mortal friends, and I continue to make new ones because each and every individual is different. They enjoy their lives, and we enjoy helping them along with their journey."

The next morning I found my friends at Mike's house playing basketball. As I strode to join them, Mike caught sight of me and demanded to know if it was safe for me to be out. I was sure it was more of a question if it was safe for him and not me. When I tried to hug him he ran away, hiding behind Heather. We all laughed as he offered Heather as the human guinea pig first. Heather, being the true friend she was, ended the joke by hugging me as she grinned back at Mike.

Of course Mike began to taunt us. "Heather *would* hug you. She has already had the chicken pox in first grade." I stuck my tongue out at him as I told him you could actually get the chicken pox more than once, which is true. Meg hooted as Matthew came barreling out of their house, charging towards us. "The plague of the pox is infesting Mike's house!" Meg hollered with glee. Mike started laughing and said, "There still would have to be one more to join before it is a full out plague." Of course he meant Tyler. Where was my cousin?

Matthew rushed over to offer me a hug. Had to admit it felt nice to be held again. I had missed this last night. Mike's comment caught us both off guard. "That is probably how you both got the pox in the first place. Man, give her some breathing room. Don't always keep your arm around her."

Matthew grinned over at Meg, which made her stiffen as he retorted. "Yeah, well you would probably like to be giving her a hug instead of me. I think you are jealous." Mike dropped his ball and promptly walked over to give me a big hug. He had that Muir look of domination on his face. Suddenly both boys were harassing each other, while Meg giggled with her eerie laugh as she relaxed. Even so, Heather looked back towards Tyler's house anxiously. I knew she was worried he wouldn't be joining us today. With a gentle tap I draped my arm around her shoulders and whispered, "He'll be out soon. No chicken pox will be able to keep you separated much longer."

She smiled weakly. "Do you think he really likes me?"

"Why would you even ask?" Her reply hit me like a lead balloon. "Because… his mom wouldn't let me talk to him for almost a week. Not to mention he caught the chicken pox at the same time as you. I sometimes feel he likes you." Matthew looked at me, allowing Mike to steal the ball. I was sure he wanted to warn me to not freak out. This misconception was something I was expecting. I knew the boys were being too protective of me, and this proved it. Carefully I considered how to answer. I knew I had to keep control or I would be in trouble with Sarah. With a tug to her arm, we headed towards the woods.

At first I was tempted to tell her the truth about Tyler being my cousin, but that wouldn't go over well. Matthew's voice commanded, *"Not now."*

"Listen Heather, Tyler really likes you. I know he does. Since I am your best friend he looks out for me too. You wouldn't want a boyfriend who didn't get along with me, would you? He looks at you with adoring eyes and he just bosses me around. I mean, come on, I have Matthew and to be honest, I am not sure I was ready for a boyfriend until he came along. I mean, did you really think you and I would have boyfriends this year? Shep and I always thought I would never have one since I am so stubborn and way too independent. You and I have always done things together and though we liked talking about guys, we never cared for their personality, not seriously. Even when we went out on dates I was never impressed."

At least she laughed. "Mike and I always thought you wanted us to get together."

"I really thought I would be a bridesmaid at yours and Mike's wedding. I guess I was wrong." We both were laughing at my shattered dream of the future. Thankfully, we were surprised when Matthew and Tyler came jogging down the path towards us. Straightaway Tyler caught Heather up and swung her around like a rag doll. I was sure he had heard her doubts and wanted to make it up to her. The minute her feet were back on the ground she smiled at me and told me I was right. The blushes to her cheeks were priceless. I was happy to see her embarrassed smile.

Matthew gripped my hand, trying to assure me everything was fine. Besides, he was happy to hear I had never felt this way about anyone else but him. Now it was my turn to blush. Gently, he wrapped his arm around me as Heather decided we needed to take a long walk out to the lighthouse. For a moment she looked hesitant as she wondered aloud if we should ask the others to join us. Tyler's emphatic "no" drew all of our attention. He seemed to squirm as he looked behind us. "They can take care of themselves. I want time alone if you don't mind."

This pleased Heather to no end. Matthew agreed solemnly as they began pulling us up to the plank path.

Suddenly we all froze as Heather asked about our spots. It had just struck her that we had no blemishes on our skin to prove we had the chicken pox. "You're right. The first time you get a lot of sores, but this was my second time I had them and I didn't get them that bad. The problem was we were contagious and slept a lot." Matthew agreed swiftly. I could have lost it right then and there. Luckily Tyler saved me by pointing out some kites, which were flying down at the shoreline.

Heather and Tyler started chatting on about the misery of her being at school by herself. I was glad they were becoming involved in their own conversation. Matthew and I allowed them to inch ahead of us so we could let them have some time to themselves. As we rounded the bend, I recognized the spot where Billy had confronted me. It seemed ages ago that I had shadowed out of control.

Matthew's grip tightened, making me fully aware he knew what I was thinking. "I am glad you shadowed that night. I was able to help you from ending up who knows where. It also allowed me to be honest with myself that I was…" He stopped without finishing his sentence as his eyes darted to the ground bashfully. What was he about to say but chose not to? A second later he perked up as he agreed Shep was right. *"You are stubborn and independent but I like that in you. Besides, your independence includes me and that's good."*

The seagulls were squealing as the waves hit the shore. Too bad we hadn't thought to bring kites. It would be a perfect day to fly them. We continued to walk down the path, only to spy Tyler and Heather sitting out on the beach watching the kites soar. They looked like such a cute couple. I couldn't imagine them any other way. Abruptly Matthew hollered for Tyler and Heather to catch up. The sight of them running while holding hands made me very sentimental. We continued teasing each other as we walked down the path to the lighthouse, making me feel normal for once.

After we arrived, I realized how strong the wind was, especially at the shore. My clothes were sealed to my body by the gust of wind. Slowly I glanced around to discover we were basically alone except for a few people. Heather informed Tyler that on some Saturdays they conduct tours of the lighthouse and maybe we could see if the docents were here. We were lucky to find them sitting at the door, just waiting for someone to entertain. I guess we were going to be their first victims of the day. Right away they all jumped up, looking pleased as we entered.

They quickly began going over the history of the area and when this lighthouse was established. Then they asked if we would like to go up five hundred feet and reminded us that if anyone had a fear of heights, they wouldn't want to. We all smirked at each other, for it wouldn't be any problem. What would be the problem was all those stairs, but it was worth it when we made it to the top. To me it was amazing how these lighthouses had been maintained. A person would run up these steps carrying who knows what in a matter of minutes as part of a normal routine. Nowadays most people got winded just going up the first flight. Luckily the docent informed us we wouldn't have to go back down too soon since there wasn't a line yet.

Most of the time Heather wouldn't go out on the catwalk, but she wasn't going to miss a chance for Tyler to put his arms around her. She stood against the railing with Tyler behind her, who was giving her a ton of information on how the environment works in this area. I was sure she wasn't hearing a word he was saying.

We watched the horizon as a barge was making its way across. When we looked down we saw people arriving below and knew it was time to head down for the new arrivals. Carefully I turned around backwards and went down the steps to get out of the lamp area. The boys obliged by helping us until we were able to turn around. When we reached the final level, Heather's leg spasmed with a charley horse. I had forgotten how her ankles were. This meant we would be here longer than we had originally planned.

The minute we reached the beach, we left Tyler to take care of Heather while I removed my shoes so I could get my feet wet by the cold waves. Matthew didn't understand why I couldn't resist this. With a grin he picked up my shoes as we walked down the beach, facing the whipping wind. The wind had continued to grow since there were no trees around. You could really feel it. When I finally walked out of the surf, Matthew and I sat down to watch the seagulls glide on the wind. Sometimes it looked like they were staying in the same spot.

Matthew rubbed my arm briskly. "So how do you feel about school tomorrow?" If I were being honest I would tell him I was petrified, but this was not the time to admit to my fear. Instead I pretended to not pay much attention to his question.

"I handled the mall pretty well, so tomorrow should be okay. Especially since I don't have to worry about Tyler and Kirt protecting me from you." He laughed in agreement, reiterating how he had felt like they wanted to pound him. And yet he made it abundantly clear that he knew they wouldn't do anything in public. This reminded me of the first day of school when I had a problem on the bus. "Matthew, were you spying on me in the woods that first day?" Anxiously he admitted he had. Then I asked him if he had seen a man at the same time and he replied no.

I could see the concern flash across his face. He wanted to demand more. "Why?"

"Tyler had said there was a man in the woods and we thought it might have been your father." Matthew became concerned and wanted to know what he looked like, but I knew nothing. Besides, I figured it had been the man in the mist, and yet there was some doubt. Then Matthew demanded to know if Shep had investigated this. I could only shrug my shoulders while reminding him Shep was always investigating stuff these days and I didn't ever know what it pertained to.

His face was full of dissatisfaction with the situation. Obviously this piece of information unsettled him. "Shoot. I didn't even know about the other realms until this past summer."

Matthew looked stunned. "That is so hard to believe, Selena."

"Yep, I spent the whole month of August learning about the Guardian ways and I still don't have all of it down. My head is on overload with new knowledge. If the truth be told, some of my teachers were from the Shadow Realm. Some were friends with my family for a long time. I didn't even know how my parents' accident had really happened until recently, and even now I know there is more that they aren't saying." For a brief moment I actually felt bashful.

"You are amazing. This has been too short of a time to learn everything you have. I didn't realize until recently your parents died, and that Shep thought it was Alexander. My dad won't tell us everything, but he and Shep both agree several of the killings had to be done by him and his cohorts. I am surprised they were successful in killing your mother with Shep around. He is a Protector, and they are very dangerous."

"What do you mean he is a Protector? He was my mom's guardian, and when I was born he and Sarah became mine. My dad's journal said he wouldn't have it any other way. In fact, Granddad said my parents went to great lengths in all three realms to make sure he was my legal guardian and able to adopt me. I know they did a good job. We had a small problem back in the summer, but Shep had it all tied up legally in all three realms. You know, Shep adopted me when I was five years and seven months, which is why my name is Martin-Goodwin."

Matthew was looking at me like something had just dawned on him. "I know why he is your Protector. My dad says Shep is one of the fiercest Protectors there are. Protectors are very loyal and usually to one family—in this case, your grandmother's family. If he was there the day your parents died, then he must have saved you. He may have witnessed something. See, a Protector guards one child and their bond is said to be as strong the parents' bond at times. A Protector will die before anything happens to his charge. They are trained to sense the possibility of danger. Selena, it is very rare for the child to ever come to any harm. He was no longer your mother's Protector but yours. He still would have been close to your mother, but his senses would have been tied to you. He wouldn't have felt any fear from you since you were a toddler. His first duty to the family is to rescue the child and not to return until the child is safe. Even if the family is in danger he has no choice. He would be like a mama bear with her cubs. You never get in between them, and if he adopted you when you were that young...I bet you two have developed the parent bond and that will make his protection of you even stronger."

The memories of Shep's recent training flooded my mind, and I felt Matthew wince upon sensing them. Without delay I tried to focus on the waves. I loved my parents. They saw the need for me to have another set of loving parents, and I do. Billy wasn't sure they had thought about the bond thing. Somehow I know they did.

"According to Drew, once this adoptive bond is created, it can never be broken, not even if the biological parents return. Sarah and I are forming the same bond. I can't see my life without her in it. I sometimes feel a little guilty. My family says my parents wanted this." With a smile over my shoulder, I quickly knocked him to take the look of amazement off his face.

"So you have his genetic markers now, don't you?"

"Yes, I do. Sarah figured it happened after the first month we were together, according to her test. That is probably why we always felt safe, because technically we were sensing each other constantly and weren't aware the bond had occurred. Sarah says she will recognize when our bond has developed, and then we will have to train, too. Technically, I think the bond is almost complete. I feel a difference lately. I wonder if it can be that fast. I'm afraid to ask. Sometimes I am sure she can read my thoughts, and I am able to keep track of her some, too." Staring at him, I knew it all made sense. Shep had said he didn't realize there was any danger until my mother had tried to tip him off. He had also said I would always be his daughter and no harm would ever come to me unless he was dead.

Matthew was listening to my thoughts and understood what he had revealed. "I'm sorry, Selena, I didn't realize you didn't know."

"I have a lot to learn about the Shadow Realm. I think they are trying to keep me safe, but it just causes trouble. I know they have their reasons. Still…would you teach me about things you think are common knowledge?" I could tell he wasn't sure if this was a wise idea. Reluctantly, he agreed.

"Let's just pray I don't overstep my bounds with Shep. He could wipe me out in a breeze. My dad says I *would* choose a girl with a special Protector. Although I don't think he realizes you are adopted by Shep legally. I imagine that would make a difference because you represent…" Suddenly Matthew became very solemn. Gently I leaned over and hugged him while feeling a sense of relief wash through my whole body. This reminded me of our trip to his special place. Matthew looked pleased that I wanted to go there with him.

Telepathically I called out to Shep to ask if Matthew and I could visit another location. "*I'm surprised to hear you ask, little one. Analease didn't catch on for a good two months. It's fine, go ahead.*" As we stood, Matthew helped me to brush the sand from my clothes. We made our way over to Tyler while still swatting the sand from each other.

"Tyler, we are going to head back." Tyler immediately started to follow, but I told him to stay and enjoy the beautiful weather, even if it was windy. Before long, winter would be here and we all would miss these sunny days at the lighthouse. Tyler reacted suspiciously as he inquired on why I was being so generous. Matthew smiled coyly. "*Wouldn't you like to know?*" Tyler scowled at him until Heather distracted him again. Swiftly we walked back down the plank path until Matthew felt safe enough to take me to his hiding place. My stomach had butterflies as I grew excited about seeing the waterfall again, but most of all being alone with Matthew.

After a while he decided it was safe, and we went into the darkening cool pines while sensing around us to make sure we weren't being watched. Matthew held out his arms and I snuggled up to his warm body. This time I heard his heart jump at my touch. With a light, amused whisper, he reminded me I wouldn't have to close my eyes with him. I felt us fading into the darkness and watched the shapes pass before my eyes. I really could understand the different forms now. We slid smoothly through and came to a stop right next to the waterfall. It felt warmer here, and this made me wonder where we were exactly. Matthew continued to hold me as a warm breeze blew across us. The smells of flowers were very strong.

Matthew rubbed his face in my hair as he told me we were off the map. I pulled back to stare at his face. He knew I didn't believe him. When he released me, I looked at the plants and their colors of vivid purples, reds, and yellows. We had to be in a forest or jungle of some kind. Cautiously I took a seat at the water's edge and rolled my pant legs up after removing my shoes again. Matthew snickered at his observation. "You never do leave your shoes on."

When my legs were immersed I was thrilled that it felt warm, like bathwater. "Just think. We can go swimming during the winter here," Matthew informed me with a huge smile. This would be wonderful, and it would be our own private place. But the thought of Meg ran across my mind. Did she know about our little oasis? Matthew seemed to snicker as he glanced apprehensively at me. "No, Meg doesn't know where I go when I need space. Of course my parents would be able to track me here if the need ever arose. Just like I am sure Shep would be able to find you here if he needed to. So for now, as long as no trouble arises, this is our private oasis as you call it." I liked the idea no one besides Shep could follow me here.

"So that means we are alone totally. No Tyler, Kirt, or Heather to hide from anymore." I knew I had to be beaming by now. My body was shivering with the excitement of not being interrupted if Matthew decided to be close to me.

"Is that what you want? For me to always be alone with you?"

The excitement in my eyes must have been showing, and I suddenly felt short of breath at trying to answer him. Feeling him so close made me want nothing more than to sit with him forever. His hands slowly caressed my face as his lips brushed mine, making my heart pound out of my chest. When he pulled away, I could see I had the same effect on him. Very slowly I leaned towards him, only to find myself being pulled into his arms as our lips continued to play with each other. His kisses felt so soft to the point I couldn't think anymore. As soon as he pulled back, my breathing was ragged and I wondered if my heart would ever beat normally again. His smile was so cocky I had to turn away. He truly affected me in a way that I wasn't used to.

Roughly he pulled me into his body while whispering into my hair. "It's alright. I like to hear your mind. I promise to help you keep this secret." Giggles escaped me like a small child. I wondered if I would be able to keep Heather in the dark. My thought caused Matthew to snort. "Probably not."

We sat there for a while in silence just enjoying the feeling of being with each other. His heartbeat against me made me feel ecstatic. Not wanting to ruin a moment with him, I hadn't moved in so long my foot had gone to sleep. Instantly he started to shuffle to help me up. "You should have said something. You need to walk it off." When he helped me up, I shook the invisible needles that were piercing my foot as he chuckled at my predicament.

I couldn't help but look at the beauty of the scenery around us. Matthew took my hand and told me he wanted to show me something else that was amazing. He walked me towards the waterfall. We came to the rock-faced wall and could go no further. Matthew asked if I minded getting a little wet. Of course I shook my head no. Slowly he started walking on a thin shelf that led behind the waterfall and disappeared. I hadn't noticed the toe ledge before. Warily, I placed my hands on the warm rock and began inching my way to where Matthew had disappeared. I continued to where the water was falling when Matthew's hand reached out and helped me step onto a sparkling precipice. The inside of the cave was filled with glittering, clear rocks that acted like prisms when the sun hit them through the water. The cave was alive with rainbows, and it was so beautiful.

"I thought you would like this." Matthew stood there proud while looking around the crystal opening. "I sometimes sit back here when it is too hot outside and rest or read a book. That is why this little oasis is perfect for me. Back here I have air conditioning and the sound of the waterfall, which can soothe a headache." Matthew was bubbling over with his love of this place. It truly was a place he needed, and maybe I was intruding by knowing about it.

Matthew acted as if he had been poked as he gasped. "You are never intruding here. You are just adding ambience to my heaven."

With his pronouncement I rolled my eyes as I continued to walk around the room, rubbing my hands along the rocks, watching how the light reflected rainbows and shadows. Matthew blocked my path while looking so deeply into my eyes he took my breath away. Abruptly, the alarm on his watch went off, surprising us both. He jerked to silence the annoying beep. It was time to head home, but I really didn't want to. Matthew acknowledged my disappointment. "We will come back soon, but in order to do that we should keep Shep happy by returning on time."

Before leaving his secret chamber, I took note of a couple huge throw pillows and a blanket, along with a very used pad of paper and pencil on the floor. Evidently he spent enough time here that he needed some comforts. Once in his welcoming embrace, I held tight to him as we began sliding through the shadows. Softly I felt his lips kissing my head. Then he tilted my chin up to softly caress my lips. I felt a warm chill run through me as he obliged. When we slowed down things became a bit bumpy, and before I even realized it, we had stopped. Instead of parting we continued to kiss. When I opened my eyes I recognized that he had shadowed us directly into my family room. "Mind if I stay for dinner?" he whispered as he trailed soft kisses across my cheek to my ear. "No, I'll just keep you as my prisoner," I beamed.

Shep came up from the basement carrying a Halloween box. Crud. Our house was going to be transformed into lots of cobwebs and loud creaky noises. Then Sarah came walking into the family room and asked how our day had been. Matthew admitted he didn't want to go back to school after a day like today. The idea of going back to school wasn't the most pleasant idea under the sun to me either. This thought alone was enough to make my stomach fall through to my feet. I really didn't want to acknowledge I was becoming a little apprehensive I would never have a normal day at school again.

To my surprise Matthew had to ask what was I thinking about so intently. I tried to act like it was nothing. But with the thought of school, I had started shielding my mind again. It didn't take a mind reader to know what had just happened. Sarah and I looked at each other as we heard the first scream of a Halloween ghoul. "Where did you say those earplugs are?" Sarah demanded. They followed me into the kitchen where I promptly pointed to a drawer where I kept a couple sets. They really weren't there for this, but it helped to make everyone laugh when I produced a pair. We all took a seat

Matthew left soon after dinner. I had to admit I hated to see him go. I watched him walk down my drive while Shep pulled me back, commenting he was a nice guy. It was funny how close I had become to him in such a short period of time. I was depending on him like I did Shep.

The next morning I was ready early, waiting on Matthew to show, for I was sure he would come. Our house was slowly turning into a haunted house with flickering chandeliers and other weird things. Even though I enjoyed some of it, the noisy junk gets on my nerves when overdone. When I was younger, this stuff kept me up at night. On the other hand, the kids in the neighborhood loved Shep's decorating, including his special effect crystal ball. He would have it at the front door before long. Maybe Sarah and I would be able to turn all this junk off if we worked together.

Carefully I went over my plan for the day. I started clearing my mind to bridge any space that would make me vulnerable to the teenagers around me. Soon Matthew faded into the room and immediately came over, wanting to know if I could use any help. He knew that was a stupid question, for I always could use his help. To my surprise the doorbell rang. We weren't expecting anybody this early. When I opened it, I was shocked to find Tyler waiting impatiently for me to answer.

"What are you doing here? You should go on the bus with Heather."

Not paying attention to what I had said, he entered the house, closing the door briskly behind him. Immediately he began accusing me of not doing what I was told. He was making it perfectly clear he was mad. "I checked to see if you were home when we returned and found you hadn't done what Sarah said." Suddenly he was demanding every detail of what I had been doing yesterday. "Heather is going to be on your case today because she wants to know where the two of you disappeared to. She has no idea how right she is. So where did you go and did Shep know you left the area?"

Matthew had been sitting in the family room quietly until his temper got the better of him. I thought they had overcome this. Matthew informed Tyler briskly he had no right to make such demands. "Shep knew and is the only person who needs to know." To my dismay Sarah walked in, in commanding form, making both boys glare at each other. She was not happy with what was going on at all.

The minute Shep appeared, he greeted Tyler solemnly. "Tyler, I knew. Matthew is safe and you both need to work together from now on." Tyler realized he wasn't going to get anywhere and left to meet Heather in a rush of anger. After the door closed behind him, Shep informed Matthew he was going to have to understand Tyler was only looking out for me and he didn't want that to change. Matthew acted like it was no big deal, but I knew differently.

# CHAPTER 17.
# THE BIG GAME

**As I climbed** out of the car, Matthew took my hand like it was totally normal for us to do this every day. The buses hadn't arrived yet, and I couldn't imagine what Heather was going to do when she saw Matthew holding my hand, acting so territorial. This reminded me of the day at the vet's office when Shep introduced Sarah. Hopefully some people had noticed us together at the beach party and we wouldn't be the subject of gossip. I had never thought about listening to others talk about me behind my back when I could actually hear them.

As we walked together up the steps, I heard the buses pulling in. I tried to focus on not tensing up as we walked straight into the foyer. Matthew didn't say a word. I don't know if he was trying to allow me to concentrate or if he was trying to assess the situation himself. The buses unloaded and I could hear the kids, but they weren't attacking my mind yet. I closed my eyes, taking deep breaths to calm my body, and hopefully my mind. Matthew's hand began to rub my back in a comforting manner as he offered his support silently. Instead of waiting for everybody to enter the building, I walked to my locker only to find I was holding my breath. To my horror, I realized Matthew was not beside me or touching me anymore. I had accidently slowed everything down.

With a breath, Matthew looked at me in shock. When he caught up to me he asked if Tyler had done that. Unfortunately this made me have to admit to him it was me. He acted absolutely delighted as I reminded him I was part Guardian. He thought it would be cool to be able to do both types of abilities. I had never thought to tell him about this one.

"It's the one ability that came easiest to me," I grinned. "Sure you don't mind dating a half and half?" With a resounding "no" he acknowledged he could handle it as long as I let him guide our traveling. The corridors were becoming full with teenagers, and I didn't seem to be having any struggles with blocking their minds.

As we were passing classrooms, some were being transformed into orange and black colors for Halloween. Once we reached my first period class, I felt comfortable with Matthew's arm about me. Tyler and Heather came bouncing up as Heather knocked me teasingly. One could tell and hear she wanted to know if I had a secret as she smiled at Matthew coyly.

"So how was your day with Tyler yesterday?" Her mild reply of "great" didn't surprise me. She patted Tyler's chest before telling him bye. By the way she was walking towards our desk, I could see she was waiting for me to be alone so she could grill me.

Tyler looked at me with pure satisfaction. "So, do you have a headache yet?" he asked before walking away. He was getting pleasure from all my pain of having to lie to her.

"No," I said.

"You will when she gets through with you." He was telling the truth. Heather wasn't going to give up until she heard every minute detail of my day yesterday.

Matthew's demeanor began to feel like ice as he smiled at my cousin. "Well, you'd better get going if you don't want to be late."

Reluctantly I sat down beside Heather, with no sign of Mr. Jensen in the room. A second later she leaned over and told me to spill the beans. She knew we didn't go home after we left them, and she never did see me come home. With a shake of my head I told her Matthew ate dinner with us and left around eight p.m.

"Fine, but what did you do with him in the afternoon, because Sarah said she didn't know where you were. If I'm your best friend, then best friends tell each other everything. We have no secrets, remember?" Heather's attention was drawn to the front of the room when Mr. Jensen called us to order. Without warning, Heather leaned over and whispered. "I know you are keeping a secret. You'd better spill later." She had no idea how many secrets I was keeping from her.

The bell rang and I hadn't even realized time had passed so quickly. Before Heather left, she looked very determined. "You and I will talk later, and I want details." As we slowly exited the door, I was caught by the crowd of students rushing to their classes, and to my surprise, no one was greeting me. When I made it to geometry, I found Mike standing in the room across the way with Meg. He didn't even notice me go into class, and I was glad. Unfortunately, Matthew wasn't in his usual seat and I wondered what had happened to him. I really wanted to have him at my side.

Mr. Cain called me over to his desk and gave me one piece of makeup homework he had forgotten to send to me. Matthew came straight to Mr. Cain's desk and was offered the same piece of missed homework. Slowly we walked to our desks as Matthew apologized for not escorting me. His last period teacher held him over to give him some of his missed assignments. I tried to convince him I understood, but he seemed to be more focused on me.

In class, Matthew kept looking at me inquisitively. "What are you thinking so hard on? I want to help." Unfortunately, Mr. Cain called the class to order early and I was not able to tell him what my predicament was. Mr. Cain turned on his projector and started showing theorems on the board and—like always— half the class fell asleep in five minutes.

When the bell rang, Matthew took my hand. Tyler met us in the hallway and wanted to walk me to biology, too. Evidently he was still ticked about yesterday. As we were walking, Tyler explained to Matthew that he could handle this. Matthew growled that he wasn't going anywhere.

Quietly as I could, I asked them why they were so concerned, because I was doing fine. They both stared at me with disbelief. Tyler whispered I had to be lying since he couldn't sense me at all. Taken by surprise, I asked Matthew if his problem was the same, and he nodded his head yes. They both agreed it was totally out of the norm not to sense my mind a little. I was doing better than I thought since I was guarding from everyone.

It took a lot to reassure them I was fine, but I had other problems—mainly with Heather. Matthew looked confused. "What is bothering you so bad you have shut down? Nothing Heather could ask should cause that."

"Heather will know I am lying and I have never lied intentionally. She also knows I have a secret and she wants to know. I don't know what to say to her. Heather is like a sister to me."

During biology, Tyler and Kirt kept whispering possible solutions, but none of them would do. They were both exasperated, especially Tyler when he figured I wanted to tell her the truth. He kept reminding me we couldn't guard her mind well enough to do so.

My next class passed slowly as I went over all the possible things I could tell her, but none would be good enough. I could feel a headache, but it wasn't due to the noise; it was just the stress of not knowing what to say to Heather. To my surprise, a crack of lightning drew my attention out the window. The day truly fit my mood. It was raining full force outside, and that meant I would have to face the lunchroom. As I collected my belongings I wondered if I could procrastinate long enough to skip lunch altogether. Miss Fleur had left it to me to close the door behind me when I left. After closing my backpack I stared out the window at the rain once more. So many things were running through my mind I wasn't sure what to focus on first. Maybe I should leave.

"I don't think you want to do that, Selena." When I jerked around I found Shep leaning against the corner, silhouetted in its darkness.

"What are you doing here?" Shep sat down in the chair beside me in the darkened classroom. He studied my face before glancing out at the storm.

"I know you are upset, Selena, so talk to me." We sat there in silence until Tyler came to the door looking for me. Shep motioned to him everything was all right and told him he would be with me for a while.

"You know, you have the boys all upset. I'm afraid you might do something you shouldn't and that might lead to worse problems. Do you understand what I mean? Heather is your friend. Tell her the general things, and if she pushes, tell her right now you need to keep some things personal. She will understand. Who knows, she might want to hear about your first kiss and then maybe she will tell you about hers." I couldn't believe it. Shep knew about my first kiss, and evidently Heather's. "I wasn't meaning to pry, but I knew you weren't where you were supposed to be. It's my job to keep my eyes on you."

Shep continued to look out the window. "Shouldn't you go to lunch?" With a shake of my head no, I let him know my fears about trying to enter the lunchroom and how I really had not had one easy day at school since it started. He listened to me without interrupting and then assured me I was handling things much better today.

"It's time for you to face your fears, especially with winter coming. You can do this. I suggest if the noise becomes too much for you, slow things down a little, just enough for you to gain control. Billy told me if you don't want someone to be affected by the slowing you can make them immune to your ability by willing them to not be affected. This way Matthew or Tyler could help you through it. Now get going."

It was a surprise to see Matthew leaning against the doorframe. He wrapped his arm around my waist as we walked towards the lunchroom together. "I hope you will pick me to be the immune one if you have to slow things down." His statement broke my somber mood. We stopped at the cafeteria door and I felt the pressure beginning to build. I continued to concentrate on keeping the noise at a distance as Matthew's hand continued to pat my hip. When I opened my eyes, I saw Heather and my other friends taking note at how close Matthew and I were. Matthew whispered he was totally enjoying this.

"Let's get it over with and face Heather's questions together." With a firm look, Matthew began to speak to me telepathically, even if we weren't supposed to. *"Selena, I wanted to ask you yesterday but chickened out. I want us to be a couple, officially. I don't want to date around. If you don't want to be with me as your boyfriend, then tell me now. Because I think we should make it official. It would also help with your problem with Heather."*

I knew I had to be blushing, but I couldn't find enough air in my lungs to say yes. He knew my answer anyway. "Good." With a quick kiss to the side of my head, we headed to our table to sit down. Once I was sitting next to Tyler and Heather, I could see the excitement in her eyes. Oh brother, what was I going to do?

Matthew looked at Heather proudly. "As of yesterday we are officially a couple. Selena is no longer available, so spread it around." Heather's mouth dropped as Mike began clapping his support, and the whole table went abuzz. Heather was so excited she definitely was sidetracked now. Matthew was smart. Heather was saying there had to be a reason we had gone off by ourselves yesterday, and she wanted to hear all about it later. I was so excited myself I didn't even notice any pressure in my head. Matthew's hand kept rubbing my back through the whole lunch period. We hadn't even eaten any lunch by the time the bell rang. When we headed off to the next period, Matthew stuck to my side.

After Matthew left, I found my seat and daydreamed for the rest of the period. Jeremy struggled forward once class had ended. He didn't look to be in a good mood. "I just heard you are going steady with Matthew." This brought a huge smile to my face as I fessed up to its validity. He didn't seem to like it, but congratulated me anyway. Matthew showed up, almost as if called, and grabbed me around my waist to escort me to my next class. His face was flushed with his own excitement.

"I think Jeremy wanted to date you, Selena. He doesn't like me much." I told him I had never shown him any interest in that way. Matthew laughed at my naiveté. "You don't have to show interest for someone to like you."

***

One whole day and I didn't have any major incidents, not even a headache. Everybody was happy for me, and even Laura teased about me going steady with Matthew. Then it hit me. How was I going home? Matthew whispered to me that Shep said we could wait together for him after school. He was going to pick us up at four o'clock. We waved bye to Heather as she insisted on me coming over to her house tonight. She wanted to hear all the details and according to the BFF code, she should be the one to know more than anyone else.

Upon arriving at her house, I was surprised to find Mike there too. What was this all about? My two best friends were ganging up on me. Mike snickered and said he was as close as Heather and deserved the lowdown too. I hedged for the next two hours the best I could.

Mike said he hadn't had the guts to try and kiss Meg yet, and we all laughed at his predicament. Who would have thought boys have it as hard as girls? Heather and I totally enjoyed listening to his misery. Finally, putting Heather under the spotlight took the pressure off me. I didn't mean to ask, but Heather gave me more information about my cousin than I really wanted. Her mind was, as Tyler said, yelling at me. It didn't matter how much effort I used, I couldn't stop the flow of my two friends' minds tonight.

"Mike, are you all going to decorate for Halloween this year?" He looked at me like I was dumb.

"Of course, what type of holiday would it be without a Muir production? I already have permission to have a party the night of Halloween for our friends with a bonfire." This all sounded like fun. Looks like we were going to be sending out fall with a bang.

Mike and I left at the same time. Unfortunately it had started raining again. I could feel it was even colder than when I came over. Before leaving the porch, Mike wanted to know if he would see me at the bus stop tomorrow. "No, Shep is going to be driving me the next couple of days. I have been suffering from headaches a lot lately." He seemed convinced and wished me goodnight as I proceeded to walk back across the yard. The night was so chilly I could see my own breath smoking out in front of me. I was amazed it was getting so cold so early in the season. Shep had left the outdoor light on for me. It usually made me feel safe, but not tonight.

Leisurely I continued to walk as I began to feel uneasy. It was almost like a warning, as if I was being watched. I couldn't even make my heart slow down as I came to a stop in between the two houses. I wanted to look off to the side. Unfortunately, I couldn't pull up the nerve. I had seen nothing out of the ordinary.

Abruptly the front door to my house opened, and Shep was out in a flash. As he walked towards me, he asked what was bothering me. I felt hesitant and uncertain what to say. "I guess it is just my imagination getting the better of me." He didn't agree. He walked me back to our home as Grandma came over and drew me inside with her. Granddad was there, too. Shep and Sarah went back out without saying a word.

Grandma walked me back to my room and asked me how the inquisition had gone. I could tell she was just trying to sidetrack my attention from what was going on outside. Gramms sat down on the edge of my bed, running her fingers through the eyelet sheet top. "Selena, talk to me. I do want to hear." I told her almost everything.

Granddad kept walking back and forth down the hall as if he was waiting for something to happen. I could see Gramms sneak a peek at my grandfather, or she would wander over to the window and pull my blind to glance out. They were nervous, but about what?

The next morning I was greeted by another gloomy day. With one glance out my window, I found a heavy fog barely floating above the ground. My morning ritual went by without any interference. Everything was as it should be, which proved it must have been my imagination. With a glance into the kitchen, I could see Shep was waiting for me like usual.

"Come on in, Selena. We just wanted to inform you that Sarah is going to be gone for a couple of days. She plans on being back by the weekend." I bet this was her way of ducking out on finishing the decorating of the house. "She is needed in the Shadow Realm to deal with an issue that has arisen recently." By this point, I knew I couldn't ask any questions. I wondered if she could take me with her so I wouldn't have to help finish decorating either.

That reminded me about Mike's party. Hopefully I would be able to stay out past midnight. Luckily Shep was enthused with the idea of a Halloween party and wanted to know if Mike's parents needed some more chaperones. I knew Shep just wanted to be at the party. This would be Chelsea's chance to get know Shep's live-in girlfriend, too, so I knew she wouldn't turn down the opportunity. Sarah had been the topic all around town for a while now.

Matthew arrived at the house along with Kirt and Laura. They had decided to abandon the school bus for a while, too. My poor cousins were also getting worn out with the buzz of minds on the bus. For a brief moment I felt hesitant about leaving. I wanted to make sure Sarah knew I loved her and would miss her while she was gone.

"I'll come back as soon as I can." Softly she brushed her hand through my hair as she kissed the top of my head. It was evident she was growing as attached to me as I was to her. It didn't feel right in letting her go. We needed her at home.

The rest of the week went pretty well the same as Monday, and I was grateful for having control. We hadn't heard anything from Sarah, but if she stuck to the rules Shep had made with me, then it meant everything was fine.

This weekend would be one of the last football games of the season. Heather wanted Matthew and I to go with her and Tyler. To my surprise, when I arrived home that Friday before the game, I found Heather waiting on my porch. As I walked around, I could see she was uncomfortable with something, but I wasn't sure what. She acted flustered as she looked over at her house, stating she had scared herself and had the terrible feeling she was being watched. Parker wasn't there, so she had been home alone. She always hated to admit to being scared, so for her to do so meant something really had frightened her. I didn't take it lightly as I volunteered to help her gather her belongings for our date tonight with the boys. With a holler to Shep, I informed him I would be at her house, but we would be back in time to get ready for the game. He waved us on with a peek out the window as we walked across the yard towards her home.

Once inside, we started going through each room. She was right; the house had an eerie feeling, especially in her room. We had found nothing out of the ordinary. Neither one of us could shake the uncomfortable feeling, though. Heather's decision to call Shep made me even more uncomfortable. Something wasn't right, and I really didn't want him to be involved. Softly suggesting that she not bother him since there was truly no reason for us to be acting so skittish seemed to convince her for the moment.

Instead, I paid extra attention to my surroundings by sensing around me. To my horror, I did sense a presence. With haste I encouraged her to follow me home. I offered we would come back when Parker returned. Regrettably, my suggestion wasn't well-received. Instead of doing as I asked, she headed back towards her room, forcing me to follow. I continued to argue with her, but she wasn't listening. Instead she was being bullheaded. I was ready to do whatever I needed to get her out of the house. As I tried to act normal, I pulled her towards the door, stating loudly how I had scared myself too much and we would have my dad come back with us. Heather stopped in her tracks immediately and looked at me strangely. She rarely heard me call Shep "Dad."

Thankfully I had succeeded in pulling her out onto the porch, but she wanted to go back in to get some clothes for the game. Why wasn't anybody running to help me? With a bit of persuasion I tried to convince her to borrow some of my stuff instead. She started to go back in when Tyler hollered out her name. This was the first sign that proved someone had felt my tension, but I didn't dare use telepathy to forewarn them.

Matthew exited his house swiftly to cross the street as I grabbed Heather's hand. She actually put up a good struggle as I dragged her down the steps. Hastily Tyler crossed the expanse of two lawns in record time. When he reached us, he grabbed ahold of her so tightly I thought he might bruise her. Matthew and Tyler were looking at me for some explanation, but I couldn't dare chance it. With a glance back over my shoulder I continued to try to involve Heather in a conversation about how we had scared ourselves. Thankfully she obliged.

Tyler directed Heather towards my house, but she was insistent she at least needed her jacket. "I'll get it for you." In the next second Heather started to follow, but Tyler did something totally unexpected. He wrapped his arms around her waist and drew her very close to him—almost like he was scared and needed to protect her. She was taken by surprise, but was in no hurry to move. Matthew volunteered to go back with me so he didn't have to watch them make goo-goo eyes at each other. For a moment I hesitated at the door.

Abruptly Matthew leaned over to whisper, "I sense the person, too."

Tyler hollered up they would meet us at my house when I had the jacket. Suddenly we heard the slam of my front door. It wasn't a huge surprise when Shep came over. Once Shep was at Heather's front door with me, I was suddenly fearful for him to enter. Without hesitation, he pulled me away from the door and had Matthew keep a hold on me as he tried to assure me all would be fine. When he went inside, he looked back at us puzzled as he muttered there was no one within the house. His concern grew as he looked anxiously back at me. *"Are you sure you sensed someone?"*

Immediately Matthew became exasperated, almost to the point of losing his temper. "There was someone in there. I could sense them." Shep studied both us carefully. "Listen, Dad says Protectors are very good at sensing. I don't understand why you can't now, but I confirmed what Selena sensed. They were there. Do your job." I was stunned since Matthew almost sounded like he was giving Shep an order. It was even more surprising when Shep seemed to accept the order.

"I stopped her from opening the door when I sensed someone else inside. They were here." Shep shook his head in disgust and said he didn't like this at all. Shep told me to get Heather's jacket. He stayed right at my side as I ran to her room and grabbed it. He looked back over his shoulder at us as we left. "They might be thinking Heather is Guardian, or worse—they are looking for you. For right now we won't assume anything, but you all stay close together. While you are gone tonight we will make a sweep of the area."

None of this could be good. What if they were looking for me, and had mistaken Heather for me? Without another word we exited the house. When we arrived back home, Heather looked around the corner at us and asked if we had found anything. Shep assured her no one was in her house, but she was welcome to stay here until it was time to leave for the game. Billy's knock on the door came with no surprise, and we heard Shep filling Billy in on what had just transpired.

Tyler looked at me like he wanted to talk, but there was no way for that to happen. Matthew finally asked Tyler if he would come over and see his new game while he picked up his stuff for the football game. Tyler answered all too quickly he would love to, making Heather ask if a game could replace her. Tyler kissed her head, so softly, as he muttered nothing could replace her. It was clear she was no cover story for him. He truly had feelings for her. The boys headed for the door once she was satisfied. I knew Matthew would let him know the horrible truth: I had endangered my best friend.

Matthew came back suddenly with the excuse that he had forgotten to tell me goodbye. With an urgent whisper into my ear, he demanded for me to do nothing foolish. Why did everybody assume I would? With a quick kiss on my cheek he left.

Heather's eyes were sparkling as she cooed over how sweet our men were. I had to agree with her—we did have the best. Once the house was quiet again, I took the chance to ask her why she liked Tyler so much. Her response wasn't what I expected. She admitted he had been tutoring her on occasion and acted in awe of his intelligence, but I knew it was more than that. As she straightened the fringe on the blanket nervously, her cheeks became pure roses. "Selena, he seems old-fashioned. Before he ever kissed me the first time, he asked permission."

At this point the boys burst back in the door and our conversation abruptly ended. Tyler looked pale and I knew exactly how he felt. He sat down next to Heather and told her he was cold from the misty rain outside. He needed to warm up by cuddling to her. She squealed at his cold hands but was enjoying his closeness just the same. I couldn't help but smile at how cute they were together. Matthew did the same to me, but his hands didn't feel cold. A moment later Billy and Shep came back into the room looking a bit unnerved. I caught the glance he gave Tyler and wondered what had happened.

***

Five o'clock came and our plans had changed. Billy and Betty volunteered to take us to the game, and Matthew's parents would pick us up.

Once we arrived at the field, we found a large crowd, since this was the next to the final game of the season, and next weekend would be Homecoming. Heather and I hadn't even discussed if we would be going. She was talking animatedly that we had to go dress shopping. I liked dances, and every year I would go with someone just to be at the dance, but this year would be different. I would be going with someone who took my breath away. Matthew and Tyler thought we would have already had everything ready. Elbowing Matthew, I asked him how I would know he was taking me to the dance since he hadn't asked. With that, he knelt down on one knee, and in an over-exaggerated manner asked if I would go with him to Homecoming. He totally enjoyed how I blushed with embarrassment as I tried to pull him up, and glanced around to see who had caught his dramatization. Tyler then proceeded to do the same.

Heather and I both were roses by the time they had finished their production. We couldn't contain our giggles. Finally they stood up as we were joined by Mike and Meg. Mike's parents had brought Meg and him to the game. His dad was huge into sports and this was our rival team, so he would be cheering harder than most of the adults. The boys stopped by the concession stand while Heather and I found our seats. We went pretty high into the stands, but I preferred it that way. I liked to be up above where you could see everything.

When the boys arrived, they had all the necessary food to feed more than just the six of us. Matthew sidled in beside me in order to share the heat of his body on this chilly night. As I began to eat my hot dog, the band marched out for the pre-game show. The team was introduced, and you could see the mist falling through the bright lights. The energy in the stadium was high and it looked like the opposing team had an abnormal amount of fans with them, especially for such a rainy night. I could tell this was a game that might go into overtime.

The band played the "Star Spangled Banner" and the game began. We were all on our feet for most of the first quarter. Our team was holding its own against our rival, but the score was tied. Heather, Meg, and I were losing our voices as we cheered. Before halftime hit, we decided we'd better head to the restrooms. As we started to leave the stands, Tyler and Matthew insisted on going with us.

As we headed towards the bathrooms, I noticed one of the overhead lights was out, which made the surrounding area vulnerable to shadows. Matthew walked with his eyes closed, trusting me to guide him as he sensed ahead. He nodded to Tyler that it was okay to proceed when we arrived at the restrooms. Heather and I entered the bathroom in a rush for the hand dryers to warm ourselves by. When we heard the buzzer, we took care of business and ran out before we were caught in the overflow to the restrooms. Both guys were at the door as we exited. Immediately they pulled us out of the way of the swarm. I pulled Matthew's arms around me while leaning into his warm coat.

He was smiling at my forwardness, but I was cold and was not ashamed to seek his embrace. The football team began running into the locker room to cheers as they passed. When Heather saw Jeremy she waved, but he didn't seem as polite as he normally did. Wonder what that was about. Matthew leaned his head down into my hair and asked if I really expected him to change his opinion so quickly.

Matthew's heat felt good. Maybe I had been too forward and tried to pull away, but Matthew didn't allow me to. Instead he held me tighter as he nodded to our side. I was surprised to see Heather cuddled up inside Tyler's jacket too. I wondered how that had happened. Heather and I truly were being forward tonight, but we did have good reason. "Better get back to our seats!" the boys encouraged. Heather looked regretful as she agreed with a nod.

When we climbed back into the stands, the band was performing their halftime show. It was really good, but with all the rain we couldn't hear the music. Once we were back at our seats we all were surprised to find Mike and Meg sharing one seat. She was cuddled up in his lap and somehow had managed to close his jacket around her. Matthew snickered that the only reason we had brought them was to steal their heat. With this we took offense as we continued to wrap our bodies inside their jackets snuggly. "Well it is a plus," I teased.

Our team finally won by one point in the final two minutes with a touchdown. On the way home, Matthew's mom invited us to come into the house for some hot chocolate. We accepted on the spot. When we pulled inside the garage, I found it to be well lit and unnaturally clean. Once inside the house it became obvious his mom was a major neat freak, even worse than me. What added to the surprise was how bright the house was with all white walls. Matthew hadn't been kidding when he said she was a perfectionist. I was glad Shep wasn't that way. We made our way into the warm dining room to enjoy our cocoa. I appreciated the warmth of the house immensely. Mrs. Sturley brought the hot cocoa out, and I warmed my hands against the ceramic mug.

Matthew and Tyler were still going over the last couple minutes of the game. Mr. Sturley seemed to be anxious, glancing out the windows, which made me wonder if they had come across anyone. I hoped not. Slowly I began to wander through their house. I loved the color scheme of the living room. Mrs. Sturley walked along behind me as we left the others to talk about the game. She clicked on another light as she offered me a seat. "Finally I can have a bit of a private conversation with the girl who has stolen my son's heart."

Abruptly my blood boiled. I hadn't thought about talking with Matthew's mom. We could hear everybody goofing off in the next room. She acted like nothing was going on but her conversation with me. With a whisper she spoke. "Have to admit, I was surprised when Matthew stayed away from home so much. Once you came home, he grew antsy, almost anxious. He usually makes friends and has dated on occasion, but this time he became totally focused on the girl across the street. Didn't know what to do with him. We weren't even sure if you weren't of another realm. He has been so taken by you. I never thought it would happen this soon with him. It is rare for you both to be the same age."

Matthew came lumbering in and sat down on the arm of my chair uneasily. "I hope my mom isn't embarrassing me." I told him he had nothing to fear as he leaned down and pecked my head. His mom smiled so big it reminded me of the

Cheshire cat in *Alice in Wonderland.* Matthew took my hand and asked if I had seen the rest of the house. I admitted we hadn't gone past this one room. Slowly he guided me up the stairs as his mom followed. Matthew pointed to the pictures trailing up the steps of his and Meg's earlier years. They were adorable. Once at the upper level, I was shown a den plus three bedrooms. When I looked into Matthew's room, he clicked on the light. It was just like I had imagined. His furniture was all black with silver, and very neat with a navy blue comforter on the top bunk bed. His mom was prattling on about how it was the hardest for Matthew to keep his room clean. For once his cheeks turned red. His mom took the hint and went into the den to straighten up Mr. Sturley's desk.

"So…how are you?" I could tell he was concerned about more than what had happened earlier today. In fact, I was certain he was concerned about his mother's interrogation of me.

"I am totally enjoying your mother's detailed list of you. I am even more pleased with not having any problems with my telepathy." Matthew acted embarrassed as he stroked my shoulder-length hair. "So, I am the first girl you really have taken an interest in?" His cheeks were flooded with color as he said I was the only girl he would ever be interested in. His blue eyes were gorgeous. I felt that wonderful, tingly feeling again as it reached from the tips of my toes to the top of my head, leaving a hole in my stomach. I could feel my breathing quicken as he rubbed my cheek and pulled me close.

"I have found what I was looking for, and I don't plan on losing you now." I felt the same. As his lips gently brushed mine, I heard his mom come back into the hallway while clearing her throat. We smiled bashfully at her intrusion into our personal moment until the doorbell rang, drawing us back downstairs. We heard Mr. Sturley answer the door. Unfortunately it was Shep, and he was drenched to the bone.

# CHAPTER 18.
# DATING

**Shep's voice** was low as he informed Victor they had run across some Shadow activity in the woods. They were not sure if it had anything to do with Alexander, but several traps had been sprung. If the truth be told, it was a clear enough trail into the neighborhood. Matthew's hands tightened around me as I felt a shiver go down my spine. When Shep caught sight of us, he suddenly backpedaled. His stutter that it could be normal activity of the portal didn't settle well with Misty. I could tell neither man believed that, especially when Misty muttered that the traps would only be triggered by someone with ill intentions or the correct markers. Shep grimaced as his eyes darted to the floor.

"I had turned most of my traps off after Selena came into her abilities. I needed to afford more travel from our home, especially through the portal areas. I had placed safeties on them for the normal traveler and children. Still…I didn't expect our enemy to be able to access the portals so easily. I wished I had made the traps inside my perimeter stronger. I may need to reactivate them fully."

Shep raised his voice, calling for Heather and Tyler to come along. When Heather entered, he informed her he had received a message from Parker. "Your dad had to leave on an emergency business trip, so you will be staying with us." Somehow Shep had arranged this circumstance, and it didn't make me feel any better. This meant he was worried about Heather's safety as much as mine. With a glance towards Tyler, one could see he had picked up on it too. I didn't think it was even possible for him to grow paler, but he did. Heather and Tyler exited to the porch, leaving Shep and I inside the foyer.

"Victor, I don't mean any disrespect but it is time for you to reclaim your rights at Embers Greene. Michael and Charles are very suited for this type of job. Don't keep putting this off. Do it soon! We need their assistance."

When we exited I found Tyler standing on the edge of the porch, acting like he was enjoying the breeze, but we all knew he was checking ahead of us. With a quick kiss to Matthew, I stepped out with Shep at my side. Matthew urged me to call him later as he hollered after us. I could tell he wasn't happy. He wanted to be with me. His dad placed a restraining hand on his shoulder as if in warning to be careful. I wondered if Matthew was thinking about turning into his Shadow form to follow or what. The door snapped closed behind us, and I could see the houses across the street were brightly lit.

Kirt and Betty were out, and I could tell they were using their special ability to scour in all directions to make sure of our safety. Billy was tinkering with the wheelbarrow, which meant my grandparents had to be somewhere lurking around, but I didn't know where. As we hustled across the street I felt Shep's hand firmly holding my shoulder. Surely he wouldn't shadow out and leave the others behind if something happened. Still, Matthew's words rang loudly in my head: *Protectors have no other choice in these matters*. Without thinking I grabbed Heather's hand from fear. I wouldn't leave her behind…I couldn't…not to face danger. The surprise of my hand catching hers drew a loud laugh.

"Selena, are you jealous?" Tyler understood what I was doing and gave her a quick peck on the cheek and ran ahead to his house. Kirt grimaced at Tyler's act of affection but didn't say one word this time. I could sense Heather seemed annoyed by Kirt in some ways. "I hope Kirt finds a girl soon so we can return the favor." I knew by holding her hand I would be able to shadow her to safety with Shep if anything happened. This helped me to feel better. I had confidence Tyler and his family were equipped to deal with this if the need arose. Granted it would take a lot of explaining, but I would rather her alive and mad than anything else.

At the door we were met by Sarah. I couldn't resist rushing forward to offer a welcome home hug. I had missed her a lot and was so glad to see her home. She greeted Heather warmly as she quickly informed us she had taken the liberty with Shep to go pick up a couple items for her; she hoped Heather didn't mind. With one glance at her darkened house, I was surprised to hear Heather admit she was thrilled to not have to go back home for anything tonight. Her mind made it very clear she didn't feel safe there.

We took hot showers and settled down in the family room with the fireplace running. Sarah joined us for the night. She made it clear she wanted to be included in any boy talk. We all hollered for Shep to leave. After a few minutes of chasing him, he finally left, dejected. The rest of the night we spent talking about everything, from boys to what we would wear next week for homecoming. Sarah offered to take us shopping tomorrow, and she would cover Heather's expense for her dress until Parker returned home.

Finally falling asleep around two, we slept hard until a big bang occurred outside. Sarah jumped to her feet before I had opened my eyes. I found myself grabbing Heather as I watched Sarah for any sign of danger. Shep hollered not to worry. A tree behind Heather's house had fallen and we could go back to sleep while he checked their property. Sarah's eyes were full of warning as she tried to act nonchalant. I wasn't so sure Shep was telling the truth, but I would try. Hesitantly I laid back down, only to find it odd how fast Heather fell asleep. Too bad I didn't. I kept thinking about what could happen to Heather if I wasn't around.

The next morning I woke up grumpy. Like usual, Shep came out of his room humming Disney tunes. It figures—he was a morning person after all. As he passed near the family room he asked if we weren't supposed to be going shopping. This woke Heather up in a flash. She was off to take over the bathroom before any of us had thought to race her there. Thankful I had Shep and Sarah to myself, I started asking everything I had questioned during the night.

"If something happens, would you leave everybody to face it without us?" Shep looked disagreeable as he and Sarah shared a look of concern.

"Who told you about that?" It didn't take a brain scientist to know Matthew had. Shep leaned over on his elbows with a serious look on his face. "We have laws, Selena, especially about charges." Shaking my head I felt nauseous as things became clearer than they should. "Listen, Selena. You are my charge and my daughter. I have a safe place I can tuck you away and would be able to return in no less than five minutes to help if something went wrong. I would need you to do what I would ask in that situation." I couldn't believe him.

"Shep, I couldn't leave everybody. I have as many—if not more—abilities than they do. I would be able to help, and there is no way I could leave someone as defenseless as Heather behind. You can't ask me to do that." I watched as Shep stiffened and his face seemed to lose all emotion.

"I don't have to ask, Selena. You wouldn't have a choice. I am your Protector and father. I will do what is in your best interest when it comes to safety. We all have worked hard to keep you safe all of these years and you will do as you're told. Billy's children have a route of escape as do the Sturleys. If we all stick to our strategy all of you will be safe. While we deal with the threat here, Heather and the others will be a priority to us. Let us deal with it. You have more to learn than you realize, not to mention you need experience, too. Matthew and Meg have excellent abilities and would be formidable, as would Billy's children. They have been practicing for years. You are new to this. I know you will do well, but I would feel better if you had more time to practice."

It was evident I wouldn't have a choice in such a situation. Moreover, it sounded like I could endanger the others more by not listening. With a look to my shoes, I didn't want him to see how mad this made me. If practice was what I needed, then practice would be exactly what he would get.

"You have something else you want to ask me, Selena, so go ahead." This was an unexpected move on his part. It had been bothering me a lot lately, and still I didn't have the courage to ask. Abruptly my anger drained like water in a sink. It was the one question that hurt to my core, and I was afraid of the answer. I wasn't even sure if I wanted the answer.

"The day my parents died…" Hesitating, I tried to find the right words but they weren't coming easily. "…Because you were my Protector and not my mother's, did I cause…I didn't understand what was going on. Could you have saved them too?" The tears were welling up in my eyes, and I could barely breathe. This made my emotions grow to a strength that might cause me to lose control of my slowing ability, and I didn't need or want that. For a moment I struggled to wrestle with my control. Suddenly Shep's arms were around me as my body shook with the guilt I felt.

Gently Shep started muttering that I had nothing to do with that. It happened so quickly because they had been overconfident. "I did get there fast, but only in time to shadow you to safety. Your parents were more concerned for you than themselves at that point. They ordered me away. I had no choice. You were safely with Sarah before I left to help them."

I had been saved because they had ordered it. That was what Shep had said. Control was a struggle. The tears wouldn't stop pouring as a storm broke loose overhead. I apologized for being so emotional, but all Shep could manage was a small mumble that he understood. We both felt helpless. Finally he gave up.

"Maybe we should call Matthew. He will be able to comfort her." He even gave his permission to shadow to our oasis if need be. Shep must have been feeling really bad to have made this offer.

The doorbell rang. I could hear the front door open and Matthew's concerned voice as he and Shep began to talk quietly. My face was still hot with tears as I approached the two. Poor Shep looked miserable and sad. It was that look that I had seen every time I mentioned my parents. No wonder he couldn't talk about them. He looked helpless. It was obvious Shep hadn't had time to explain things, for Matthew wanted to know what he could possibly do to help. Without offer I leaned heavily into his embrace. "Can you take me to the oasis…please?"

He pulled me into the dark corner and started shadowing more gently than I thought possible. The tears didn't seem to be stopping and when we were finally still in the oasis he held me tight without saying a word. His hands continued to rub circles on my back as I tried to explain, but no words would escape my throat. I felt exhausted. Slowly cradling me in his arms, he gently sat down. I don't know how long we sat there in silence. His strong arms seemed to hold me together as I bawled. This was the first time in a long time I had allowed myself to think about my parents' death.

Matthew's mouth tightened into a grimace, knowing he was the one who had informed me about Protectors. For once I lifted my hand up and rubbed my fingers across his lips, trying to get them to unclench. He looked sick. "I am so sorry, Selena. Sorry about everything…"

*"No, you didn't do anything wrong. I just wanted to know if Shep could have saved them. I don't understand these rules. Can't they be broken?"* I knew I was pleading from my own hysteria.

Matthew only winced as I continued to babble, but his troubled blue eyes grew calm. *"I wouldn't want them broken if it meant you wouldn't be safe. Besides, Shep is right. We all have been doing this longer than you and we have our escapes down pat. So don't worry, we all will be fine. But you have to abide by the rules."* With a quick glance towards his eyes, I could see the torture I was putting him through and knew I had to stop being so emotional.

*"Matthew, I always wondered how I survived the crash and my parents didn't. It never made sense to me. If our car plunged into the lake, then how did I get out*

*of a car seat with only a gash on my face? Now I know some of the truth and it makes sense. Evidently Shep did see who was there. He said my parents ordered him to take me to safety. That meant they survived the crash and were alive when he left. I need to know more, but I wasn't strong enough to ask or listen this time. I had nightmares when I was younger and now I see things differently. I hate being weak."*

His arms tightened around me and I could hear his heartbeat in my ear. It had become one of the most soothing sounds to me. We talked for a while, helping my tears to cease.

With a look to his wristwatch, Matthew announced we needed to leave before we drew too much attention from Heather. He helped me to stand in order to shadow us home. Sweetly he swept me against his strong chest and faded into shadow.

Instead of finding myself in my house, he had taken me directly to the family room of his house. His dad didn't look surprise as he greeted me. "I heard you would be arriving here today. Shep called and told us what happened. He thought you and I might have a talk. I know what it is like to lose a parent in a traumatic way." Victor guided us up to the study as he explained that Tyler arrived before Heather was out of the shower and told her his family wanted her to go with them to the mall. "Shep explained to Heather you had to pick up something you had forgotten here the night before and you would meet her at the mall later." This made me happy, for I knew if Tyler was in the equation then she hadn't given me a second thought.

For the next couple of hours we discussed things I didn't understand, like what it meant to be a Shadow and the different rules. We also discussed how he felt when he lost his mom. "I can't exactly say I understand but I do understand how it feels to lose a parent to murder. You were a toddler when they died, which means you don't have a lot of memories. I think that would be something to be thankful for. You may have survivor's guilt, but that is unnecessary. I can tell Shep has done right by you, especially since I understand by all legal standpoints that he and Sarah are your parents."

I agreed I really hadn't missed much except really knowing my parents. I didn't really even remember their faces except from a picture, and sometimes I felt guilty about that. Mr. Sturley assured me he would have wanted Matthew and Meg to not feel guilty or to grieve for him. The matter of fact tone with which he spoke proved that to me. Mr. Sturley seemed to be an assertive man with no doubts over anything. When he spoke of his mother or his wife and children I saw love and devotion, but still—that underlying strength was strong and had no doubts.

When he began to explain laws and Protector laws to me, I was shocked when he pulled a huge, old hard-bound covered book from a locked cabinet. It was funny how he poked his finger and placed blood on the door, and then used the key to unlock it. The book looked worn from wear as he began to turn to the page he was looking for. When he found it, a look of pure glee crossed his face. "You..." He pointed at me, and then motioned for both Matthew and I to step closer. "You were a charge, and no ordinary charge just like my children. Our realm Protectors will do whatever they must to ensure your safety and mine too, not that I require that. Yet, it is a requirement by law, by house. Our people are strong and we are not weak by any means, but still we need Protectors and stewards to keep us safe. Shep at that time was following his orders. Nevertheless, when the adoption took place, you became his daughter. And when the bond was sealed as father and daughter, you became even more than a charge; you became a Protector's child. No one wants to ever endanger a Protector's child. Their abilities are deadly and meant to be feared. In my experience I find them to be some of the gentlest by nature. Jared and Analease knew what they were doing."

A second later Mr. Sturley demanded for me to call him Victor as he continued to teach us about Protectors and the laws we abide by as Shadows. Our discussion had made me feel much better about everything. I couldn't hold myself responsible for a decision that was made for me.

Before we left, Victor informed us that Mike and Meg were at the mall with Mike's parents. Not only were they dress shopping, but they were buying stuff for the Halloween party. Matthew let out a sigh of disgust as his dad laughed, proclaiming they didn't know what they were getting into with Meg shopping. Matthew walked me home. With a quick peck on the cheek, I began to feel a bit bashful. I was a bit surprised as he took both my hands in his and pressed his cheek against mine. "I'm sorry, so sorry about all of this. Please stay safe while I'm gone."

I walked in to see our den had flickering lights, which meant Shep was on the computer. When I peeked in, I found him staring at a blank screen. With a soft rap on the door I went in and gave him a hug as I apologized for being so insensitive and stupid. His hug was strong, almost so tight I couldn't breathe. He tucked his head into my hair as he muttered he wished things could have been different. I murmured that it was hard for both of us as I assured him I didn't want it to be different.

Shep pulled back and carefully cupped my face in the palm of his hand as he forced a weak smile. "I love you little one and you will always be mine, I promise. I just need to protect you better, that's all. Did Matthew and Victor help you any?"

Briefly I explained to him how Victor had showed us some laws of our land and how he had called what we were suffering as survivor's guilt. This seemed to help Shep relax. "Victor suffers from it too." With this admission, Shep grimaced. "But Shep, he was right. I had no control over any of the decisions, and as a Protector, you didn't either. I understand that now. It still hurts to think if I hadn't been there they might have survived."

Our conversation then changed to the rules of being a Shadow Protector, and I realized that in this short morning I had received a crash course in some of the laws that pertained to the Shadow Realm.

We both felt relieved as Sarah came in and announced she was ready to do some shopping and have her share of chocolate. Shep rolled his eyes and pulled Sarah and I into a big bear hug as we tumbled onto his lap. Then Shep announced loudly for all to stand back; we had an arrival coming. Sure enough, Matthew faded into the room.

We spent the night at the mall, and I found a royal blue dress with sequins for Homecoming. We also met up with Mike's family, and Shep of course helped with buying Halloween party favors. By the time we left, Shep had bought one of those fake coffins to add to his graveyard scene. Sarah and I had a hard time keeping him from buying more junk. Mike's parents were getting along well with Sarah, which made me happy.

On our way home I fell asleep on Matthew's shoulder. Shep kept the garage door open and asked Matthew if he wanted to be escorted home. Matthew almost acted insulted. "No thanks, I can take care of myself if the need arises. Don't want to start that…I have a hard enough time with my parents. I like to do things by myself."

I was shocked at his ramblings as he exited the garage. Shep looked across the car to Sarah, who acted very concerned with what had just happened. Her voice was soft but I heard every word. "He will adjust. He has no choice when he returns home. It won't be easy for any of these children who grew up outside of our culture, but they will have to adjust." She was trying to convince herself.

Billy and Tyler arrived home a few minutes later and walked Heather into our garage. I was sure they were keeping a close eye on her. Going over, I helped her in with her homecoming outfit. She had bought a beautiful, red taffeta dress. Sarah came out to offer snacks to anyone who might want something, but we all were tired, especially since we were expected at Mike's house tomorrow to help plan the party. The rest of the night nothing happened out of the ordinary, thank heavens.

Before we left my house the next afternoon I started sensing around in the general area to make sure there was no danger of bumping into anyone we didn't want to meet. As we passed Heather's house, Tyler came running at us from behind. He had succeeded in scaring Heather to death. Abruptly the front door to Mike's house opened and Meg was standing in the doorway already. She had to be spending all her time over there lately. I wonder if her mom felt the same way about Mike she did about me.

Mike's house was decorated on the inside like mine was. Mike and Shep really did make a Halloween pair. Meg seemed to fit right in with the Muir family. As

Meg greeted us in her airy voice, Heather whispered that all she needed was Goth style clothing and she would be naturally scary. Matthew came around the door and pulled me in while telling Heather not to talk about his sister that way, especially since he was the only one allowed to do that. We all laughed at his joke.

Meg and Mike had gone all out, down to even setting the dinner table with those silly skeleton hand goblets with fruit punch in them. They were a true pair. We spent the afternoon planning the food and type of music we wanted to play. After we delegated chores it was decided we should go collect some of the downed brush in the woods to help with the bonfire. All of the houses in this area had wood-burning fireplaces, so we were stocked on wood, but starter material would help.

With a step out of the house, one could see the flaming fall colors of the forest. It was true: fall really was here. We would start receiving tourists just for this beautiful sight of leaves, but what I don't understand is why they enjoyed the cold.

The leaves were crunching under our feet as we entered the woods. I knew everybody who was not Mortal was checking every so often to make sure we were not being followed. Heather was chatting with Meg on how she hoped Homecoming would be fun this year. To Meg, it didn't matter how it was decorated just as long as you were with the right person. I heard Mike holler out a hello to someone and turned to see Jeremy Baker and his brothers walking down the path. They said they had heard we were planning a party and wanted to know if they could help. Heather thought Jeremy was here to cause trouble. When she reached me she whispered that Jeremy had been trying to muster up the courage since last year to ask me out. With a heavy sigh I shoved her hard. The last thing I needed was this.

Matthew had been over with Laura picking up brush, but now he was wandering towards me. By his facial expression he was not happy. Not wanting to get too close to Jeremy, I kept pushing forward, hunting for debris to use in the fire. Josh and Jeremy were teammates who had played together through the years. Jeremy had been more Josh's friend than Mike's, and for some reason Andy never did seem to like him. It was unusual for Jeremy to have stumbled upon our hunt for wood unless he had come over to play.

Matthew grunted and I knew he had to be listening in on their thoughts. Mike was grinning from ear to ear and accepted the help that the Baker boys offered. Jeremy bumped into Matthew's shoulder as he asked if he minded some competition for me. Matthew stood up and I saw a glint of something I had never seen in his eyes. They looked darker and like their shape may have been changing. Quickly I changed my direction in order to move closer to Mathew. To my disappointment, Jeremy intercepted me. He jerked me to a full stop. I was shocked to feel his hand restraining my elbow.

He acted nervous as he asked if I really enjoyed the woods after being lost here back in the summer. "Sure, I don't have a problem with it. I just don't want to be out here after dark is all." He continued to jabber on about the previous game, but I was barely able to listen. In order to get away from Jeremy I simply began to move around, gathering more tinder. I tried to show no more interest in him than being courteous. So far he wasn't taking the hint, and I could see Mike flash a grin at me as Matthew continued to grow more agitated. Finally, I told him I was busy and needed to see if Matthew and Mike needed some help. He couldn't take a hint. I didn't want to cause Matthew to do something he shouldn't, so I began to walk away from Jeremy when he grabbed my arm again. Instantly I jerked my arm away from him, only to feel his grip tighten. I stared in astonishment at his face. He began talking about Homecoming and maybe I would like to join him at the dance. Meg chimed in with that eerie voice which even drew Jeremy's attention without causing a scene.

"You know very well..." She picked up another branch as she continued, "she is dating Matthew exclusively." She had shocked me with how close she was to us. I hadn't seen her walk over. Jeremy smiled sarcastically at her while arguing with her that I had never been exclusive with anybody. "Well, she is now, so stop acting like a puppy by demanding attention."

Matthew was making a beeline for me as Kirt and Tyler joined in behind him. Then I heard Jeremy's thought loud and clear. He wanted to show me he was better than Matthew, and who wouldn't want to go out with one of the more popular athletes in school? Good gracious, why was he doing this? I had never encouraged this behavior. I had known him all through school and we were just friends. Boldly I informed him I was with Matthew and didn't have any plans on changing my mind.

Jeremy's brothers began snickering at his play for me, but it wasn't amusing anymore. Mike, however, came to the rescue by playfully hitting Jeremy in the stomach, commenting he had waited too late to do this now. It had become obvious to Mike and Andy that this was no longer a friendly situation but was fast growing into a ticking time bomb. Andy was actually plowing through the woods like he was ready to defend us both. Andy and Josh had always been very protective of Heather and I, and especially Mike if he was outgunned.

By this time Matthew stepped in front of me, making me feel panicky. "You all need to settle down. Jeremy, I am dating Matthew exclusively. Thank you for the offer, but no." Nothing seemed to register in his fat head, making me decide that now would be a good time to use my slowing ability so I could pull the guys away. Unexpectedly, Tyler grabbed my arms and pulled me back behind Matthew. He whispered for me to let Matthew deal with it. I truly wanted to argue the point, but I knew my argument would only fall on deaf ears.

Matthew stood very still and told Jeremy he was sorry, but he had known from the first time he met me that I was the one for him. Threateningly, Jeremy's fist clenched, causing me to jerk in Tyler's grasp. Matthew didn't even seem to flinch at the gesture. "Listen, Jeremy, we don't want trouble. Let's just part ways while we can. You don't want to be the cause of a disturbance. Selena has made her choice clear, so go find someone who wants your attention. There are plenty of girls who do."

When Andy arrived to aid Mike, the Baker boys had moved forward too. Slowly Jeremy backed off when his elder brother growled for him to cool it. It was too bad I could hear his thoughts that this wasn't the end of it. Matthew stepped back, not taking his eyes off of Jeremy and his brothers as they departed.

"We're going to have to deal with this sooner or later. Jeremy is not going to let this go," Matthew whispered urgently to me. As Mike turned to Meg, he simply stated maybe they had better try to find a date for Jeremy. The snarl on Meg's face was priceless. "I don't think any girl in her right mind would tolerate a beast like that. She would have to be needy or stupid to accept after what happened today." Mike began to laugh nervously as she walked away from him.

Suddenly Matthew jerked away from everybody but me. I was surprised to see darkness swirling in his eyes. It made me wonder if all Shadows were such a dead giveaway when angry. Tyler punched him as he growled for him to get a grip. Meg ran to her brother's side, chiding him. For once her voice sounded strained and raspy—almost normal. "Hey, you know Selena wants to be with you and not that over-muscled freak. Settle down. You have never lost control like this before. You can't, not now. Heather and Mike are following."

Matthew continued to walk away while shaking his head in frustration. There was no gentleness in his tug as we tried to get away from the other kids. It was hard to see him struggle for such control. I could hear Kirt and Meg bring Mike and Heather to a halt. They were encouraging them to give us some space so Matthew could cool down. Once we were far enough away from the others, he stopped with his back still turned from me. When he finally looked back up, his eyes were swirling with darkness, but his normal eye color was returning. We hadn't realized it, but Tyler and Kirt had remained with us. Kirt asked if it was normal for a Shadow's eyes to swirl like that. Matthew growled it was, as he jerked us in the opposite direction of my cousins. He needed space.

Unfortunately Kirt wasn't about to give in. He continued to rant how he would have welcomed a fight with those goons. I tried to shush him as Matthew began mumbling over and over again that this was becoming too irritating to deal with anymore. Tyler agreed a good fight would help to release some of the tension we all felt, at least for them.

While walking further away from the group, Matthew continued rubbing my hand, trying to convince his body to relax. He looked at me knowing he had insisted that Jeremy liked me. With a flash of his bright smile, his eyes almost changed back to the norm. He was shaking his head in disbelief, explaining how he felt when Jeremy had approached me, let alone when he had grabbed me. "It took so much effort not to use my abilities." I could tell it frightened him in a way. He didn't mean to lose control, but he had never felt attached to someone like he did to me. His eyes seemed to be searching for something from me, but I wasn't sure what he needed me to do, let alone say.

My mind wandered back to my discussion with Meg on relationships, and even further back to August. He took both my hands and asked what I was thinking. He didn't need to ask. I knew he already knew. He was the one I would spend the rest of my life with. My heart knew before my mind did that I was in love with him. I was his match.

Matthew sighed in relief. "I figured that would be your answer, but I also had felt your confusion for the past couple of weeks. I didn't want to push you. I wanted you to come to your own conclusion on...who I am to you. You are my heart. You are my true love, my match."

I had always thought teenagers could only be infatuated with each other. Certainly they couldn't fall in love, but I knew he was my true love. I wouldn't have to look around. Matthew's smile was sparkling as he added that in the other realms, relationships happened at our age. "We fall in love once, and this is it for us." His voice was so sincere, as he promised it would be forever. We still would have to wait for the appropriate age because of living in the Mortal Realm, but even his mom knew I would be his companion for life. Matthew was grinning as he squeezed my hands nervously. It was evident he was letting this sink in.

"That is why I have been so protective of you. I didn't want to scare you, but I can't lose you now that I have found you, either. For some it takes centuries to find their match. My heart was breaking since I had caused you so much pain with your new knowledge of your parents." Matthew reached forward and pulled me tight into his embrace. I really knew everything he was saying was the truth. I knew I would be his forever. I could feel his body moving closer to me as he took my face in his hands. I watched as his eyes came towards me and he began to press our lips together gently. The pleasure was even stronger than the first time we had kissed. I was his and I felt complete.

I heard Kirt moaning at our PDA as Heather came tramping through the wet, cold earth, grumbling. "I can see you!" Matthew informed her we weren't trying to hide. She was curious if I was all right, but could see things were well in hand. Matthew looked at her teasingly as he asked if he had her approval. This excited her to no end as she gave her hearty approval with the condition, of course, that she would hunt him down if he ever hurt me.

Unfortunately, back at the house Heather had to tell Shep and Sarah about the almost-fight with Jeremy. Shep was shaking his head, especially when she had caught that Matthew's eyes seemed to grow darker when he was angry. They both looked at each other questioningly. It seemed strange for them to wonder about that. Sarah commented it would be normal when you loved someone.

I couldn't help but bring up Tyler at the mention of love. I had to admit it was satisfying to see her face go blood red as she glared over at me. Shyly she admitted she had never felt this way before. It was odd to see her drop her eyes bashfully to the table, acting so meek. One thing about Heather was that there was no room for meekness, only brazenness. In a way it made me happy to see how she felt about my cousin, and yet it depressed me too. Meg was right about one thing: who would want to marry a Mortal only to outlive them for centuries? Maybe I shouldn't encourage her to think this way. Tyler wouldn't want to lose his spouse so young. Suddenly my own frustrations began to surface. Luckily I had a handle on them, or at least as far as Heather could see. I was beginning to wonder if Sarah wasn't inheriting the parent bond like Shep. She seemed to glance sharply at me as I pressed my depressing thoughts back into the trunk they belonged in. For as long as I could remember, I always felt like I had trunks in my mind to help me deal with my emotions, especially with the ones I wanted to forget.

When Sarah dropped us off at school the next day, she placed a restraining hand on my arm while the others left the vehicle. "Selena, I need to let you know that Shep, Victor, and Billy have placed special securities around Heather's home. We are still debating on the traps in the immediate area. There are so many factors and risks that we aren't sure what will be appropriate. We need to keep a clear path into our neighborhood. It is going to take a lot of thought on how to improve our inner boundaries and keep a path open for Guardians to travel." Sarah sounded worried.

As I exited the car I practically jumped right into Matthew waiting arms, causing us both to laugh at my awkwardness. He made it worse when he pretended to be a cowboy and added he had been glad to be of assistance. With a rushed glance towards the building, I saw Jeremy and his brothers heading in. Sarah's warning was stern. "Matthew, you will behave no matter what that Mortal does. Do you understand?"

I watched as his hands fisted. "Understood." Matthew reacted suspiciously as he looked back at her. "I always behave." We both could see she was not convinced.

As we walked in I didn't feel any pressure, so I had to be doing well. My only problem would be English class. There I would have to deal with Jeremy alone.

I had made it through my morning classes and lunch, but when it came time for English, dread filled my body. I truly wasn't looking forward to dealing with Jeremy at all. Tyler hovered closely behind us in the hallway, knowing he would have to prevent any problems if Jeremy tried anything. When I arrived at the door, Jeremy was already in there waiting on me. Everybody in the classroom looked from Jeremy to Matthew in anticipation of what might happen. Carefully I placed my hand against Matthew's chest and leaned over to give him a kiss. Matthew was shocked, but he didn't show it on his face. I was glad he hadn't. Jeremy turned red. He became furious but kept his temper in check at least. Tyler was at the side of the door and warned Matthew to let me handle it. I could tell this was very hard for him, especially having to leave. Finally he managed with Tyler at his side.

Carefully I searched the room for a seat far from Jeremy. Thankfully I found one and sat down. The student beside me moved as Jeremy walked towards his desk and jerked his thumb, ordering the kid out. Great. I was going to have to deal with this jerk after all. Jeremy tried to start a conversation, but I politely pulled a book out and acted like I was reading. Suddenly my book was wrenched from my hands. As I looked to Jeremy, he began thumbing through my book asking if it was any good. "Jeremy, may I please have my book back?" Instead of handing it to me, a stupid cocky grin spread across his face, for he had been successful in getting my attention.

"You and I have been friends since kindergarten so why don't you come to Homecoming with me?" Unluckily I could feel the pressure in my head as I struggled to be polite. The bell rang as the teacher called class to order. Regrettably the class droned on forever, forcing me to have to listen to Jeremy's thoughts. They kept bubbling to the surface, and I could tell there was going to be no nice way to get rid of him. When the bell rang, he grabbed my hand. Immediately I jerked it away, furious that he kept insisting on touching me, and most of the time it wasn't a touch, but a grab of possession in many ways.

"Listen Jeremy, I only look at you as a friend. I have never looked at you any differently. Please leave me alone and don't do this anymore." His face was like stone, but I hadn't convinced him. My movements towards the door were rushed and rude as I struggled through the grouping of kids. Once outside of class I was grateful to see Kirt standing there with a serious look on his face as he studied the situation. In the next moment Matthew swept his arm around me, Kirt smirked, saying that it took both he and Tyler to keep Matthew from breaking Jeremy's face. I tried to offer Matthew some encouragement by warning him I had handled worse. He simply scowled at that and wanted to know who else he could beat up, or at least make them afraid of the dark. When the school day was finally over, Laura offered to ride on the bus so I could handle Matthew's rage in the car.

As I pulled my backpack out at home, I realized my reading book was missing and Jeremy definitely had it. This was a dilemma. I wish I had thought to demand my book back. I didn't want Matthew to do anything stupid. All of a sudden I heard Kirt yell out a curse as Matthew demanded to know what I was missing. "It's nothing...Really, I can get it later." Matthew's face became infuriated, since he already knew what Jeremy had done: he had my book—my favorite book. Sarah ordered Matthew to get a grip. She reminded him over and over again that Jeremy was only Mortal. Otherwise it would be different. His agreement made a shiver run down my spine. The tone he used sounded frightening. Kirt volunteered to stay at Matthew's house to make sure he behaved, but Matthew told him he didn't need to worry; he always behaved like his family expected.

Once the boys had gone home, Sarah told me a story about Shep and another person who had been interested in her. She said it is wonderful to have a man who was jealous. We both laughed. It made me feel a little better.

Heather came home around eight thirty. Luckily I had already taken a shower. When it was time for bed, Heather kept going over the saga with Jeremy. I could barely stand him anymore. Shep and Sarah had been sitting with us in the family room, occupied by books they were reading, but they both looked up. Heather met their eyes. "He is turning into a real piece of work. He is becoming a bully, and not just with us, but with a lot of others."

"Then you two will stay away from him. If he becomes a problem, Parker and I will go to the school."

The next morning Matthew showed up on our doorstep with my book in hand. I was afraid to ask him what he did. Shep was clearly amused. He was patting Matthew on the back like they were enjoying an inside joke.

When we arrived at school, I didn't see Jeremy right off the bat, which surprised me. By the end of the day, Jeremy hadn't bothered to come to school either. His brother had said he had a rough night last night.

The rest of the week went by without incident, and I was happy. Even so, I did wonder what had caused the change or better yet, what had Matthew done?

Saturday would be Homecoming and the boys had been warned to not come near the house until around two or three. Sarah was totally enjoying the mothering thing. Heather and I worked on our hair, but like normal my hair continued to fall through like silk. That was the one bad thing about fine hair. Heather's hair had a natural wave and curl, and it only had to be put in place. Sarah finally helped me manage my hair into ringlets on the top of my head with a sequin clip that she assured me would not fall out. She helped us both with our make-up, and I had to say she did a wonderful job, but I wasn't used to so much. I really liked the natural look. They both assured me I was fine, but I had to try to tone it down since it really wasn't me.

Finally feeling pleased, we ate lunch. Shep kept snapping pictures here and there as he promised Parker he would. Sarah and Heather were working on her nails as I slipped out into our backyard, wondering if Laura was doing the same. She had been sly and surprised us all with the news that she had a date, too. Betty about fell over with the thoughts the boys were having. It had been an amusing scene. Laura wouldn't even tell us who it was. She wanted us to be surprised. Besides, she was afraid of what the boys might do. I agreed and told her to keep it to herself. I needed a bit of space and walked further into the backyard to get a breath of fresh air.

Once back at the fence, I climbed over. I hadn't been to the portal in a long time and tonight the drawing was very strong, almost like somebody needed me. When I arrived I looked at the weaving of the design around what was supposed to be an ordinary grouping of trees. I hadn't realized it, but Tyler had followed me. "I sensed you leaving the house. You seemed so focused but on what?" He acted a bit concerned and I wasn't sure I should even confide in him, but I had promised, hadn't I?

"I sometimes feel drawn out here, almost like I am needed." I scuffed the toe of my shoe in the dirt as I tried to avoid his eyes. He carefully touched the nearest tree to us and I could feel him sense it.

"I didn't want you to be alone out here." By the way he was acting I knew I had made him concerned. When I mentioned to him that Heather would take his breath away, he shook his head as he looked away from me. "She already does without all the glamour." My dear cousin wore his heart on his sleeve.

"Tyler, you know Heather is Mortal. Maybe you should slow down."

"I know, but I like her. It doesn't mean anything more than that. Don't worry, Selena. She isn't looking at me any more than a boyfriend for the time being." This made me feel protective of him. Gently I placed my hand on his shoulder as the wind picked up in the wet, cold forest. Tyler and I both felt it and we drew back behind a tree, waiting for something to happen. It felt like the night at Heather's house.

Being as quiet as possible, we scanned around us. We both sensed two others nearby but we did not recognize them. To my shock, they were shadowing. Tyler grabbed my hand while pulling me back towards the houses as quietly as possible. We could hear them discussing that they needed to figure out if the girl was really Jared's daughter. They felt it was a possibility since Billy Martin was here. "One of his sons is always with the girl." They didn't want to mention it to their boss until they were certain.

We stumbled to the ground at the mention of Jared. Unfortunately, we fell on some creek stones that were embedded there, too. I hoped the men hadn't heard us as Tyler covered me with his body. I could sense he was drawing for any animals in the area. Tyler stopped me as I began to slow down the area around us. Huskily he whispered it would prevent the others from helping that weren't immune. Fear coursed through our eyes as the voices drew closer. For right now they were not aware of us.

Suddenly we heard a large animal off to the west of the men. They abruptly changed course towards the sound. Shep faded in beside us with his eyes swirling. We didn't dare use telepathy, but I knew Shep knew what I was thinking. I tried concentrating on my dad's name as Shep covered Tyler and I with his shadow. He shadowed us to the other portal in the woods, only to point towards the shelter and whispered for us to stay. Quickly we followed his instruction. Tyler and I didn't say a word as Shep shadowed away.

Mr. Sturley appeared a minute later and motioned for us to come to him. He shadowed us to his home where Matthew was waiting anxiously. Mrs. Sturley had closed all the curtains and waited near the door, as if listening for something. The doorbell rang, only to reveal Betty's fidgeting form. When she came in she informed us that Billy and Granddad were trying to track the Shadows down, but Shep said they had left the area because they had sensed Tyler's ability. Shep shadowed into the room looking quite fierce.

Tyler finally spoke up and told them the bad news. "They mentioned Uncle Jared's name. They did recognize our family and they think Heather is his daughter. They said they had to be completely correct before revealing her to their master."

Matthew's arm tightened around my shoulders and I could feel him trembling against me. Shep and Mr. Sturley both agreed it was good they were misguided. They thought we might be able to fool them if the Sturleys and I could play Mortal. Tyler asked about Heather, and they explained the men wouldn't hurt her because they would see she was Mortal, no matter what they threw in her way. Matthew slid into the chair with me. Immediately he grabbed my hand to pull it up. I hadn't realized I sliced it when I fell. To my misfortune, I was dripping blood all over my jeans. I was a mess. He quickly grabbed a tissue from the table and was pressing it against the cut. Tyler laughed weakly, saying he might need a Kleenex, too, since he had scraped up his knees. When I looked in his direction I noticed he also had a scratch on his face welting up. What a great duo we were.

A knock came on the back door as Mr. Sturley hollered for them to come in. It was Billy and Granddad. Granddad paled even more at the sight of us. "I can handle anything thrown my way, girl." Shep informed them about the men looking for Jared's daughter, but that they had been misled by Tyler always being around Heather. This made them all feel better, for they felt it would be enough for the Shadows to give up on their search if they proved Heather was Mortal.

Shep then gave them a menacing look as he growled he had a plan. It required that the Sturleys and he would have to stay out of sight, for their look would give them away. The rest of us would have to act Mortal, no matter what we sensed. Billy seemed pleased with the plan, but Granddad wanted to know how Tyler and I had received our injuries. As we began to explain, Granddad scowled at the two of us. "You shouldn't be walking back near the portal."

"While we were trying to not attract attention we fell on some rocks," Tyler started, but was interrupted by Billy demanding to know why I was spending so much time at that one portal. I know I must have seemed hesitant.

"It seems to be a place of comfort, and at other times I feel drawn there. I can't explain it. It must be that I would like to see where it leads." Billy looked at Shep while shaking his head. He started to say something, but Granddad put a restraining hand on his shoulder. This was the second time somebody started to say something and was stopped. What was this secret that Shep, Granddad, and now Uncle Billy had?

# CHAPTER 19.
# HOMECOMING

**As we sat** there in the living room, I realized if there was no immediate danger, I really needed to get home so I could repair the damage I had done to my appearance. Matthew's cheeks flushed as his eyes flashed to meet mine. It was funny to see his cheeks redden at the comment. He still hadn't released the pressure on my hand since it was continuing to bleed.

Shep knelt down to look at my hand a little more thoroughly as Victor hovered over his head trying to look at it, too. Shep tilted my head back as he looked deep into my eyes. I felt he was looking into my soul these days, which made me uncomfortable. I tried to pull away but stopped when I saw a look in his eye. Something was wrong. He excused himself, grumbling he needed to find Sarah so he could get her opinion as he slapped Mr. Sturley's shoulder. "Why don't you check her while I find Sarah?" I had just cut my hand. It wasn't like I was dying. I couldn't understand all the mystery.

Victor took Shep's place with a grave look of concern as he glanced towards his wife. He tried to grin, but it was more of a grimace as he asked if he could take a look. I figured I really had no choice. He repeated what Shep had done, plus his hand turned to mist over the cut. This took me by surprise. I should have realized he was a healer too.

Matthew looked directly at his dad and demanded to know what was wrong, but we heard no reply. A few minutes later Sarah arrived, and we both could tell Victor was already giving her warning of something. The bleeding had nearly stopped when she took Victor's spot. Sarah looked at my hand and then into my eyes. She fumbled a little while on her knees as she swiftly looked to Victor, who hadn't left her side. She then began a funny misty movement around me as if she was sensing my whole body or something. She finally looked at Shep and announced his assumption was correct. "What assumption?"

Mrs. Sturley seemed to understand what was going on and wanted to know if she could check Matthew, too. She admitted they had been suspecting the same with him lately. Now Matthew and I both wanted to know what they were discussing in front of us without our understanding. Sarah repeated the same procedure she had done with me and agreed it was true. Victor groaned that he had been afraid to mention it earlier, but he felt it was a little worse than Sarah thought initially. He knew he was going to have to explain. Shep took a deep breath.

"Do you remember what I told you about Shadows staying on this plain for long periods of time?" With a slight nod I reminded him of my dad's journal where he was concerned with my mom needing to return to the Shadow Realm to recharge.

Instead she announced she was pregnant.

"That is correct. You need to understand—a Shadow can stay on this plain for long periods of time but does have to return occasionally to recharge, for the lack of a better term, especially after a major use of abilities. Since you and Matthew have never been in the Shadow Realm and were born here, you will need to travel to the Shadow Realm. You both are showing signs of having the need to return. This will help you maintain your human forms. I was hoping with Selena her father's genes would prevent the need, but it isn't working now that her abilities are growing by leaps and bounds." Shep was acting flustered, especially with the way his hand kept sweeping his bald head.

"The Sturleys confided in me…They had noticed the same signs with Matthew, but not so much with Meg. These were warning signs we would have to travel to the Shadow Realm soon, especially with the special circumstances surrounding the two of you. We will have to plan a special trip to guide you both there. Many safety precautions will have to be arranged. We will take this time for all of us who are of the Shadow Realm to rejuvenate."

Billy looked very serious as he interjected.

"We will want Guardians with you when you travel. We can't take any chances." Shep seemed to understand there was no option on this key point. I couldn't resist but to ask, since everybody else seemed to know what I didn't. "What if we didn't make the trip?"

To my shock Matthew answered for everyone. "We would fade away into nothing. That is one way for a Shadow to die," he stated simply as he nuzzled my head. "We might be able to survive a bit with the darkness from deep within a cave, but if a Shadow needs full charge then there is no choice." The sound of his answer drew a deep silence from everyone present in the room. The silence was deafening as the tension rose. Finally Betty broke the silence by wanting to know how soon this trip would need to take place.

"We should not push it. They both are still strong but with the stress level of our surroundings, I think we should take an early Christmas vacation. This definitely can't wait any later than the end of December."

Sarah began examining Matthew again with her hands. She seemed to be re-evaluating her assumption of him. "Fine, then it's settled. We will plan the trip for the second week of December," Mr. Sturley announced. "My house will be willing to help in our protection. We do talk occasionally. They have wanted us to come back before, but we didn't think we could endanger our children, at least not until we had no choice. Our families have never seen the twins. To be honest, they don't know the twins exist technically. The last meeting I had with them was sort of interrupted." Mr. Sturley winced as he looked in our direction, forcing Shep to groan.

"We need to set another meeting up soon. Victor, you need Michael." Victor grimaced as he agreed softly. Both men seemed lost in their thoughts—almost desperate.

Finally the men separated off to discuss our future plans. Matthew continued to hold the Kleenex on my cut until Sarah asked him to remove it so she could work on it. Sarah's hand changed to mist, which she swept over the cut repeatedly. The burning sensation left. Still the cut was obvious. Sarah used the herbs and ointments on my hand that Betty had provided and wrapped it tightly. She announced she would be shadowing me back home so I could finish getting dressed for my big night. I couldn't help but smile at Matthew as I told him I would see him later. The concern on his face changed into a bright smile before I faded from the room.

When we arrived home, I found Sarah had shadowed us into the master bathroom where the shower was running. Sarah reminded me she had to tell Heather something so she wouldn't become suspicious of where I had disappeared to. She had made the excuse that I didn't like how I looked and had started over. We both giggled as Sarah helped me do my hair again. With a hard look into the mirror I asked her if it was really that serious about recharging our batteries. Her curt nod was all the answer I truly needed. I watched as her expression seemed to look grim.

"As a Shadow becomes older you won't have to recharge as often, but since Matthew and you are of the Shadow Realm and have never been there, it is a necessity for you to do so now. You don't have to worry. You will be back for school. The worst scenario is that you might need to be there for four weeks. Besides I have a lot there I want to teach you, and I am sure Shep has stuff he wants to show you, too. It actually will be easier for you there than it is here to gain control over your Shadow abilities. Don't worry. They will make sure both of you are safe."

Sarah was a miracle worker. She had my hair looking like it was always well-behaved and not flying all over the place. She raised my hair up in ringlets and placed sequin flowers in the center of each. My hair looked fuller and was not falling down. Heather began calling from the other room for help, so Sarah ran giggling. With another look into the mirror I applied my makeup the way I liked it. My eyes popped in a way I didn't expect. I must be maturing. Lipstick was the final touch before pulling on my dress. Carefully I pulled it on and zipped the low back. When I glanced next, I was surprised at my appearance. Normally I didn't feel good about myself. Tonight, however, I felt pretty.

Sarah came in and gasped that I looked marvelous. She had brought in a small jewelry box with her. When she opened it she revealed a beautiful heart locket with delicate sequins embedded in it. It was engraved on the front with the words "love endures."

"This was your mother's locket. She would want you to have it." Carefully she opened the delicate locket to reveal a picture of my mom and dad. Then she unclasped another set of pages. "This page is for you and your love." She closed it back up and hung it around my neck. For a brief moment I felt sentimental as I touched the small locket. This was now my most prized possession, since the last person to have worn it was my mom. I had never had anything so personal. "Shep has placed a genetic marker on it so only we can open it."

Sarah left and went out and hollered at Heather. Evidently we needed to come out to let Shep take pictures. Slowly I picked up my black lace shawl with one last glance into the mirror. I could see the shadow of my parents' appearance in its reflection, even if it was only a shimmer. I stopped for a moment to study my features a bit better and could see Shep and Sarah's influence in me too. The darkness that surrounded me seemed to fit.

As I came closer to the family room I could hear Heather posing for pictures but this was not my forte. When I peeked around the corner, Shep looked aghast. "You look…incredible," was all he could mutter. The way he was staring at me made me feel awkward. Heather commented that Jeremy would blow his stack tonight. Quickly Sarah jerked the camera from Shep so we could take some pictures together. Before long, my awkwardness subsided until the doorbell rang. Shep hollered for them to come on in. Sarah quickly flashed a couple more with Shep before he answered the door.

It turned out to be the Muirs and the Sturleys. When Mike stepped into the family room, his jaw dropped. "The two of you no longer look like the little girls I have known all my life. You really look nice." Matthew sounded his agreement as he came rushing over to my side. I felt like a princess, and for once I felt beautiful too. I wish I had this confidence more often. I didn't know what to do about all of this praise.

As was tradition Matthew, placed a wrist corsage on me while everybody kept taking pictures. I guess on nights like this one might get a dose of what it is like to be a movie star. Matthew leaned over to whisper in my ear that I looked gorgeous. Of course he got the response he wanted when goose bumps ran over my skin as my heart beat out of my chest.

"You look quite breathtaking yourself." My statement drew a bright flush to his face. If you ask me, he looked cuter when embarrassed. Matthew looked at my locket as I explained to him it was my mother's. I felt a bit anxious as he tried to open it, and received something like an electric shock. "Sarah said they placed something around it to keep anyone from opening it. Matthew looked closer but insisted I hold it for him.

"We placed a genetic marker on it so only family can open it without receiving a small shock. If someone was to force it there would be worse results than the static electricity you felt. We can't have anything that might identify her as unprotected, but Shep felt she deserved to have this item. Most people won't know anything about it unless they were extremely close to Analease. If you open it up you can see there are small leaflets all ready for more pictures." Sarah looked hesitantly at me as she continued. "The one picture that had been placed of Selena we removed, but in the future we will return it like the other. Analease planned on having other children, and as tradition she would have replaced it with the picture of Selena with her spouse—you," Sarah said in the direction of Matthew.

The doorbell interrupted our small conversation. I wanted to ask about the baby picture but wasn't sure if I should. Suddenly Sarah cupped my chin as she drew my eyes to meet her gaze. "Even your baby picture would help a Shadow to identify you now. As babies, some things give away identifiers. To me it is surprising that when Shadows were near they hadn't identified you."

Shep had joined our small group, looking pleased at my locket. "She's right. You are easily identified even now, but I keep your appearance a bit distorted to any from our realm along, with Heather's and Mike's as well. I started that as soon as I realized the three of you probably share a special bond."

We were interrupted by the doorbell again, and this time it was my family. Tyler walked in first and immediately went to Heather with her wrist corsage. To my surprise, Laura and her date were in the group. The boy's name was Kyle, and he was in my grade. I wondered how Kirt was taking this. My grandparents stood at the back of the room proudly. One could see in many ways this was an emotional night for them as they clung to each other. I could see tears in their eyes as they continued to watch me and my cousins.

Laura was beautiful in her white-blue, sheer dress. I could tell she felt very good about her appearance, too. It was definitely a change for her to look so delicate. It was nice to see her blush as she admitted she felt beautiful. Then her eyes darted towards her brother filled with warning. "But no one is to give us a hard time. Do you understand?" Tyler smirked as he nodded.

The doorbell rang again, but this time I didn't know who could be here. Shep hollered our limo had arrived for our little group. The adults had surprised us. We all thought our parents were going to have to drive us. Everybody left the room but my grandparents. Grandma walked over very slowly. She definitely was struggling tonight. Carefully she reached towards me with shaky hands to straighten my locket as a tear escaped its confines.

"Jared would have said you take his breath away. That was something he always said to your mother. You are beautiful and your mother's locket is a fine addition to the ensemble."

Granddad couldn't resist touching my face. I could tell he studied it a lot these days. "You are a good mix of all your parents. I like that. Your heritage is growing too strong to hide much longer. I can see it in your eyes." Granddad hugged me before trying to slap himself out of his sentimental state. "We'd better get outside. There are more surprises." It was funny how he immediately acted mischievous as he scampered out the door.

Outside we saw that Kirt had invited Maymie Jean as his date. When did he find time to do that? As we were being ushered into the limo, I saw a familiar face I had not expected. It was Tyler's older brother, Dillon. He was acting as our chauffeur tonight. I was sure that was part of our security.

I was amazed by the amount of room inside as I climbed in. This was something I had always wanted to do. It would be nice to be rich. The interior was lit by twinkling lights, and there was a TV and a fridge to boot. We all were able to fit and still had space between us. Matthew still leaned next to me with his arm over my shoulders as Mike hollered that the fridge was stocked with pop. We all waved goodbye to our parents as we pulled out. It was fun driving around town while watching some of our friends walking to the school or coming out of the restaurant after eating. We even saw Cassidy and Dr. Owen siting on a bench to watch all the couples.

We drove around in the limo for an hour before entering the school. I had to admit it was fun. When our limo stopped, the door was opened and the boys acted like gentlemen by helping us out. Since I had on a T-length formal, I tried to slide as gracefully as I could. Matthew was beaming when I stepped out. His eyes seemed to shine in the moonlight tonight.

As we walked up the stairs we entered a candlelit arch brocaded with white flowers. The smells from the flowers were light but fragrant. When we stepped through the arch, a picture was taken and we were given a card in order to see the proof later. Jennifer was the photographer for the yearbook and newspaper, while Cory stood at her side interviewing people for the school newspaper. They were quite the pair. One of these days I expected to find them married, with as much time as they put into their job together.

As we entered the gym, we were on the top shelf area of the bowl. Our surroundings had vines brocaded with white flowers hanging from the rafters, and in the center was a net which held nothing but white and red balloons over the dance floor. Those were our school colors. Meg, Mike, Kirt, Maymie Jean, Laura, and Kyle were off to the dance floor as soon as the next song began. Heather and Tyler stayed with us as we took in the scenery. The student council had done an outstanding job. Heather punched me in the ribs and pointed towards the opposite side of the gym. "You have an admirer." I started to look in the direction she pointed but Matthew informed me it was Jeremy.

Heather's laughter only irritated Matthew. "No, Heather, he looks mad." We both looked to find he was right. Tyler grabbed her hand in an irritated fashion, announcing they were headed towards the dance floor before she could cause any more trouble. Matthew whispered in my ear. "Heather is right. You are so beautiful tonight. Jeremy isn't the only one upset. There are other guys you have never even noticed...but they notice you now." He took my hand and escorted me to our table so I could lay my shawl down. I had forgotten I would have to remove it to dance. Matthew smiled an evil grin as he vowed that if he was going to be disliked for being with me, then he was going to show them all what they were really missing. I froze for a second as he seemed to stare deeply at me. I knew I had to look pale. My shoulders would only have the spaghetti straps around them and my back would be totally exposed. Matthew laughed as he assisted me in removing my shawl.

The feel of Matthew's hands so close to my bare skin made me shiver as he removed it. When I looked around it felt like everybody's eyes were on me, even though I knew it was all in my head. Mustering up some courage I turned around to look at Matthew as I asked if he liked my whole outfit. Matthew's eyes were huge as he eyed me from head to toe. Carefully he reached forward and fixed the chain on my locket since the clasp had ridden around to the front. His eyes betrayed that he was enjoying this way too much.

Matthew took my hand once again before escorting me towards the dance floor. When I looked across the way, I found Jeremy and his date. I felt guilty about the way I had treated him lately. "It's unnecessary to feel bad. He doesn't understand the word "no," let alone other things. If he doesn't find his moral compass I am afraid he is going to head down the wrong path for his life," Matthew stated firmly.

We arrived on the dance floor in time for a slow dance. The slow song began, and it sent chills up my spine as Matthew's hand slid down, landing on the small of my back. This reminded me of when we traveled by shadow, which right now, might not be a bad idea. Matthew let out a low laugh at this, and commented that too many boys were looking for us to get away with it. Jeremy entered the dance floor from the opposite direction. Unfortunately he wasn't looking at Mary, his date. She did look beautiful tonight. Matthew drew my attention back to him, reminding me this night was for us and not any of my silly concerns.

That night the glowing lights seemed to make his eyes shine more deeply. That was strange. I had thought the same about my eyes tonight. Could this be one of those warning signs Shep had seen? Matthew thought it was because we had each other. His mom always said the eyes were the windows to the soul.

*"How do you always know what I'm thinking? I can't do that around large crowds. Right now you're showing off."*

*"Why wouldn't I? I have you and that is all I need. Besides, you and I are connected so well I don't have to try to guard against anyone else here because your mind is a part of my essence now. They say it will get stronger the longer we are together. When you are more practiced with guarding your mind from the crowd, you won't have any problem. I know when we are in small groups you know my thoughts. I can tell."* I could hear him but his mind never interfered with mine. He swiped a piece of hair back over my ear that had fallen down. I felt extremely comfortable in his arms as I stared around the floor. So many couples were dancing, and I wondered how many of them would be together a week from now.

Gradually I closed my eyes as I laid my head on his chest, only to feel disjointed from the whole room. I no longer could even feel the buzz in my mind. Matthew's voice sounded a warning in my ear not to accidentally fade into a shadow. Instantly I lifted my head to look straight into his eyes, and I know he could see fear. Still swaying gently to the music, he explained that is how you feel right before you change forms.

Immediately I took inventory of my body as he laughed. *"Is that how you found each of your abilities?"* I felt embarrassed to admit to him it was true. His eyes became huge as he demanded for me to explain, but this was not the place to do so. *"They do happen usually by accident."*

With a rushed glance to the stairs, I saw Heather and Tyler headed towards our table. Off to the side of Heather, I had the strong urge to look closer at where she was standing. For some reason I felt uncomfortable. Not knowing why I felt that way, Matthew turned us in the direction so I could have a better look. Eventually Matthew stopped swaying before guiding me to the stairs. As we were walking past a group in the stands, they were commenting on how cold it felt. Matthew and I both quickened our steps. Once we reached the top we both tried sensing around the area, searching for any sign of anything unusual. There were too many people around for us to be able to distinguish between them. Even though we were using our eyes to scan the wall, we found nothing out of the ordinary.

For the moment we were letting our imagination get the best of us. We joined the others at our table as Heather pulled her shawl back over her shoulders, complaining she was getting cold a lot lately and it was becoming annoying. Tyler leaned over and tried to warm her. The rest of our group showed up, bubbling over with the excitement from the dance.

The night was a beautiful one. We spent as much time as possible dancing. When the dance was finally over, we headed towards the parking lot where we were met by our limo almost immediately. To my dismay, I found myself too tired to keep my eyes open. Upon arrival at the cul-de-sac, Matthew and I discovered we had fallen asleep together. Mike took it upon himself to wake us with some of his crude jokes.

Matthew walked me home, stating we had both better get some rest tonight since it was obvious we couldn't keep our eyes open. With a quick peck goodnight, I couldn't help but lean against him, willing him not to leave. Softly his hands brushed up my arms. "Shep is waiting." Matthew looked towards my front door. I watched him depart across to his home as Heather and Tyler were in the front yard saying their goodbyes. I headed straight to my room and quickly undressed and fell straight to sleep before Heather even entered.

A little bit later Heather and Sarah came in the room and decided they wouldn't bother me, so they went back to the family room. After their abrupt departure Shep came in and started checking me. I didn't even have the energy to complain.

His mind entered my thoughts as he questioned me about if I used any abilities tonight. He already knew I hadn't except for trying to sense for trouble. Shep rubbed my cheek as I fell into a deep sleep.

The next morning I woke to a silent house. I didn't even hear Heather around. When I began to sense through my house, I heard Shep saying everything was fine and to not use my abilities right now. I immediately stopped. When I started moving I found I was still too tired to roll over. I continued to lie still until I fell asleep again.

I wasn't sure how long I had slept this time. My blinds were down and I couldn't see what the weather looked like today, so I crawled out of my cozy, warm bed. As I went down the hall I yawned out the word "Heather" and was met by Sarah explaining she was over at Mike's with some of the other kids, finalizing the Halloween party for next weekend. As she continued talking to me, she was doing that funny hand movement around me again. Finally I mustered up the energy to tell her to stop because it was driving me nuts. She halted as I marched off to the kitchen. Not feeling particularly hungry, I began to regret snapping at Sarah as I laid my head down on the cold table.

Upon feeling the coolness against my forehead, I whispered aloud I was sorry. Her voice responded right next to me, making me jump. She started laughing but I could see she was more concerned than anything else. Without needing to, she offered to fix brunch for me. This startled me when I realized it was close to noon, and I really didn't feel like going to Mike's. Shep came in and started asking if anything had happened last night. I couldn't think of anything as I rubbed my head. Sarah chose to fix some toast and scrambled eggs but when they were placed before me I really didn't feel like eating anything. This didn't make either one of them happy. It became evident I had no choice so I ate a, little but it wasn't enough by the looks on their faces.

Once back in my room, I sat down at my desk and pulled out my dad's journals and began reading them. The journal I began reading was one that I've never read. For some strange reason I was feeling sentimental and needed only silence. This was an early journal describing my father's visit to my mother in the Shadow Realm. Traveling through the city, he was amazed at all the different time periods that were related to each individual lot. Some homes looked like they were modern and others looked as old as Camelot, he stated. When he arrived at my mother's house, he said it fit her personality to the letter. Carefully marking the page, I leaned back in my chair and decided I really needed to call my friends to let them know I wasn't coming today. I was feeling a little under the weather. Still sitting there I began to feel extremely comfortable and light. Shep charged into my room, calling my name sharply, but I could barely hear him even though he was inches from my face. When I looked at him everything returned to normal. As his hand ran across my forehead, I stiffened as he explained that Matthew had sensed me doing the same thing last night. "You have another ability appearing, and we will have to do some work on control today or you won't be going to school tomorrow."

Great, this was exactly what I needed, another ability. I just wanted to scream. Sometimes these abilities were a pain to have. I didn't know if I really cared to have them. Shep, knowing my distress, reiterated that eventually I would have all my basic abilities under control and that would become the norm for me. He patted me on the back as he tried to reassure me things would become normal very soon. "I'll call Mike and let him know you are under the weather." When I had my room back to myself I felt like hitting anything and everything. I forced myself to become compliant even though there seemed to be a tug of war going on inside of my head. I began to dress in a pair of jeans and sweatshirt. I pulled on a pair of dirty tennis shoes since the outside would definitely be muddy if we tracked through the woods. To me, learning a new ability sounded more like a chore than fun today, and what did he mean *basic* abilities?

Sarah informed me Matthew was at home today too. She was hoping that would make me feel better but it didn't. I was grateful for her help since I felt dejected as I headed towards the kitchen. A moment later Shep came into the kitchen in a rush. "We aren't going to be practicing in this area today." He looked very determined as I faced him. "We will be practicing in an area we set as a safety point for our house. It is the same place we practiced your shadowing. The teaching quad was set there a year ago for you. I had used it as a Protector quad for myself when in need. It has special boundaries around it that only someone with my permission can pass through. Even Shadows who are traveling in the Mortal Realm are aware of the warning beacons that are placed around a Protector station. The difference with this one is it has the mark of a Protector along with our Inner Circle marker. We have several placed strategically throughout the Mortal Realm. It will be a safety or safe zone for you, which means you could always enter."

Shep picked up his dirty tennis shoes to put them on. "Now I want you to follow me and learn how to arrive there on your own if the need ever arose." When he looked to me, I could tell he was expecting me to answer.

"Ye...yeah...I can do that." I was shocked that he expected me to shadow on my own. The past week I had improved in this area, but if I knew Shep's tone of voice, he was challenging me so that maybe I wouldn't be in such a foul mood. He reminded me I would have to sense and watch the patterns while I traveled, plus keep him in my range of sensing. Going over the rules with Shep on how I was to sense his essence and follow, I could see how he was concerned. Matthew had told me once that shadowing was a skill he received around the age of eight, so to him it was as simple as adding. I should have learned this long ago, not when I was a teenager.

Shep began to fade into the shadow and I followed his departure. Carefully watching the patterns had become easy, and to my surprise I could feel Shep's presence without any problem. Luckily I was able to follow without much difficulty. When I sensed him come to a stop, I did the same. Even my halts were becoming better since I was no longer fumbling around. We practiced the route several times to make sure I understood the path enough to do it on my own if I ever needed to. Shep was waiting on me and approved of my improvement. He offered the explanation that children should be able to follow their parents easily because of the genetic bond, though he hoped my skill was actually more than that. But in order to figure that out we were going to need someone that wasn't related to me.

Shep's eyes raised in amusement as another Shadow appeared. "Ruth has come here to help us today." She seemed very enthusiastic and happy to meet me. "She grew up with your mom. They were inseparable as children and are considered sisters. She has been helping us from time to time in your care, so you can trust her." I could feel both grow sad as my mother must have been passing through their thoughts.

"Thank you for coming today, Ruth. Maybe later you can tell me about my mom. I understand she was a handful." Thankfully this brought them out of their somber moods as they winked at each other. Ruth's smile was soft.

"They had hoped that by introducing me to your mom I might be able to curb her ability to find trouble. Instead she taught me how to find it. Before I met her I had never been a problem—always shy and meek and firmly grounded, staying away from adventures. But that all changed. Not many were allowed to spend time with your mother considering her rank. I didn't care about that and became stuck with keeping an eye on a girl younger than me. I was to babysit her. Even so, I didn't do a good job." Shep winked again as he agreed solemnly. She slapped her hands on her hips as if trying to pull away from the memories that hurt. I wish I could have helped but I didn't know how. From the looks of things, I brought her a lot of pain.

"Well, don't expect too much from me today. I am not very good at shadowing, and trust me, I don't look for trouble either. From the sounds of it I am more like you than her. I pretty well stick to books and my closest friends and rarely have I ever outright disobeyed. I think the only one who brings that out in me is Dre…"

Suddenly I bit my lip, since I remembered some of what Sarah had told me about my security. They had made sure that most did not know more than one person's identity who knew about me. Shep placed a comforting hand on my shoulder as he smiled. "Ruth knows about Drew. You don't have to worry. She knows about our neighborhood, too. She helps keep security there."

Grateful that I hadn't endangered somebody, I began to feel shaky and unnerved as I looked around my surroundings. "Actually…Ruth, don't expect me to be a natural at this stuff. I seem to be failing miserably and I am not so sure I will ever get these shadowing basics down. I am almost afraid of asking what is after the basics." I truly felt weak and uncertain that I could handle who I truly was, to the point I wasn't even sure that the mixing of my two halves didn't work against me. Japeth and the others had said it was hard but worth every challenge. Still, they hadn't exactly shown up to help, and in a way I knew I needed them. Where were they? Suddenly that small voice I was used to calling my Jiminy Cricket resounded in my head. "*All is as it should be. Trust yourself and me, we will survive this, and they will demand to be in your life soon whether Shep wants them around or not.*"

Ruth reassured me that nothing would be easy to learn here in the Mortal Realm, especially if you had to do everything in secret. She almost seemed perturbed as she glanced at Shep. "Master Goodwin, I do believe the Shadow Realm would be advantageous to her training. You can't expect to learn much if you are not free to practice." Shep cut her off before much more could be said. He was practically yelling it was not an option while glaring at her. We both were startled by his sudden reaction. She apologized quickly, stating she understood, but it wouldn't last forever. "So…where do we begin?"

Shep rubbed his bald head as he glanced around our surroundings. "The area is a ten mile radius. You will keep within the bounds of the safety. I have raised the child safety bar so she cannot leave here without me, so that should make it safer. I have also set an emergency alarm if our boundary is broken through. If this happens, whoever is closer is to take responsibility for taking her to our second planned safety. You will not deviate from this order. Have I made myself clear?" Ruth nodded with understanding as she smiled at me. "Begin when ready, and I will be keeping tabs on you both."

Ruth began her travel, and a half a minute later I tried to follow. I could barely feel her, which made my trip rough, but when she stopped I found that I could see her. She was a good thirty feet away. Ruth faded again and I tried to follow. This time she was quickening her pace. Still, I was able to maintain a sense of her. This time when we stopped I was still closer than either of us expected. She seemed surprised by this. We tried several more times, each being more difficult than the last, but when she came to a stop she flashed a grin at me, almost as a challenge as I watched her fade. This was sort of fun; it was like hide-and-seek. She traveled for a much longer time, but I still followed through all the shades that passed me. This time when she stopped I was closer than I had ever been before. She did not leave this time as Shep faded into view. He was smiling and asked what I thought about this ability.

For a moment I felt perplexed. "Well…I can sense her but, it is harder than you. Yet, I can do it. I sort of like it." He and Ruth both shook their heads with disbelief. "You did an outstanding job whether you realize it or not." Then they both agreed it was time to rest a little, and then we would try to change into a full-body shadow at will.

They explained there were many types of Shadow form, and that a normal body shadow was the easiest. As I sat under a tree, I wondered what Matthew was doing. *"I am at home resting, unlike you. You might say I am keeping tabs on you though. I hope you don't mind."* I felt him all the time now, but didn't realize how close of an eye he was keeping on me. This made me wonder how far away I was from home.

My reply came instantly from Shep. *"The two of you shouldn't communicate for too long, and definitely not about our distance."*

*"Are you not feeling rested today, Matthew?"*

*"I'm fine, but I felt like reading a book instead of running around."*

Again Shep interrupted us to reiterate that our use of telepathy was only for inside our safety. I knew it was to prevent us from continuing. It was clear telepathy wasn't a good idea. *"It's time for her to return to practice, Matthew."* I could feel Matthew press into the background, yet he remained firmly present. I could tell Shep even noticed, for he looked surprised at me.

"Well we need to begin again. Like with everything you have to relax to control the shift between the three forms we have as Shadows. You are beginning to understand your natural Shadow, but now we need you to learn about your mist form and the separating of your Shadow essence from your physical. The last is very dangerous and is something we discourage, but as you saw from previous experience it is something that is used to mend major injuries. Matthew has it down very well. A person cannot stay separated for long. Otherwise your physical human form dies. Today we will only be practicing with your mist form, though." He motioned for me to make myself comfortable. Hastily I searched around for a dry spot among the flickering rays of the sun.

"When you feel light, your vision will change slightly. You can move anywhere, even on a ceiling if you want, but remember: if you are trying to not be discovered, you must react like a shadow should react," Shep firmly voiced. When I concentrated on the feeling I had earlier, nothing happened. Opening my eyes, I found I was still in the same place. Fine. This was not going to happen today and I really didn't care. Shep knelt down with concern as he held my hand. "Close your eyes allow your full Shadow form to become a part of your surroundings. I mean, down to every shade, and stop letting your bad mood influence you." Now I knew I was going to have a problem. As I tried to relax, I closed my eyes and listened to my own breathing, but instead I fell into sensing around me instead of fading into a Shadow form. Shep continued to guide me with helpful suggestions, but nothing worked. Instead my temper was close to its boiling point.

"Stop! I can't do this. I need a moment, please." Without thinking I stood up and walked away quietly. I wasn't intending to be rude, but I needed a moment to breathe. I didn't feel good, and I didn't like the distance that stood between Matthew and me. Thankfully Shep didn't make any objections.

Once I was out of sight of Ruth and Shep, I sat down and created a breeze to help me clear my mind. My wind ability always felt right to me, like it fit, just like my slowing did. So why didn't my basic shadowing skills fit? After all, I was half Shadow too. My breeze continued blowing softly, helping me to relax as I sat cross-legged on the ground. Slowly I began to intensify the breeze to work on my control with it. Thankfully it reacted at my whim as it should. The wind was like a small lake breeze, which successfully blew my bangs from their clip. I truly did enjoy this sensation. Finally feeling like I wasn't under scrutiny, I rested in this position. It helped me to stretch out my aching muscles, and even though my eyes were closed, I could see the sun flash on me. A sensation of comfort and lightness ran through my body as my blood seemed to cool.

I hadn't realized that Shep was calling out my name. When I opened my eyes, I was shocked to see a slight film there. I could still see colors, but they were not as bright as before. Panic gripped my insides and I dropped back into the position I had been in before I turned into a Shadow form. Shep was running towards me and asked why I had done that without his supervision. I hadn't intended to. It had been accidental once again.

Suddenly Shep straightened as he read my thoughts. "It's okay." We sat there in the peace and quiet for a few minutes as he seemed to be in deep thought. "Let's try to recreate what just happened. Stop putting so much pressure on yourself. I don't expect anything from you, so don't assume I do. I will mimic you no matter what you do. You won't be alone and don't have to be frightened. I know you miss Matthew, but I can help too. Trust me."

This time I was able to accomplish the solid Shadow form with some of the variations in color to mimic the surroundings. Matthew had advised me on how important that was when I traveled with him. He would purposely travel with me around the small oasis so I could feel the varying degrees. Shep and I continued to try off and on throughout the day. I was able to do it whenever I felt safe, or if I became too relaxed. Considering how school had been, he felt I would never be too relaxed there, so I could go. Instead he was going to have to worry when I was at home.

It was decided we had enough practice, and we told Ruth goodbye and thanks for her assistance. She had been a good friend for the entire day. She would tell me stories about my parents when Shep wasn't around. There had been an awkward feeling every time Shep drew near. She didn't exactly seem comfortable with him, almost like she was afraid of him. I followed Shep back to our neighborhood, but instead of going home I focused in on Matthew. After Shep gave his approval, I followed through with my plan. Not knowing exactly where in his house he was, I zeroed in on his essence. When I faded in, I found I was in his room where he was sitting on the floor playing some video game, which immediately clicked off upon my appearance. Quickly he turned around and smiled at me as he patted the floor beside him for me to come sit. "*I was hoping you would come.*"

"Do I need to let your parents know I am here?" We heard a shout from his mom stating she already was aware, and I was welcome to stay for dinner if I wanted. Right away I took her up on the offer as I continued to sit next to Matthew and enjoy his company. He looked better than he did last night, but still looked drained. Carefully I felt his forehead and felt no fever. He said he wasn't sick, but I looked like I was. I had forgotten he had been keeping an eye on me today.

"So how did I do?" Unfortunately I really didn't feel good about my progress. He took a moment to consider it, and then shocked me with his answer. "Your following was excellent, but taking your full Shadow form needs some work. Your varying degrees of color aren't quite right and you need to mimic what real shadows do, not what you think they do. Personally, I think you are holding yourself back due to your own fear of the unknown and of being the boogeyman." He snickered at his addition of the boogeyman. I guess I did have a fear of being that. He nudged my shoulder gently as he offered that things would be different if he was the one practicing with me. It would be different, for I truly could sense everything Matthew sensed when shifting between forms. I had his heart there with me if I became frightened. He wouldn't ever let me lose control. Technically I knew Shep wouldn't either, but Matthew held me when practicing and he knew me more intimately than Shep did somehow. When we shadowed together, it was like we were one, unlike when I shadowed with Shep or anyone else. Finally I confided in him I really didn't feel comfortable and I was so tired. On that note we decided to go to the study and watch a show.

I flopped down on the couch as Matthew picked out a movie. His father must love movies since there were shelves upon shelves of them. Mr. Sturley came to the door and wanted to know what we were going to watch. Matthew chuckled as he held up a show about the supernatural. It was some kind of TV series. Mr. Sturley smiled broadly. "She will get a kick out of that. Most of the time they deal with ghosts and urban legends. To be honest, I get a kick out of the show. Sometimes they hit on things that are possible. Enjoy. Selena, if you need my assistance with feeling a bit better, I could try to help."

Mr. Sturley left as Matthew took a seat next to me in order to cuddle. It felt good. The show did have a unique look at the supernatural, but I wondered if they ever dealt with shadows like us. Matthew snorted they do a little later, and it was far off from the truth. We continued watching until we fell asleep.

I don't know how long we had been asleep, but at one point Mr. Sturley came in and was shaking both us awake. The look in his eyes made me wonder what was worrying him. Suddenly he smiled weakly at me as he informed us that dinner was ready. Going downstairs, the smell that wafted in from the dining room was delicious. Once there, Matthew pulled out a chair for me and then seated himself next to me. Evidently Meg and the others were finished with their plans for the party. "So how did it go?" Meg didn't even look up from her plate as that small smile of hers spread.

She informed us that everything was done except for the actual setup. Matthew inquired if anybody was upset we hadn't been there. She informed us they had been speculating that we just wanted time by ourselves. Then she giggled and stated that was obviously what was happening. If anybody noticed me here tonight, it would look that way.

Matthew's mom had fixed a wonderful spaghetti dinner. She excused herself to do the dishes as I offered to help. She turned me down firmly. "You should spend some time with Matthew instead." Meg informed us all she was going back to Mike's house to help him put together the music and would let them all know we missed them today. On this note, Matthew picked up a pillow and threw it at her. She faded in and out so quickly it was definitely a practiced trade.

With a quick look to Mrs. Sturley, I questioned if they were always like that. It was funny to see her wipe her hand across her mouth as she tried not to smile. "You should have seen them as toddlers. When they started shadowing I thought we were going to have a nervous breakdown. Being who we are, their abilities started earlier than most…and of course, they are much stronger than the average Shadow." I had never thought about that. I imagine it had been a challenge to keep two Shadow children in line here.

Matthew hooked his arm around me, and immediately I found myself shadowing to our oasis. A welcoming warm breeze hit me, causing Matthew to seem pleased with himself. *"What are you smiling about?"* He chortled, "*Meg just tried to follow, but that was one thing she has never been successful at.*" I was surprised to hear I was able to do something that Meg couldn't. He looked at me with such a serious look that it made me feel uncomfortable. *"See, I told you things come easier to you than you realize."* I appreciated his compliment greatly.

*"So do you do everything perfect?"*

*"I haven't found too many complications in learning my natural abilities. Some are harder to learn than others, but you have to practice until you understand it."* He was beaming with excitement as he stated it was harder to act normal when he had moved into my town. Evidently he had had a hard time.

He began the story of the first time he noticed me. Of course it was the night I arrived home, and he was able to hear my mind whirling. "*My family couldn't understand for a while. Meg was the only one who believed me that you were a Shadow. My mom knew I was telling the truth, but she could not figure out why. I was the only one who was hearing your mind. Now I know that they assumed it was…you know. That we were a matching pair since it happens that way among our people. The other thing was that my mom never was able to see you plainly like me, and this concerned her. She was anxious for my dad to return. She was going to stick to protocol in order not to endanger us or you. From what she has admitted lately, she already suspected who you were. She left several times trying to locate my dad, but never did.*"

With a wink in his direction I admitted I had noticed him too. We both were relaxing while enjoying our memories of the first sight we had of each other. We spent a large amount of the evening enjoying the coolness of the cave. After several hours, Matthew glanced at his watch, announcing it would be bedtime at home and we should leave. Before we left, Matthew wanted to know if I wanted to learn the way. In a way I did—and I had been studying it most times he brought me here—but tonight I was only interested in being in his arms. He grinned as he held up his arms and I melted into his body with my ear listening to his heart.

With a quick peck on top of my head we began to shadow back home. As we landed gently in his study, I could sense only family around. I guess our sensing while shadowing was becoming even easier for me. We both fell onto the couch together as Matthew's father looked at us from his desk chair, wanting to know if we felt better. Matthew squeezed me tight, simply stating he felt awesome. I had to agree; I felt very relaxed too. His dad suppressed a grin as he warned us that Mike had called wanting to speak to me.

So Meg did tell him we were together. Matthew slammed his fist into the couch but said he didn't expect anything less from her. As I leaned against Matthew's chest, I laid my hand gently in order to caress him while he tried to find peace again. Before I realized it, Matthew had fallen asleep. He truly wasn't well, I could tell. With a worried look to his father, I inquired why he wasn't acting normal. I could see the underlying concern on Victor's face as he moved closer. "I believe Matthew may need to go home sooner than expected. He seems to be draining faster than he should without a new ability being the problem."

About an hour later I pulled myself up off the couch to go home, for it was dark now, and Shep did have rules. Cautiously I leaned over and kissed Matthew, not expecting a response, but found him kissing me back as he pulled me onto the couch. *"Where do you think you are going?"*

*"It's late and we have school tomorrow. Besides, you need to go to bed."*

Defiantly Matthew shook his head. "Don't leave. I can sleep right here sitting up if I must. I don't sleep well when you aren't next to me. I know it's strange but it is true." I could see he was serious and was uncertain how to respond, for I understood in a way. My sleep was becoming more and more restless with every passing day. The only time I felt true relief in my sleep was when I was with him. I tried to make a joke out of it, but he knew better. I pecked his cheek as I stood up and shadowed home. Thankfully my evening had been much better than my morning.

The next day came, and I felt as tired as always. Today I was to ride the bus for the first time since the catastrophe at the beginning of the year. I wasn't sure I was ready for this, but I didn't really have much of a choice. Slowly I walked towards our bus stop, only to be met by Matthew on my porch with Tyler. They both were waiting on Heather and me. Once at the bus stop I was definitely pleased to realize I was dealing better with keeping their minds at a distance. Even if the bus ride was long, it was tolerable, which meant I finally had the control I had longed for.

When we arrived at school, it was decorated in orange and black since Halloween was on Friday. The elementary division would be having their annual walk-through in their cute costumes. They were always adorable.

When we arrived at our lockers, Mike made his way towards us. "So what did the two of you do all day yesterday? You certainly didn't help finalize the party." The air became charged as Matthew answered.

"If it is any of your business, we were under the weather yesterday. We watched TV and spent time with my parents." Mike continued to rag on how he couldn't believe how Shep was dealing with this. He had always thought of Shep as an overprotective parent with me.

The rest of the week went well except for English, where Jeremy continued to try to sit next to me constantly. He had truly turned into a bully. Tyler and Kirt had to help Matthew keep his temper in check as this situation continued to strain my patience. Jeremy was pushing the limits. What was it going to take to get rid of him?

Friday finally came, and the school had been packed with parents coming to celebrate with their children at Halloween parties. To my great relief, I had no problems keeping everything under control. Back at home I had been practicing inside the house to take Shadow form, but I hadn't been successful at it. Matthew kept encouraging me, but I was sure he and Shep were right: it would be second nature once I understood it. The varying degrees were a pain to copy, and I was only successful when Matthew accompanied me.

Trick-or-treat started at six p.m. and ended at eight. Shep, Parker and the Muirs had succeeded in freaking a ton of kids out with their creepy costumes as they peeked out from behind their doors. The whole night they continued to rehash about the poor little kindergartener who was dressed up as a cow and had gone screaming from their houses. They probably had traumatized him to where he would never go trick-or-treating again.

Around six we walked over to Mike's house where we could hear Shep's outside surround sound blaring haunted house sounds in the front, while in the back you could hear party music. The backyard was aglow with orange and black Chinese lanterns that lit the boundary, while a bonfire was burning bright at the back. The air was cool as the wind added to the frightening ambiance, along with several small wind chimes Meg had placed. Meg and Mike had done a beautiful job of decorating.

Our friends arrived in droves, and the party was in full swing by eight-thirty.

The Muirs had rented a wooden dance floor that had candle stands lit with dark candles. Matthew and I danced by ourselves for most of the night, until Jeremy arrived. When he entered, his mind made no qualms about trying to get me to dance with him. Shep, however, intervened so Matthew and I could escape to the people at the bonfire.

Unfortunately, Matthew was angry and could barely stand the sight of Jeremy. When he finally sat down behind me, he held me securely against his chest. I was barely able to breathe, let alone move. Tonight he was totally possessive and he didn't care what anyone thought. Tyler brought Heather over and we chatted about how well things were going, until Heather reminded us it might only be temporary if we couldn't keep Jeremy away. Several agreed sourly who were not even a part of our regular group. It seemed to me that Jeremy was beginning to get a bad reputation. At least his brothers had never gone this far.

Tyler leaned over, whispering to us that Kirt was already on it. "Mike and Kirt have been preparing for this all week. Meg gave Mike an ultimatum. He is to keep Jeremy away from the two of you. That girl has a way of making her points well understood without saying too much. Besides, you know Meg. She meant it. I think Mike really likes her. He doesn't want to lose her." Tyler actually sounded glum with the last part of his statement.

A nervous twitch from Matthew surprised me. "I owe her," Matthew commented miserably.

Strategically we had sat in a position so we could see anyone new who was joining the ghost stories. Mr. Muir was outstanding with his presentation of the scary tales tonight. Meg had evidently been working with him, not to mention the atmosphere was perfect. Things seemed to blow or crack at just the right moments, and I could tell they were not natural phenomena. When Matthew whispered, "I told you she was overdramatic," I giggled.

John had done an outstanding job. He seemed very pleased with our praise as he offered that Meg had practiced with him a lot. Meg had to know what we were saying because she smiled as a limb behind us cracked. Heather let out a scream and everybody jumped with fright.

It had been a cold night, but fun. Kirt and Mike had managed to keep Jeremy at bay. Thankfully he had to leave with his older brother, which made it easier for us to help with cleanup. The night grew colder as the other kids began to disappear. Cleanup was fairly easy. The biggest issue would be the bonfire.

We all were discussing how well things had gone when all hell broke loose. Matthew and I were cleaning the debris from the bonfire when he froze to his spot. A second later he rushed over to me and jerked me to face him. His whole body was trembling as he tugged me along. I didn't know what he was up to. I was tired and we needed to finish soon. The wind seemed to be picking up, which meant we needed to get the bonfire completely out before something bad happened. I didn't have time to goof around. I stopped dead in my tracks as I struggled against his pull.

"What do you think you are doing? We need to get this fire out. It could cause a huge fire if any embers make it into the woods." As I jerked to return to the bonfire I saw what Matthew must have already seen. Two Shadow forms at the edge of the woods. Matthew jerked me around before I let out a squeal and placed his finger up against my lips as he pulled me against his warm body. He continued to pretend to flirt with me while keeping a watchful eye behind me. "Let's go into the house, *now*." Matthew hollered to Tyler and Heather to follow us, but I could see that Tyler understood when their eyes met and he looked in the direction that Matthew motioned.

Thankfully Heather didn't put up a fuss at being forced back to the house. Shep had already appeared and was on his way to where we stood. Sarah was right beside him. They seemed not to notice what was evidently right behind us. When we reached Shep, he told us to keep the others inside while they investigated. Shep's dead tone sent a shiver down my spine. "We will take care of this if the need arises. Now get in."

He must have grabbed Matthew's arm a little tight because Matthew winced a little at Shep's touch. He said something to Matthew, but it was so low I could not hear him. Matthew wrapped his arm around my waist as we left Sarah and Shep to face whoever was out there. I hoped they were friends. Otherwise that meant they had either found Matthew's family, me, or worse, were trying to make Heather reveal herself as a Guardian. They had mistaken her for me, and no matter what they would do, she wouldn't be able to stop them. I thought the safe corridor into the neighborhood was guarded, so maybe they were just passing through. Back inside the kitchen I demanded to know what Shep had said to Matthew.

"He told me not to leave your side. If any problem arises to go to our…" Without Matthew finishing, I knew exactly where he had been told to take me. I didn't need any further explanation. Just as I was about to lose it, Laura and Kirt came in wide-eyed. Tyler looked nervously around as he informed us on more instructions he had been given.

*"My parents are already in the woods, heading for the point behind the bonfire. Granddad is coming to get us, but he wants Meg and Matthew to come too. Your parents are already in Shadow form and are converging on the same spot. If the strangers are passing through they will not reveal themselves, but if they are a part of Alexander's lot, then they want you to shadow us to the portal. Man, I never saw Shep look so scary. His eyes did this funny thing similar to Matthew's thing the other day."*

Matthew asked if they had changed shape and color for a moment and Kirt nodded. "That is because he is not a normal Shadow. Shep is a Protector—of Selena in particular. You have to be nuts to take a Protector on especially since he is her father. See…"

Heather walked in before he could finish his explanation. There was a sudden clap of thunder and lightning outside as the sound of rain started hitting the windows. The whole house shook with the thunder. Most of us knew this was not a normal storm and began to look worriedly around for trouble. The doorbell rang, and we heard John greet Granddad. He came in asking the Muirs how the party had gone. "I'm here to escort the children home, including the Sturleys."

Mr. Muir glanced appreciatively out the door. "I'm sure glad we got the dance floor and electronics inside before that hit. I declare, we are having the worst luck this year with abrupt storms." Andy stood out on the porch without paying a bit of attention to his girlfriend. When he glanced back, he muttered that something wasn't right. We all could have groaned in agreement at that, but none of this would make sense if we did. Granddad acted puzzled as he looked towards Andy. "Son, it's just a normal storm. Probably will be…" Andy shook his head no as he cut Granddad off. Andy was rarely rude, and to an elderly person in particular was surprising.

"No, it's not. Something has been wrong around here for a while. I can't put my finger on it, but it is bound to get worse. Come on Chel, let's get you home while the rain has lightened."

Granddad motioned for us to come while looking perplexed at Andy. We excused ourselves with a promise to return tomorrow to help. We walked out onto the front porch and waved goodbye as we all huddled together. This was definitely one of Shep's storms. I remembered the downpour on our way to my training area when he didn't want me to see where I was going. Come to think about it, I never did find out where we had been. Matthew held me tightly in his grasp as I sensed the two strangers in the back. They were not even aware of the others about to descend on them. Instead of any of us going home, we stopped at Heather's house to drop her off. I hadn't thought about her being unprotected.

Matthew murmured in my ear they had placed security around the house. Still, I pulled loose to hug Heather goodnight. I couldn't help but hold her tight as I searched her house for my own reassurance that she was safe. I was thrilled to find there was no one there that shouldn't be. When I released her, I found myself back in Matthew's waiting embrace. He hadn't even given me a second to slip back to him on my own. We headed towards Uncle Billy's house, and once safely inside, we found Grandma waiting anxiously for us. She had a look that one should think twice about confronting her. She ushered us all into the dining room where cups of hot cocoa were waiting.

The next hour we all sat in silence listening for any warning that we would need to make a run for the portal. Suddenly there was a crash of lightening that made us all jump to our feet. Granddad went to the bay window in the living room while Kirt was evidently doing his sensing of things around us. The crack had to be a bad sign, announcing a fight had broken out. I scoured the room for a shadow so I could use it to go grab Heather. Matthew and Tyler both knew what I was thinking and responded by grabbing my arms. I hadn't been fast enough. If only I could change into Shadow form they wouldn't be able to hold onto to me. Grandma, seeing what was happening, demanded to know what was going on. Tyler tattled on me as Matthew stepped in behind me encircling me in his strong arms. Grandma became very stern with me as she added that precautions had already been made on Heather's behalf and not to act impetuously.

Matthew held me tightly, not giving me much room to move. I was sure it was to remind me I couldn't shadow without taking him with me. Matthew's urgent whispering was firm that if necessary he could stop me, even in Shadow form. "Calm down."

Listening to him I stopped struggling. I knew I was defeated and would have to pray the precautions were enough. Slowly he relaxed as I waited in misery like everyone else. Forms began taking shape in the hallway, who thankfully turned out to be our parents returning. They were all soaking wet, but said the strangers had been there to see if Heather could be provoked into using her abilities. When the storm hit, it seemed to discourage their effort. They didn't even realize the storm was not natural. Mr. Sturley said Alexander's thugs were definitely not intuitive. Mr. Sturley, Billy, and Shep felt the person behind these guys was definitely the one who would have seen through what they had done today.

Relief flooded my body as they continued to inform us of all they had learned. Since everything worked out, we all went home. Tomorrow would bring new plans for how to deal with this impending threat. Andy had been right: things were bound to get worse.

The next week everybody was running us through drills of how to deal with different type of attacks. I hadn't even been able to take proper Shadow form yet for fear of acting as a beacon. School had been a pain for all of us. We could have done without the additional responsibility. To add to our problems, Jeremy had continued harassing Matthew every chance he had. Luckily Matthew hadn't responded to any of it yet, but I was sure the restraint wasn't going to last much longer. Even Kirt and Tyler were taking bets on when Matthew would shadow him somewhere and teach him a real lesson.

Staying close to Matthew had been my top priority. We spent a lot of time at our oasis, and I had learned how to reach it by myself if necessary. I still made mistakes sometimes, but Matthew was always there to help. Thank heavens Thanksgiving would be soon.

# CHAPTER 20.
# BATTLE

**It had been** a cold, dreary day. Actually, the whole month had been. Winter hadn't hit hard like it usually did at this time of year. The temperature was remaining in the fifties most days. Thankfully we were three days from Thanksgiving vacation and I couldn't wait. We all truly needed a break.

Matthew and I were taking daily walks trying to enjoy the last of the tolerable days of the season. Shep and Sarah had gone on a trip to try to uncover who our visitors had been the past couple of months as I stayed with Heather under the close supervision of Billy. Tyler spent most of his time at Heather's house anyway, and this helped Billy out with his surveillance. Tonight was the first basketball game of the season. We were all excited about seeing Mike in his first game as a starter. Our Saturday had been planned around this event. Parker was going to drop the four of us off at the game while Meg was going with Mike earlier, along with Laura and Kirt to help him stay relaxed. We all decided to meet in the stands later to cheer him on.

The school parking lot was overcrowded and busy. For the first time in a long time I could feel a little pressure in my head from keeping everybody's mind at bay. Matthew continued to smile, although I could tell he felt the pressure, too. Poor Matthew had been having a harder time than me lately. It was evident we both were in need of being reenergized, as Shep put it. Each day was making it more obvious, according to Victor and Sarah's analysis. As we were walking into the big gym, the buzz of activity grew to intolerable limits.

Heather wanted to purchase a school spirit shirt, so she left it up to us to find and save seats for our group. In many ways our gym looked like a coffee cup the way the stands were set, and our school colors of red and white were all over the place with a big Spartan head painted on the far wall. As I looked across the stadium, I thought I saw something against the wall, but I had to be mistaken. After all, we were in a crowded room. No one would dare follow us here. Matthew, noticing my stare, began scanning across the way. He didn't see anything.

A half hour later, Heather returned with her school spirit shirt with Tyler keeping a hand on her. She didn't seem to mind his possessiveness, and by her thoughts she felt it was the next step in their relationship. As she took her seat with Tyler, she asked if we had seen the others yet, but there had been no sign. When the buzzer rang, the two teams took the floor to warm up. Mike came zipping out, waving with a big smile on his face. Somehow he found us with ease.

We watched the players go through their intimidation tactics, as I called them. They ran their squat routine with their loud voices while we all clapped. Meg,

Laura, and Kirt entered as I waved to catch their attention to where we were seated. Then I saw it again, but this time it was a different shadow. Matthew immediately looked and shook his head. Obviously he didn't see what I had. The Shadow moved quickly and it didn't act like the other shadows in the area. Could there be a Shadow following each group of my cousins? The upper edging of the gym did have cement walls, and many shadows played on them. Hopefully it was my imagination.

When they headed over in our direction, I didn't see anything obvious following them. Heather stood up, making a show of where we were seated. "Selena, help me. Why did you stop waving? They will never find us." She sounded perfectly disgusted. Meg came down like nothing in the world bothered her. Something about her gave a person the feeling that there was a lot more to understand. She didn't dress Goth, but her black hair and sophisticated dark clothing gave the appearance of it.

When the band started playing, it became painful to tolerate all the noise in our heads. My ears had become extra sensitive lately. Matthew bent his head down as his hand automatically went through his thick black hair, proving how miserable he was. Without thought, I leaned over and rubbed his back. The next twenty minutes were probably going to be the worst part of the night.

Finally, the game officially started as the color guard marched the flag out to center court. When the pledge was finished, the players were announced. Mike was the third one to run out. Of course he was a show off; he had to for Meg. He flipped while waving excitedly. She actually enjoyed his cockiness. It was odd to see a glimmer of excitement as she bounced, waving proudly back to him. Matthew grinned and remarked that Mike must be rubbing off.

To my satisfaction, our team immediately showed the caliber we were used to seeing in our teams. We may have been a small country town, but we were stronger than even the big city schools. It was a rare event for us not to place in the top three of any athletics we took part in. It looked like we were going to mop the floor with them.

By the time we had made it to halftime, we were already twenty points ahead. Mike was no longer looking up to find us because he was totally in the "zone" as Josh called it. One thing that was nice for the Muir brothers was that they each thrived in different sports, and this was Mike's. He had been made captain this year, and that was truly unusual, being only a sophomore.

Matthew mentioned he needed to get a breath of fresh air. He was perfectly miserable. Carefully we extricated ourselves from the bleachers, only to have Tyler and Heather join us. They felt this game was over; there wasn't much to watch since our team had better skills. When it came to games like this, it became boring or painful to watch.

We walked towards the back doors to get our hands stamped so we could reenter later. Matthew looked tired. His appearance was beginning to concern me. I had a strong inclination we were going to have to make our trip at Thanksgiving instead of Christmas. Once outside, Matthew whispered not to worry. He assured me firmly that he was fine. I wasn't convinced by any means. The heat of his hand felt good as we walked out into the cold. "You worry way too much for your own good." With a soft reminder that I knew him too well to believe him only made him smile.

Suddenly Heather decided she needed to go to the restroom. Instead of going back inside, she volunteered to go to the restroom building out near the science center. This building remained open during any activities. The boys waited against the wall while we went in. To my dismay, the building seemed abnormally cool and even Heather shivered. This building had its own heating system, so something had to be wrong. Maybe it needed to be reported. Heather surprised me when she asked if Matthew was starting to get headaches like I did at the beginning of the year. "Yeah, I don't think he is adjusting to the varying weather here."

Heather nodded in agreement. "I bet he has allergies. How are your headaches doing?" She caught me off guard, for I hadn't expected her to think I still had headaches. She continued to prattle on as I tried to deny her accusation. "Don't try to lie to me. You are not good at it. We have grown up like sisters for far too long for you to keep secrets, and I know you are. AND, don't think I haven't noticed those dark circles under your eyes most of the time. Not to mention you are tired all the time these days. Maybe you need to go to a migraine clinic."

Heather continued talking when I noticed the room acquired an eerie feeling as well. This was becoming all too familiar to me in the past month. Heather grabbed her shoulders and remarked it was too cold to be out here and she was going back to the game. We probably needed to let them know the heater wasn't working out here. When she walked past me, I noticed the movement of a shadow that did not match, and this time I was certain of what I saw. I tried not to panic as I assured her she was right. With the suggestion she head back inside to inform the staff, she acted puzzled.

We walked out to find that Matthew had gone off by himself into the woods. I couldn't believe Tyler had let him. Tyler merely shrugged his shoulders while looking perplexed at me. "Tyler, you need to take Heather back inside so she can report the heater doesn't seem to be working out here. It really should be." I had high hopes that he would take this opportunity to invade my privacy with this hinting stuff, but he didn't which made me frustrated.

To my horror I noticed the Shadow must have followed us outside. Its movements were sloppy, delayed in their reaction to the flickering lights. It didn't take a brain surgeon to see it. I stepped a bit closer, hoping Tyler would notice. Finally he caught my hint and I could see fear creep into his stature. "You two go back to the game. I will find M…him and be in soon." Even though Tyler seemed calm, I knew his words weren't a statement but an order.

He shoved Heather towards the gym. For once I agreed without arguing. I would take care of my best friend. Hastily I began to drag her towards the well-lit door as the noise of the crowd rose with cheers. I bet we had scored. As I walked my best friend towards the gym, a deep darkness surrounded us. It was like dark ink taking over our surroundings. Heather squealed that the lights had gone out as we were totally enveloped. "I'm scared Selena. Where are you?!" I was scared too, for this was not normal, and it was definitely Shadow related. A second later I managed to grab her shirt, and then I lost her again. Not being able to use my eyes properly, I swung my hands around until I hit something hard. Slowly my eyes began to adjust to the darkness, and what I saw was frightening. The darkness was swirling like a whirlpool of ink. To top it off, I could see it was about to close in around us. I had just this one moment to pull us to safety. Heather was ice cold as I dragged her towards the only possible exit, or at least it looked like an exit. We continued to struggle towards the sound of Tyler's shouts at the last of the opening. It was like stepping out of an overly stuffy room. The ice cold air felt good against my skin. We both stumbled as we took deep breaths. Suddenly I began to lose my grip on Heather's hand and turned around to see the darkness approaching us again. I had to act Mortal and not use my abilities, but this was beginning to become impossible. "Heather, stop acting like a baby. Come…ON!" I pulled with both my hands as her grip tightened. We started to run towards the gym, only to be joined quickly by Tyler. "Where's Matthew?" I hollered.

"He's still in the woods." Tyler tried to make a grab for me, but I whipped around in the opposite direction too fast, a move I had learned from him this past summer. I dashed for the woods smoothly, jumping the fallen logs. My training was really coming in handy tonight. When I looked back, the darkness was still close but wasn't moving. Heather was almost to the door with Tyler when I glanced back. Tyler would take care of her, but for now I had to find Matthew.

Tyler began hollering something at me. Once I was in the shelter of the trees, I tried to sense where Matthew was, but instead a hand grabbed me around the waist, interrupting my thoughts. It was Matthew, and he didn't look well. "What are you doing? Were you attacked?"

He stuttered, which was not normal for him. "Yes." That was when I heard Heather hollering she didn't like the dark and she wanted me to answer right now because she was afraid. Staring back through the trees I saw the darkness reaching towards her once again. Why weren't these Shadows giving up? It had to be obvious she didn't have a clue they were even there. Tyler hands began to move in an effort to keep the Shadows from changing forms. I could hear him calling to Kirt, shouting they were in danger. I had to help. Matthew agreed this time. We both could see the danger plainly.

This was one time it didn't matter if anyone found out. I couldn't stand by and let anyone get hurt. "Matthew, I can use my slowing ability. I don't know if I can make you immune. I hope I can."

He shrugged his shoulder in defeat as we heard Heather letting out a horrifying scream.

"We'll do what we can, but stay close." With this he stood up to prepare himself for the charge. Again Heather screamed when she looked behind her, but Kirt came running out of the gym straight for her. He was moving very fast and tackled Heather. Instead of falling she was being dragged into the woods by him.

Without delay Tyler stopped and ran for the woods in the opposite direction. Matthew pulled me back and whispered we needed to not draw attention to ourselves since they were safe. The darkness continued creeping towards the place where Kirt and Heather had entered the woods. They weren't convinced. Why? Tyler passed by us and motioned for us to stay as he continued towards the last place we had seen Kirt and Heather enter. Matthew stayed hunched over while following Tyler. If they thought I was going to stay out of this, they were wrong. This time I had to control my emotions in order to keep everybody safe. I didn't want to give away our location. It would be hard but it was the only way to ensure their safety.

I kept telling myself to not allow my thoughts to give us away. My mind was feeling numb. Whether it was from fear or stupidity, I don't know. I could see Heather backed up against a tree with a look of horror plastered across her face. She was petrified. The Shadow had taken human form in front of her. Surprisingly Kirt swept the attackers feet out from under him so she could run. As he hollered she seemed to jump from fright. Suddenly the man bounced back with a gymnastic move I had seen long ago. Shep did that move. The man struck Kirt hard. Just at that moment it hit me how I could help this time, especially when I saw another form rolling in. This one was still in mist and was inching towards them but I successfully slowed him down. Luckily Heather had her eyes closed and looked to be holding her breath while waiting for the inevitable. It was obvious she was expecting to be struck. At that moment I chose to make Tyler immune since he was the closest to her. Tyler charged at full speed and grabbed her. Instantly, I released my hold and mouthed to Matthew my apology. He smiled as he lunged forward, smoothly taking me to the ground. He landed on top of me in the midst of a lot of debris. It was no surprise to hear the Shadow curse as he hollered with outrage. "I thought you said it was only kids! They aren't acting like babes! The mix is too dangerous… we have to pull out and try again later! He's on his way!"

Meg appeared about twelve feet away and caught Tyler and Heather as they dashed through the woods. When Heather looked at me, I could see the horror in her eyes. Suddenly my heart dropped, and the only thing I could manage was to mouth I was sorry. Matthew held me tight as he nodded his head to Meg, and she vanished with Heather in tow. "She'll be alright," Matthew whispered.

Tyler looked relieved and headed towards the other assailant. Abruptly, we heard Kirt holler out in pain, causing us all to look to the source of the cry. Kirt was on the ground holding his midsection. He was hurt but, how badly was still unclear. I watched as Matthew began pulling debris around. I didn't know he could do this, and evidently he didn't either, for he looked just as shocked. With the use of my wind I was able to blow dirt into the assailant's eyes. I watched as the debris gathered close enough for my wind to spin it out at him. Our little windstorm would help disable the attacker.

Hopefully Kirt would recover enough to hide. As I looked around I saw a lot of brush and another pile of sand and dirt. Again I used my wind to help stir up the dirt and sand together. I began blowing harder as Matthew seemed to be concentrating on moving the pile I had pointed to. With a sudden rush of energy Matthew and I managed to throw the debris at the attacker with our abilities. Kirt saw what was coming and covered his eyes as he rolled off to the side. It was working well, but was taking an awful lot of energy to do. Kirt jumped to his feet and ran further into the woods.

Suddenly we heard Laura's shout of warning. When we looked towards her we saw another attacker we hadn't noticed before. "They're babes, take them…stop goofing off! I wish to return home you fools," the man shouted. We rolled to our back to see Laura struggling to hold a Shadow in his Shadow form. She had saved us, even if it was for the moment.

The next couple minutes were a blur and my energy was giving out. I felt exhausted as I fell to the cold, wet earth with Matthew at my side. His sweaty faced was smudged with dirt as we both lay there panting. Suddenly he shadowed over beside me and placed his body against mine protectively. His body was trembling and I could feel his ragged breathing against my shoulder. He was in pain. I could feel it. To my horror I could hear another group coming. I sensed it was my family. It was Billy and Betty appearing with Shep and Sarah. Their faces gave you the feeling they were deadly but it was too late. Unfortunately the Shadow located us before anything could be done. His approach became ungodly fast as he shadowed towards us. Matthew jerked with the awareness of the encroaching danger. He hadn't seen our faces, so my secret could still be salvaged. He whispered, "He thinks you are Heather." Matthew pulled me tighter than ever against his body as we began shadowing. I could feel the attacker's essence following us as the air around us whipped. Matthew kept my face against his chest, barely allowing me room to breathe. I was sure he was trying to keep my identity a secret, but was it worth it? We made several jumps to different areas, but we weren't shaking him. Our pursuer was too good. Matthew was looking more worse-for-wear than ever before. I wanted to help, but he wouldn't let me take over the shadowing. We always seemed to be a little ahead, and yet not far enough to lose the attacker.

The last time we were motionless, lightning came out of nowhere as Shep appeared in his Shadow form. He immediately turned into a blur and became entangled in the attacker's form. It seemed like they were tussling around. There were zigzags and flashes of brilliant light all over the place. The sounds were utterly horrifying. Some of them sounded like monsters or wild beasts fighting. The air was ripping over us as the rain began pouring down in a sheet. Before I could help Shep, Matthew grabbed me around the waist and told me very harshly not to fight him since he could handle it.

Seconds later he shadowed us into another area where I could not sense a pursuer. Unfortunately, Matthew had done all that he could handle. This time he lost his grip and we both fell hard to the ground. He was breathing heavy with a wheeze. When I looked at his eyes, they were no longer normal. This time it was my turn to protect him. We were both soaked, cold, and in pain. I needed to come up with a plan on how to get Matthew the help he needed.

I was pretty sure we were not being followed since I couldn't sense the stranger anymore. Shep and the others must have been successful in diverting their attention. Suddenly I heard Matthew fall back against a tree with a thud as he tried to stand. When I looked at him he was sweating profusely and his eyes were swirling with darkness. He didn't make any noises, but I could sense he was in pain and exhausted. He had been using his abilities too much to keep us safe and my identity hidden. Now it was my turn to take care of him. Gently rubbing his body, I tried to warm him as I whispered for him to trust me. I needed a moment to collect my thoughts so I could find the portal near the beach. I would take him to the Shadow Realm myself. I had a general idea of how to wind up close to Sarah's home. Hopefully once we arrived there would be somebody to help us with Matthew's condition. He seemed to be struggling now to maintain his form. For the first time I was thankful to have both sets of abilities.

Suddenly I felt a calming presence within me, which almost seemed to be assisting me in my endeavor. It also helped me to calm myself so I could concentrate on how to use my abilities to benefit us. I was careful as I leaned over and put my arms around his shoulders while lifting him up. His weak smile made my heart jump with misery. To my shock he began to cough as he tried to speak. "Wha... what do yo..uuu...think you are doing?"

"Don't worry." With as much strength as I could muster I pulled him into my embrace and took over the shadowing. He had done enough. Surprised I had done this so well, I continued to hold Matthew to me in case we needed to leave suddenly. Once we arrived at the portal, I saw the man from the mist nearby. This startled me, but his eyes looked very kind and concerned. He didn't say a word, but motioned for me to come to him. I couldn't see his face really well since the collar on his coat was up with the scarf covering his mouth. He pulled his hat lower over his eyes. It was evident he didn't want anybody to see his face. Matthew tried to pull back, but I was stronger. The man walked out of the mist in solid form to offer help. Matthew's weight and size was a challenge.

At least with my Guardian ability I would be able to open the portal since no one else could. I began reciting the script I had been taught. It weaved itself beautifully. Even the man in the mist was appreciative of my execution. Matthew began objecting to my performance, but no one was going to stop me from taking care of him. From all I understood, Sarah went home through this portal. The man was still supporting Matthew's large body as he came forward.

As soon as we entered, I muttered the word agape like I had been instructed. I was startled as I heard a vacuum noise and light seemed to light our way as a boom sounded. I was astonished when I heard the sound at the far end of the tunnel. It sounded like an alarm and wind. I wondered if someone would appear from the shadow to help. I was thoroughly disappointed when the cavalry didn't arrive. The man from the mist touched my shoulder and without saying a word, he pointed towards the subdivision. Carefully I watched the man and knew I would do whatever I needed to take care of Matthew. Maybe he was the cavalry. Shep had said to trust him and do whatever he instructed me to do if I was in trouble. Even though he hadn't spoken a word, somehow I knew he wanted Shep to know what I was doing. Telepathically I could feel Shep was dealing with our threat, so it had to be quick. I thought of my mom's locket, man in the mist, and the simple word "home." Surely he could figure it out.

This, however, did make me wonder if I needed to use actual words. My breathing was becoming labored and I wasn't sure how much more I would be able to manage. Hopefully Shep would understand. The strange man took my hand while supporting Matthew's body. We started walking through the portal.

Slowly the feeling of our surroundings disappeared as we were fully encompassed in the portal. I didn't care right now. I was more concerned about Matthew than the darkness surrounding us. Anywhere else had to be safer than where we had been. Somehow I knew I could trust this man. The man squeezed my hand, and for a brief moment I felt something from him. He shook my hand, and then I realized he wanted me to state the word again.

"Agape." I suddenly saw a change in light as the door behind me snapped shut.

***

When I arrived at the end of the portal I found myself at the edge of a tree line, and the sun was shining bright. How could that be, for it was night back home? Suddenly I could see a large, manicured lawn with a white Victorian house and gardens in front of me. They were absolutely beautiful. Even the rock fence fit. Suddenly I dropped to grab my knees as I attempted to calm the pain and dizziness that had smacked me. It felt like I had been hit in the stomach. The man appeared concerned at my sudden weakness and grabbed me with his free hand to steady me. As I stood up, I tried to assure him I was all right and to give Matthew to me. The man pulled Matthew back to my side. Gradually I began to support his weight again. When I looked up, the stranger pointed towards the back of the house where I could see a cobbled sidewalk. "Thanks," I said. He still did not respond. Shoot, he barely moved. Instead he touched my face, being careful not to show his own before he turned back to enter the portal. I knew his touch, I know I did, but I couldn't place who he was.

He entered the portal as I uttered the script, and it closed behind him. Shoot, Matthew was really hard to handle now. I wasn't feeling too good myself. Hopefully the man from the mist had brought us somewhere safe. Somehow I knew deep inside he had. This had to be a place of safety for us, and surely somebody would be able to help us.

It was a struggle to head towards the walkway. It seemed to take forever and the feeling of being watched was heavy. When I reached the sidewalk, I saw two blurs coming towards us. I couldn't help but slow things down out of fear. To my own surprise I recognized Tommy, my teacher, from the summer as one of the men approaching us. I released the hold and found that this use of energy brought me to my knees. Evidently I had used the last of my reserve. My head felt like it was spinning, and pain was raging through my sides. Before I hit the cobblestones, Tommy and the other man rescued us from falling to the ground. Tommy held me tightly as he tilted my head back and commented that my eyes were definitely showing signs of a major drain. His concerned look was evident as he grumbled under his breath. Something about wishing she wasn't always so right about these things, and something else about the vortex.

"What is a vortex?" I mumbled.

Tommy hushed me. "It is a place where Shadows reenergize when the need arises." The man who had accompanied Tommy was trying to support Matthew all on his own, but I didn't want to let go of him. I was afraid. In fact, I was truly horrified for Matthew. He seemed to be fading from sight.

"Selena, let Collin take the boy. It will be faster." I no longer felt like I could support Matthew's body anyhow. He was right: I was being a hindrance. Tommy reassured me we were not too far from where we needed to be, but I had to let Collin support Matthew.

When I released Matthew, Collin grimaced, but I watched as he began to support Matthew's form. "I have him, sir. Sir, he looks to be an heir."

Tommy was half carrying me into the yard while the other man was struggling with Matthew. A third blur approached us and I could hear chatter, but I could not understand it. When we entered the courtyard, a white building at the end was being opened and I saw a swirl of black velvet flowing inside. This was a beautiful sight, but frightening too. Tommy, sensing my fear, explained to me that this was the vortex and not to be afraid. My family had been using this one for ages and I would be safe. Matthew somehow had gathered some strength and grabbed my hand. I couldn't stress him out any more than he already was, so I feigned a smile.

"I know we can trust them…trust me." With a look to Tommy, I asked what we had to do to enter.

"You will need to stand in front of the doors and take full Shadow form. The vortex will take over from there." He could tell I had never done this intentionally and became concerned.

"You will have to let go of the physical universe while mimicking the shadows around you. If the sun reflects, you shift. Oh dear. Collin, I will have to go with her..."

Matthew shook his head as his breathing began to sound like a rattle. "She... can...stay with me." This was the only way I had been successful in taking complete Shadow form unless it was by accident. Tommy asked if I could stand. I lied and said "yes." Barely being able to hold my own weight, I wobbled over to Matthew. Tommy—seeing how unsteady I was on my feet—followed very close behind me in case I fell. I could sense he was truly upset as he began giving out orders for the house grounds to be closed and for all to report to duty.

Matthew tugged us in front of the entrance as we struggled to stay standing. As I turned, I was amazed with all I saw. People of all periods were rushing around like you would see in the movies. They looked as if they were preparing for battle. To see people shadowing or running in from all different directions was overwhelming, not to mention the noise that surrounded us. Loud bangs and orders were being shouted out.

I cuddled up against Matthew's chest to hear the comfort of his heart beating in my ear as I felt myself releasing into the void behind us. Once again I saw a heavy mist start covering my eyes and it darkened. I could no longer see Tommy or the others. That was when I realized I didn't know how to exit. I no longer heard Matthew's heart or felt his warmth. Panic took over, especially when I realized I couldn't feel my hands. I had forgotten in Shadow form that I wouldn't technically feel. Coldness was creeping in around me, and I didn't feel anything but frightened and alone. To make everything worse, I could hear something all around me and I couldn't tell what it was.

*"Settle down, Selena. I'm here with you. Michael is too. He will take care of us. I promise. Michael is here."* But I couldn't, and who was Michael? I didn't realize until now that I couldn't see any light, and I didn't like that either.

Then the darkness no longer seemed to be swirling around me. Suddenly I wondered if *I* wasn't the darkness. It was like being in a cave when the guide wants to show you complete darkness and you are totally blind. The only difference was that I could no longer feel anything physical, not even the cold.

Then I sensed someone else entering the vortex. It was Shep. He gave me the feeling of reassurance that everything was all right. Slowly I relaxed and no longer felt or thought anything. I was safe. *THE BLACKNESS WAS ALL I KNEW NOW.*

Light started coming towards me in the deep darkness that surrounded me. It was like waking from a deep slumber. Slowly everything around me was becoming clearer. To my shock I felt someone next to me, and his heart was pounding vibrantly. It was Matthew. I recognized his feel, especially of having his warm body against me.

Abruptly we seemed to be removed from the vortex. Shep, Mr. Sturley, and others were standing there waiting for us. When we started to slump to the ground, I felt the strong arms of Shep and Matthew's dad catching us. A smile of relief crossed everyone's face. Matthew wasn't letting go of me, and I realized I hadn't let go of him either. Shep and Mr. Sturley began assuring us we were all right and to let go of each other. Quickly Matthew pecked my head as we released one another. With one glance at Matthew, I was shocked not to see his normal blue eyes. Instead his eyes were swirling in an abnormal way, and the darkness within them was an odd color like nothing I had ever seen before. I wondered if mine were different too.

Shep was whispering to me that it was normal, and in a couple days our eyes would return to their original color. People were mumbling to each other, and from the sounds of it there were a lot. I wished they would all go away and leave us in peace.

Suddenly I realized Sarah was near for I felt her kneel beside me. "Here sweetheart, drink this for Mommy." I felt water dribble into my very dry mouth. I hadn't realized how thirsty I was. Matthew's mom was doing the same. Matthew was looking at me as if to ask if I was all right. I tried to smile but wasn't quite able to manage much more than a weak one. I hoped it would let him know I was fine. Sarah's voice was becoming clearer as I heard her say the disorientation was lightening. Mr. Sturley tried to help Matthew into a standing position. Evidently he was in a weakened condition. Sarah whispered to me it was normal to be fatigued physically when one exited the vortex. "Your body goes without its normal nourishment." Her voice sounded strained as I tried to focus.

So far I was only catching bits of information here and there. I was startled by a loud resounding thud as the doors of the vortex were shut. It was clear I had grown accustomed to the noises I had been hearing when in the void. Shep laughed at my surprised reaction. "I wish things could have been easier for them. She seems to have done well, but she is still frightened." Apparently they had planned to prepare us for what to expect. Nonetheless, our overuse of abilities had weakened us too much and had caused this disaster. Gradually I began to realize that Shep was picking me up like a baby. I tried to resist his embrace but was unable to. Instead I felt like a rag doll. With a glance back, I was surprised to find Matthew had managed to stand. He looked wobbly as a man raced forward to assist Victor in helping Matthew to walk. They were following us into the house. Then I happened to notice the rock fence that was at a distance from us. I thought it had been closer and shorter, but it was not. It looked to stand taller than any privacy fence I had ever seen, and to my amazement there was a large wooden gate. Now everything was shut tight, and the feeling around us was one of pure agitation.

Once inside the house, I noticed it was definitely decorated in an elegant Victorian style. Normally I would have been enthralled by its appearance. Today, however, I couldn't even concentrate. I felt so tired I couldn't keep my eyes open. I wished I could. The last person I saw was Matthew hobbling in behind me. I wanted to be with him. I needed to be with him.

The next morning I found myself in the fanciest bed I had ever seen outside of a historical museum. The room was pale green with a high, vaulted ceiling. It was brightly lit by the sun shining through the floor length windows. I pushed myself up into a sitting position. Abruptly my stomach rumbled because I was starved. When I glanced down at myself, I was shocked to discover that someone had changed me into pajamas.

Gradually I was able to pull myself off the edge of the bed. At first I was hesitant. I wasn't even sure my legs could hold me. After finding I could stand, I wandered over to the window to enjoy the warmth of the sunlight and to see what lay before me. Cautiously I peeked out through the window to find four very tall hedges, which created a box for privacy. There was a weeping willow directly in the center, and Matthew was sitting there quietly, resting with his eyes closed. Without thinking, I jumped back to the side of the window as he jarred awake. To my own surprise, my body shadowed me directly to his side. I practically pummeled him to the ground when I landed on top of him. He laughed as he gripped me tight so I wouldn't fall.

"How did I do that?" I gasped in astonishment.

"Our abilities are stronger here, I think. Like earlier, I just thought of you, and whoosh! I was in your bedroom before I realized it. By the way, you're pretty cute when you're asleep. Anyway, I was afraid I would get in trouble, so I shadowed out here under the tree. I didn't want to be too far away from you. We were in so much danger before, I couldn't stand to not be near." He smiled nervously while draping his arm around me securely. This was mortifying in some ways, for I felt embarrassed by my obvious need to be with him. The heat immediately began to burn through my cheeks as I looked to my hands. Gently he squeezed me tight as he assured me it was fine, because he understood.

"I like knowing you wanted to be with me so bad your ability took over for you and found a way, even with all this sun." I guess that *had* been a feat, I thought as I glanced back to the window and only saw thin shadows that I could have followed to have plowed into him. This was so bad I began to laugh at my predicament. Instantly I hid my face in his shoulder as I tried to gain control. His hand pulled my face towards his and this time his kiss was soft as his lips parted mine with his tongue.

My heart began racing with the excitement of his touch. I wasn't even sure if my heart wouldn't explode. Cautiously I could feel his hands begin to caress my shoulder as I felt my body lean heavily into his, almost as if I had no strength to move away. Not wanting to break his embrace, I allowed my hands to travel up his chest as I wrapped my arms around him. His body felt strong and comforting as his hand rubbed down my side, pulling me against him while sending chills through my body. When we finally parted, his cheeks were flushed with the same excitement I felt. It was the first time I could sense a little shyness or hesitation in him, and yet his own need was charging forth, taking control of him. His eyes were glistening with his lust as he melded my body even tighter to his. It was hard to restrain ourselves but somehow I managed to pull slightly away.

"How long were you waiting?"

Matthew acted perplexed. "The closest I can figure is an hour. I'm just not sure my watch is right." In that amount of time he had seen no one since he woke, so he wasn't completely confident in his watch.

It felt cozy to be cuddled so tightly against him. We both rested against the tree together while his hand kept rubbing my shoulder as he explained how he had felt so helpless when I made the decision to trust the stranger in the woods. He actually sounded a little irritated with me. Obviously he wanted an explanation, and I guess I could explain some of what I did know. "I sort of know the man who helped me carry you through the portal. I mean…Shep knows him. He is a family friend. Shep told me to trust him, especially if I had no one else to depend on. So I did. I am not supposed to let anyone know about him. The man is a secret, and now you have to help me keep his secret."

Needless to say, Matthew was curious about these instructions and the fact that I didn't even know who the man was. It troubled him. I had to admit I did feel stupid, but then I was reminded of one of Tyler's favorite phrases: "I will know who he is when Shep feels I need to know." Boy, that did sound brainless, but nonetheless it was true. To our surprise, Shep and Sarah came walking through the opening in the square holding hands. They were a perfect couple.

"Thought I felt you wake up, how do you feel?" Shep's voice boomed with an echo.

"I'm starved but feel fine." Matthew agreed he was starved too. Their faces looked pleased as Sarah came over to affirm our condition. A moment later Matthew's parents arrived. Victor waited patiently in his light, billowing robes, holding Misty's hand like a gentleman would have from long ago. His smile was as bright as his wife's.

"They are fine. The vortex has successfully enhanced the stability of their Shadow essence. We can safely let them resume the practice of their abilities." After Sarah's announcement, Victor growled that it was time to go to the kitchen for nourishment.

As I struggled to stand, it struck me odd to see Misty dressed with such flowing robes similar to her husband's. Both of them were wearing emblems on their shoulders, but what type I couldn't discern with the way the sun kept blinding me. Misty's dark hair was down for once, and she actually looked much younger than when we were at home in Empire. Matthew tapped my side as he stared towards his mother's form.

"She likes being home. She doesn't have to hide who she is here. She intentionally tries to look older there." All four of the adults wore bands on their person somewhere and emblems on their shoulders. The bright gold and bronze glinted with the sun's rays, making the designs of the bans totally indiscernible. It was unfortunate I couldn't see them closer, for I was sure there were emblems all over them. Victor made a loud cough as if trying to distract me, while Shep muttered it was time to eat, not to study.

As we began walking, I asked if everybody was all right and was informed they all were well and anxiously awaiting news on the two of us. "In fact, they wanted to come make sure you were both fine, but I explained the way the vortex works and that we wouldn't know when you would exit. Meg is also here, and her time in the vortex was much shorter than yours. She hadn't overextended her abilities. In reality, you two have been gone for a long period of time, longer than we anticipated, due to the circumstances of your departure, I'm sure." Victor began to grumble, and I could see the stress pass through Misty's anxious eyes.

"We were fine. You didn't have to worry. Matthew did an excellent job of confusing our pursuer and causing him trouble. Although he became really ill and I knew he had to come here to the Shadow Realm."

"We know, Selena. I was aware of your travel and I knew you would be safe. A friend let me know what you were doing."

"You mean…"

"Yes, but we don't want to talk about him. I must ask you both not to." Shep sounded strained as he whispered this reminder to us. Then it hit me. "Shep, you said Meg's time wasn't as long as ours but I didn't feel anybody else enter the vortex but you."

"Meg and her parents returned to their family's vortex and did not use this one. Mr. Sturley's family made special preparations to take care of their own. They were disappointed with not meeting Matthew, though. On the other hand, it has been decided that Matthew's identity is now as important as yours. You two are a match, and Alexander's group would use Matthew to get to you. New rules have been put in place for his protection as well. Sarah has taken him as a permanent charge."

Misty looked hesitant as she spoke. "We figured you wouldn't mind." It was a surprise to see her look anxiously towards Matthew's stiffening form. "Matthew, I feel much better knowing you have a personal Protector." It became obvious they had been concerned about our relationship and the added danger. Matthew was trying to be polite, but we all could hear the irritation in his statement of being able to take care of himself.

Sarah laughed lightly as the sun hit her tan skin. "Matthew will have to get used to having me around." Unfortunately Matthew's thoughts betrayed him by screaming loudly.

"Matthew!" I couldn't believe I had actually drawn attention as I jerked on his arm. "You say it makes you feel better to know I have Shep. Well, it makes me feel better to know you have Sarah, so cool it. Besides, it is not that bad." Nevertheless, he was very clear in his statement that he would be the judge of what was bad or not.

Matthew then made a strange inquiry about time and how it worked here. I started to ask why when he showed me his wristwatch. The date showed December 22nd, which was a complete shock. This time Mr. Sturley piped up that that was why everybody was getting anxious about us. "You have been gone close to a month. We told everyone the two of you had mononucleosis."

Wonderful, that was all I needed. "What about school?"

"Luckily you didn't miss too much with all the snowstorms that have been occurring. On the other hand, you both were in bad shape when you arrived here, and it took longer for you to reenergize than anticipated. Nevertheless, you won't be able to return home anytime soon, and not without a lot of explaining to the leading factions here." Matthew started to ask about the three Shadows that had been pursuing us, until Shep offered up the explanation that we were quite safe and had not been followed.

"Regrettably, I did kill the more aggressive one who was pursuing you. Heather, however, is fully aware of us not being normal Mortals. She is dealing well with the little knowledge we have given her. Alas, she has a lot of questions for you. Not to mention she has been hounding Tyler for answers, but he hasn't given much. Heather is a true friend, I would say. As for the other Shadows, they disappeared, but not before we hurt one badly. The only positive thing we do know is they did not travel back to the Shadow Realm, which makes it so we can hunt them down for once. The injured one will have to return soon to a vortex since his injuries could kill him unless they find another way. We know the enemy does not allow their Protectors to have specific knowledge for creating of vortexes, so we are pretty sure they don't have an easy road ahead of them at least. Specific Guardians are keeping watch over all the portals to ensure they do not return here. They won't be a concern much longer. Besides, Billy took his family to a safe location for Christmas break, and we convinced Parker to let Heather go with them."

"So, what happens now?" Matthew inquired sourly.

"For now we do some practicing, touring, and you both relax under our close supervision. We have you safely protected here. This will give Selena time to refine her Shadow abilities. This realm will make it easier for her to gain control of them. We figured you could help her."

Matthew was satisfied with that.

Made in the USA
Monee, IL
17 June 2022